THE BEAST   THE CITY

THE BEASTS OF THE CITY

A THOMAS BERRINGTON TUDOR MYSTERY
BOOK 4

DAVID PENNY

RIVERTREE PRINT

Publisher's Note: This is a work of fiction. Names, characters, places, and
incidents are a product of the author's imagination. Locales and public
names are sometimes used for atmospheric purposes. Any resemblance to
actual people, living or dead, or to businesses, companies, events,
institutions, or locales is completely coincidental.

2024.10.06: 1808

For little man Sam

ALSO BY DAVID PENNY

The Thomas Berrington Tudor Mysteries

Men of Bone

A Death of Promise

The Hidden Dead

The Beasts of the City

The Thomas Berrington Historical Mysteries

The Red Hill

Breaker of Bones

The Sin Eater

The Incubus

The Inquisitor

The Fortunate Dead

The Promise of Pain

The Message of Blood

A Tear for the Dead

The Thomas Berrington Prequels

A Death of Innocence

The Thomas Berrington Bundles

Purchase 3 full-length novels for less than the price of two.

Thomas Berrington Books 1-3

The Red Hill

Breaker of Bones

The Incubus

Thomas Berrington Books 4-6

The Incubus

The Inquisitor

The Fortunate Dead

Thomas Berrington Books 7-9

The Promise of Pain

The Message of Blood

A Tear for the Dead

Writing as DG Penny, the Wilde and Ward Crime Thrillers

The Murder Trail

Unit-13: WWII Paranormal Spy Thrillers

An Imperfect Future

LONDON
SEPTEMBER 1503

ONE

A faint light leached into the eastern sky as Thomas Berrington approached London. Clouds offered a grey welcome, and a light rain fell. The stench of the city carried to him on an easterly wind. Thomas had forgotten how putrid the place could be. Unfortunately, he also knew he would grow used to it before the day's end. He thought of the sylvan fields and clean rivers that lay close to his home near Ludlow and considered himself a fortunate man. He had left its sweet air three days since to travel alone. He had ridden through the night, aware of the urgency of his coming.

Two letters had arrived within days of each other. One was a demand, the other a request. The first, from King Henry, was brief and offered no explanation. A king did not need to explain why he wanted someone to attend them. Come to The Tower at once, it read.

The second came from Catherine of Aragon, the young princess Thomas had accompanied across wild seas to

England at the bequest of her mother, Queen Isabel of Castile. This letter was longer and more personal. It asked after Thomas's children, Will and Amal. Also, after his companion, the eunuch Jorge. It went on to tell of Catherine's new life following the death of her even younger husband, Arthur, who was meant to be king one day when his father died. Now, Arthur lay in his graves. His body in Worcester Cathedral, his heart hidden in St Lawrence's Church in Ludlow.

Only at the end of the second page of her letter did Catherine approach the topic of why she wanted Thomas to visit. Though she took pains not to state it directly, it concerned what was to become of her now she no longer had a husband.

At its end, the message said, 'Come to Durham House as soon as you can, my dear friend.'

Neither summons could be ignored.

Approaching Ludgate, Thomas looked around, expecting to see people even this early in the morning, but there were none. His mount, Sombra, walked slowly, as if aware of Thomas's unease. His old horse, Ferrant, now grazed sweet meadow grass beside the river Teme. The thought of Ferrant and the strange lack of people made Thomas think about growing old. It came to all, beast and man alike, and could not be avoided. There were aches in his body that had not been there a few years earlier. Man was mortal, and Thomas, too, was mortal. How long he had left was a mystery, and he was glad its answer was unknown to him. To be aware of one's fate, one's day of dying, would not be a welcome gift, however far in the future that day might lie.

Thomas had few ambitions left. Ever since he had made his way south to Moorish Spain, he had lived a charmed life and found a place for himself in that world. Surgeon. Physician. Punisher of death. His life – and the world – had changed beyond recognition. Moorish Spain was no more. Queen Isabel and King Fernando sat on the throne of a reunited Spain. The glorious palace of Alhambra no longer echoed to the sweet laughter of water and concubines. It remained a place of great beauty, but its heart had been hollowed out. Just as Prince Arthur's heart, at the prince's final request, had been hollowed from his body by Thomas himself. No, Thomas thought, not Arthur's final request. He had made one more.

"Take care of Catherine, Tom, for I can no longer do so. Watch over her for me so we may be reunited in heaven."

Thomas had agreed to care for the young princess. He had first made the same promise to Queen Isabel in distant Spain when Catherine of Aragon had crossed wild seas to marry Arthur, Prince of Wales. The man who was meant to be king.

At the Bel Savage, Thomas dismounted and led the black mare into the stable yard beside the inn. The ostler, a lad of no more than fourteen years, took the reins, and Thomas slipped him a penny, promising more if he took good care of the horse.

"You are Harrold, are you not?" Thomas asked.

"I am sir. I recognise you from when you stayed here before. I will make sure your horse is well cared for."

"It is quieter in town than I expected," Thomas said as the boy started to wipe Sombra down.

"Folks are afeared of the dark these days."

"Since when? I recall the streets were never empty, day or night." Thomas turned to look through the gate. A few people had started to pass along the street, but he would have expected more.

"Since the beasts came to the city," said Harrold.

"Beasts? There are no wolves now and few bears."

"Beasts that cannot be seen, only heard. If I might advise you, sir, you should go inside, and I will shut the gate again. Until the sun is fully risen, London is no longer safe."

Within the Bel Savage, Thomas saw a girl in her teens washing the stone floor tiles by the light of half a dozen guttering candles. She glanced up when she heard Thomas and offered a half-hearted curtsey.

"We are not open for an hour yet, sir, but you can sit and wait if you want. I can pour you ale if you have thirst."

"Where is Peggy?" Thomas asked.

"Goodwife Spicer is abed, as all righteous men and women are these nights. Except those such as me who have to prepare for the start of a new day." She pushed her mop about, but it was unclear if it left the floor any cleaner.

Thomas knew there was little point arguing with the girl, so he arranged two chairs, which allowed him to stretch out and close his eyes. Over a day and a half without sleep soon sent him into a dark, dreamless place. He was woken by a scent too pungent for most to wear and warm lips pressed against his own.

He opened his eyes to see Peggy Spicer.

"What was that for?"

"To remind you how a real woman kisses, Tom. You cannot have forgotten me so soon, can you? I take it you want a room?"

"Somewhere quiet if you have such."

"I am sure I can squeeze you in somewhere."

The clear challenge in her gaze caused Thomas to shake his head and laugh. "I have a woman of my own now, Peggy." He no longer spoke the truth, but she needed to be discouraged. Things had not been good between him and Bel Brickenden for several months, and he did not altogether know why. What made him feel worse was that he did not regret the change in their relationship. He believed Bel felt the same.

Peggy laughed. "And I am married, Tom, but that did not stop us tupping together that once."

"I had no one then."

Peggy brushed a hand as if about to slap him. "Get away with you, Tom. I will have you again, I wager. Once tasted, never forgotten, is what they say about Peggy Spicer's ample charms. Do you want to see your room, or are you happy there?"

"I need food first, then perhaps to close my eyes for an hour. Is there anything to eat?"

Peggy turned to the girl who had finished with the floor. "Has the baker been yet?"

"Not yet, Peggy." She glanced at the windows. "I will fetch bread once the sun is fully up and folk are about, but..."

"Away with you, girl. Nothing stalks these streets but

fear. Get this man some bread before he expires from hunger."

The girl made a show of putting her mop and bucket away, an even slower show of finding a cape before making her way to the door. She was saved when it opened, and a young man entered carrying a basket of warm loaves.

"Bread, cheese and ale, Tom?" Peggy asked as she sat on the chair Thomas had been resting his feet on. "And there may be some pottage left from last night. I can heat it up. It is always better the morning after." The familiarity came easy to her, as it did Thomas. When he had first arrived in London, he had spent a pleasant few hours in bed with her until she betrayed him. But Peggy did not let such a thing spoil a business transaction.

"Anything will do, Peggy," Thomas said. "I need sleep more than food."

"Then that is what you shall have. Once you are settled, I will bring the food up. How long will you need the room for?"

"That I do not know. Let me say five nights to start, if you can accommodate me that long."

"That I can, Tom. Do you wish me to show you it now?"

"Tell me where it is; I am sure I will find my way." Thomas glanced down at a heap of pamphlets left on the table by the baker's boy. "What are these, Peggy?"

She waved a hand as if in dismissal. "Gossip of the worst kind, but my customers like them." She picked up one of the sheets. "Here, take one."

Thomas took the paper, where tiny letters were pressed

too tightly together for him to decipher without a glass. His sight for reading was less sharp than it had once been. Another sign of age.

An acrid scent rose from the paper, which he suspected came from the ink. When he ran his thumb across the sheet, the words smeared. He made to hand it back, but Peggy shook her head.

"It is no use to me now you have smudged it. I will add the farthing to your bill." She smiled as if they were old friends, which was almost true. "What brings you to the Bel Savage again?"

"A summons."

"From whom?"

"Is my business."

Thomas ignored Peggy's scowl as he rose. He ascended the stairs and turned right at their head, before opening a door at the end of the narrow corridor. The room was better than those he had used before. How much Peggy intended to charge might have concerned another man, but Thomas, despite his appearance, did not lack in funds. He dropped his bags on the floor and tested the bed. The horsehair mattress was firm and dipped in the middle. No matter, he hoped not to be there long.

The single window was glazed, for which he was grateful because it looked across Watling Street, where men, women, children, and hawkers were starting to appear, many calling out as they set out their wares. On the far side, a butcher had live chickens, geese, and lambs penned. Children and dogs ran between the legs of adults. Sound still penetrated the room, but less so than without the glass. Whatever fear had emptied the streets when he arrived had been banished by daylight.

As Thomas looked out, he tried to decide which summons to answer first, although he knew there was only one. Not the one he wanted, but rather the one he had to respond to. Catherine would have to wait a while longer.

When Peggy Spicer entered the room, Thomas was fast asleep on top of the covers. She set his food down, removed his boots, and closed the door behind her as she left.

When Thomas emerged onto the street, he was late for his appointment with King Henry, who he knew liked to discuss business early. He might have remained asleep, but Peggy had come to wake him with a sultry expression and an offer of sin he had turned down. As he followed the streets, the stink of unwashed bodies assaulted him from all sides, as well as raised voices from the throng and those of the vendors, which rose above everything as they tried to outdo each other. Thomas pushed through until the crush eased a little in the wide square beneath St Paul's Cathedral. The wooden sides and slim towers soared to reach closer to a God Thomas had turned his back on many years before and missed not at all. Some considered him a heretic, but he ignored them as much as he could. Except when in the presence of the King, where he would make a pretence of holiness. He knew the words and actions and could put on a good-enough show of faith when necessary.

Crossing the square, Thomas turned into a narrow

alley that would take him to Cheapside. He slowed when he saw a man at a table with a stack of papers similar to those Peggy had offered him. As he approached, the man picked up one of the sheets and waved it.

"Want to read all the gossip, sir?" He fluttered the page and grinned. "Learn where to find a good woman. Even better, where to find a bad one." He cackled at his joke, poor as it was.

Thomas turned away. He thought the man might follow, but he did not. He would no doubt find other ready buyers for his wares.

Thomas was aware that Durham House lay closer than the Tower, but he continued east. There was no guarantee King Henry would be present, but Thomas knew no other location. As it was, Thomas was fortunate. When he announced to the guards on the postern gate who he was and who he wanted to see, they admitted him at once.

"Your best chance is the White Tower, sir. Do you know where it is?"

"I do."

TWO

Thomas drew his robe more closely around himself as he entered the shaded interior of the Tower. The weather had turned even colder as the year slipped from a cool summer into autumn. Already, ice-covered many ponds, and there had been snow on the hilltops around Ludlow before Thomas left. Jorge had complained his bones were meant for the heat of Spain, and Thomas could not disagree with him. Though he reminded his friend that neither of them was likely ever to tread the dry ground of southern Spain again. It had not been what Jorge wanted to hear.

Now, Thomas stopped a passing servant and asked if he knew where the King was.

"He is about to take his midday meal. Is your business urgent?"

"That I do not know, for it was the King who summoned me."

The man nodded curtly. "In that case, no doubt it is.

You will find him in the Queen's House. Would you like me to show you the way, sir?"

"I know where it is."

The man turned away, and Thomas went in the other direction. He followed the outer wall to its eastern end, then entered through a narrow opening. Lamplight showed from within the Queen's House, and Thomas knocked on the door. When he gave his name, he was admitted at once and led to a familiar dining room where not only King Henry and Queen Elizabeth sat, but also their children. Thomas nodded to the girls who he knew by sight, but young Harry rose and came across. For some reason, he had taken to both Thomas and his son. Though Thomas suspected more to his son than himself. Which was confirmed when Harry spoke.

"Are you alone, Tom, or is Will with you?"

"Will remains in Ludlow, sire, so it is only me this time."

Harry reached up and slapped him on the shoulder. He had little need to reach far. Despite having only twelve years, he was tall, only six inches shorter than Thomas, who was taller than most men.

"Perhaps trouble will find you again, and then you will need him at your side."

"I hope that will not be the case."

"What are you doing here, Tom? Is there news from the Marches? Father says the Lords there are a constant thorn in his flesh. There is one here today to petition for something."

"The Marcher Lords are relatively quiet of late, sire."

"Father claims that is your doing, and grateful he is for

it. And stop calling me sire. You know my name full well, so use it."

"I also know my place."

Harry grinned and turned away. "Papa, look who has come. Did you send for him?"

The King, a man of medium height with dark greying hair and a sallow complexion on whose face seemed a permanent scowl, turned away from the robed men he was conversing with. Thomas recognised one as Sir Geoffrey Blackwood, one of the King's advisors. Thomas had met him several times before but still had no clear grasp of who the man truly was. He seemed a will-o-wisp, his manner changing depending on who he was with. He had heard rumours the man was deviant and obsessed with alchemy. Thomas knew he himself was beneath contempt and to be ignored. As he was now. The other, Sir Richard Croft, he had not expected. He wondered if Harry's question regarding Marcher Lords was due to his presence.

King Henry turned and beckoned Thomas forward, but Sir Geoffrey continued to whisper in his ear. Sir Richard stood back and nodded in recognition of Thomas. In the end, Henry took four paces away. Sir Geoffrey hesitated before taking two to follow, then stopped, as if belatedly aware that to keep pace with the King would break protocol. Instead, he placed his hand on Sir Richard's shoulder, and the two walked away together.

Henry grasped Thomas's hand. "Well met, Thomas. You must have ridden like the wind to get here so soon."

"I have a new, young horse, Your Grace. And would

have been here sooner had I not slept like the dead when I arrived."

Henry smiled, but the expression sat uneasily on a face unused to it.

"You will eat with us, yes? I have several matters to discuss, some rather delicate." Henry glanced at Blackwood who remained close enough to overhear their conversation. "We have finished, yes?"

Sir Geoffrey leaned forward, then back. "There may be matters we must conclude later, Your Grace. Send for me when you are ready."

Henry turned back to Thomas. He leaned close and said, "That man is hard to like, but he knows everyone and hears everything. He has his uses.

"I cannot say I know him well, Your Grace."

Thomas turned away and kissed the Queen's hand, then each of the daughters, before grasping Harry's hand. He would want to keep the boy close because one day he would be king in his father's stead. Though as the thought came to him Thomas realised that would be many years away yet, and doubted he would be alive to see it.

Henry ignored them. He had attained his crown through battle and took little heed of the niceties of power.

"Come, Thomas, we will eat in a side room, just the two of us. Did you come alone, or did you bring some of your family and friends?"

"Only myself, Your Grace."

"Good. The less who know what I want to discuss with you the better."

"I did not expect to see Sir Richard with you, Your

Grace," Thomas said as they approached an ornately carved door.

"He presses me regarding a tract of land he wants the title to. I told him to come to you. The matter is beneath my attention. Has he been giving you trouble?"

"I have seen little of him for some time, which does not mean there is no trouble, only that I am not aware of it."

Henry grunted. "It is your job to know about trouble."

"These days, my son deals with such matters, Your Grace. And if there had been any, he would have informed me."

When they entered the side room, it was hardly small, but smaller than the dining room they had left. Three servants had set food and wine on the table and now stood against the wall, their gazes fixed on the floor. A fourth hovered nearby, ready to serve. A capon and a side of beef and pork sat on the table. Vegetables were arranged on platters. Wine had been poured, though the King ignored his and drank water.

Once their food had been carved and set before them, the King came directly to the point.

"Catherine's future is becoming a problem. You know her as well as anyone in England. What am I to do with the girl?"

It surprised Thomas the King asked him. True, he did know Catherine as well as his own daughter. He also knew her parents, Isabel and Fernando, but considered it wise not to make judgements on princesses, kings or queens.

"Well?" asked Henry when Thomas failed to respond. "You must have an opinion."

"It is not my place to have an opinion, Your Grace."

Henry almost smiled. "I am asking you all the same. My advisors tell me only what they think I want to hear. You possess subtlety, but also honesty. Sometimes too much of the latter. Tell me, Thomas, do I keep her a prisoner in Durham House, marry her off, or send her home?" He held a hand up. "That last is not an option. I cannot – *will* not – return the half of her dowry I hold and would welcome the rest being paid."

"Money is not my strength," Thomas said.

"As several people have observed. It is one of the reasons I appointed you Justice of the Peace in Ludlow and now Coroner for the district. You are the first holder of those posts I can trust not to line their own pockets. Whatever your opinion, speak it, for there are only the two of us are here. No one will ever hear what we discuss in this room."

Thomas tried not to glance at the servants, their eyes downcast better not to meet the gaze of their master, but they would hear all and, he was sure, speak of it amongst themselves. Another matter was whether what they heard would pass beyond the Tower walls. Secrets, once known, were difficult to keep. Men and women were known to dangle from a gallows pole for speaking them, however mundane they might be. And this matter was not mundane. It concerned the future of both the English crown and that of Spain. Thomas wondered if Henry was deliberately creating a crisis. He had fought pretenders to his throne, uprisings and plots, but things had been quiet of late. Was Henry one of those men who thrived on chaos? Thomas did not know but set the question aside for now because he saw the man was waiting for a response.

"It is true I know Catherine well, Your Grace. I held her in my arms on the day she was born, and she grew up as much in my own house as she did in her parents' palaces. She is devout, clever and honest. And she loved Arthur greatly."

"Never mind about cleverness and honesty – is she obedient!"

"I believe so."

"Good. Love is not a requirement in a royal marriage."

"I apologise if I speak out of turn, but I believe you and your queen are much in love."

"We have been fortunate, and I a fortunate man, for she is a great beauty."

Thomas suppressed a smile. "That always helps, Your Grace."

"You know Elizabeth is with child again?"

"I noted it when she came to the table. I am a physician, and we see such things. She is due early next year, yes?"

"According to the midwives, in February or March. Such things are a mystery to a man, as they should be. Though not, it seems, to you. Were many children born in this harem you served, Thomas?"

"Less than might be expected, but some, yes. Though I was only ever called upon if there was a danger to the life of mother or child."

"Do you miss it?"

"Miss what, Your Grace?" Thomas was still waiting for the King to come to the point. Catherine's fate was important, but he was sure there must be more than that for them to be in this room away from the others.

Henry waved a hand. "Spain. The harem. Your work as a physician."

"Yes, I miss Spain, but am surprised at how much I have grown to love England again. More so than when I left it many years ago. Perhaps, as children, we do not appreciate the beauty around us. I do not miss the harem. It was always a burden to me, as was serving the sultan it belonged to."

"Heathens. The Spanish have done the world a service expelling them."

Thomas said nothing.

The King sighed. "There are questions other than Catherine on my mind, but whether you can offer advice on them is another matter. Though one is connected, of course."

"Your son," Thomas said.

"Yes. Harry is a clever lad, but less studious than Arthur."

"He is strong and has a generous heart, Your Grace. He is popular with both men and women." Thomas made no mention that Henry himself was not. A good king, but unpopular.

Another sigh. "Sometimes too much so. For a lad who has barely twelve years, he may be too popular with some ladies. I need to get him married as soon as he reaches an age, which will be a year or two off yet." The King stared at Thomas until his meaning became clear.

"You have, of course, considered Catherine," Thomas said.

17

"I have. But..." A wave of the hand. "Matters are complicated. She is the widow of Harry's brother, and there would need to be a dispensation from the Holy Father. The Spanish monarchs would have to agree, of course. Apart from which, we have received advances from royalty throughout the continent. Spain might be in the ascendancy, but England also wields great power. I hear much gold and silver has been brought to the shores of Spain by their adventurers."

"Many of whom have been lost both to the ocean and the natives of those distant lands. But England also has settlements in the New World."

"It does, thanks to Henry Cabot, but they are far to the north, and an abundance of fish is not the same as an abundance of gold."

"Except we cannot eat gold, Your Grace, and we can eat fish."

"Salted and rank from the long sea crossing. Besides, we have a surfeit of fish around our own islands."

"You also have riches, Your Grace."

Henry glared at Thomas. "See – only you, a man with no interest in wealth, could say such a thing. A great deal of silver is required to run a kingdom. A king can never have enough of it, nor fish, meat, or fowl. So a new alignment with Spain would benefit both our countries."

"Perhaps it would, Your Grace."

"No perhaps about it. In addition to approaches from the continent regarding Catherine, there are also plots and dangers. My position is not as secure as it may seem. Burgundy still ferments trouble, as do the Dutch. And Scotland ... well, I am negotiating with King James for the hand of Margaret as his queen. It will cement an alliance between us and hopefully keep him quiet and north of the border."

"Does Margaret know of this?"

"Margaret is a devoted daughter and will do as her father demands. Besides, I hear James is a handsome and sturdy man. He will give her many children, so she will be too busy to miss England. But that is a simpler matter. I need to settle Catherine's fate first."

Thomas waited, knowing it was not his place to comment. The marriages of princes and princesses were far above his station in life, even if that station had been enhanced these last years.

"Have you spoken with her about these matters, Your Grace?"

"Of course not. Like Margaret, Catherine will also do as she is told."

"Except she is not your daughter, but that of Isabel and Fernando."

Henry scowled. "Do you think I am not aware of that? It is another reason you are here. I intend to send you south. You are known to the Spanish monarchs. Rumour has it you are even a friend to them." Henry's expression hinted he did not altogether approve of such a thing. "Diplomats will attend, of course, but it would also help to have someone there who they like. What say you, Thomas?"

"To go to Spain?" Thomas deliberately set aside this thought as it came into his head, for he knew the temptation might prove too great. It was the land he had made his own – Al-Andalus rather than Spain, but it was all Spain now. And while Catherine remained in England, he could not return there. He had made a promise to Isabel that could not be broken.

"I want you to go to Spain on my behalf."

"I have responsibilities here, Your Grace."

"Responsibilities I bestowed on you and can just as readily take away."

"You would need to appoint a less honest man in Ludlow in that case."

"It would not be the first time. I hear your son is as honest as you are, also your daughter. You should be minded to find a husband for her before she turns into a spinster."

"Amal has but fifteen years, your grace."

"So more than ready to push babies out. Do you agree?"

"To what, Your Grace?" Thomas was confused about which subject they were talking about.

"To going to Spain on my behalf. To smooth the way for Catherine to marry Harry when he is of an age. It will be a few years yet, but she will have to wait. I need her here, in England, and married to my son."

"With a dispensation from the Pope," Thomas said.

"Of course with a dispensation from the Holy Father, but that is being sought as we speak."

"And who will manage matters in Ludlow if I go?"

"I hear your son and that eunuch are doing as much work as you. Apart from which, we are talking about matters of state, and whatever happens in Ludlow pales into insignificance."

"And if I want to take my son with me? He too loves Spain and its people."

"I would forbid it. Take that creature with you. What is his name?"

"Jorge."

"Yes. Take him."

Thomas was unsure if Jorge would want to accompany him. He complained enough about England but had made a place for himself here – a place for himself in Ludlow, where he was regarded with both admiration and curiosity.

"I will consider your request, Your Grace. I would like to speak with Catherine before I make a decision."

"Speak with her? She will do as I demand."

"I would still speak with her. With your permission, of course. I can smooth the way by raising the possibility. If I am allowed admittance, that is. I understand Doña Elvira controls those who can see Princess Catherine with a rod of iron."

"I will provide you with a letter telling whoever might stand in your way that you *must* see the princess. You know where she is, I take it?"

"Durham House."

"Indeed. As for this Doña Elvira, whom I am unfamiliar with, she will also do as I command. Where are you staying?"

"At an inn, your Grace. The Bel Savage."

Henry grunted in amusement. "Gods, Thomas, but you'll catch the pox if you stay there too long. I will call on my keeper of houses. I am sure he can find something suitable, and staff for it. A man of your standing cannot be seen to sleep in a tavern. I will send you a message when it has been arranged. Now, let us eat our food and sample this fine wine. We shall talk of more pleasant matters." Henry speared a slice of beef and chewed. After swallowing, he said, "Tell me more of this harem. How does it work? Were the women beautiful? Were they skilled?"

It was not the first time men had asked the question. In truth, Jorge would be better suited to answer it, for he had served as a eunuch there for many years. But Thomas was familiar with the harem and those who lived within its confines, and had created a story long ago so when asked he could both titillate and inform.

THREE

As Thomas passed through the looming gates of the Tower, a man barged past him without apology. Thomas watched him go and wondered what could be so urgent. King's business, no doubt. That always seemed urgent, even when not important.

He turned away and took an alley north to return to Cheapside. Fat spots of rain began to fall but barely reached the ground, so close did the roofs almost meet above. The alley split in two, and Thomas took the left path because two men were blocking the other as they argued, pushing at each other. When one shouted, Thomas slowed and turned his head. The next thing he knew, he was on his back with a woman atop him. The two men laughed, put their arms around each other and walked away.

"I am sorry, sir, I did not see you." The woman clambered off him before looking back along the alley.

Thomas sat up and then climbed to his feet and offered his hand. "Are you hurt?"

"No." She looked up at him before accepting his help. "And you, sir?"

"I have been hurt worse," Thomas said. "What were you running from?" He looked beyond her but saw nothing obvious. At the far end of the alley, people passed along Cheapside, but here, the two of them were alone. He studied the woman for the first time. Her face seemed made of angles, and though it lacked true beauty, she was attractive. Her pale yellow hair had pulled loose from a knot behind her head to hang past her shoulders. Her dress had been torn, and she preserved her modesty by holding the ragged edges together with one hand. "What happened?" he asked.

"Nothing you can help with, sir. Again, I am sorry. Are you sure you are not hurt? You fell hard.

"No, I am not hurt. Now tell me what you were running from."

The woman glanced along the alley once more, then came to a decision.

"We were attacked by three men. They are most likely gone now I have escaped, but I fear for Luke."

"Who is Luke?"

"My man. My assistant. He could not get away. I was going for a constable."

"Perhaps I can help."

She looked Thomas up and down. "You are not young, sir, though uncommonly tall. Are you strong? Can you fight, for if those men are still there, that is what it may come to."

Thomas smiled. "I am strong enough, and have been told I can fight well enough, as well."

Her gaze took him in. "And brave?"

"That has also been said of me. Why?"

"As I say, the men are most likely gone."

"Three, did you say?"

"It is too many." She started to walk away. "I will find a constable. If not, I will raise the hue and cry."

"Take me to where this happened," Thomas said. "We can watch from a distance, and I will decide if I can help." He expected more resistance, but she nodded and turned back the way she had come.

"Do not approach them if they are still there. They are dangerous men."

"I see your clothes are torn. Did they want your body?"

A smile quirked her lips. "One of them tried to grab me to stop my escape and my dress tore." She tugged at the rip. "It will repair easily enough." Her gaze rose to meet Thomas's. "And I cannot allow you to accompany me. It is too dangerous."

"You are afraid they are still there? Which is where?"

"At the head of this alley where my printworks sits. I will not approach until I am sure they are gone."

"I will accompany you. And I may be old, but I can still protect a woman."

"If you are sure, sir." She slipped her arm through his.

When they were halfway into the alley the woman slowed.

"Where is your house?" Thomas asked.

"I told you it is a printworks, sir, not a house. Though

we sleep there, too. It is there." She pointed to where a small wooden sign showed a drawing of a book.

"I see no men," Thomas said.

"Nor I. But we should approach with care."

"I will go first. You stay here."

When he reached the printworks he saw a man lying on the floor. The woman pushed past him and knelt. She shook the man, without response, before looking up at Thomas.

"He is dead, sir. Stabbed. We will need a constable, after all."

Thomas knelt beside her and felt the man's neck. After a moment, he felt a steady pulse. Leaning closer, he saw blood leaking from a blow to the man's head, more from a knife wound on his shoulder but the wound was shallow.

"Not dead, only knocked out."

"Then we need a physic. I know several, but the best are Moors and the very best some distance away."

"I am a physician. Let me look at his wound."

"You are no Moor, sir. I will send for Timothy, for he is Moorish."

Thomas was tempted to walk away but knew he could not. There had been many times in the past when walking away would have been the right choice, but he had never done so.

He pushed the woman aside and tore the man's shirt to reveal the wound. The knife had entered his chest high on the right side. The wound was clean, but blood welled from it. Not enough to indicate a major vessel had been cut, but more than he could afford to lose if it went untreated.

"Do you sew?" Thomas asked the woman.

"Sew? Are you an idiot?"

"I told you what I am. Do you?"

"I am a woman of limited means, so of course I sew."

"Fetch me a needle and thread, hot water and a candle. I will sew his wound shut."

"Is there anything else you want? My livelihood, perhaps, or my virginity?

Thomas suppressed a laugh. "I have my own livelihood and suspect I am too late to steal the latter. I ask only for a needle and thread. The longer you take the longer he will bleed."

He put an arm beneath the man and half-carried him into the rear of the small shop. There was little space spare, and he stumbled over a tall wooden staff such as might be used by a shepherd. It clattered to the floor and as Thomas moved to avoid it he stubbed his foot against a heavy wooden chest and cursed.

"Are you sure you can manage?" asked the woman with a smile.

Thomas thought she should take her man's injury more seriously, but had seen the same reaction before. Sometimes it was difficult to accept what had happened, and humour covered over the concern.

Thomas found a chair and sat the man in it before turning back to the woman.

"Bring me what I ask if you would see your man recover."

"I would have him live, but I do not know who you are or why you came to my aid. What use can you be to Luke, even if you are a croaker?"

"If you have an alternative, let me know and I will be on my way."

"Hot water, you said, and a candle?"

"And needle and thread. I prefer gut, but thread will do. I will return to remove it in a week." He looked around. "Will you still be here in a week?"

"That depends whether those men return."

Thomas wanted to ask more about the men, but he needed to close the man's wound first. Any questions could wait.

At last, the woman went into a small side room. When she returned, she carried most of what Thomas had asked for and set them down on the wooden chest. She picked up the staff and propped it back in the corner.

"The water is on the stove, sir. It will be a minute or two yet."

"Then fetch me rags, cold water, and soap if you have it."

"Soap?" But she went into the back room again to emerge with a small bowl, a small bar of soap and some relatively clean rags.

Thomas soaked one before using it on the man's wound, then the soap to clean the area around the wound. The man winced, and the woman reached for his hand.

"I have nothing with me to ease his pain or I would use it." Thomas took the needle and thread. "This will hurt only briefly and be less painful than if the wound should turn bad." He glanced at the woman. "Do you have a length of leather he can bite down on?"

She went through for a third time, emerging with a

square of thick leather and another bowl, this one holding hot water, steam rising into the air.

Thomas turned the leather over, then cleaned it before returning it to her to offer the man. He wetted a fresh rag in the hot water and pressed it as deep into the wound as possible before pulling the sides apart to allow him to peer inside. He reached in and pulled out a few tatters of the man's shirt that had been forced into the wound by the thrust of the knife. Then he washed it again, threaded the needle and began to sew it shut. After a short time, the man's eyes rolled back in his head, and he passed out.

When Thomas was finished, he stood back to judge his handiwork. It was not his best, but would do, and already, the bleeding had stopped.

The woman stared at him wide-eyed.

"How did you learn to do that, sir?"

Thomas laughed. "It is not difficult, but I learned it, and much more, in a land far to the south." He glanced around. "Is this your trade?"

"Mine and Luke's, yes."

"What did the men want?"

She scowled at the reminder. "Should we lie Luke on our bed, sir? He looks all twisted on that chair."

"He will wake soon, but yes. Show me."

Thomas put his arms beneath the man and lifted. It was a strain he would have barely noticed five years before, but time passed, and nothing could stop its effect. He was still strong enough to carry the man to the back room, where a narrow bed was pushed against the wall. Thomas laid him down as gently as he could. The movement brought the man awake, but only for a moment. He stared up at Thomas and the woman before closing his eyes again.

"I have something at the Bel Savage to help with the pain. I will bring a little and show you how to prepare it."

"Are you staying there, sir?" The woman drifted back into the main room, and Thomas followed.

"For the moment, though the King has promised to find me a house."

"King Henry has offered you a house? Who are you, sir? Someone far too important to come to the aid of poor traders such as myself and Luke." Once more, her eyes went wide. Striking eyes, hazel-grey. Thomas estimated she had barely twenty years.

"My name is Thomas Berrington, and I have little importance other than the King wants me to help him in a certain matter. And I would come to the assistance of anyone in need. So tell me, who are those men, and what do they want with you?"

She looked around. "We will have to leave here now. I fear they will return on the morrow and make more demands. And there is so much to move."

"I will see if I can arrange help, but you may not have to move. I will come here in the morning and stay to see if the men return. If they do, I will dissuade them from whatever action they intend to take. I can be persuasive. But I am still waiting for you to tell me who they are, and what they want with you."

"Who they are I do not know, sir. They came three days since with a proposal. I considered it and gave them my answer when they returned today. It was not the one they wanted. So the threats started, and then they grew violent. If I refuse to do what they ask, they will destroy my business. They are bad men, sir."

"That I gathered. What do they want of you?"

"To produce a book for them. They believe that I will work for them because we create works of a particular kind. And I may have done until I read the book itself. Written in multiple hands, as though it has several authors. It is a book of demonology and beasts, and profane. I want nothing to do with it. Let them find another print works to produce their deviltry, if they can."

"Printing is your trade?" Thomas asked.

"Of course it is, sir. Do you not recognise a press when you see one?" The woman seemed to remember her torn dress and pulled the parts together again. She smiled. "I will have to ask for that needle and thread back."

"Will you be safe if I go to the Bel Savage to fetch the tools of my trade to treat your … husband?"

She laughed. "We live as man and wife but are not married. I hope I do not shock you, sir."

Thomas smiled. "I have lived in much the same way myself, and some of my friends might shock you more than you can ever shock me."

"I doubt that, sir. I think you might find the nature of my work shocking."

Thomas took a few steps and turned his head to study the long sheets of paper hanging over a wooden rail. Each contained what looked to be several pages of a document. He counted four on each side of the paper, which he now realised was hung there to let the ink dry. He had never seen a printworks before, and to his eye it looked a complicated set of tools and equipment.

"I see you print in English. That is unusual."

"Some may think so, but our ... pamphlets are meant to be read by any man or woman who can do so, and spoken to those who cannot read."

"Lock your doors until I return. Is there anything I can bring back?"

She shook her head.

"My thanks, Thomas Berrington. At least we get to live another day."

"You will live more days than that, I promise...?" He left a question at the end of his words for he realised he did not know the woman's name and, for some reason, he would like to.

"Look at me, so ungrateful. My name is Eleanor Cooper. And my 'husband'," she smiled, "Is Luke Thatcher."

"You are incomers to London?" Thomas heard the countryside in her accent.

"Out of necessity, but that is not unusual these days. I will do as you ask and bar the door until you return."

Except, when Thomas entered the Bel Savage, Peggy Spicer came bustling across to him.

"A man is waiting for you, Tom. He says the King sent him to take you to your new house." She scowled. "And you have barely arrived."

"Which man?" Thomas asked, but that became clear as a tall, well-dressed individual crossed the room. His sour expression showed he was unused to being kept waiting.

FOUR

"Did he offer a name?" Thomas asked Peggy before the man could reach them.

"Does he look like someone who would give his name to a goodwife?"

Thomas watched the man approach as if he had all the time in the world. His expression did not improve.

"You are here for me?" Thomas asked.

The man's gaze studied him and came away unimpressed.

"If your name is Berrington, and you are Justice of the Peace at Ludlow, then yes, I am here for you. I have a note for you in the name of the King that will offer you access to Durham House. Secondly, I am to take you to the accommodation you will stay in while you remain in London. Can you come now?"

"Do you have a horse?"

"Of course I have a horse."

"In that case, I need to pack my bags and saddle Sombra. Can you wait a little longer, sir?"

"If I must." He looked around the taproom. "I will be outside. I do not understand how you can stay in a place like this."

"I am a simple man with simple tastes, sir."

"So it seems."

Thomas did not rush or attempt to draw out his packing. He paid Peggy Spicer extra for the loss of a tenant, though he was sure she would find another soon enough. No doubt men who, unlike Thomas, would also pay extra for the favours of one of her girls, or even Peggy herself. The man was astride a rowan mare when Thomas rode from the stable on Sombra, his possessions slung across the saddle in front of him. The man turned away without a word and headed east, away from Ludgate.

The square fronting St Paul's Cathedral was busy, as usual. Less with the devout and more with those hungry for gossip. Traders sold hot pies, meat, fried fish, oysters and pamphlets. As they passed the entrance to the alley where Eleanor Cooper's printworks lay, Thomas knew that he would have to return to complete on his promise once he had been shown his new lodgings.

"Is it far to this house?" Thomas asked as he rode beside the equerry.

"Not far, no." The words slid from the man's lips like treacle, as if reluctant to leave his mouth.

Thomas was used to entitled men and ignored his attitude. "How long can I stay there?"

This time, the man glanced at him as if in surprise. "Am

I meant to know that? As long as the King requires your service. Though what you can offer his grace is beyond my ken."

"Oh, I am a man of many talents, sir. Thank you for the permission to attend Princess Catherine, a close friend of mine and my family." It was petty to point this out, but the man annoyed Thomas. He had met too many of his kind and feared there were ever more of them surrounding the King.

Beyond the square in front of St Paul's Cathedral, the man turned his horse to the north, and Thomas had to fall behind in the narrow street. He considered attempting conversation again but dismissed the idea. He did not care about the man's opinions. They followed Frydaystrete until it met Cheapside, then turned left to enter Milkstrete, where the man stopped.

"Your house is here, Berrington. You have been assigned suitable staff, so my work is done." There was no farewell, not even a nod before he turned away.

Thomas dismounted and patted Sombra's neck. In the late afternoon light, he studied the frontage of a substantial house It sat alone, a strip of grass on one side beyond which sat a small church. To the left, a narrow alley led towards what appeared to be an orchard, with a two-storey workshop set to one side. The house itself was more than suitable. He wondered how many other houses the King owned in the city. No doubt many.

He knocked on the door and waited, but not for long. A short man opened it and stared at him.

"You are Sir Thomas, yes?"

"I am." It was easier to accept the title than make an explanation. Apart from which, it might offer him a little more respect. Thomas was not unused to staff. When he was appointed Duque of Granada, a position bestowed on him by Queen Isabel, there had been a household of a score, as was expected for a man in such a position.

"Take your steed along the alley towards the empty shop. You will find a gate at the back that leads to the stables and garden. Jack will take care of your horse and show you the rear entrance. Will you want to eat tonight?"

Thomas was sure a 'sir' should have been added to the question, but he ignored the slight.

"I have something to do, so no, not tonight. But I would like to introduce myself to the rest of the staff. You can start with your name."

The man seemed taken aback for a moment, then recovered. "I am Hardwin Steward. You will deal with me on most matters. It is unlikely you will need to know the names of the other staff unless you are the curious type." He sounded as though he did not approve of curious people.

Thomas turned away and took the alley, barely wide enough to lead Sombra along. He glanced at the empty workshop in passing, and a thought came to him. A possibility, in any case. Behind the house, another alley ran to the promised gate, which led into a yard with a substantial garden set with apple and pear trees. A skinny boy of about seventeen years trotted up to him.

"You are the new master, sir?" He glanced at Sombra and rubbed the horse's nose, which brought a snort and made the boy laugh. "Fine steed, sir, fine steed indeed. Shall I take her?"

Thomas passed the reins over together with a penny, which the boy handed back.

"I am paid to tend the horses when we have them and to do any other task Master Hardwin gives me."

Thomas took the coin back, knowing he could offer it again once the boy knew him better.

"I was told there is a back entrance to the house." Thomas thought he would be more likely to use that in the future.

"Beyond the stable, sir. The door should be unbarred and will admit you to the kitchen. I do not know where your room is, but Winnie can tell you the way from there. Welcome, sir."

Thomas smiled because he had already learned the names of two of the staff. No doubt Hardwin Steward would disapprove. The kitchen was warm and fragrant, with still-warm bread on the large table. A tall woman kneeled to take a second loaf from a wood-fired oven. She glanced over her shoulder before returning to her work.

When she eventually rose, she said, "I take it you are the new master. Bedlington, is it? Welcome, sir." She gave a perfunctory curtsey.

"Berrington," Thomas said. "And you are Winnie?"

"Winifred is my given name, sir, but everyone calls me Winnie, other than Hardwin. Have you eaten?"

"I have no hunger, but my thanks. Is there someone who can show me to my room?"

"Rooms, sir. This entire house is yours now. Give me a

moment to set this bread to cool and I will show you around. Hardwin will not do so, but we are a small and hard-working staff."

Thomas waited, watching as she tidied up. He recognised her as someone who enjoyed her work, though he did not know what the staff here did when there was no master in the house. He had questions he might ask but was unsure if Winnie would be willing to answer them even if she could.

Finally, she dusted her hands on her skirt and told him to follow her into a short corridor leading to the front door.

"Hardwin has his rooms on this floor, sir, to the right of the entrance door. There is a dining room on the left at the end, then a sitting room. The best rooms, your bedroom and study, are on the first floor. Do you wish to see them now?"

"Please."

Winnie led the way up the wide staircase. At the top, she pointed to a small door. "Beyond that is a narrow staircase to rooms on the top floor where the staff sleep. Call out if you ever need one of us at night, and someone will come." She turned right. "All the other rooms along this floor are for your use, sir. Sleeping, washing, guests, entertaining. Whatever you wish to use them for."

"Has the house been empty long?"

"Half a year. It is not unusual. Sometimes, it is one master after another. Other times, there are long periods when it is only us. I hear you may be more permanent." She opened a door at the end. "Your chamber, sir. As you can see, the bed is large and already made up." She glanced at

Thomas. "Should you wish for a woman to visit, ask me, not Hardwin. He disapproves but will not stop it. I know the best whores around these parts, those who will not give you the pox."

"I need no woman," Thomas said.

Winnie laughed. "All the men who stay here say that, but they all weaken before long. The King puts men here and then forgets about them. Time can pass slowly while they wait for him to remember what he put them here for."

"I doubt time will pass slowly for me, Winnie. I have much to do. I have another question."

"Look at you, sir, all questions. Most of the masters give orders, not ask questions."

"The empty workshop next door belongs to the house?"

"It does, sir. Do you have a mind to go into trade? We are close to the Guildhall here. The shop should be used, but Hardwin prefers to keep it empty."

"And if I asked to use it? Not for me, but someone else?"

"If you ask it, he will have to allow it, sir. But you will make an enemy of him." Her expression did not show whether she would be concerned about that. Which most likely meant not.

"I think I can bear the risk. I need to go out for an hour or two, perhaps longer. Will I need a key to get back in if I am late?"

"Knock, and someone will let you in, or come around to the stables. Jack sleeps in a small room at the back of the yard. He can admit you into the house."

When Winnie had gone, Thomas laid his clothes out

and checked his leather satchel where he kept his medical instruments and dwindling supply of hemp and poppy. He would make time while in London to search out a Moorish physician if possible. He had heard several had settled in the town, which might allow him to purchase what he needed. It would also please him to speak Arabic again. The language sounded sweeter in his ear than English.

Noting the lack of a lock, Thomas left his room and descended the stairs. He passed out through the front door without seeing anyone. He left Sombra where she was in Jack's care. Both his destinations could be reached as easily on foot.

FIVE

When Thomas reached the small printworks, he found Eleanor and Luke packing trays of metal typeface into boxes. The printed pages that had been hung up to dry were now rolled, tied and set to one side.

"Have the men who threatened you come back?" he asked. "Is that why you are packing everything up?" He looked at the heavy print stone and wondered how that could be moved without more hands to help. Luke should not be working. Thomas looked him over and did not like what he saw. Not that Eleanor looked much better. She was pale and unsteady on her feet. He wondered if the shock of events was dawning on her.

"They have not, but they will surely come before long," said Eleanor. "By which time we do not intend to be here." She pushed her hair back from her face as she looked around. "You can help if you want. Already my head pounds, and we will be hours yet."

"I can help more if I fetch you men and a cart to carry everything in."

Thomas walked fast to Ludgate and then into the Bel Savage. As expected, the taproom contained a score of men. He stood in the doorway and clapped his hands to get their attention.

"If any among you wish to earn five pennies each for an hour or two of work, follow me."

He saw Peggy Spicer scowl because she would lose trade. Thomas crossed to her and put a silver coin in her hand. "They will want to spend the money I pay them when they return, Peggy," he said. "And this is for your loss of trade until then. Do you know where I can get a cart at short notice?"

Peggy slipped the coin into a pocket on her dress, laughing at her good fortune.

"We have a cart in the stables, Tom. You can hire it for another six pence. Harrold will sort it out."

When Thomas turned back to the room, he saw five men standing by the door. It would be enough.

One of them stopped Thomas on his way out. "Payment in advance, sir."

Thomas reached into his purse. "Two pennies now, the rest when the job is done." He stared into the man's eyes and saw him decide not to argue.

"Aye, all right. Two pence now." He held his hand out.

Thomas found Harrold in the yard and had him put a horse in the cart's stays. The lad also offered to drive the cart for him. They drew curious stares as they crossed in front of St Paul's, a group of seven men, a horse and a cart, but

Thomas ignored the looks. Light was already leaching from the sky, and he wanted to finish before it was fully dark.

The cart barely managed to pass down the alley, and blocked it once they reached the printworks. Eleanor directed the men while Thomas and two others manhandled the dismantled printing press. The hardest item to move was the large and deep press stone. It took four of them to set it in the back of the cart, which creaked alarmingly when it was placed there. Harrold assured Thomas the cart was sturdier than it might look.

As the last of the items were loaded Luke went through to the back and brought sacks holding their clothes and personal belongings. Thomas went to him and took them, then turned to Eleanor, who stood giving orders.

"Where are you planning on taking all this?" he asked.

"South of the river. Luke says he knows a place we can set up there, though it will not be as good as here. All the printers work within shouting distance of the cathedral.

"What if I told you I could find you somewhere better?"

"I would wonder why you offered, sir."

"Because I can and because I do not like men who bully honest workers. What will they do when they return and find you gone?"

Eleanor shrugged. "That depends on whether they have others in mind they can bully into doing their work. If so, they will most likely forget about us. If not, they will make enquiries regarding where we have gone. Where is this place you have in mind?"

"A little north of here, in Milkstrete. Do you know it?"

"It is close to the Guildhall, which would make it a

favourable location. And I ask again, what do you want in return?"

Thomas grasped what her concern was and laughed. "Only what I have told you. I would see you set up and earning a living again before the week is out."

"Sooner than that, I would hope, sir."

"Call me Thomas or Tom. I mind not which."

Eleanor shrugged, but whether she intended to do so was unclear.

"Luke," she called out, "we are staying this side of the river after all." She turned back to Thomas. "Do not speak the street's name to these men. They do not need to come with us once the cart is loaded. We can unload everything between the three of us at the other end. If you are willing to help, that is."

"I am. And I may be able to find a few to assist us when we get there."

"How do you know of this place, si–" – she broke off – "Tom?"

"It sits hard against the house I have been offered by King Henry while I am in London."

Eleanor was unimpressed. "It sounds like it will cost too much if it belongs to Henry. He would take a cobble up from the street if he thought there was a penny 'neath it."

"It will cost you nothing, for it is empty. I believe no one will move you out once you set up there and find customers."

"I hope you speak true, Tom, for it is indeed a fine location for us." She looked around. "We are done here, we should go."

The men were pleased enough not to be asked to help unload when Thomas paid each their three pennies and sent them back to the Bel Savage. Harrold remained with them. He appeared to be excited at the clandestine nature of what they were doing. They helped Luke onto the cart, where he perched precariously on the yew box which had taken three of them to lift onto the cart.

The air was growing thick with the coming of night when Thomas and Harrold took the stays and turned right onto Mayden Lane, then almost immediately left into Frydaystratte. It took them almost to their destination. As they crossed the wider Cheapside, Thomas commented on the scarcity of people. One or two passed, hurrying on their way.

"I told you, sir, it is the beasts," said Harrold. "Darkness is when they stalk the streets. All good men and women lock their doors and close the shutters."

"Exactly what are these beasts?" Thomas asked Eleanor as they turned into Milkstrete, almost at their destination. He pointed out the alley that would lead to the stables behind his house and then to the abandoned workshop.

"All I know it the talk of them," said Eleanor. "But I know what they are not. Folk claim they are demons and devils, but there is no such thing. Whatever they are will be men, like you, though maybe not as honest as you appear to be." She offered a smile, then looked up as the cart came to a halt. "Is this it?"

"Will it do?"

"I need to see inside, but I believe so." She glanced up. "It looks as though there is a room above as well."

45

"I do not know. I have never set foot inside, but it appears there is. You and Luke will have a place to lay your heads at night. I expect everything is filthy, but I suspect neither of you are strangers to hard work, though Luke needs to rest his wound for ten days at least. I will be able to help with some of his duties in the meantime."

Eleanor cast him a coquettish look. "My, what manner of duties do you have in mind, Tom?"

"The work," he said, trying not to smile.

"We are no strangers to hard work." Eleanor's gaze went to the nearby house. It was broad and tall, with lamp-light showing in the windows, even on the high top floor where the staff had their quarters. "This is where you live?"

Thomas nodded.

"Are you a rich man?"

"I live here due to the generosity of the King, nothing more. I have another house, which is mine, in Ludlow, but you will not know of that place."

Eleanor stared at Thomas. "You are wrong in that, for I lived near there at a place called Croft."

Thomas frowned. "I know it well. But I do not recognise you as someone I have met before."

"If you had, I would have been young. I ran away eight years ago when I grew weary of the master's attentions."

"Who was your master?" Thomas asked, though he already knew.

"The master of Croft Hall, Sir Richard Croft himself. He might be an old man, but his blood still runs hot. He also has a fine house in London, but I make sure to stay well away from it these days when I know he is in town. Now, we had best start work."

"Croft is in town at the moment," Thomas said. "I met him only this morning at the Tower."

"I am pleased you told me. I will take care. If I need to go anywhere I will choose the hours of darkness when few are about."

"You are not afraid of the dark?" Thomas asked.

"I told you, these beasts are only men, not demons. Men with mischief on their minds."

"Tell me about them," Thomas said as he started to carry some of the goods they had brought inside.

"Not now, for the night is upon us. These tales need speaking of in daylight."

Thomas went into the stables to find Jack and asked the lad if he would help, and if he could find some lamps. He readily agreed, and between them they unloaded the cart and moved everything into the workspace on the ground floor. Luke carried only a few lighter items and spent most of the time sitting on a stool that the previous tenant had left.

Once they were done, Harrold turned the cart, and Luke came out and shook his hand. "Don't hang about, lad. There will be few on the streets by now."

"I can take care of myself," said Harrold, urging the horse to walk. With the cart empty, he would make good time back to the Bel Savage.

Thomas followed Luke back inside, where Eleanor was dragging the heavy press stone to one side with Jack's help. Her hair had come loose from its ties and hung in disarray about her face. Thomas believed she had made the right decision to leave the employ of Sir Richard Croft. He knew the man well enough to know he could be affable with men but unable to resist a pretty face, however young or old it might be.

"Is there anything I can help with?" he asked.

"You have already helped more than we can ever repay, Tom," said Eleanor. "In a day or two, we can start work again."

"You never did tell me what manner of work you produce."

"And will not do so now. It is not suitable for a gentleman such as yourself."

Thomas laughed. "If I was a gentleman, then perhaps not."

Eleanor stared at him with a curious expression but said nothing.

"Have either of you eaten today?" he asked.

"When have we had time? I think some of yesterday's bread and a piece of hard cheese are here somewhere. Do not concern yourself with us, Tom. You have a fine house next door and good fare, I reckon. Our thanks again." Eleanor lifted up and kissed Thomas on the cheek, which unsettled him.

"Do not thank me yet. I want to look upstairs to see if you need anything."

"We have bedding," said Luke, his face pale, and Thomas knew his wound was ailing him.

"I still want to check, and then I will bring something from the house to help you sleep." Thomas went to the open staircase and ascended through an opening onto the second floor. It consisted of one large room with an old mattress pushed beneath a small open window. There was a broken bowl which must once have been used for washing.

Eleanor's head emerged from below. She glanced around. "It needs a good clean, but I can work and sleep up here. I have never had a space of my own before." She stared at him, looking into his eyes. It made him uneasy. Even more so when she said, "Are you an innocent, Thomas Berrington?"

"Far from it. Why?"

"You asked what we produced, so instead of telling you, I will show you. Come, I have some of my work downstairs."

As Thomas followed her down, he wondered about her saying it was her work. Did Luke not help with the printing?

When he reached the ground floor, Eleanor knelt to reach into a small box. She pulled out three sheaves of paper and handed them to Thomas.

"You can read these later, Tom. They are my own words and may shock you, but we make a good enough living selling them to a certain kind of man, of which I suspect you are not."

Thomas looked at the top page. There was a title and what he assumed was a false name.

They read: *A young woman's travels through Arabia, penned by The Moor.*

Thomas did not have to read any more to glean the

content, and he looked at Eleanor. She stood tousled, innocence on her face.

"It is not all we produce," she said. "We also take commissions, but not the kind those men want us to print. These little pamphlets attract a good return and are fast to write. The work pays enough for us to eat and live well. Does it shock you a woman could create such material?"

Thomas shook his head. "It does not. I have met many women who might make you blush. I was even married to one for a time."

"Then you are a fortunate man. Was this in Ludlow?"

"Spain," Thomas said. "Moorish Spain."

Eleanor stared at him. Luke had found a chair and sat pale faced. From his expression, Thomas decided to make a fresh tincture before leaving them for the night.

"I would welcome hearing your stories of that place," said Eleanor.

"I have a friend you would be better asking, for he was a eunuch in the harem of al-Hamra, which is no longer. The harem, that is. The palace still stands but seems lessened."

Eleanor shook her head. "Yes, we should talk. Is your friend in London?"

"He is not, but I will bring him to you if he comes. He, like me, is not as young as he once was, but still the most handsome man you will ever have seen."

"Luke is also a handsome man."

"That he is, but Jorge shines like the sun."

"I expect you have your own tales, do you not?"

"I may. Now, I will make a fresh tincture for Luke and fetch you some food. I would invite you to eat with me in the house, but I have only been here since noon and do not know what I can and cannot do."

"Are you not the master here?" asked Eleanor.

"That is to be seen. I will return soon. Make sure Luke does not try to do too much. It will be a week before he can lift anything heavy, and that press stone is indeed heavy."

Thomas knew they were watching him as he left the shop.

SIX

If Winifred thought it strange Thomas should ask for food to take to the workshop next door, she kept her opinion to herself. Thomas sat at the kitchen table as she prepared the food, which consisted of a small selection from their supper.

"Can I ask you something?" he asked.

She glanced over her shoulder at him. "Ask all you like, sir, but I may not have an answer. I am a plain woman who cooks and cleans. What do you want to know?"

"The shop next door, why is it empty?"

"Empty no longer, I hear."

"That is true." A thought occurred to him. "Do I have the right to bring in new tenants?"

"That is not for me to say, but I suspect Hardwin will have an opinion on the matter. It is empty because he does not want trade so close. You are the master here now and the building is part of the house, so I suspect you can do as you see fit. Ben says he saw many large wooden items being taken in. You, a lad, and a woman and man, though he says the man appeared to be sick."

"He was attacked earlier today. I treated him, so I expect he will live. Who is Ben? I have only been here a few hours and am still learning who everyone is."

Winifred smiled and Thomas hoped she might be warming to him.

"Ben is my husband, sir. He works in the garden and does any repairs around the house. Hardwin, you have already met." Her expression soured, but Thomas knew it would not be her place to offer her opinion of the man – at least not until she knew him better.

"I spoke with Hardwin about the workshop and told him I had a use for it. I could see he wanted to say no but could not."

"You are master of the house, sir. Much as…"

"Much as what, Winnie?"

"Nothing sir."

"Tell me about the other staff."

"Why, sir?"

"I would like to know."

Winnie appeared to think about her response for a moment, and Thomas wondered if she might refuse.

Then she said, "You met Jack, the stable lad. Then there is Eliza, the scullery maid. No doubt you will come across her before long, though she takes fright easily and will avoid you if she can."

"Is your husband a strong man?" Thomas asked.

"As an ox, sir."

"Would he be willing to offer help next door? Luke must not exert himself and there are a few heavy items that need assembling. I will help him."

"You, sir? And yes, I will call Ben to help you once I have prepared this food."

So it was that three of them took the few short steps from the back door of the house to the workshop. Ben did indeed look a strong man. Not tall, but broad and bow-legged, his arms muscled. Winnie came as well, carrying a tray with the food on, no doubt curious about the new neighbours. Even so, as they crossed the short distance in the dark she looked around nervously.

Only Eleanor was in the ground floor room when Thomas entered. She was attempting to fit the horizontal wooden beams into the vertical of the press but lacked the strength to raise them high enough.

"Ben, can you help with that if Eleanor shows you how?"

"I expect so, sir. Here girl, let me have at it."

"Where is Luke?" Thomas asked.

"He was feeling unwell so went to lie on the bed." She turned to Ben who was struggling with the wooden beams. "You need to do them both at the same time or they won't lock together. Help him, Tom. I do not feel much better than Luke."

Thomas had noticed she was pale, but had taken that as her natural pallor. He wondered if the shock of being attacked had upset her more than she admitted.

He went to Ben, examined the beams, then between

them tried again. Eleanor stepped closer to show them how and the beams dropped neatly into place.

Thomas went to the middle floor and found Luke sprawled on his back on the unmade mattress. Thomas shook him, then sat him up and made him drink the liquor he had made, which held enough poppy and hemp to ease his pain. It would also bring sleep, and that was a good thing. Once Thomas was satisfied Luke was not going to bring it all up again, he went back to the ground floor to find the press almost complete. Only the heavy stone remained, propped against the wall. Thomas knew they had lifted it out so assumed between him and Ben they would be able to lift it back into place. Eleanor came to give instructions and they heaved the stone up then laid it into the opening for it. Winnie had set the food on the side table and stood waiting for her husband to accompany her back to the house.

With the press stone in place, Eleanor said, "My thanks to you, Tom, and to your companions. I can finish here on my own if you want to return to the house."

"I would like to stay and help. I need to check on Luke again before I go to my own bed, but you may go back now, Winnie and Ben."

The man nodded, his eyes on the equipment he had helped assemble. He glanced briefly at Eleanor and frowned before turning to follow his wife.

Eleanor had not missed Ben's study of her, and his reaction.

"He is unsure of me, Tom, as many men are. I think a strong woman working for herself goes against all they believe in." She laughed. "They are sure it will bring down society itself. And his wife is sore afraid of the night. The same as most in London. But not you, Tom."

"I cannot be afraid of something I know nothing about."

"Then you are unlike most."

"Can you explain it to me?"

"I will if you can help me finish up." Eleanor pushed her fists into her back and Thomas expected it ached from the efforts of the day.

"Of course, but let us eat this food Winnie prepared."

Eleanor glanced at the platter on the table. "Aye, that is a sound idea. I will set some aside for when Luke wakes."

There were no chairs, so they stood at the table and picked at the food, Eleanor less than Thomas.

"Those men who came to our printworks must be part of the reason for the fear that grips the city," said Eleanor.

"The lad Harrold who brought the cart said something to me when I arrived at the Bel Savage about beasts that keep people indoors."

"The beasts of the city," said Eleanor. "They are what everyone fears." She chewed on a tiny slice of goose. "No, not everyone fears them. There are those who find excitement in searching for the so-called beasts. A certain manner of man. Wealthy men with power for the most part."

"Such as whom?" Thomas asked.

"I doubt you would know any of them. They gather around the King and whisper plots in his ears."

"What about the men who attacked you and Luke – are they that type of men?"

"Of course not. They were rough men no doubt paid by someone to threaten us. It is why they came to me. These beasts are written of in a book. A book, like my own poor scribblings, written in English. I have never seen a copy, and not many have. Though if I had agreed to what those men demanded that would change. They wanted me to print copies. They would take them away and I was not allowed to sell them."

"But you refused. Why?"

"I am not a good woman, Tom, and my own pamphlets pander to men's baser desires, but better they slake them on my words than act them out. Did you even look at the sample I gave you?"

"When have I had time?"

"There is that. What did you do with it?"

Thomas thought back. It took some time before the memory came to him.

"I left it in the kitchen," he said.

"In plain view?"

"On the table, so I expect so."

"Who in that house can read, other than you?"

"I do not know, but likely the Steward, Hardwin, but possibly not even him. Why? I gathered their nature from what you told me, but they are not illicit." Thomas looked into Eleanor's eyes. "Or are they?"

"The Church would not approve, and I doubt King Henry would either. But many of my regular customers are priests, judges and titled men. Some women, too. It seems that the higher a person rises the more base their interests become."

"As Sir Richard Croft has become," Thomas said.

"You know him well enough, then."

"He all but boasted to me of his desires and conquests. Or what he refers to as conquests. I doubt the women had much say in what he did with them."

"Which is why I had to get away from his house. But while I was there I used to go into Sir Richard's library, which is indeed fine and contains many erudite tomes."

"I have seen it."

"It also contains a number of more unusual works. I read them in secret, for Sir Richard at least gave me the gift of reading, and at first they shocked me. Then I came to learn that men would pay good coin for such debauched tales. Which is what I now do. I am not proud of it, but nor am I ashamed. There are good-looking women in this town – and yes, I am aware of how I look, and of how men regard me – who earn their living by selling their bodies. At least I have avoided that fate."

Thomas could not condemn her. In fact, he admired her intelligence and strength of purpose.

"Sir Richard was with the King this morning," he said. "Together with a man I have taken an instant dislike to by the name of Sir Geoffrey Blackwood."

"I did not know Croft was in London, but Blackwood spends all his time here. He is a rogue of the worst kind who flatters King Henry with sweet words. All he wants is power." She looked into space for a moment. "No, not only power. Like Croft he is dissolute in the worst way. Even more so than Croft, I believe, and he dabbles in alchemy, though I suspect not well."

"How do you know him?" Thomas asked.

"How do you think? On several occasions Croft brought me to London with him and I was introduced to his friends. There were expectations. I would kill them all if I could. As I would those men who attacked us."

"I take it they did not want you to produce lewd stories for them."

"They did not, but even if they had I would have turned them down. I can earn more by making the stories and printing them myself than doing so for someone else. It may come to that one day, but not yet." She looked around, then out into the dark alley. "I know not what the true purpose of the book of beasts is, or who its author might be, though it is possible they may."

"And you say you do not know what this book contains? I do not understand why a book read by so few can empty the streets of London."

"Few may have read it, Tom, but rumour spreads through the dark and taints the daylight hours. Fear runs rampant and few know the reason. Once such rumours start it is hard to shut them down. They have a life of their own. I suspect whoever is behind them wants the fear to deepen. As I say, I know not the reason, but it feels as if someone wants to spread chaos. It could be a move by plotters to unseat the King. Henry is not popular and holds his wealth close. He taxes the common man more than some can bear, yet he keeps asking for more. There are those who wish he did not sit on the throne."

"I knew there were plots against him, but he told me they had been quashed."

"You have spoken with the King?"

"I spoke with him earlier today."

Eleanor stared at him. "Are you a titled man, Tom?" She shook her head, "Listen to me, talking this way to you, confessing the wanton nature of my work." She turned away.

Thomas reached out and grasped her wrist, then released it almost at once when he realised she might take his touch the wrong way.

"I am not an important man, Eleanor. Not anymore, though I expect I was for a time when I lived in Spain. In Ludlow I have a lowly position, but know my place, as many often remind me I should."

"You are no lowly man if you converse with the King, Tom. Far from it. What do you speak of, or can you not tell me?"

Thomas recalled his conversation with Henry. Some he could not repeat, but some he could. Though he knew to do so would negate almost everything he had just claimed regarding his position.

"Were you in London last year when Prince Arthur married the Spanish princess?"

"I was. Catarina, was it?"

"Catherine. Princess Catherine of Aragon, the daughter of King Fernando of Aragon and Queen Isabel of Castile. At one time I was appointed Duque of Granada by Queen Isabel, who I consider a friend."

Eleanor shook her head, wonder in her eyes. "Not an important man, Tom?" She put a hand to her mouth. "Or must I stop using your name that way? Do I need to bow in your presence and ensure my gaze remains downcast?"

"I am but a lowly man, but my life has been beyond strange. I seem to have found myself an ordinary man in extraordinary places and events. None of it was my doing."

Eleanor smiled, and this time it was she who touched his arm. "Sometimes it is the times that choose the man. You will have made brave decisions, I am sure, just as you did today. You did not need to help us but you did. It is actions such as these which placed you in your position, or am I wrong?"

"Not wrong, but it was never something I sought. I would be content to remain unnoticed. I expect it is my nature that involves me, and always has. I cannot see a wrong and not try to right it."

"Those men would have killed you had they still been there, Tom."

Thomas laughed. "They might have tried, but so have many others and I am still here."

"Yes, you are still here, for which I am grateful. Thank you, Tom, for all you have done for us. Now, you must go to your bed. You look exhausted, and are no longer a young man."

"You look tired yourself. Do not spend all night working down here. And make sure to bar the door. I will call and check on Luke again in the morning before I go to see Catherine."

"You mean Princess Catherine, do you not?" Eleanor said with a smile.

Thomas returned it. "My family refer to her as Cat, but

do not repeat that to anyone or Henry will likely hang my head from London Bridge."

"I think he would not do that." Eleanor lifted up and kissed his cheek. "Besides, it is too handsome a head to waste in such a manner."

She pushed Thomas away and he went, aware of a deep tiredness filling him.

SEVEN

"Why do you want to follow him so soon?" said Amal Berrington. "Pa has been gone but four days and will barely have reached London. Surely even he cannot have found trouble already."

Will Berrington stared at his sister before turning to Jorge Olmos. All three sat before the dying embers of a fire, in the kitchen of the large house Will and Amal's father had built for them all. Kintu lay in front of the fire, so close Will was surprised her fur did not burn. She was a gift from Sir Richard Croft after her father, Kin, had died in his sleep on the last day of June. It had been no surprise, for the dog was old and his life had been hard. Not so hard he had not been able to mount one of Sir Richard's bitches, who presented him with six puppies. Kintu was the smallest and youngest, and Amal had chosen her. Or perhaps it was fairer to say they had chosen each other.

"Should I go?" Will asked Jorge.

"You know, as do the rest of us, that Thomas can find trouble quicker than a snake can bite."

"But they do not have many snakes in England, do they," said Amal. She was short, slim, exotic and beautiful. Her mother had been a Moor in southern Spain, herself a daughter of a Moor and a Northman, the giant, Olaf Torvaldsson. Fearsome to his enemies, but gentle to his family. Amal's brother, Will, took after Olaf. He also was tall and fearsome, but soft inside.

"But every snake there is your father has managed to find," said Jorge.

"Which is why I think we should follow him," said Will.

"We?" Both Amal and Jorge spoke at the same time.

"Me and Usaden," said Will.

"What if I want to come?" said Jorge.

"To London?"

Jorge stared at him. "Why not?"

"Because you are needed here, as is Amal. I am Justice of the Peace in my father's absence. You can be Justice in my absence. Amal is needed to administer that justice."

"People like me, but they do not respect me as they do Thomas or you," said Jorge.

"They will."

Jorge shrugged. He was a eunuch, made that way by Thomas many years before. He had done so to save the boy's life. How and why they became such friends was a mystery to both of them. Jorge was tall, light-haired, the handsomest man most people had ever seen, with a personality to match. Everyone loved Jorge – women even more than men. But despite his constant teasing, Jorge had remained faithful to one woman for over a score of years. Belia. Not Moorish, but more exotic, from further east. She now lay upstairs in their bed, their three children sleeping in adjacent rooms. Older now, so the boys shared one, and seven-year-old Leila had her own.

"Will only wants to go on the chance he can see Cat," said Amal with a smile.

"As if that would be allowed," Will said.

"Pa told us he is going to see her."

"If he is admitted. You know she is a prisoner in Durham House, and if Doña Elvira has anything to do with it, he will be tossed out on his ear."

"So I should come," said Jorge. "I can charm Elvira like I can charm any woman."

"Have you ever met her?" Will asked.

Jorge stared at him wide-eyed. "Does that matter? It is me we speak of."

Amal laughed. "I am sorry to disappoint you *tio*, but even you could not charm Doña Elvira. She is one of perhaps five women impervious to your charms."

"As many as five?" said Jorge. "Are you sure? That seems a lot."

Amal shrugged. "All right. Four."

"Three?"

"Four," said Amal with a laugh. "And even if it was but one, that one would be Doña Elvira."

"I think I have to follow Pa," said Will, bringing the rambling conversation back to what lay on his mind. Both Amal and Jorge were right. It would be difficult for him to gain access to Durham House, but he would take that slim chance if it meant he could see Catherine. The girl they all called Cat because she was as much a sister to them as any other member of their family. Except there were times past when Will had not thought of her as a sister. He suspected there had been times Catherine had not thought of him as a brother. Those days were long in the past, but friendship remained, he was sure. He had liked her husband, Arthur, and had felt no jealousy. Now, there was talk of Catherine marrying Arthur's brother, the young Henry, and again Will told himself he would feel no jealousy. Catherine was meant for great things, and Will was not.

"You are going anyway, whatever we say," said Amal. "So ask Usaden in the morning and he will come with you."

"I am not so sure these days. He has a wife and child. Responsibilities here in Ludlow."

"Which is uncommonly quiet these days," said Amal. "Usaden misses the times it was not quiet and his skills could be used. Ask, and he will come. You know he will."

"Yes, I do. But now I have decided I do not want to wait until morning." He rose, kissed his sister on the lips, kissed Jorge on the cheek, then said, "Tell everyone I have gone, and where and why."

"And Silva?" asked Amal, rising to her feet. The top of her head barely reached her brother's chest.

"We are..." Will shook his head. "No, I do not know what we are anymore. She is strange, but I have always known that. I think she finds me too ordinary." He smiled as if the idea pleased him.

"Then she is a fool," said Jorge.

EIGHT

Thomas slept without dreams but woke with a start in darkness, his heart beating fast. He lay in the wide bed, the master of the house's bed, even if he was master only at the King's pleasure, and wondered what had dragged him from a slumber deeper than the ocean. And then he heard what it was. A scream, high-pitched and filled with raw agony. Thomas threw the covers back and went to the window but saw nothing even when he leaned out. There were lamps set in sconces at the front of the house, more along the street, but nobody was in sight. He listened, waiting, but nothing more came. He thought of what Eleanor had told him, that he was a man who could not turn away from trouble. Was this trouble? He had heard but one scream. Had there been more before he woke? He looked up, but there was no moon, only stars punched through a velvet sky. The rooftops of London ran away in all directions. He thought the scream had come from the north. The town ended in that direction, not far from where he stood, The wall and ditch beyond marked the edge of safety. Or once had. Did the scream come from beyond that wall or within?

The beasts of London. The memory of Eleanor's words came to him, and as they did there came shouting and then more screams, but of a different nature. Thomas dressed and descended the stairs through the sleeping house and left the rear door to the stables. There was no sign of Jack, and Thomas had to unbar the gate and leave it unlocked. He ignored Eleanor's dark workshop and took Milkstrete north. He reached a meeting of four roads with a well standing at their junction. The shouting was closer here, but now only came occasionally. He went on. A conduit stood in Aldermonbury, with the grounds and bulk of the Guildhall to the right. Beyond it, where the street widened, Thomas saw a small gathering. Two men and a woman. The men wore robes over their nightclothes. The woman had taken the time to dress. What they gathered around was hidden from Thomas but as he came closer he saw blood on the cobbles. A great deal of blood.

One of the men turned away and threw up in the gutter. He saw Thomas and held his hand up.

"Come no closer, sir. What has been done is terrible. We have sent for a watchman."

Thomas ignored the man and pushed past. What he saw was worse than terrible. The body of a man lay face up on the ground. At first glance he appeared without injury, but as Thomas approached he saw the blood. A great deal of blood. And yet still no wound.

And then he saw it. Or rather the lack of something.

The top of the man's head had been opened. Thomas knelt, but it was too dark to make out much.

"Someone fetch a lamp," he said.

"Who are you?"

"I am Thomas Berrington, a Justice of the Peace and physician. I need light to see what has been done here."

"It is plain what has been done. A demon has come and torn this poor wretch's skull open. It has taken his brain to feast on."

Thomas shook his head. "If someone fetches me a lamp, I will judge what has been done here." He stood and faced the men and woman. The woman turned away. Beyond them, more people appeared. A short man with dark hair and wearing a black robe approached. Behind him came four others, watchmen. He glanced at the body, then at Thomas.

"What happened here? And someone bring a light."

"I have sent for a lamp," Thomas said.

The man looked him up and down. "And you are?"

Thomas offered the same introduction he had before. The man did not appear impressed, but he did say, "Physician, you say? If so, how do I not know you?"

Thomas realised the man was not a watchman. "I learned my trade in the infirmaries of Malaga."

The man's lips curled. "Malaga? Everyone knows that the finest place of scientific learning is Padua, in Italy. Spain has only heathen medicine."

"And where do you think Padua learned its science?" Thomas asked. The man annoyed him, but before a pointless argument could break out, the woman returned with a lamp and Thomas took it.

He knelt and held the light to examine the head more carefully, but the newcomer pushed him aside. Despite his annoyance Thomas held the lamp high to illuminate the gaping skull.

"Physician, you say?" said the man. "If you speak true, then what do you make of this?"

"Have you seen the like of it before?" Thomas asked.

"Have you?"

Thomas thought he detected a note of suspicion in the man's voice.

"I have seen men torn limb from limb in battle, and worse where madmen have assaulted men and women, but never this."

"I have seen its like three times before in the city." The man looked at Thomas. "Not exactly the same, but all featured the head. In one case, the entire skull was missing. In the other it was the same as this, the skull sawn open."

"I would need to look more closely before deciding a saw was used," Thomas said. But if so it would have taken time. I have opened skulls, but only after death." He glanced at the victim, the grimace of horror and pain on its face. "I would say this was done while he still lived. Do you know who he is?"

"Sir Charles Cunningham. A minor gentleman much given to various vices. I treated him for gout four months ago, and the pox a year since. He failed to take my advice or salves in both instances. And I agree – based on the fear shown on his face, he was alive when this was done. I will take the body to the infirmary, but I doubt it will tell me anything more than we see here."

"I would accompany you if I can, sir."

The man stared at Thomas once more. "You would, would you? Malaga is where you studied, you say? How does an Englishman learn his science in a heathen country? Or was this event more recent?"

"It was over forty years ago, but I have kept my studies up since."

"Hmm. As any man of science should. Very well, you may come, but do not expect to learn anything."

"Who are you, sir?"

The man almost smiled.

"I, too, am a Thomas, as are many men in England. Thomas Linacre, physician." He did not offer his hand, but nodded, as if finally accepting Thomas's claims. "Have I met you before, sir?"

"I believe not."

"The name Berrington is familiar, but I do not recall from where or when."

"Do you ever attend King Henry?" Thomas asked.

"I meet him now and again, but mostly his son, young Harry, to whom I teach Latin and Greek. He is a bright lad but has little interest in learning.

"He prefers to fight and flirt with the ladies of the court."

Linacre frowned. "Is that where I heard your name?"

"It is possible. I believe I amuse Harry, so he may have mentioned me. I would like to question the people here to see if they witnessed anything."

"Why? The watchmen will do that and report to the Constable of the city."

"People will have heard the screams of this man's dying. It is important to find out what they heard and saw."

"That is the job of the watchmen," said Linacre. "And people will tell them a demon did it."

"Is that what you believe?"

"I am a man of science, sir, and make my decisions based on evidence. All God-fearing men know that demons exist, so it is a cause that cannot be dismissed. There is talk of such hellish creatures stalking the streets of London of late, but what brings them here is unknown. Perhaps they are a judgement on our un-Godliness."

"The beasts of the city," Thomas said. "I have heard the rumours and dismissed them for what they are, the prattling of the mob. Men killed this man. Now, I must speak with some of these people."

Beyond Linacre more watchmen entered the small square. There was little point in raising the hue and cry, but they might prove useful in waking people to discover what they witnessed. Some of those who lived here would have heard the commotion. Whether they would admit to it was another matter.

"There is nothing for me to do here," said Linacre. "If you insist on this course of action, I will leave you to waste your own time. Perhaps we will meet again in the Tower or elsewhere. I also visit Princess Catherine at Durham House twice weekly to instruct her in the classics."

Thomas started to form a reply, but before he could, Linacre had gone to instruct three of the new arrivals. He got them to shroud the corpse and carry it away. When Thomas asked for the help of the others at least half decided they wanted nothing to do with what had happened. Of the remainder, another half recalled an urgent duty they must attend to. Thomas was left with only two men, but at least they listened to him and knocked on doors. Gradually, lamp and candlelight appeared through the windows. Most doors remained closed, and little was learned from those that did open. One of the watchmen approached Thomas with an old woman at his side. She had pulled a robe over her nightclothes, her feet pushed into wooden clogs.

"This is goodwife Constance Parker, sir," said the man. "She claims to have been woken in the night by the sound of horses. She got up and peered through her window."

Thomas looked at the woman, who met his gaze with a stern expression. She did not look towards where the watchmen were wrapping the body, and Thomas took her elbow and led her away so they were out of sight.

"Which house is yours?" he asked.

"That one there," she pointed. "The small one. I run my business from the ground floor. My husband grows vegetables on the common land north of the city wall."

"Did your husband hear anything?"

"He does not live at home in the week. He has a hut on the field and sleeps there."

"So you were alone?"

"Of course, I was alone. What do you think I am?"

"An honest goodwife," Thomas said, relieved when she uncrossed her arms. "Tell me what you saw."

"Horses, sir, and demons. Three horses, two demons and one man. His hands were tied in front of him."

"You say demons. Can you be sure?"

"If you had seen them, you would believe that is what they were."

"It was dark," Thomas said.

"It was, sir, but a torch is always burning near the well if someone wants to gather water at night. They were close enough to it for me to see."

"Tell me what they looked like." Thomas was sure the woman was mistaken, however much she believed what she saw.

"They were scarlet, sir, with horns on their heads and gruesome faces with long snouts, though their hands were like those of ordinary men. But demons are sneaky beasts. Everyone knows that."

"Did you hear any words spoken?"

"I did not, sir, and pleased not to. It is well known that hearing a demon's voice can send a person mad. And then everything turned bad. One of the demons used a cudgel on the bound man. Then another knelt and used his talons to open his skull. He screamed, of course, but not for long once the demon reached in and pulled out his brain" She glanced along the street, but the body had now been moved. "There was a great deal of blood. Then one of them turned as if it knew I was watching. I stepped back from the window just in time."

"Which direction did they come from?"

She thought a moment. "From the river, if someone

were to go that far. Whether that is where they came from, I do not know."

Thomas thought it unlikely but not impossible.

"Did you see which direction they left in or what they did with their trophy?" *If trophy it was*, Thomas thought. The alternatives were too gruesome even to consider.

"I am thankful I did not."

Thomas knew he would have to ask the watchmen to widen their search if they were willing, but the two remaining could not do enough. If someone else had seen these demons leaving, and where they went, Thomas might never know. There would have been bloody flesh, wild-eyed horses to keep calm, and two demons. Thomas smiled grimly and wondered if the demons flew away into the dark sky above London. If not, someone must have seen them. It was too late to start asking questions now. It would have to wait until morning.

NINE

As Thomas stepped from the house the next morning, the nearby church bell struck six times. Which meant he had managed less than an hour's sleep after returning from the slaughter site, but felt the excitement of the chase. It might come to nothing, but then again, it might.

The doors of the new printworks were closed when he passed, and he walked on. When he reached the well, he saw that someone had washed the cobbles clean of blood. There was no sign that anything monstrous had occurred there. The night before the watchmen had reported back after an hour, but only to inform him that nobody had seen anything. It did not surprise him. Most ordinary folk preferred their lives to continue undisturbed, even if it meant ignoring what was happening before their eyes. He walked north to the city wall in the cold morning light but saw nothing he might associate with the slaughter. Whoever had taken the brain from the man should have left some sign. He walked east along the wall to Cripplegate and asked the gateman if anyone had passed through in the night, only to be told that people no longer walked the streets after dark, and he was asleep in his bed.

"The gate was locked?" Thomas asked.

"Of course it was locked. What kind of gatekeeper would I be if I left it open?"

Thomas looked at the gate's height, the wall's face. It would not be impossible to climb them, but awkward if someone carried a burden. Thomas had witnessed men's skulls opened in battle, and knew a brain was weightier than expected. The old woman had told him those she called demons came from the direction of the river, so Thomas turned and walked back along the streets as far as Queenhithe, but again found nothing. He knew there were too many streets and alleys, any one of which could have been taken. Wandering aimlessly was wasting time. He needed to know what action had been taken the night before. The person who might know would be the Beadle for the ward. Thomas did not know who that was, or where they lived, but he went and asked until he found an address.

The man who eventually opened the door was enormously overweight and his face almost purple with a surfeit of blood.

"You are the Beadle for the Guildhall Ward?" Thomas asked.

"Who is asking?"

"Whoever I am will not change what you are, sir." Thomas waited.

Eventually the man said, "If I am?"

"There was a murder in Almonbury last night. I

wondered if the watchmen passed the information on to you."

The man stared at Thomas so long he started to think he would not answer. Then he said, "I have heard of no murder."

The door shut. Thomas stared at it, his fist half-raised to knock again, then he lowered it. The man owed his position to money or connections. Thomas knew he would give little thought to that position, only to the power it might bestow on him.

Thomas considered approaching the Constable, but expected he would know all about the Beadle. He expected both would be as bad as each other. Their attitude would pass down, Constable to Beadles to Watchmen. Little would get done. Crime would be ignored. It was little wonder that so-called demons were allowed to terrorise the streets at night.

Thomas needed to know more about these beasts of the city and knew of only one person who had been honest with him. So he returned to the house, intending to check on Luke and speak with Eleanor about the book. What Thomas wanted to know was if it was possible obtain a copy. Cheapside was as busy as ever when he crossed it, stalls filling over half the width. Men, women, children, dogs and horses travelled in both directions. The noise and crowd only thinned as he entered Milkstrete. He took the alley to the printworks where he was stopped by Jack, who was waiting for him.

The boy dropped down from where he sat atop the stone wall.

"Master Hardwin wants to speak with you, sir."

"I will call when I have finished next door," Thomas said, going to pass the lad.

"I am sorry, but he insists."

Thomas thought to ask whose house this was, then realised he had little position here and was only under its roof at the King's pleasure.

"Show me to him, lad, and I apologise if I sounded rude."

Jack said nothing, only turned and led the way. Thomas sent Jack away and knocked on the door to Hardwin's rooms. It took the man some time to answer, and Thomas suspected he had been kept waiting on purpose.

"You wanted to see me," he said when the door eventually opened.

Hardwin looked along the hallway. "Come inside where we can speak in private." He turned away, and Thomas followed.

"What is this about? There was a death last night, and I am searching for the culprits."

"If you mean the man killed by demons, then good fortune with that. The fool should not have been out after dark. I need to speak to you about your putting tenants in the workshop next door. It is not your place to let out the building. You should have come to me."

"And what would you have said?"

"I would have told you it cannot be done, of course. We do not welcome riffraff so close to an honest house."

"They are not riffraff but a hard-working couple."

"They have to leave. Today."

"No. I apologise for not consulting you, but time was short and their need pressing." Thomas stood his ground, despite being unsure how firm it might be.

"They must. I am responsible for this house, the workshop next to it, and the orchard. I cannot have people making decisions for themselves."

"Then I will take the matter up with the King. In the meantime, Eleanor and Luke remain where they are. If I discover you have thrown them out, I will be obliged to report your action to the King. I am sure he will be displeased" Thomas looked around the elegantly furnished room with an elm desk at its centre. Through a half-open door, he glimpsed a bedroom, equally well-appointed.

"You have it good here, Hardwin. I suggest you look after the house and stop trying to pretend you own it."

"Neither do you own it, Berrington. You are here on sufferance, and not for long, I wager. King Henry soon tires of wastrels."

Thomas fought to control his anger. He suspected Hardwin had less power than he was trying to project, but he did not know that for certain. And annoying Henry so soon after arriving would cause problems.

"I go to visit him as soon as I change my clothes. I take it I can still use my rooms?"

"You may not wish to visit the King at the moment."

"That is my business, not yours."

"A message came for you." Hardwin turned away, opened a drawer in the desk and withdrew a sealed paper.

Thomas flexed it and saw the seal had been broken and re-applied.

"Do you read all the private messages that come from the King?"

"Only when they affect the running of this household." The man showed no shame.

Thomas turned away before he was tempted to hit him. In his room, he unfolded the paper and read the note. It was permission from Henry to admit him to Durham House. Thomas knew he should be grateful. Even though it was not the King he was visiting, he changed into the clothes he used when he pretended to be a gentleman. They sat uneasily on him.

He left the house. Instead of going to the stables to ask Jack to saddle Sombra, for Durham House was some distance away, he first entered the printworks where he found Eleanor at work.

"Welcome, Tom," said Luke from where he sat on a stool, his back against the wall and one leg up on the heavy yew chest. "My thanks for tending to me yesterday. I feel much better today."

"You should not be working yet, and I need to examine your wound."

Luke laughed. "If you can find it. Let us do it in the back."

When Thomas went after Luke, he had removed his shirt. Thomas touched the bruised wound, which showed an inflamed red mark around it, which concerned him.

"You need to wash this well and keep it clean. If it becomes infected, you will regret not doing so. Get Eleanor to do it for you."

"I will do as you ask, Tom."

"Does it hurt?"

"Not as much as it did. Whoever struck me used too short a knife."

"Long enough to make you bleed." Thomas peered at the wound. "The stitches are holding for now, but I will need to remove them soon. It will hurt when I do so."

"I can stand a little pain," said Luke as he drew his shirt over his head.

"I hope you are not exerting yourself already."

"I only fetch what Eleanor asks me to, no more. We had some stuck-up arsehole here telling us not to get too comfortable."

"Hardwin Steward. I have also had a run-in with the man. I intend to ask the King to confirm you can stay, so ignore the arsehole. I will sort things out. But I have a question before I go."

"Ask away."

"I would like to get my hands on a copy of the book, The Beasts of the City, if possible."

"You are asking the wrong person. Speak to Eleanor. She has the better head for these things. I am but her slave."

Thomas smiled. "I suspect you speak false in that, Luke, but I will do as you say."

He found Eleanor standing at a high desk on which sat a wide wooden rack holding four lines separated by low wooden rules. Three of the lines were already filled with lead type. He watched as she started on the bottom line. Her hands reached out to pick up each piece of type while her eyes remained on a handwritten sheet of paper.

"Is this one of your tales?" Thomas asked.

Eleanor turned briefly to him and smiled. "Did you read the one I gave you?"

"I am afraid not, but I will, I promise."

"You may be shocked at its bawdy nature."

"I think it takes more than a saucy tale to shock me. Can I ask you something?"

"Do not mind if I continue to work. I would like to have some of these printed before dark."

Thomas watched her complete the last line, only then noticing that he could not read the type because it was assembled upside down.

"Move aside, Tom. Luke, this plate is ready."

He took the lines of type from her, knocked them against his raised knee to settle them into place, then slid them onto another board where others already sat. The ease with which he did such an awkward task told Thomas both were adept at their work. It also told him Luke must indeed feel better.

"Tell me what you want to know, Tom," said Eleanor as she took the empty board from Luke and laid out new lines.

"I want to obtain a copy of this book of demons."

She stopped for a moment and turned to him. "Why would you want such a thing? It is profane. People say that about my work, but that book is beyond evil."

"A man died last night not far from where we stand. I believe the book might be involved. A witness claimed his life skull was broken open by demons, and I heard there had been other killings the same."

Eleanor stared at him before nodding. Whatever her opinion of his foolishness, she kept it to herself. "I will make enquiries of some other printers. Once I lay this last plate, I will go and ask Jack to help Luke work the press. A walk will help clear my head. You can accompany me if you wish."

"I would like to, but I have an appointment with a princess."

Eleanor laughed. "You know the King, and now a princess? And yet..." She looked him up and down. "I was going to say you do not look like an important man, but I see you are wearing better clothes and may change my opinion. I will leave a note for you if I find something out."

"I do not trust Hardwin to pass it on to me. I will call back here when I finish."

"Aye, do that. If we are abed, you can try again in the morning. And return home before dark, Tom. I do not believe in demons, but something evil stalks the nighttime streets of London, and people are dying."

"So you do know of others?"

"Rumour only, the same as you heard. Most of London is no more than villages and people stay close to their own, but this rumour has spread to infest the entire city and beyond."

"Tell Luke not to overexert himself. I did, but he might listen to you better than to me."

Eleanor laughed, the sound sweet. "I suppose there is the first time for such a miracle." She lifted up and kissed his cheek. "Take care, Tom. You look rather handsome in those clothes. I hope your princess is impressed."

TEN

When Thomas returned to the stables, Jack had saddled Sombra and stood patiently with the reins in his hand. Thomas rode south to Watelying Street, then west to pass in front of St Paul's Cathedral and, shortly after, out through Ludgate. Here, the roads were rougher and the houses set further apart. Durham house sat solidly beyond the river Fleet. Thomas handed Sombra over to a groom before approaching the main entrance. The house had a forbidding appearance, and he knew it had become more a prison than a home for Catherine, despite having her Spanish ladies around her. Unfortunately, one lady in particular knew Thomas and held no love for him. Once King Henry's message gave access to the house, he discovered Doña Elvira standing with arms crossed, blocking his way. He could have walked around her, but she knew he would not.

"You are a long way from Ludlow, Berrington. What business do you have here?"

"I request an audience with Princess Catherine, Lady

Doña." Thomas reached into his coat. "I have permission from the King himself." He held the note out, but Doña Elvira did not glance at it.

"The Princess is busy with her lessons. You will have to wait. Out on the street. I will send for you when she is free."

"How long will her lessons last?"

"Some time yet." The information seemed to please her. She stared at Thomas for a moment longer, then turned and strode away. A small woman with enough spite in her to fill ten people. She knew Thomas of old in both Spain and Ludlow, but familiarity had never softened her dislike of him. Why, he did not know, but suspected she disliked most men, and women too. The friendship between his family and Catherine no doubt also added to it. She bore her duty of protecting Catherine like a suit of armour and never bowed down beneath it.

Thomas crossed the street to a small inn which sat on the corner. He ordered ale and a pie because he had not yet broken his fast. He watched farmers pass on their way into London with carts piled high with produce, others trying to control flocks of sheep, gaggles of geese and sounders of pigs, much to the amusement of watching passersby and children, who took delight in foiling any attempt at keeping order. Time passed, and he was starting to nod off when he saw two figures approaching from the direction of Durham House. He recognised one of them from the night before, so rose and approached.

Both were deep in conversation, but Linacre glanced up and offered a smile.

"Now here stands another namesake, More, another

Thomas among the thousands. He claims to be a physician but says he learned his craft in heathen Spain, so how skilled he is might be questionable." The words were spoken with good humour.

"I am Thomas More, sir," said the other man, who stepped forward and offered his hand. He was short, clean-shaven and with dark hair cut long, most of which was covered with a black felt hat. He wore a cloak that reached his knees and wore dark boots cut from fine leather rather than felt.

Thomas shook the proffered hand, then did the same for Linacre when he offered his.

"Is there any news on the events of last night?" asked Linacre. "You told me you were going to make enquiries, and you struck me as a man who does what he says."

"Nothing yet and I doubt anything will come of it. I visited the Beadle but the man was uninterested."

"That, it seems, is the job of a Beadle," said More.

"London is a large place, and whoever the culprits are they will have disappeared among the throng. Even so, I will not give up. As educated men, I assume neither of you believe demons committed these murders."

"What is going on?" asked More. "Another death?"

"Yes, another death. Another man with his skull opened," said Linacre, then explained what had happened.

"London is not safe once the sun sets," said More. "Only God can protect us from these devils, be they men or demons. They are, as promised, truly beasts of the city."

"You know of the book?" Thomas asked.

"I do, sir, and have a copy which I study to see if I can

make sense of what is happening, but it is written in riddles."

"More is adept with riddles," said Linacre, "and it annoys him he cannot decipher these."

"Perhaps I can help," Thomas said. "I have enquired about obtaining a copy of the book for myself, but would be most grateful to see yours if possible."

Linacre punched More on the shoulder. "Invite him tonight. He has lived among the heathen, so he will be familiar with demons."

"Would you not be afraid to cross London after dark?" asked More

"Wild rumour will not kill me," Thomas said.

"But wild men may," said Linacre. "If you are not tracking the guilty, what brings you to this place?"

"I was hoping to see Princess Catherine, but Doña Elvira turned me away, saying she was at her lessons."

Linacre smiled. "Indeed she was, and before you stand the most exalted tutors in all of London." He clapped Thomas on the shoulder. "With luck, you will be able to see her now." Both men walked on, heads together as they talked. Watching them go Thomas was pleased at More's offer to show him his copy of the fabled book.

Thomas expected Doña Elvira waiting to block his access again, but she was nowhere to be seen. Perhaps she knew she could not confront him again so soon.

He was taken into a large room with couches, elegant chairs and fine tables. Tall windows looked across the Thames. Doña Elvira stood beside Catherine, of course, their backs turned to him. Catherine was the first to turn and came towards him with a smile but stopped abruptly when Doña Elvira coughed into her hand. Thomas saw the joy drain from Catherine's face as she rebuilt the mask of a princess. It pained him to see it, and he determined he would attempt to restore the joy he knew lay within the girl if he could.

"King Henry has sent me to speak with the Princess," he said. "To speak in private, Doña Elvira."

"It would not be seemly."

"I suggest a groom and one or two of Catherine's ladies be present, but our conversation must be private. The King has insisted." Thomas doubted anyone would check with him so the untruth would never be discovered.

"Wait here. I will have to make arrangements."

Doña Elvira took Catherine by the arm and led her away, leaving Thomas alone. He should have been annoyed at the formality and protocol but was well used to it. All self-important people relied upon it.

He walked to the windows and stared at the river, which ran hard against the stone wall lying beyond the wide terrace laid with shrubs and trees. Wherries crossed to and fro over the stained, ruffled water. Detritus drifted from left to right with the incoming tide, the objects possibly only reaching the sea weeks or months in the future. A shaft of sunlight illuminated the grey water, but only for a moment. The sky promised more rain, and Thomas feared the coming winter would be harder than the one past and people would grow even hungrier.

He turned his back on the Thames and studied the tapestries on the walls. Most depicted hunting scenes, men chasing stags, boars, bears, and wolves, some of which no longer walked this land. The only bears Thomas had seen were those at the end of a chain being used for baiting, a spectacle he did not find entertaining.

He heard footsteps, and then Doña Elvira and Catherine appeared, this time with two grooms and two ladies in waiting. Thomas recognised the latter from his time in Spain and acknowledged them with a brief nod. The grooms were, no doubt, English, which would be to his advantage because they would not understand the Spanish he would speak with Catherine.

"I will need an hour at least," he said, even though he would not. But the longer he could spend in the young woman's company, the better for her and him. Catherine had played with his children and shown much affection for them, him, and the members of his extended family. Even Jorge. Thomas believed the nature of those close to him had opened Catherine's mind to cultures and peoples other than those now accepted in Spain. Most of the Moorish settlers had been despatched across the narrow sea. Others had fled to distant parts of Europe. Many had come to England, the majority to London. Which reminded him he still needed to find a Moorish doctor who might be able to provide him with both poppy and hashish.

"Perhaps we can walk alongside the river," said Catherine, speaking in Spanish.

Thomas responded in kind. "It will be my pleasure." He offered his arm, and Catherine slid hers through it with a smile.

A groom led the way along a corridor to a wide staircase.

The stink of the river rose to meet them, but at least they were outside the confines of the house. Thomas discovered that once they had descended the steps, the air was less miasmic.

"I need to speak with the Duke of Granada in private," said Catherine, deliberately using the title her mother had bestowed on him. "Remain close, but avert your gaze, and should we disappear for a moment among the pillars, it is not as if we can escape this prison."

Catherine encouraged Thomas to walk at her side, their arms still linked.

"How are you, Cat?" He hoped none of those standing close would hear the name he used for her, but use it he and his family had for most of the girl's life.

"How do you think? I am a widow and still miss Arthur, my love."

"And love him you did. We all know that."

"Not everyone in this place," she said. "It seems love has nothing to do with the marriages of princes and princesses."

"You speak true. It is even less of a concern to those who believe themselves better than others."

Catherine smiled. "Whereas I know there is none better than you, Thomas." She glanced back. "Quick now, while we are not observed. Embrace me, Uncle Thomas."

It was a dangerous request, but Thomas did not hesitate. He slipped his arms around the short, painfully thin girl and held her tight, his chin resting on her red-blonde hair. She, in turn, squeezed him back. They remained that way for several minutes before only slowly untangling themselves.

"Thank you," said Catherine.

"I miss you, Cat. We all miss you."

"Is Will or Amal with you?"

Thomas shook his head. "They remain in Ludlow. I am alone in London."

Catherine touched his arm. "No, you are not. You will always have a friend in me." She laughed. "Listen to us, but you know I consider you more a father to me than my own ever was. You certainly treated me more kindly."

Thomas had no need to say it had not been difficult. King Fernando was a hard man with little give. After his only son Juan had died five years before, he had turned his back on his daughters, other than to arrange the best matches he could for them, and that was little of his doing.

"I told my tutors you would visit."

"The other Thomases?" he said with a smile. I met Linacre last night and believed him unimpressed. He told me he visited Durham House as your tutor."

"Greek and Latin, but you know my Latin is already passable. Greek I find difficult, but they insist. Are you here at the behest of the King to speak of my future?"

"I am here to see you, Cat. But yes, Henry has asked me to talk to you. I do not think he knows quite what to do with you."

"Oh, I think he does, but I expect I have no say in his plans. The boy is pleasant enough, but wild at times. More and Linacre tutor him as well, and I suspect he is a less amenable student than am I. But my ladies all love him." She came closer and lowered her voice. "Some more than they should, I suspect."

"He has only twelve years, Cat. Surely, he is too young for what you suggest."

"Is he? He is tall for his age and fine handsome. But rumour has it he was spoiled by the women around him when he was younger, and even more spoiled now. If we are to be joined together in marriage then he will come to it more experienced than his brother did."

"It was something Arthur learned soon enough, though."

A blush coloured Catherine's pale cheeks. "Perhaps, but he was never an enthusiastic convert to married life."

"But you loved him, I know you did."

Catherine nodded. "With all my heart, body and soul. But…"

Thomas waited, but when Catherine said nothing more, he said, "But what, Cat?"

She offered a great sigh. "Everyone believes I am ignorant of what is being talked about, but I have my spies in the Tower and Westminster and know what they say. If I laid with Arthur as his wife, I cannot marry Harry." She raised her gaze to meet Thomas's. "I may have to ask you to set aside your honesty and lie for me, for you know Arthur and I had a full marriage."

"Do you want to marry Harry?" Thomas asked. He knew what she spoke of, and what she was asking. He also knew that lying would be hard for him, but in this instance he would do so if Catherine asked it.

"What I want is never discussed other than with you. What I want is my imprisonment to be over. Harry has barely turned thirteen, and no marriage can occur for years. I fear this imprisonment will be the death of me."

"No, it will not. I will not let it be."

"You saved my life at the start of the year but could not save Arthur's. Even you cannot save everyone."

Thomas smiled grimly. "But I can try. If ever you need me, send a message, and I will come at once."

"My body aches, and my belly hurts."

"You need to eat more."

"Food has no pleasure for me these days."

"Then do not eat for pleasure but for health. Eat to live, not die! Shall I speak to your cook? I can suggest some recipes from Spain, though whether all the items required can be found in London is another matter." Thomas smiled. "Perhaps I can bring some herbs and spices back for you. The King has asked me to speak with your mother and father on his behalf."

Catherine stared at him. Thomas was aware their chaperones had come closer but remained at a distance. Protocol must be followed, and these men and women were well versed in its requirements.

"To Spain?"

"Yes, to Spain."

"But ... but there are others who deal with such matters, you know there are. Why send you?"

"Because the King is aware that I know both of them well. That I am their friend, and they will trust my word over that of ambassadors who have their own demands."

"Oh, if I could but come with you," said Catherine, her expression pained. "To stand in the sun of Spain once again.

To walk through the palace of Alhambra with my mother at my side. But I know that will never be allowed."

"It would not. But I can speak on your behalf if you tell me what lies in your heart. Would it be your wish to become queen to Harry's king one day?"

"I was meant to be queen alongside Arthur, but that can be no more. Harry is handsome, but more importantly he is clever and sharp-witted. Young yet, but he works hard at his lessons, I am told."

"Is it the two Thomas's that tell you this?"

"They should not, I am sure, but sometimes I will ask an innocent question, and they answer honestly enough, I think."

"That is because you, too, are sharp-witted, Cat. They will appreciate such."

"Some of that is your doing, Thomas. Do you recall all the times I sat in your house on the slope of the Albayzin and read the books you had a surfeit of. Do you still have them?"

"Most remain in that house. At least, I hope they do, for some would be difficult to obtain these days."

"Your heathen books."

"No knowledge can ever be judged as godly or profane. I hope I taught you that." Even as Thomas spoke, he was reminded of the book he wanted More to show him. If it was as he suspected, then that was truly profane. But would he burn all copies if he could? He did not know. "Do the two Thomas's find you a good pupil?"

"Sometimes I pretend it is hard for me, so they are pleased when I do well, but the exercises come easily." She raised a gloved hand to her mouth. "Is it a sin of pride to say that, Thomas?"

"Never in you." He looked at her pretty face, her red hair so much like her mother's, and the likeness between them in appearance, manners, and intelligence brought an ache in his chest. "Tell me, Cat, for you can speak true with me. If you were to marry Harry, how would you feel about it? Not how you would act, for I know you would behave as a true princess and queen. How would you feel in your heart?"

"The truth, Thomas?"

"Between us, always."

"Mother said she could always speak the truth to you and knew you did the same in return. So I would not be crestfallen or put upon. Harry is a sweet boy. He is young, but sometimes he acts older than his years. He is clever, kind, and brave. Sometimes he is foolhardy, but am I not looking at someone who can behave in the same way?"

"Only when called upon," Thomas said.

"As Harry would be, I am sure. So no, it would not displease me. Whether Harry would want to marry someone five years his senior is another matter."

"Harry will do what his father demands. You know that is the way of it."

"As I have done what my parents demanded, though I regret nothing but the loss of Arthur."

"As do we all. I will tell the King I agree to his request. I will travel to Spain again and work as hard as I can for you, my true princess."

ELEVEN

As he returned to London, Thomas considered his conversation with Catherine. She found her imprisonment in Durham House hard – all the more so because nobody called it that. She was well cared for, and if that meant never leaving its confines, that was all to the good as far as King Henry and Doña Elvira were concerned.

He wondered if there was some way of allowing her to escape the confines of Durham House even for a short time. He determined to think more about it, and who might help. Sombra found his way as Thomas fashioned the words he would write to the King in his head, telling him of what he had learned. He did not allow himself to look forward to a possible journey to Spain, unsure whether he welcomed it or not. His heart was pulled in too many directions, and none of the choices offered were easy.

Instead of entering the house, he went to see if Eleanor was in her workshop. Luke again sat on a chair in the corner, his face pale, and Thomas went to him first as Eleanor continued working the press. He felt the man's head and neck, fearing that a fever might have developed, but he was cool.

"How do you feel?" Thomas asked.

"Tired – more tired than after the attack. It is not like me, Tom. Am I sickening?"

"It is not unusual. You might think your wound is minor, but the body knows better. You will feel this way for some time yet. It is best not to fight it. Sleep, eat and drink, and try not to exert yourself."

"And if those men find us again?"

"I suspect they will look for someone easier to persuade to do their bidding next time."

Thomas turned to Eleanor and waited for her to finish transferring the type to paper. Once she had hung up the finished sheet, she pushed back her hair, which had fallen loose. A sheen of sweat made her pale skin glow.

"I might have a chance to study that book I was asking about," Thomas said. He was reluctant to name it, as if to do so would give the words power over them.

"That is good because I have not had time to do anything about it, though you did only ask this morning."

"It was not a judgement, and I apologise if it felt like one."

"Where did you find it?"

"I have not yet, but I met a man called Thomas More who—"

"The lawyer? I know him. He has a fine mind and a fine pen when he turns his mind to it."

"I do not know whether he is a lawyer or not. I met him

at Durham House where he and another Thomas, Linacre, were tutoring Princess Catherine."

Eleanor shook her head. "There you go again, dropping the names of princes and princesses like leaves from an autumn tree in a gale. I also know of Linacre. He is a physic and a good one, it is claimed."

"We spoke a little of the science of the body, but I judged him not to accept that I knew much in comparison to him. Which may be true. It has been many years since I learned my craft."

"You knew enough to fix Luke; that is all I care about. So More has a copy of the book, does he?"

"He claims so. I only called here to tell you to make no further efforts to find one for me. He has offered to let me study his copy tonight. He told me how to find his house, but I realise the directions were from Durham House. No matter, I can go there first before following them."

"Do you have the name of the street?" asked Eleanor.

"He told me it is in Chaunceler Lane, but I do not know exactly where that is."

"It runs close to Lincoln's Inn, where More is training in the law, so his lodgings will be nearby." Eleanor thought for a moment. "If you go to Cheapside and turn west, you will eventually find Holborn Street, a wide roadway. I think Chaunceler Lane runs south from it. A tavern named The Antelope sits on the corner, but I would advise you not to frequent it."

"My thanks."

"Let me know if he has a copy, Tom. I would also like to

examine it. A printer can often tell another's work. The information might be useful to you."

"I will make notes and tell you what I learn."

Thomas nodded to Luke before leaving the workshop. He hesitated a moment to the side of the house, considering whether to saddle Sombra again, but he knew he could walk the distance, which was less than a half mile. Unless Eleanor had led him wrong. Also, he did not want to cross paths with Hardwin if he could help it. He glanced at the sky before setting off, judging there to be enough daylight to get there and back before full dark.

After asking several people, Thomas found More's lodgings and rapped on the door, which was opened almost immediately.

"I was not sure you would come," said More, ushering Thomas inside, "but I have the book you asked about on the table, together with some notes I made." More shut the door and looked at Thomas. "I should have asked before what your interest is, but I trust Princess Catherine's proffered opinion on your piety. It is not a tome to which all men should be granted access. I assume you know that?"

"Linacre first mentioned the book to me in passing, and it sparked my curiosity, which often gets the better of me."

"I would say take care, for when studying it I feel as if something has wormed into my mind and planted a seed of doubt about my life. You say it sparked your curiosity, but is that all?" More held a hand up. "I do not mean to insult you, Berrington, but you are a stranger to me for all Princess Catherine tells me you and she are close, but this is a different matter."

"You are right to question my motives, and I take no offence. You do not know me." Thomas held his hand out. "Thank you for your time. I will take my leave. I have a friend who may be able to obtain a copy of the book for me."

More ignored Thomas's hand. "There is no need to go. The Princess told me you are a clever man who speaks many languages, including Spanish, Arabic and Latin. Do you have Greek as well?"

The question confused Thomas. "Only a little, but the other languages, yes. If I am honest, I would say that until the fall of Moorish Spain, I was more comfortable in Arabic than in my native language. Why do you ask?"

"Many of my associates believe a man must understand Greek to understand the world."

"Are you one of those men?" Thomas asked.

"Many great books are better read in the Greek they were written in, including Socrates, Aristotle, Homer, Plato, Plutarch, and many more."

Thomas smiled. "I see you prefer Philosophy over science. I have read those works, but also Archimedes, Claudius Ptolemy, Democritus, Euclid and Thales of Miletus. I have also read many erudite Arabic works that scholars in more northern lands ignore."

More studied Thomas, who studied him in return, wondering what the man saw. A man in his sixties who he might suspect was not as sharp as he once had been. Thomas might agree with the judgement, but intended to give as good as he got. What he saw in return was a man barely in his twenties and clearly in possession of a great intellect.

Finally, More shrugged and smiled. "Only a scholar would know of those men. As to Arabic studies, I admit ignorance, but Linacre has told me that when he studied medicine in Florence, some of the titles held there had been translated from that language into Latin or Greek. So come, Thomas Berrington, sit at my table, and we can discuss this deviant book. Shall I send to the tavern for ale?"

"Not on my behalf, but do so for yourself if you wish. Do I assume this talk of Latin and Greek mean your copy of the book is in one of those language?"

"No, it is written in English, but it has the feel of being a translation. I suspect it was originally penned in Latin, and in a monastery, despite the subject matter."

"I have known monasteries and abbeys where profane titles could be found."

"It is interesting you say so, for I have heard the same. My faith is strong, but there are times I question whether the Church might have lost its way."

Thomas took a seat and stared at the closed book. "May I open it?"

More sat beside him, his hands on the tabletop. "Of course."

Thomas made no immediate move. Instead, he studied the frontispiece. It was a crudely drawn image of a tailed demon confronted by a monk.

"It is the battle of St Cuthbert against the Devil," said More. "But in this case, it is more of a temptation, an advertisement of what might be found within."

"You told me the book is written in riddles. Have you managed to solve any of them?"

"One or two, but even when I have done so, I am unsure if they are meant to be easily solved to lead me in the wrong direction."

Thomas glanced at the frontispiece again. "Where did you obtain this? My contact told me copies are extremely rare."

"I did not find it; rather, it found me. It lay in the middle of this table one day when I returned home. My door is always locked, for I possess several rare titles, as you can see. I asked the goodwife who rents these rooms if she had let anyone in, but she said not. So how it came to be here is one more mystery."

"Presumably, whoever left it wants you to study the book," Thomas said. "Do you have a reputation in the arcane or profane?"

"I am not sure I welcome being questioned in such a manner, sir." More straightened, his expression changing in an instant.

"I apologise. I meant nothing by it. I was merely curious as to why you were chosen. Is it perhaps because you are a tutor to Princess Catherine and Prince Henry, so have a connection through them to the King?"

"That I do not know and can see no reason for it. Why would King Henry be interested? It is possible it was given to me because I am known as a devout man. I almost entered an order of the Carthusians when I was younger before deciding I could be more useful in other ways. It may be that the book has been sent to tempt me, as the Devil tempted our Lord Jesus himself. But see what you make of it, Berrington, and I will send out for ale."

Alone in the room, Thomas opened the first page and then flipped through the others. Each showed a hand drawing in the top corner of a profane nature, each one different. When he reached the end there was a final page, the illustration on this different. It was less dark, and the text offered a promise.

"Eternal life?" Thomas said, turning to More. "Am I reading this right?"

"You are," said More. "It is a promise that whoever completes all tasks will reveal the ultimate prize." More snorted a dismissive laugh. "It is the grail of all alchemists but can never be achieved. God would not allow it."

"And science would not allow it," Thomas said.

"God is more powerful than science, but I suspect you are right. I am sure Linacre would agree with you. But there are men out there who believe what is written here. Men who work in cellars to turn lead into gold, to reveal the location of the Philosopher's Stone, and to gain eternal health and life. I am familiar with a few such men through my studies at the Inns of Court, and they would benefit from treating their bodies more kindly, rather than seek childish answers in a book such as this."

Thomas turned back to the start and began to read. He wondered if the book had been printed only in England, or if copies were distributed in other parts of Europe, each a translation into their own language. Though he was aware Latin would suffice in most places. It was, after all, the language of the Church. And if More was correct and the intended audience were men of status, they too would most likely be able to read that same language.

The first page described a location, but, as More had said, the exact place was not named; it was only couched in terms of a riddle. It read: *An apostle raised high to reach for heaven. When bells toll, the time will have arrived, and Mammon will rise to take those who refuse any holy contribution.*

Thomas had no idea what it meant, or even how to start deciphering it, so it was fortunate that there came a knock at the door and More returned carrying two leather tankards. He set them on the table and pulled up his chair.

"That one is easy enough," he said, touching a finger to the riddle.

"For you, perhaps, not me."

More smiled. "Where do bells toll?"

"In churches. But there is a surfeit of churches in London."

"A city can never have too many places of worship. Tell me, who may the apostle be?"

Thomas shook his head. He could have named all the apostles at one time, but no longer. Prior Bernard – now Abbot Bernard – had made certain he studied the bible even as a lad. But which apostle was referred to here?

"Who is the most exalted apostle? Come on, Berrington, have you forgotten your bible?"

"That was long ago, and I admit to being a poor pupil as a boy."

"Saint Paul," said More, "is the highest apostle. And the tolling, of course, refers to the bells that ring in St Paul's

Cathedral. And Mammon is a demon of hell who tempts men with great wealth. The demon comes to punish those who give too generously to the Church in hopes of entering heaven. You must know that rich men and women purchase indulgences to pay for their sins to be wiped clean. Except God sees all, and when their time comes, those people will be taken down into Hell to burn forever."

"So this page refers to the area around St Paul's?"

"I believe it does."

"Has anyone been tortured or killed in its precincts?"

"Not that I know of, but perhaps they will be."

Thomas smiled. "Yes, perhaps they will be, but I would rather we catch whoever is behind this before any more deaths occur. Are you sure you have no idea who might have left this book for you?"

More shook his head. "I made extensive enquiries and am not without contacts, but nothing. Nobody was seen entering the house who should not have been here, and—"

Thomas interrupted. "Could it have been left by someone who lives here or comes and goes, such as a cook or cleaner?"

"Students such as myself are in and out of this house all the time," said More. "Some stay for a few years, as I have done. Others might come and go within a few weeks. So I suppose you are right. It could have been left by someone familiar with the lodgings, but someone new, not a regular. And if it were a person such as that, they would have already moved on."

Thomas considered More's words. Was it worth trying

to find out the names of those who had stayed for only a short period when the book was left?

"What manner of person were these students?" he asked.

"I assume you mean the temporary ones. They were many and varied. Some will come to use the libraries in London but choose to lodge here because the cost is less. Others will be from universities, as I once was. I stayed here a month after I studied at Oxford. Yet others are religious men. There have also been those in trade. We are not within the city wall, but the houses of various guilds are not far. We have had goldsmiths, physicians, printers, candlemakers, embroiderers, saddlers and a surfeit of other trades."

"All of them men?"

"Other than the goodwife who lets out these rooms, no women are allowed beyond the door, as is right."

Thomas did not comment. He considered it a waste of time attempting to track down those who had stayed here if, as More said, there might have been scores or hundreds.

"What date was this book left for you?"

"It was left on midsummer morn, just two months ago. When I first saw it, I thought it had been left in this room in error, but nobody else was expecting such a gift when I enquired."

"Who would know your room was vacant?"

More shrugged. "Almost anyone who lives here, and many outwith. I visit Durham house twice weekly to instruct Princess Catherine. The same with Prince Harry on one day. I spend the rest of my hours at Lincoln's Inn studying for the law. Mostly in the library, but also observing cases and speaking with qualified lawyers."

"Do you think you could ask the goodwife, for I assume she may have the information, who of the short-time lodgers resided here at that time? Let us say only those who stayed a month or less. I suspect whoever left the book for you would not want to stay around long afterwards."

"But why leave it for me?" asked More.

"If we knew that, we might know who it was or who put them up to it. You said you considered entering the Church. This book is the opposite of what the Church stands for, so perhaps it is meant as a temptation. Princess Catherine tells me you have a fine mind."

"I cannot claim that, but it has been said of me."

"Then they might expect you to decipher the text and glean some meaning from it."

"I have done some of that, but not so much yet." More reached out and touched the open page. "Let us go through it together. A man of your experience might notice something I have missed."

TWELVE

Three hours had passed before Thomas left More's room. Outside, he was surprised to discover dusk spreading across the city. Pools of shadow lurked in alleys and wrapped around the corners of houses. Already the streets held few people, and those who passed Thomas avoided his gaze and walked with eyes downcast as if searching for something ... but what?

The pages he had studied were burned into Thomas's mind and left a foul taste in his mouth. He had witnessed much through his long life, but what was described in the book was beyond debasement. It truly was the work of a demon, if not the Devil himself. Between them, he and More had deciphered five more riddles. Each of them related to both a place and a practice. Many were alchemical, the obvious being the transmutation of lead into gold, but others were more arcane, beyond the experience of either of them. Blood used to offer eternal life. Tinctures prepared that would make a man hard for hours. Others to make a woman fall under the spell of even the most disgusting man. Certain organs of the body that could cure illness – claims Thomas could easily ridicule. All of them referred to where such treasures, if such they could be called, might be found.

What had drawn his attention were several passages hinting that the flesh of the human brain could increase a man's knowledge. That partaking of it would, somehow, transfer the experience of one person to another. It was nonsense, of course, but men were known to believe nonsense too often for the good of the world.

Thomas also not had a list of six locations that, he believed, would attract a certain kind of man. And men they would be, he was sure. He knew that members of the female sex could be evil and had personal experience of such, but in general, he considered them to indeed be the fairer sex.

He passed even fewer people as the last of the light faded from the sky. His feet carried him without thought, and when he finally looked around, he found Ludgate ahead and three men blocking his passage. He examined them as he came closer, not slackening his stride, which would show fear. They stood shoulder to shoulder, their eyes on him, and he knew there would be a confrontation. He wondered what they wanted with him. Were they rough men taking advantage of the deserted streets to pick on the few using them? Or were they something more sinister? Eleanor had said three men attacked her and Luke, and now three men blocked Thomas's way through the gate. The same men? If so, how did they know who he was?

Thomas ran a response to an attack through his mind. Except when he was six paces away, the man in the middle stepped aside, leaving just enough room for Thomas to pass through. He took the bait, expecting to be grabbed as he pushed between them, but passed without issue. Two of the men fell in beside him, with the third behind. It was a skilled move aimed at blocking his escape other than ahead. Thomas knew he could ignore them, but better to discover what their intention was now.

"Do you want something? I have no coin on me, and as you can see, my clothes are hardly worth stealing."

"You know what we want. Where is the printer Eleanor Cooper?"

So these *were* the men who attacked her, the men she could not describe? It made sense. How they knew who *he* was and where he would be did *not* make sense. Eleanor was hardly likely to have told them where he would be. He might have suspected they kept watch on her and had seen them together when they were moving her equipment, but he thought not. He too had kept watch in case they turned up. There would be little point moving her printworks if they saw where it was moved to.

Thomas continued walking. "I do not even know of who you speak. Now begone." He glanced to one side, then the other. He let his gaze take in the man to his right, who was tall and well-built. Not as tall as Thomas, but younger and stronger if it came to a fight. But, no doubt, less experienced.

"Do you think us stupid? We saw you with her. We want to speak to her, nothing more." The man sounded reasonable. If Eleanor had not told him they attacked Luke, he might even believe him. "We have a proposition for her that will benefit everyone."

"Then it is a pity I have no idea who she is or where she could be found."

St Paul's Cathedral lay ahead, but Thomas turned aside instead of crossing in front of it, and made for the Bel Savage. The men came with him. Thomas entered the inn, which was surprisingly busy. He saw Peggy Spicer take note of his entrance, but before she could ask if he had returned to take a room, he moved his hand to silence her and ordered ale.

"And one for each of my friends, Peggy. From your special stock, if you would. Has my room been cleaned?"

"It has, sir. Do you want me to send your ale upstairs? And a woman, perhaps? Sally told me only this morning when you left that she wanted to lie with you. And she is clean. Well, fairly clean."

"Yes, send her up." Thomas turned to look at each man, who wore uneasy expressions. "You can pay for your own whores, but the ale is a gift from me. Peggy serves the best ale in London. She also has the best whores. I will leave you now. My thanks for your company and conversation."

Thomas turned and made for the inner door. Once in the corridor, he left through the back door, entering the stables. He found a dark corner and stood waiting, but the men did not appear. He waited a few more minutes, then went to the street, only to find another shadowed space to conceal himself in.

The men appeared before long, as he expected. He watched them stop and look around. A conversation took place, which was not entirely friendly. The man who had done all the talking said something, then walked off. The two others remained, talking more reasonably. When they moved away, Thomas waited until they were almost out of sight, then followed. He glanced back in case the argument had been a ploy, but there was no sign of the third man. Had it been Thomas and his son Will, or Usaden, that is what they would have done. Split up to follow the follower.

The men continued on foot into Cheapside, almost deserted despite several lanterns burning from sconces. Market stalls were closed up, and only a few candles showed in windows. Thomas suspected people had moved to rooms in the rear of their houses to huddle away from an unknown peril.

At the great conduit at the eastern end of Cheapside, the men took the left of the three streets and walked along Bradstrete. Some distance ahead, the men appeared to be conversing, but he could not hear their words. Thomas wondered if their destination lay within the city walls or not. He knew they could pass through either Moorgate or Bishopsgate if they continued along their way. Beyond, lay a scattering of religious houses and homes for those who served them, and a few larger residences of those rich enough to build their own manor houses out there, away from the stink of the city. Thomas recalled coming this way a few years before when he was in pursuit of an evil woman and her even more evil father. Both had burned to death in a windmill they had taken refuge in. Thomas hoped what was happening now did not lead to something similar. He was growing tired of righting wrongs, of causing the death of evil men and women. It was not a path he had ever chosen, but it seemed the path had chosen him.

When he looked up, only one man continued to walk along the middle of the empty street. Thomas glanced to either side. To his left lay the Austin Friary and, on his right, houses. He passed an alley, but no one emerged to confront him. He suspected the men had split up, one to go to his lodgings, the other to theirs. Except, as he had been many times in his life, Thomas was wrong.

Another hundred paces and the lone man stopped and turned back. Thomas saw his hand drop to his waist and draw something. It was too dark to see what, but a knife made sense.

He slowed to a halt and looked back, unsurprised to see the other man approaching with a sword. He was grinning.

"Kill me, and you will never discover where this Eleanor Cooper is," he said.

"You still refuse?"

"I still refuse."

"Then you are no use to us and have seen our faces."

Both men closed on Thomas, and he had a decision to make. He could call out for help but doubted anyone would respond. Apart from which, it was not in his nature to ask for aid. So he ran at the man with the knife, on the assumption he would be easier to deal with.

Which he was.

A thrust from the waist was meant to gut Thomas, but he jerked aside at the last moment, unaware he was going to, not knowing how he could do such things, only that he could. One day, he would fail and die, but not tonight. Cold certainty filled him.

He wrapped the man's right arm in his robe, then ran his hand down the arm to his wrist. He twisted, and the knife clattered to the cobbles. Thomas put his foot on it, then punched the man hard between the eyes. He fell backwards, his head making a loud crack as it hit the ground.

Thomas went to one knee and picked up the knife. He stayed there as the other man ran at him, the hilt of the sword held in both hands, ready to swing down. Except, before he was close enough, Thomas pushed hard, flying horizontally to run the blade of the knife across the back of the man's ankle to cut through the tendon. It was not a killing blow, but it was painful and would hobble him for a month or more. If the man had any sense, he would visit a Moorish doctor who could treat the wound so he might regain some use of his foot.

Thomas had no regret about crippling a man. If the tables had been turned, both would have taken Thomas's life. Which raised the question as to why they wanted him dead. Unless they did not like to be crossed, and that was reason enough. He knew he had to speak with Eleanor again to press her as to why she had been chosen and whether she had found him a copy of the book. Despite having gone through More's copy, Thomas wanted one for himself to study at leisure.

He thought of putting his foot on the hobbled man's leg and questioning him, but he was too tired and sure he would learn nothing. So he left both in the middle of the wide street and walked back towards Milkstrete.

When he reached the house it was locked, and all the windows dark. Thomas went to the stables, but there was no sign of Jack. He had no option but to knock on the door to gain entry. It took some time, but eventually, candlelight showed, and Hardwin said, "Who is it knocking at this time of night? Begone with you, knave."

"It is Thomas Berrington. Open up and let me in. My temper is short."

The door opened to reveal Hardwin in a nightshirt, his thin hair sticking out from his head. He tried to assemble his features into something close to amenability.

"You are out late, Sir Thomas."

"Indeed I am, so my thanks for admitting me. Would it be possible to have a key so I do not have to disturb you again?"

"A key?"

"Yes, a key. They fit in the locks and mean I can admit myself. One for the door from the stables would suffice."

"This is the only door with a lock. All the others are barred from within."

"Then a key for this will be acceptable."

"We only..." Hardwin started, then remembered his place. "I will have a copy made, sir. Do you need anything else? Should I wake Winnie to make you something to eat?"

"Let her sleep. All I need is my bed. Goodnight."

"Goodnight, sir." But the words came out like cold rancid treacle poured from a pot.

Thomas left Hardwin to lock the door again and climbed to his room. He was barely aware of removing his clothes, not aware of his head hitting the thin pillow.

THIRTEEN

When Thomas entered the printworks the following morning he found Eleanor operating the press. He watched, unobserved for a moment, as she pulled a lever down, then used another to press inked type against a sheet of paper. Muscles in her slim arms stood out at each stage. He was impressed at the strength he had not witnessed before, and her easy skill. Transferring the ink to the paper took mere seconds before she peeled it off and hung it over a wooden bar to dry. When she turned back, she saw Thomas and smiled.

"I did not hear you come in, Tom. Is it me you want, or Luke?"

"Luke first. How has he been?"

"Tossing and turning all night, but he says he feels well enough to help later today. Did you go to see Thomas More?"

Thomas saw no point in telling her about the men who attacked him on his was back into the city. Eleanor seemed happier this morning and would not thank him for a reminder of the attack on her. Thomas would ensure he was more vigilant.

"Yes, and he showed me his copy of the book."

"And...?"

"I will tell you once I have checked on Luke. Is he still in bed?"

"He is, though his lying there till noon will have to stop before he gets a taste for it."

Thomas climbed the narrow stairs, little better than a ladder. Luke appeared to be asleep, but roused when Thomas knelt beside the pallet and shook his arm. He was naked beneath the coarse blanket, making it easier for Thomas to inspect his wound. He did not like what he saw.

"Have you been doing as I asked and washing it four times a day?"

"Mostly, yes, but there are times I forget. And I sleep so much it leaves little time to wash."

"Then ask Eleanor to do it for you."

When Thomas pressed his fingers against the wound, Luke winced. It showed redness around it, which had spread since the day before.

"Does it hurt when I do that?"

"Of course it does. I was stabbed."

"I do not like the look of it, but I have none of my herbs or salves with me. I did not expect to need them."

"Time is all I need. Give me another day or two and I will be hale again."

"Not if the infection spreads. Do you know any

Moorish doctors in London? I have heard tell of them but have never needed one myself."

"Nor me. I have never been sick a day in my life, but Eleanor might know of someone." Luke turned over, Thomas dismissed.

Downstairs, Eleanor continued to work. Pages of text, four on each sheet, came off the press at regular intervals. Thomas went to where she had hung one and turned his head so he could read the text.

"I take it this is one of your tales?" he asked.

Eleanor laughed. "Is it the bawdy nature that gives it away?"

"It is indeed bawdy. Perhaps more than bawdy. You have regular clients for this?"

"Indeed I do, which is why I will not stop work, but being a woman I can talk at the same time."

"As I see. You asked what I learned from the book last night, so if you can listen as well as work I will tell you. But I have a more pressing matter first. Luke's wound is festering and must be treated, but I do not have the salves I need with me. He said you might know of a Moorish doctor in London."

"I know of several, but there is only one I use when I need a remedy."

Thomas looked her up and down. "I would say you are as hale as anyone I have ever seen."

"There are times my head hurts something fierce, and I have pain with my bleeding." She spoke without shame, which was unusual from a woman to a man. It pleased Thomas that she did so.

"My daughter mixes fine remedies for both," he said. "Unfortunately, she is not here."

"Is she clever like you?"

Thomas laughed. "More clever."

"What age has she? Older than me?"

"I do not know how many years you have, Eleanor, but Amal has sixteen."

"Then ten years less than me." She drew another sheet from the press and hung it up. "The Moor I use can be found beyond the northern city walls at a place called Bas Court. Do you know your way to Cripplegate, Tom?"

"I do."

"Then pass through it and stay on the road north. You will see Bas Court once you are beyond the wall. Ask there, and they will take you to Timothy. He has a small workshop in their grounds."

"Timothy?" Thomas said. "I need a Moorish doctor."

"Which you will have. It is not his given name, but I believe he uses that because his true name is difficult for people to speak."

Thomas understood the reason well enough. When he returned to England after more than forty years away, hair almost blonde from the southern sun, face dark from the same, people had been wary of him. Even more so because of the clothes he wore and the long tagelmust wrapped around his shoulders and head.

"I would speak with you on my return," he said. "I want to ask you about other printworks and who might have taken a contract to produce the book."

"And who stopped printing it," said Eleanor. "Which I presume is why those men came seeking a new printer."

Thomas was glad he had not mention them. As he left the workshop, he heard the press continue. He took the street north and passed through Cripplegate. As promised, he saw Bas Court ahead and, when he enquired, was led to what appeared to have once been a stable.

Thomas rapped on the open door and entered.

"I am looking for al-Timani," he said in Arabic, hoping his guess at the name was correct.

A dark-skinned man in his late forties looked up from the bench he was working on. Glass vials and mortar bowls held a range of herbs, spices and liquids.

"I no longer go by that name," he responded in kind. "And I suggest we speak English in case we are overheard." His eyes tracked Thomas. "You appear to be an English gentleman, so how do you know my language?"

"I lived for many years in Moorish Spain, and it became my language more than my own."

Al-Timani continued to stare at Thomas without expression.

"An Englishman who lived in Moorish Spain. Did you also train at the Infirmary in Malaka?"

Thomas smiled. "I did. My name is—"

"Thomas Berrington." Al-Timani rose and came around the bench. He hugged Thomas and then stood at arm's length. "I never had the honour to meet you, but every physician in al-Andalus knows of Thomas Berrington. What are you doing here? You do not need my poor skills."

"I judge you are as skilled as I am," Thomas smiled again. "Which is to say, better than any English physician."

"I know of one or two who have made strides in accepting what you and I know. I assume you have come because you want something other than conversation?"

"I have a need for raw alcohol, hemp, poppy, garlic and bile salt. Onion I can find."

"You intend to make Bald's eye salve? Who has an infection, and how bad is it?"

"A printer by the name of Luke Thatcher. His wound festers. It is not bad yet, but if left another day or two, it will turn very bad. I will not have my patient die for lack of what he needs."

"Then let me find them for you." Al-Timani rose and went to a tall set of shelves attached to a brick wall. He, like Thomas, no longer wore Moorish clothing, but he did not move like someone from England. Thomas wondered if he moved the same way. Perhaps the heat of southern Spain softened the tendons and muscles of a body.

When the man returned with what Thomas had requested and set it on the bench, he said, "Do you want me to make the salve up for you?"

"I would be grateful. I am a visitor to the city, so I do not have my equipment here."

They talked as Al-Timani worked. Thomas discovered the man had lived in Cordoba for a time, and their paths might have crossed if fate had looked on them more favourably. As a half-hour passed, Thomas felt increasingly comfortable in the man's presence. When he was handed a small pot containing the remedy he put a silver coin on the bench. Al-Timani pushed it away.

"To meet you is payment enough, Thomas Berrington. And before you go I will give you something for Eleanor Cooper as well."

Thomas smiled. "She told me she knew you and used your remedies."

"She and Luke have lived together a long time, but there is only one master in that house and it is not him. Eleanor suffers from bad headaches and I supply a little poppy for her to use when they become too much to bear."

"She told me she has pains when she bleeds. She mentioned pain in her head but I had the impression it was not so bad."

Al-Timani shrugged. "Perhaps she does not want you to know, in which case do not say I mentioned it. I think there are times she suffers a great deal. She even once asked me about trepanning, but I told her I would never countenance such barbarity. Tell her the poppy is for her bleeding pains. Perhaps I forget myself, but it is good to speak with a fellow Moorish physician."

"I will say nothing," Thomas said. "What is this place you work alongside?"

"It was once the home of a wealthy man. When he died without issue, he left his wealth to a religious order and instructed it to be a place of healing for all. When I arrived in this land ten years ago, along with many of my countrymen after Granada fell to Spain, I found my way here and have stayed ever since."

Thomas pushed the coins across the worktable. "Then

take the silver and add it to the coffers of Bas Court. And if you would allow it, I would like to visit again when my need is less pressing."

Thomas took the bag into which al-Timani had placed hashish and poppy resin, together with a pot of Bald's eye salve. When he returned to the print works Luke was still in bed, and Thomas woke him, ignoring his grumbles. He washed the area of the wound, then rubbed some of the salve al-Timani had produced into the wound itself. He considered removing the stitches to press it even deeper but decided to try this approach first. Then he mixed the hashish and poppy with wine and made Luke drink it. He would sleep again now, but with good fortune, it would be a healing sleep.

When he descended the steep stairs, it was to find Eleanor hanging up the last pages she had produced.

"When can you print on the other side?" he asked.

"Not until the morning. How is Luke?"

"He should be asleep already, but I will not know how his wound is until tomorrow. Al-Timani also gave me some poppy for you." Thomas passed the small cloth bag across. "You did not tell me your headaches were bad enough to need poppy. I can examine you if you wish?"

Eleanor looked shocked for a brief moment, and then she smiled. Thomas thought she may have misconstrued his comment.

"They are not so bad, and the poppy helps."

"Do not get too used to it."

"I will not. Now, I have an idea that might help you find a copy of the book you seek. You asked which other printers might have produced the diabolic tome, or those who refused to do so. I intend to visit all the works I know of, starting with the most well-known, to see if they have been approached. Most of their owners know me, though I admit not all approve of what I do. We share a profession, so I can at least ask the question. You will come with me, Tom?"

"If I am allowed. Where do you intend to start?"

"The Caxton press in Fleet Street is far and away the most prestigious because it was the first."

"Do you intend to visit some of the smaller printers as well as Caxton?" Thomas asked.

"Of course. I would be surprised if John Wynkyn would allow a profane book to be produced at his works, but I know of others who are less particular."

"Or more in need of the income. Do you have one of your tales you have not yet printed?"

"I have a dozen. It takes me no time to scribble them but longer to set them in print. Why?"

"Fetch two or three. We can use them to judge the manner of the smaller printers."

Eleanor went to a wooden box with a heavy padlock which she opened with a key hung from a chain at her waist. She moved so Thomas could not look inside and pulled out several sheets of paper, which she slipped beneath her shirt before resetting the lock. She wrapped a shawl around her shoulders, for the day had turned cold. The whole year had been cold, as it had been for several years. Crops were failing, and many were going hungry, but still the King demanded taxes from all.

They left the workshop. Eleanor closed the doors then

secured them with another padlock. As they reached the street, the front door of the house opened, and Hardwin emerged with something in his hand.

"This came for you." His gaze took in Eleanor, and Thomas knew exactly what he was thinking.

Thomas took the note and turned it over. The seal had once more been broken and crudely replaced, but he did not confront the man. He broke the wax and read the note. Then he slid the message into his coat, took Eleanor's hand and led her away, leaving Hardwin on the stoop.

"He thinks you are about to defile me, Tom," she said with a laugh.

"Indeed he does. Should I peck a kiss on your cheek while he is watching?"

She laughed again. "Oh, what a wicked notion you have. Yes, please."

He stopped and kissed her cheek, and she put a hand behind his neck.

"Is he still looking?"

"He is."

"Then put your arms around me and put a kiss on my lips this time."

Thomas was concerned the show of affection might be as much for Eleanor as Hardwin but did as asked. It felt strange to embrace a woman so slim and young, and he felt uneasy. He had a woman. Except Bel, his first love, had been acting strangely of late. She had returned to her house outside of Lemster, and he wondered if it was some harbinger of things to come. He realised he was overthinking matters, which was not unusual. Eleanor laughed, took his hand and pulled him along the street.

FOURTEEN

The print works founded by William Caxton filled the entirety of a three-storey house on the corner of Fleet Street and Old Bailey. As they passed beneath Ludgate, Eleanor informed Thomas that Caxton had died eleven years before, but his name was so well known the business had retained it. She told Thomas that Caxton had fought hard to stop others setting up in the same trade, but he could no more do so than stop the Thames flowing to the sea. Even then, England had far less printers than the continent. When Caxton died, John Wynkyn, late of Bruges, took charge of the undertaking. As they entered the works, Thomas saw not the single printing press Eleanor owned but five, and by the sound of industry filtering from the floor above, more were being used there. The smell of ink filled the air, and great stacks of paper stood precariously in any spare space. Dampened sheets hung from rods ready to be used.

A tall man with thick, tightly curled hair approached.

"Have you come to accept the position I offered you, Eleanor?"

"I have not, John, but keep asking because one day I may relent." She winked at Thomas. "This is my friend, Thomas Berrington, and we have come to ask you a few questions if we may."

"Well met, Thomas," said Wynkyn. "Can I offer you both a tankard of ale while we talk?"

"You are not too busy?" asked Eleanor.

"For you, never. Come to my study. It will be quieter there, and in truth, my workers prefer it when I am not standing over them watching every move."

John Wynkyn led the way through the noise and enterprise to a room at the back. Most of the noise died away once he closed the door. A large glazed window offered a view across the work. Wynkyn poured ale into three clay beakers and then sat behind a large desk where several proofs of works in progress were laid out, together with hand-written documents.

"I see you are busy, John," said Eleanor as she took one of the other chairs.

"Which is why I need to find workers I can trust. But no mind. What is it you want to ask?"

"There is a demonic book in London that Thomas has seen a copy of. Have you produced copies yourself or been asked to?"

"If it is the title I believe you speak of, then I am sore upset you need to ask such a question. It has nothing to do with me." Wynkyn turned his gaze on Thomas. "May I ask where you saw this copy?"

Thomas considered the question before replying. "I would prefer not to say at the moment. Its owner may not wish the information to be made public, and might fear for his life if it was. I am aware of several deaths connected to the material printed on the book's pages."

Wynkyn leaned closer. "May I ask what your interest is in this book?"

"It is not the book itself, only its effect on the people of London. But the book contains clues, and if I can decipher them they may lead to whoever is doing the killing. Have you seen a copy yourself?"

Wynkyn shook his head. "I have not, and if offered the opportunity to do so, I would decline. I have heard that weak-minded men have lost their wits after reading what it contains. If you have seen it yourself, you must agree."

It was an erudite statement that deserved an answer.

"Yes, the words caused me discomfort," Thomas said. "There are also illustrations meant to shock, but these had less effect on me."

"That is what I have heard." Wynkyn turned to Eleanor. "I apologise if I have been unable to offer what you seek."

"It is as expected, John," said Eleanor. "I could not believe you involved in such an enterprise, but I am sure you know of other printers willing to take payment for producing such a book."

Wynkyn smiled. "Only those you no doubt also know. The usual suspects, though I doubt any will admit to dealing with such blasphemy." He turned back to Thomas. "Tell me, sir, what exactly is your interest in this book?"

"Until I entered London two days ago, I had none, but Eleanor—"

She reached out and touched Thomas's arm to stop him.

"I am sure John does not want to hear about my troubles, Tom."

"Very well. In that case, my interest was sparked when I saw a body with its skull laid open. I also heard of others attacked in the same manner."

"Not all quite the same," said Wynkyn. "I was told of one where the entire head was taken. Another where the damage was to the back of the skull and the face looked completely normal." He glanced at Eleanor. "I am sorry, my dear, if this is too much information for you."

"You know I am strong, John. Do not be concerned for me."

Wynkyn nodded. "I hear that was the first death but not the last. And there will be more, mark my words."

"Do you know the names of any of the victims?" Thomas asked.

"I do not."

"Who would?"

Eleanor touched Thomas's wrist, a gesture that did not go unnoticed by John Wynkyn. "John is hiding nothing from you, Tom. It sounded as if you were making an accusation."

Thomas glanced down and pulled his hand away. "I do not know enough. I only thought John might have known more that might help."

"I do not, sir. Visit the Constable and you may have more luck, but these deaths are nothing to do with men. What can be done against the demons of hell?" He made the sign of the cross to ward off evil.

"I will do whatever I can, sir. It will not be the first time, but I hope perhaps this may be the last. The King must be aware of these events."

"You would not expect me to know that, would you?"

"I apologise. I will raise the matter when I see him tomorrow."

"You are known to the King?"

"He knows of me. Whether he *knows* me is another matter. But I have been fortunate in my friends, and one of them is Princess Catherine."

Wynkyn only stared at Thomas, his mouth open as if searching for words that would not come.

Eleanor smiled and touched the man's arm. "Do not concern yourself, John. Tom is not a titled man, nor wealthy. He happens to know people who are, that is all. You can trust him. Now, you are sure no one has come here asking if you can produce the demonic book?"

"I told you they have not, and I pay little heed to other printers who might have been. Caxton Press is the most respected printer in England, perhaps in all of Europe, for as you know, my old master learned his trade there."

"You must be familiar with all the reputable printers in London, John. Perhaps you can ask a question about the book at your next meeting."

"Those of us who want to create a Guild of Stationers are due to meet in a week, but they would not welcome such a question. The city's main guilds do not yet accept us, and to raise such a topic would harm our bid to become members of the Guildhall." Wynkyn stared at Eleanor. "I would recommend you to print only religious texts and the classics."

Eleanor smiled. "I cannot afford to do that, John. Perhaps in the future."

"You are a fine setter of type, my dear, and if your business ever falters, you know where to come."

"And give up my own work?" asked Eleanor.

"What you do in your own time would be up to you. It is your soul you are risking."

Wynkyn's demeanour changed, and Thomas knew the man held deep religious beliefs, as almost everyone in England did. He did not look to see Eleanor's reaction but wondered whether she shared them. If so, how did they fit with the nature of the bawdy tales she produced? They might have a conversation regarding the matter, but it would have to wait.

"Are you sure you do not know who the author of this profane work might be?" he asked, his eyes on Wynkyn.

The man's gaze slipped away as he looked across the industry beyond his room, and Thomas knew that whatever his reply, it would not be the entire truth.

"I will ask, for Eleanor," said Wynkyn. "I will not raise it officially at the Guildhall, where we are due to discuss the creation of our new guild. Many do not consider what we do as a trade."

"But it is," said Eleanor. "If they doubt that, they should visit your works."

Wynkyn smiled sadly. "Yes, they should. And if we are to succeed, I regret to say you will never be admitted. Firstly, you are female. Secondly, there is the nature of your publications. Were it my decision, it would be different."

Eleanor laughed. "You are a sweet man, John. By the time the Guilds decide, I suspect you and I will be long in our graves."

Wynkyn crossed himself again. "May that be many years from now."

When Eleanor rose, Wynkyn walked them through the workshop and out to the street.

"I have a question of my own, if I may ask it," said Wynkyn.

"As long as it is not another request to work for you," said Eleanor.

Wynkyn smiled. "One day, my dear. This concerns the theft of a set of type and letter punches to create new sets."

"A theft from here?" asked Eleanor.

"An entire set of lead type and punches were taken. Have you heard of anyone trying to sell them?"

Eleanor shook her head. "I have not, but will ask others. Thank you for your help, John." Eleanor kissed the man's cheek, which caused him to blush.

Eleanor started off then stopped. "Wait here for me, Tom. There is something I forgot to ask John." Without waiting, she turned and strode into the printworks.

Thomas stood in the street and stared at the sky, where fresh clouds loomed tall and grey to the south beyond the river. Eleanor was gone longer than he expected, and when she appeared, it was from a side alley a few paces along the roadway, not from the door of the printworks.

"Did you get what you wanted?"

She smiled. "I believe so. John is too accommodating."

"Only for you, I suspect," Thomas said, and Eleanor laughed.

Once they had gone some distance along Fleet Street, Eleanor said, "He always asks me to work for him, and I always refuse, but it is not only my skill he wants."

"You cannot blame him. You are a fine-looking woman. Do you think he knows more than he said?"

"Of course he does. The Caxton Press is the most prestigious printer in the land. John knows everything that happens in the trade and everyone who works it. He knows the type I use was smuggled into the country, and if the fact were ever to be discovered, both myself and Luke might be hung for contraband. That is why he asked me about his missing type and the tools to create more. He would not dare ask such a question of those in his supposed guild."

"Why would someone steal those things? Can you not import type from the continent?" Thomas was aware he knew little about the trade Eleanor followed. He wondered if he had been right to set her up in the workshop directly linked to the house he used at the King's pleasure. His residence was temporary, and whoever lived there next would likely evict her. Hardwin, he was sure, would do so the moment Thomas vacated the property. Which meant they should seek somewhere else for her to set up in. But not yet. The author of The Beasts of the City had to be exposed first so she could work without hindrance.

"To import type is against the law," said Eleanor. "The apparatus you see around you, the print stone, the press, the stacks of paper, all mean nothing without type. Some who trade under the covers, like myself, have been known to create their own, but it is both an art and a skill, and it is easy to see the crudity of what is produced. Luke went to Bruges and paid a great deal of silver for a full set of English type, punches and letter presses. He smuggled it across the sea, hidden inside sacks of grain. Now, it is my stock in trade. I want another set, but it would be risky to do the same again. Wynkyn has people who fashion type for him, which is of the highest quality. Those who recognise type can tell when something has been produced at the Caxton Press."

"And you would never work for him?"

"For John? No. I admire him a great deal, but he and I are as chalk and cheese. All would be well for a while, then he would make demands I could not meet."

"Demands?"

Eleanor smiled coquettishly. "You did say I am a fine-looking woman, Tom. And there I was, thinking you were too old to appreciate a pretty girl."

"I might be old, but not dead. I assume you mean demands of an unsavoury manner."

"He would not be the first nor the last, but a girl learns to look after herself. And I have Luke to protect me – at least I will once you have made him well again. He will be well again, Tom?"

"Yes, he will." But Thomas was unsure if he spoke the truth, which he could not do in front of this woman. Luke's wound had festered more than he expected or liked. Sometimes, wounds did, and whatever was done failed to work when that happened. But there was always hope.

"Shall we visit more printers, Tom?" Eleanor asked, unaware of the doubts running through his head.

"Yes, and then we will return to see if Luke is recovering."

FIFTEEN

By the time they had visited six printers both Eleanor and Thomas were tired. He asked if there were others worth calling on.

"There are, but I do not expect better fortune. All will deny knowledge of the book."

"You cannot be the only printer those men approached," Thomas said. "So either they are lying, or we have not spoken with one who was."

"There is one more, someone who will print anything. I was hoping not to have to go to him, but we have had no luck elsewhere. Then we return to Luke, yes?"

"Agreed, one more."

"It is south of the river, operated by a man and boy, but they are not father and son. Their reputation is that they will print anything. Blasphemous treatise far stronger than the bawdy tales I produce. If anyone has been contacted, it will be someone like them. We should cross at the bridge rather than take a wherry. The river will be running fast by now."

Thomas realised he gave little thought to the turn of the tides and their effect on the Thames, though his experience had taught him perhaps he should. He knew how chaotic the river could be when the tide rose or fell hard.

They emerged into Southwark and turned east, skirting Winchester Palace and then taking Maiden Lane until it turned south. Eleanor entered a narrow alley, running in the opposite direction. The printworks, consisting of a small wooden hut which lay halfway along the lane. Some of the equipment stood in the alley, covered with canvas to protect it from the elements.

A short man with long, greasy hair going thin, grinned when he saw Eleanor. He opened his arms to embrace her but she managed to twist aside.

"What brings such beauty to my humble works?" His eyes dragged themselves away from Eleanor to study Thomas. He seemed unimpressed.

Behind him, a boy of no more than twelve years worked a heavy press. He looked too slight for the job but managed well enough.

"I have had some bad luck, Gray. Men attacked me and Luke. They damaged our press. I wondered if you had time to set some of my stories and print them for me." Thomas recognised the lie but assumed this man would not.

Gray's smile widened, and he held out a hand. "Let me see them, then."

Eleanor drew the pages from inside her shirt, the man's eyes on her the entire time. When she passed them to him, he raised them to his face and inhaled the scent of her on the paper. Thomas glanced at Eleanor to see her reaction, but she played along for now.

The man turned away and took a chair, scanned through the pages, and then stood again.

"Aye, I expect we could print these. They are tamer than I am used to but arousing enough." He handed the sheets to the boy, who took them and laid them on a small bench. "Set them so we can print all three at a go, Harrold."

The boy pulled out a type case and began picking letters, his eyes only on the hand-written pages while his fingers worked with practised familiarity.

"I did not mean for you to do it now, Gray," said Eleanor.

"Work is work, girl. It will cost you, mind. How many copies do you need?"

"Three score to start with. Let me see how they sell."

"Six shillings then. Come back the day after tomorrow, and they will be ready, but I need half the payment in advance." His manner had changed, and now he was all business.

"You would rob me?" said Eleanor, her voice sharp. "I will pay half."

"You will pay all of it, or I tell Harrold to stop now." He started to turn. "We have enough work to get on with. I am only doing this as a favour to a good friend."

Thomas reached into his coat, drew out six shillings and handed them to Eleanor.

"Six shillings, then, though I still say it is robbery. Have you no other work on?"

The man she called Gray took the coins, which disappeared into his pocket. Thomas suspected the boy might see a few pence if he was lucky.

"We are busy enough, but I will make an exception for you, my dear. Tell me about these men who ransacked your works. Were they after something, or was it simple mischief?"

"Evil, more like," said Eleanor. "They wanted me to produce a book for them, but I told them I was not interested when they told me its nature."

Gray laughed. "But your tales are bawdy enough. Why turn down work? I never would."

"Have they not been to you, then?" she asked.

"They may have done, but unless you tell me what they wanted you to print how can I know?"

"I take it you have scribes for the usual pamphlets you sell?"

"I do, but they work only for me."

"I do not want to steal them. I have read their product. The book these men wanted me to print was unlike what you and I produce. It was darker, hellish even."

"If you mean The Beasts of the City, no one has asked me to produce copies. They must already have a printer, for I hear the title has been distributed to select gentlemen."

"A few copies only is what I heard," said Eleanor. "I suspect whoever they employed to produce them realised the true nature of the work and stopped. Or something happened to them. I would be grateful if you could let me know if they come to you."

Thomas watched her and the man, with the occasional

glance at the boy, who worked almost as fast as Eleanor. He was a stranger here and was content to let Eleanor take the lead. So far she had done an excellent job, raising the book's topic without sparking Gray's suspicion.

"I will consider doing so for a small additional payment," said Gray.

Thomas made no move, and Eleanor shook her head.

"No mind, it is not important. The day after tomorrow?"

Gray made no response, no doubt considering the contract already sealed.

Later, crossing London Bridge, Eleanor said, "If Gray ever drops dead, which would not surprise me, I will try to employ Harrold. He has a fine hand and is fast, but the quality of the type he is forced to work with is disgraceful. I will pay you back the six shillings as soon as I can, Tom."

"Consider it a gift."

She looked at him, her head tilted. "In return for what?"

"The money means nothing to me."

She laughed. "For a few shillings more, you could buy the whole of Gray's workshop and press. I would not want you to think paying the money puts me in your debt. I know men look at me with lust in their eyes, but I admit I did not think you were that kind of man."

"Oh, I have known lust, but am old enough now to have set it behind me."

Eleanor laughed. "I would not regard you as old, Tom, and I suspect you could still rise to the occasion if required. At least you will save yourself the balance of payment, for I have no intention of returning. Let him sell those tales and earn himself a few pence. I have a hundred more I can scribble. It is not difficult to do."

Based on his brief perusal of the copy she had given him, Thomas was unsurprised at her words. Their content was not high art. Or even art at all. But it had a market, and Eleanor no doubt wrote to that market and did so with some measure of success. He wondered if she harboured higher ambitions or was content with her lot.

When Thomas and Eleanor turned from Cheapside into Milkstrete he saw Jack sitting on the stable wall. The lad dropped down and ran towards them.

"Thomas, sir, you have to come. I returned from an errand to find men in the lady's workshop, shouting and screaming. I dared not enter but did not know where you had gone, so I had to wait for you. Come. Come quickly."

Thomas ran, leaving Eleanor and Jack behind. When he saw the open doors to the workshop and what had been done, he turned back to stop Eleanor from coming closer. She pushed past him, then stopped with an expression of rage.

"How many?" Thomas asked Jack.

"I saw three, sir."

"How long since?"

"An hour."

"Did anyone call the watch?"

"It is not my place, but I told Hardwin what was happening. He sent me back to the stable. I could do nothing on my own, sir. There were too many. Big men with clubs, swords and knives."

Eleanor had already entered and gone upstairs. As Thomas reached the foot of the steps, he heard a cry of anguish and went up two treads at a time. At the top, he saw Eleanor on her knees, Luke's hands in hers. He was not moving.

Thomas knelt beside her. "Let me see."

She turned to him. "They have killed him, Tom. All your physics, and they have killed him."

"Let me be the judge of that. Go downstairs and see what can be salvaged. I will call you when I am finished." He tried to push past her, but she remained where she was. "Go or stay, then. It is all the same to me."

He reached for Luke's neck, laid two fingers on his throat and waited. There was a heartbeat, slow and strong.

"He is not dead, so let me see what is wrong." He pushed at Eleanor. This time, she rose and went downstairs.

Thomas opened Luke's shirt to examine his earlier wound. Thanks to al-Timami's salves, it was less inflamed. Whatever he had mixed, Thomas wanted the knowledge of it, aware of how much he had forgotten since the fall of Moorish Spain. He wondered if he ever knew as much as he believed he did. Al-Timani had been born into that world and learned since he was a toddler, most likely at his father's side.

Thomas pressed on the wound and saw Luke wince, but he remained unconscious. Thomas felt beneath his hair and found what he was looking for. There was a fresh lump on his skull, and when he drew his fingers away he saw blood on them. He checked the rest of the man but found only the one new wound. He looked around and found a brooch on the small side table. He took it and poked the pin into Luke's arm, pleased when he saw a reaction. He had lost his wits, but they would return soon enough. There was nothing more Thomas could do, so he rose and joined Eleanor downstairs. She stood in the middle of the space, hands on hips and a look of despair on her face as she surveyed the damage to her livelihood.

"Can it be repaired?"

"I do not know. Perhaps. They have broken some of the spars of the uprights, but any carpenter can replace them. The worst is they have snapped the press stone into three. That cannot be repaired. A new one must be found or fashioned."

"We can think about that on the morrow," Thomas said.

"We?"

He smiled. "I am thinking I may go into the printing business. Go up to Luke. He sleeps but will eventually wake. He needs to see your face when he does. Take water and wash him. There is a fresh cut on his head. Clean it and apply some of the cream I used on his other wound."

"What are you going to do, Tom?" Eleanor stood close, looking up at him. Once more, he was reminded of her strange beauty, but also something fragile beneath it.

"I intend to find out what those in the house know about what happened. Someone other than Jack must have heard or seen something. I will return later to see if Luke is awake and check on him again, but he will live."

Walking the short distance along the alley and into the stable, Thomas wondered why Luke was still alive. Men with clubs, knives and swords, Jack had said. So why did they use a club on Luke and not a knife? He had been cudgelled and stabbed the last time they were attacked. Did that make it the same men? Thomas tried to think of a reason why they had left him alive but could not. He knew he did not know enough and needed to change that.

SIXTEEN

Thomas found Jack sitting on a pile of sacks in the stable. The lad's face was pale and his hands shook.

"You are afeared?" Thomas asked.

Jack nodded. "Aye, sir. I thought the men might have attacked me so I hid. I should not have been such a coward."

"You could have done nothing against three strong men, Jack. You did the right thing. Did you see their faces?"

A shake of the head. "I did not want to, sir. I hid in here and hoped they would not come looking."

"Did you hear them speak?"

Another shake of the head. "But they laughed like it was the greatest entertainment. I was about to ask Master Hardwin what to do but you and the lady arrived. I was sure you would know better. I am sorry, sir." Tears showed in Jack's eyes, and Thomas squeezed his shoulder before entering the house.

He went along the hall and knocked on the door to Hardwin's room but received no reply. When nothing came after a second knock he tried the handle, but the door was locked. He turned and made his way to the kitchen, where he found Winnie with the makings of a beef pie on the table. Her husband, Ben, sat at the far end with a mug of ale. He gave Thomas a perfunctory glance before returning his gaze to the blank wall.

"Do you know where Hardwin is?" Thomas asked, hoping it did not sound like a demand, but his blood still sang from witnessing the violence done in Eleanor's workshop.

"He went out an hour since," said Winnie.

"Where?"

"He does not tell the likes of us his business."

Ben said nothing.

"Did either of you see men entering the workshop next door?"

"The place where you set your woman up?" said Winnie without looking at Thomas as she cut the slab of beef into cubes.

Thomas started to object, then stopped. Whatever he said would not change her mind.

"A man has been attacked, and Jack tells me men destroyed much of Eleanor's equipment. There would have been a great deal of noise. I want to know who heard it or who saw the men." He looked at Ben. "You were gathering fruit when we left earlier this morning. Were you still in the orchard when the men came?"

Ben shook his head, and Thomas wondered if the man was incapable of speech.

"Ben came in to eat his midday meal, sir. He was in the

orchard, but only to bring in apples for a pie. He has been repairing a door in the servant's quarters on the top floor since you left. I could hear him hammering from down here, so I do not believe he would have heard the hounds of hell if they howled right next to him. Who is injured?" The question was belated.

"A man named Luke Thatcher – he is Eleanor's husband."

"I have seen her, but not him," said Winnie.

Ben pushed himself to his feet and donned his hat. "Got work to do," he said. "I will be in the orchard if anyone wants me." He walked close to Thomas as he left, the proximity almost a challenge to their positions in the household.

"Luke has been unwell," Thomas said to Winnie. "They were attacked in their previous location, which is why I offered them the empty workshop here. Are you sure you heard nothing?"

"I am, sir. Have these people done something wrong for them to be subject to two attacks in as many days?"

"She may have upset powerful men."

"Is this anything to do with the book? Jack told me he heard you and her talking about it when he helped move their belongings in."

"It is possible," Thomas said. "Do you know anything about The Beasts of the City?"

Winnie's normally rosy face paled. "Do not mention its name, sir, or the Devil may turn his attention on this house."

"So you do know of it."

"Everyone in the city knows of it. Which is why the

streets and alleyways are empty after dark. The King should be doing something about it. Take control of the city. Put men on the street to capture these demons." She frowned. "Though if they are demons, they will need clergy to exorcise them from London. I care not where they go afterwards."

Thomas sighed, aware he would get nothing sensible from Winnie.

"Does anyone have a key for Hardwin's rooms?"

"Of course not. No one would enter without his permission."

"Not even the master of the house?"

Winnie stared at Thomas. "You are here by permission of the King, sir. Hardwin is the master of this house. Others come and go. Some stand on ceremony, full of their own importance, but I admit you have not shown yourself to be that kind of man."

Thomas took a breath to control his anger and tried again.

"And you are sure you have no idea where Hardwin has gone?

"None." Her response was curt enough to verge on insolence.

Thomas suspected she was lying, but she would not reveal the lie unless he made threats he could not carry out. He also suspected threats would carry no weight. Winnie was right – Thomas was here on sufferance and would eventually be replaced by another resident.

"Hardwin does not like that I have offered the workshop to Eleanor, does he."

"You would have to ask him that, sir."

"But he complains of it, yes?"

"He complains of a great deal, but yes, he does."

"To members of the household, or others outside it as well?"

Winnie shrugged and looked away.

"Do you know where he goes to drink ale?"

"How would I know that?"

"What about your husband?"

"Ben drinks his ale here, at this table."

"But might he know?"

Thomas was starting to see Winnie losing her patience.

"I doubt he would. Ben is not the curious type."

It was possible, Thomas thought, that Hardwin had complained of Eleanor's presence when he was out, wherever that was. And if the men who broke her equipment were the same ones, which was most likely, they might have heard of her moving in and her comings and goings. Hardwin had gone out. Had he let slip Eleanor and Thomas had left the house, that it would be empty? Thomas did not know. He was aware there was too much he did not know, but was content with his suspicion of Hardwin.

"Where can I find Eliza?" he asked.

"Laying the fires, of course. She is a good girl."

Thomas failed to understand what Winnie meant. Then it came to him. Did the woman think so little of him? Perhaps she did if she had already assumed he and Eleanor were lovers. It made him wonder what else she had said concerning previous occupants of the house. Men with inflated ideas regarding their station in life and who possessed an arrogance that would see them take whatever pleasure they wished with the staff. He suspected Eliza had been a target for such lusts in the past, and no doubt Winnie, too. There were times Thomas despaired of his fellow man, even after all he had witnessed. Or more likely because of what he had witnessed.

He left Winnie to her baking and searched the downstairs rooms first, but there was no sign of Eliza. He was about to climb the stairs when he heard a noise from the front of the house. When he followed it, he discovered Hardwin's door stood ajar and pushed it open. Eliza knelt before the fireplace, scooping still-warm embers into a metal bucket. She turned and looked up at him in surprise.

"Oh, it is you, sir. I thought it was the master returning. Do you want something?"

"How did you get in here?"

"With the key, of course, sir. It hangs in the space 'neath the stairs. The Master does not like me to lay his fire when he is here, so I always come after he leaves the house."

Thomas wondered why Winnie had not told him about the key, which she must have known of. Was she protecting Hardwin from his intrusion? She regarded Thomas as an interloper, so it made a modicum of sense.

"Does he leave often?"

"Once a week, sir. Sometimes more. There is no reason to it"

"Where does he go?"

"How would I know that, sir?" But colour pinked her cheeks, and Thomas believed she did know. Her response hinted where the man went – to see a woman. Perhaps even to the Bel Savage, where girls could be bought for a few pence, with a few pence more for a room. Hardwin struck Thomas as the kind of man who would want the comfort of a bed while being serviced.

"Is Hardwin a good master?" Thomas asked.

"He is the only master I know, sir."

"Does he ever—" But Thomas stopped himself from asking the question because Eliza would never answer truthfully. If she answered in the negative he knew he would be able to tell the lie, but did not want it presented to him. Instead, he tried again. "The workshop next to the house has been attacked. Did you hear or see anything?"

"Heard nothing, sir, but I saw three men pass the dining room window while I was in there."

"Can you describe them?"

"Describe them, sir? They were rough men."

"Tall, short, fat, thin, weak, strong? What did they wear?"

Eliza took a moment to think, still on her knees, still staring up at him like a startled hind.

"Neither tall nor short, sir. Neither fat nor thin. They wore hats with wide brims. Two had leather jerkins, the other a coat. He..." She broke off, thinking, "...He appeared to be in charge of the other two, sir."

"Can you describe him at all?"

Eliza shook her head. "It was a glimpse, only a glimpse."

"In that case, you did well. My thanks."

Eliza's blush deepened, and she offered an uncertain smile before turning away. Thomas looked around the room – a desk, shelves holding books and papers, and another door into the bedroom he had glimpsed while last here. His fingers itched with the desire to search them, but he knew he could not while Eliza was there. When she left, she would lock the door behind her – except now she had offered the knowledge of where the key hung.

When Thomas returned to the hallway, he was unsure what to do next. There had been no response from the King regarding the note he had sent. He considered visiting Thomas More again but did not know if he would be made welcome and, even if he was, what good it might do. He needed to know more. This meant knocking on the street doors to see what other people might have seen. He was about to leave through the front door when a voice called to stop him.

"I am sorry I was short with you, Tom. What happened is not your fault and not your doing."

Eleanor stood at the far end of the hall, the door to the orchard and the stable open behind her. Jack stood beyond her, and it would be he who had admitted her. Thomas knew she would not enter without permission.

"I bear some responsibility. I should have been here, or found someone to offer protection."

Eleanor shook her head. "I can protect myself. Come outside with me, Tom. You said you wanted to see Luke again when he woke, and he is showing signs."

SEVENTEEN

When Thomas ascended to the small room above the workshop, he found Luke sitting up and leaning against the bare wooden wall. He was pale, but began to rise when he saw Thomas, who put a hand on his chest to push him back down.

"I recognised two of them this time," said Luke. "When they came before they must have snuck up behind me because I recall nothing at all. Today, I saw their faces. There is a tavern near our old workshop I used to frequent, and I saw them there several times. They are rough men who make it known they are willing to do anything for payment. Anything, Tom."

"So why are you still alive?"

"Luke is strong," said Eleanor, standing at the foot of the thin mattress.

"Not so strong now," said Luke. "They could have killed me. They had steel, and I was too weak to fight." He looked at Thomas. "I do not understand why they did not."

"Neither do I, but intend to discover the reason. You say you know two of them. Which tavern did you see them in?"

"The Saracen's Head, beyond Newgate. We should go and see if they have fled there."

"Hardly fled," said Eleanor. "Did they destroy my tools before or after they knocked your brains out? And have I not told you to drink only within the city walls?"

"The ale is good there," said Luke, as if that was reason enough.

"You are going nowhere," Thomas said. "Not until I am sure you are fully recovered. I want to wash your wound again and then give you more poppy. It will help with your headache as well."

"I can stand without aid if only you let me."

Thomas glanced at Eleanor, who shook her head.

"Let us see how you are on the morrow."

"I did not know our equipment was damaged," said Luke. "They came up the stairs without hesitation, so they must have known I was here and alone." Luke looked at Eleanor, and his gaze softened. "It is fortunate you were not here, my love, or you might be lying downstairs with your throat cut."

Thomas applied more of al-Timani's salve to Luke's wound but saw it would not be required much longer. Then he mixed hemp and poppy with wine and made him drink it.

"I will wait downstairs until he is asleep if you can stay with him," he said to Eleanor, who replaced him at Luke's side.

Thomas surveyed the damage in the workshop. He saw

the heavy stone plate shattered in three pieces. Someone had tried to set fire to a stack of paper, but the flames had failed to take hold and only charred along one edge before going out. He thought it would still be possible to use it. However, the printing press was an issue, and the lack of type even more so. From what Eleanor had told him, obtaining type would be the hardest task. Thomas thought of offering to purchase a set from across the sea. He could afford it but knew he had a habit of offering his wealth, aware it was not always welcome. His daughter, Amal, had pointed it out to him.

"You have so much silver and gold, Pa, that you do not realise how offering a tiny part of it can be seen as an insult to those you offer it to. Gift people your knowledge, time, and skill, but not your silver."

"Why not, Ami?" he said. "I possess more than I can spend in a score of lifetimes."

"Then when you are gone, Will and I will spend it for you, but not to buy the love or friendship of others."

"I do not do that."

Amal had smiled. "You think you do not, but you do. Great wealth can be both a blessing and a curse."

"What will you do with it when I am dead?" Thomas had asked. The thought of being dead sat strange in his mind. To not be. Perhaps those who believed in a God and heaven were happier towards their end.

"Build a hospital, perhaps," said Amal. "Or houses we can rent at a reasonable cost people can afford. We can do good without rubbing silver under people's noses."

So when Eleanor descended the stairs and touched his

arm Thomas said nothing about buying a new set of type for her. But it did not stop him thinking how such might be possible without her knowing he was the benefactor.

"Luke sleeps now." She looked around. "Something may be salvaged from this." She kicked her foot against the shattered press stone. "John Wynkyn will know where I can get another of these, and a skilled carpenter will be able to repair the press." She nodded at the stacks of paper. "Those are useable. I might even make a positive from the charred edges." She laughed. "I will work it to my advantage and tell my customers the heat of my prose set the paper alight." Her expression turned serious as she looked at Thomas." How long will I be allowed to remain here? I know this is not your house, and you are here at the courtesy of the King. I do not suppose we will be allowed to stay once you leave."

"There must be other places you can use. How much space do you need?"

"No more than this, and somewhere to sleep." She looked around. "It will be a shame, for this is almost perfect, and I have already been asked to print leaflets for several guilds once they knew we were here. I should look for somewhere beyond the city wall. London is outgrowing its constraints, and already businesses, taverns, and houses spring up along the roads in all directions. Even, as you saw today, south of the river." She smiled. "I will even take ordinary work to pay my bills. I thank you for all you have done, Tom. You have been a good friend to both of us."

"That sounds like a dismissal."

Another smile. "It is not, but you have other matters to

deal with. Let us take responsibility for ourselves. I hope you will remain a friend, but you should not take on our woes."

"It occurred to me that you might move out of London altogether. I live in Ludlow, on the border between England and Wales. As far as I know, there are no printers outside London. It may be time to change that."

"But would there be business there, Tom?"

He shrugged. "That I do not know, but they sell books, bibles and pamphlets in Ludlow and the towns around, so someone must bring them in from elsewhere."

"I believe there is a printer in Oxford but know of no others. Let me think on it, but I suspect we will stay in London. It is where the work is and where the other printers are. When John manages to set up his Guild of Stationers, London will be the place to be." She lifted up and kissed his cheek, then pushed him away. "Now go, do something other than worry about us."

So Thomas did the opposite. He walked west until he passed through Newgate and found the Saracen's Arms a few paces beyond. Luke was right; the ale was excellent. Thomas sat in a corner with a wide-rimmed hat pulled low to obscure his face and watched people come and go, watched them talk, argue and, in two instances, fight.

And then three men entered, pushing through a standing group of men even though there was space to go around. They crowded the ale table and demanded food as well. Then they pushed two men off a table and took it for themselves. He studied their faces but none were familiar. They were not the same men who had threatened him the night after Eleanor and Luke were attacked. He wondered how many groups of them there might be, and if they all had the same orders. This group was too far away for Thomas to hear what they said. He waited, because soon they would have supped their ale, eaten their food, and leave.

He wanted to know where they went.

EIGHTEEN

The men took longer to leave than Thomas expected. By the
time they rose and left the Saracen's Arms, none of them
were walking steadily. The night outside was pitch black,
clouds covering the moon and stars. The only illumination
came from an occasional torch set in a sconce. Fortunately,
the men headed for Newgate, where more light glowed
around the entrance. Thomas held back until they had
passed through before making his way there. He nodded to
the gatekeeper and tossed the man a penny.

"Do you know those men?"

"What men?"

"The three who—" Thomas stopped when he saw the
man's expression. It would put his life in danger if they
found out he had talked. No mind, Thomas thought. He
would find out who they were and who their master was.
He knew they would be the kind who needed a master to
control them. Had they none, they would have been in gaol
by now or dead. He expected them to report back to

someone on their day's work. If they had already done so, they would lead him to their lodgings, and he would return the following day and the days after if necessary.

But they did neither.

Instead, they headed west along The Shambles to Bladder Street, where they found a dark corner and stopped. Thomas had to do the same or risk being seen. He did not know if the men had noted him in the Saracen's Head but could not risk being recognised. He took Panyer Alley, holding one hand out. His fingers ran along the front of the houses because the darkness was so dense he could see nothing. At Paternoster Row, some light came from Cheapside, and he squatted by the conduit at the junction of four streets. If the men looked his way, they would not see him.

They remained where they were, talking among themselves. They were too far away to overhear, and Thomas dared not get closer, so he waited. Eventually, the men turned and approached where he hid. As they came near, he overheard part of their conversation.

"...said the place is unlikely. There are too many houses around, and the beasts here are not alluring enough. We should try..." The words rose, then faded once the men passed. Thomas watched as they continued along Cheapside before turning into Milkstrete, in the direction of his house.

He rose and ran after them, closing the distance because he feared they might return to Eleanor's workshop. Which they did.

Fortunately, the men's gaze lay ahead, which allowed Thomas to move closer. He reached for the knife at his waist only to discover it was not there.

The men turned down the narrow alley behind the houses towards the orchard and Eleanor's printworks. They slowed and disappeared into a dark corner once more, but the light from the workshop reflected on their faces. They stared into where Eleanor was trying to assemble the broken press. There was no sign of Luke, and Thomas assumed he still slept after the poppy he had been given.

The men spoke softly, once more their words not carrying, but they did not appear to be arguing and made no move to cross to the workshop. After a time, they turned away and came directly towards Thomas. He backed fast into the stable entrance. As they passed, one of the men stopped and looked in, but Thomas was now hidden behind the wall. When he heard them start again, he waited, then followed, aware of how close he had come to being discovered. A few minutes later, he cursed himself for not going into the house to arm himself, but it was too late to turn back now or he would lose them. Following them through deserted nighttime streets made Thomas's task even harder. The men returned to Cheapside and took Bradstrete, which curved towards the north. They were not the only people on the streets at that time of night, but those who passed averted their eyes as if in guilt at being out in the dark. The men swaggered, showing no shame.

Eventually, they entered West Smithfield Market Place. Here, a single lantern hung outside a small wooden hut. A watchman sat outside the hut to ensure the closed-up stalls remained undisturbed. He would not see the men enter through the West gate from his position at the centre of the large open space. Thomas hung back and watched the men open a stall close to the gate. They were but a moment then emerged, each clutching a sack. They looked around, then came towards Thomas, who had to move quickly again to avoid being seen. Once the men had passed, he followed again, expecting another long trail through the streets of London, but they stopped in a small garden almost at once. Here, they disrobed, opened their sacks and pulled out new clothes. Once they had donned them, headpieces were added until all three looked as if they had stepped from the fires of Hell. These men, Thomas realised, were the beasts of the city. He felt a thrill of excitement run through him. Tonight, he might discover how they worked and what victims they chose.

The men tucked their old clothes into the sacks and left them in the corner of the garden, where each picked up a heavy, knobbed staff before walking brazenly along Dukstrete.

Thomas risked getting closer. He wanted to witness their attack. The broken skulls made sense now. The staffs were heavy enough to knock a man senseless, but they would also need a means of sawing open a skull and that he did not see. Perhaps they had a lair where they took their victims to do their bloody work. Come dawn, Thomas expected the men to have a new home in Newgate prison.

He wondered if the demons were their idea but suspected not. They did not strike him as the kind to have that much imagination. Which meant they were directed by someone else. But who, and to what purpose? Perhaps that, too, would be revealed in dawn's grey light.

Ahead of him, the men entered the city through

Newgate. The gateman was nowhere to be seen. Almost at once, two other figures could be seen. A whore with her back against a wall while a customer serviced her. The men started barking like dogs, howling and screaming as they ran at the pair. Within seconds, their coupling was broken, and both raced away; then the man almost fell over his hose as he tried to pull it up. The men were on him in a moment. One cracked his staff against his skull, not hard enough to kill but hard enough to shake the wits from his head. If he possessed any.

The three stood over him, and Thomas moved even closer. He wanted to see what came next. But what came was nothing. One of the men poked the man with the end of his staff.

"Be ye God's man or the Devil's?" The voice was coarse and guttural.

The man stared up at him, and Thomas could see he did not know how to answer.

"Answer me, or I call my master!"

"God's man," the man said as he rose.

"Come to me, Satan. Eat this fool's brain, poor fare though it might be."

The staff swung harder this time, and the man fell to the ground, unmoving.

Now?, Thomas thought.

But they were finished. They left the man where he was and moved off in search of other prey. Once they had disappeared into the next street, Thomas ran to the man and felt for a pulse. He found it, which meant the blow had been held back. He put his hand beneath the man's arms and dragged him to the side of the street. He propped him against the wall of a house where he would eventually come around.

As Thomas rose he turned to find himself confronted by the three men, who had returned.

"What did you do that for?" asked one. There was no guttural voice this time.

A staff swung. The blow was hard but not enough to knock Thomas out. All the same, he let his knees go weak and tumbled to the ground. As he lay there, he examined his next move. If they left him, as they had the man, he would do nothing. If they came at him again with intent, he would respond. His head hurt, but he knew he was strong enough to deal with them.

"Do I hit him again?" said one voice. "He looks like a gentleman."

There was a moment while the question was considered.

"No. This is the wrong place, and whoever he is, he is not on our list. There is no plague pit near here marked on our map, so we leave him with a bad head and a lesson learned not to walk the dark streets of London."

"Can I not stick him but a little?"

"Our task is to terrify, not kill. That is left to another. Now come, we have the night ahead of us and work to do."

Thomas lay still as he heard their footsteps move away. He waited longer before rolling over and opening his eyes. The street was dark and empty. Ludgate stood lit by torches, but still no sign of the gateman. Even he feared the night.

Thomas rose. For a moment, he remained still to test how steady he was. He walked slowly, keeping to the shadows, watching for another attack as he considered what he had heard. The fact he was dressed as a gentleman seemed significant, but then their leader had said he was not on their list and there was no plague pit nearby. What was the significance of that? He vaguely recalled Linacre mentioning a plague pit that lay near the killing Thomas had seen. He suspected More or Linacre might be able to provide information he did not possess himself.

And what list did the men possess? From what he had heard it included those who were to die? And who was their master they spoke of? It would be a list provided by that man. There was too much Thomas did not know, but there was no way for him to learn more. At the moment he had few clues, and none offered

NINETEEN

When Thomas arrived at the house he expected Eleanor's printworks to be closed up and dark, so was surprised to find her still working in the light of the approaching dawn.

"You look like something recently dead, Tom," said Eleanor. "What have you been doing, sleeping in a ditch?"

"I feel like something long dead. And not sleeping. I was knocked out."

She came across, gripped his chin, and moved his head from side to side.

"I see nothing."

"Here," he said, touching his head.

Eleanor parted his hair and peered at the lump she found.

She pulled a face. Who did this to you?" She stroked the spot as if she could soothe it.

"The beasts of the city."

Eleanor paled and crossed herself. "Do not jest."

"I do not, and they are neither beasts nor demons. They

are men dressed to look satanic. I watched them crack the skull of a man, then when I tried to help him they crept up and did the same to me."

"Did they kill him? Open his skull?" Something was sharp in her eyes, as if fear still ran through her.

"They did not. And fortunately, they did not attempt that with me, either."

"Perhaps you are not the right kind of man."

"And that matters, does it?" Though Thomas knew the question was sound. It reflected his own thoughts concerning his attacker's mysterious list.

"You said you witnessed a murdered man recently. How was he dressed?"

"As a gentleman," Thomas admitted. "Why would they only choose people of position and wealth? I do not believe those alone are enough. I overheard them speak of a list. People they must know, must recognise. I would like to see this list. It could save many lives."

"You will have to ask them to show it you next time you meet them." Eleanor laughed. "Though I would suggest you do not follow them again. You are getting deep into something dangerous, Tom."

"I have to know more if I want to uncover what this plot is."

She reached out and gripped his hand. "Do not, Tom. I have grown fond of you and would not see you dead."

"It will take more than three men to kill me." Though he admitted they could have done so tonight had they not stayed there hand. Thomas saw fear on Eleanor's face so changed the subject. He could always consider his questions later when he was alone in his bed. "You have done well here. Your press looks ready to start work."

"It would be if we had any type."

"What about John Wynkyn? Caxton Press must have a spare set."

"Oh, they do, but they will not offer it to me. Type and the tools to make it are our stock in trade and held close."

"So what will you do?"

Eleanor smiled. "Luke says he will take a ship to Flanders to buy a set. There are a plethora of printers there and their type goes missing all the time. It will carry some danger because those who steal it are rogues."

"Did you get your previous type the same way?"

"Together with all the peril associated with it, but we have no other choice."

"Who makes type? Could a skilled blacksmith not create a set?"

Eleanor laughed. "It requires someone skilled in the art, not a maker of ploughshares. Anyone who has not done it before might try, but the result would be unacceptable. I would rather obtain a set from abroad if Luke can find one and the tools to make more. It is the punches that are more valuable. Once you have those, it is a matter of melting lead and pouring it into a form."

"Finding all that will take time, will it not?"

"It will take at least a day to cross the sea, at least two or three days more to contact someone, and another day to return. I will have to wait until then, but I can use the time to write more of my tales ready for that day. I worry Luke may not be strong enough and would ask you to examine him before I decide to send him."

"Gladly. Is he upstairs?"

"Still out visiting printers, but he will return by noon."

"In that case, I will try to sleep. If I am not here by noon, get Jack to fetch me."

When Thomas entered the house, he found Hardwin standing at the foot of the staircase, arms crossed over his chest.

"You have been out the half night," he said.

"What I do and where I go is no business of yours."

"That depends on what you have been doing. You may have brought disrespect to this house, which I would be honour bound to report to the King. You are here at his will, sir, and mine, for I make it my business to maintain an honest house."

"Which I admire. Has any message come from King Henry for me?"

"I have not checked for messages today. If there is, where will you be?"

"In bed. Put it under my door, and if I have not come downstairs by noon, send someone to wake me."

Hardwin did not appear to approve of a man who would sleep the morning away, but he turned and went into his rooms. Thomas climbed the stairs. He did not bother to undress but removed his boots before lying on the bed. He stared through the small window at the sky, watching as clouds scudded across, promising more rain to come. It seemed it had not stopped raining in weeks. He spent some time examining how he felt. If he had a patient struck hard on the head, he would recommend that they stay awake for a few hours. But he had always been a bad patient, so he let a deep sigh loose and closed his eyes. He started to work through what he had heard and seen but knew it was not yet enough to draw any conclusions from until he learned more.

When he opened his eyes, he heard a knock on the door and wondered if it was the second or third one. He rose, washing hands across his face, and opened the door to see Eliza standing there with a metal bucket filled with the tools of her work.

"Master Hardwin told me to wake you, sir. Can I make your room up now?"

Thomas nodded. "Did he give you any messages for me?"

"Oh, yes, they are here." She reached into the bucket, pulled out two sealed notes, and handed both to him, slightly smudged with soot.

Thomas slipped them inside his shirt, pulled on his boots and went downstairs. As he passed through the stable yard, Jack came out.

"You have not ridden your horse since you came here, sir," the lad said. "She grows restless. Would you like me to exercise her?"

Thomas knew he had neglected Sombra and should have used her more, but in the crowded daylight streets and alleys, a horse was more of a hindrance than a help, not that it stopped so-called gentlemen from always riding. But that was a matter of status rather than convenience. Even so, Jack was right. Sombra could be high-spirited, and a gallop would do her good.

"You would do that, Jack?"

"Of course, sir." Jack tried to look disinterested, but Thomas sensed an excitement in him.

"How about taking her north to the open fields and letting her have her head? An hour should do it."

"Yes, an hour, sir. Can I use your saddle?"

Thomas almost laughed before noting the seriousness of Jack's expression.

"Yes, use my saddle. When you return, there will be three pence for wiping Sombra down and cleaning the leather."

"You are too generous, Master Thomas. It is my job to tend to the horses. Are you visiting your friend in the workshop next door?"

"I need to check on Luke. I assume you have seen no one hanging around the place today?" Thomas knew Jack was sharp and would take note of strangers.

"No one, sir, but Luke left an hour since. He looked hale, so I expect he has recovered."

TWENTY

Thomas found Eleanor kneeling beside the repaired printing press, adjusting something beneath it. She looked up as entered the workshop.

"Jack told me he saw Luke going out again," he said. "When will he be back so I can examine him?"

"Not for at least a week. He has taken money and gone to find passage to Flanders. He returned with news that there is no type or the makings of it to buy anywhere in London."

"Did he visit the works in Southwark you took me to? That man struck me as not beyond selling his own for enough money."

"I told him not to go south of the river because Gray is not someone to be trusted. I am not yet desperate enough to resort to dealing with him. Here, Tom, help me lift this stone. I cannot do it alone."

Eleanor shifted to one side, allowing Thomas to reach the solid print stone.

"Where did you manage to find one?"

"Stones are easier to come by than type. I had a mason working on a church cut a piece of granite for me. It is heavier than the sandstone we had before but will be better for the job."

Thomas worked his fingers under the edge of the stone and tried to lift it, but the angle was awkward, and though he managed to raise it a few inches, he could not lift it any higher.

"We need another strong man," he said.

Eleanor laughed. "Or a strong man." She reached out and stroked his head. "But I forget, you are an injured man."

Thomas scowled at her, which only made her laugh the harder.

They stared at each other, their faces close. Thomas felt the heat of her, the want to press his lips against hers.

He leaned back. "Wait here. I will see if Ben is willing to help."

"Who is Ben?" Eleanor straightened up but remained on her knees as she pushed hair back from her face, which was flushed.

"The gardener next door. He may or may not. I am not altogether sure he likes me."

"Liking you is not necessary in this instance, is it?"

Thomas went to the kitchen where, as expected, Ben was sitting at the table while his wife prepared vegetables for the coming evening meal. It reminded him that he had not yet eaten in the house he was supposedly master of.

"Do you want to earn a few pennies?" he asked.

The man looked up. "For what?" He made it sound as if Thomas had proposed something unsavoury.

"Eleanor next door cannot lift the print stone into place. It needs two men. I thought you might be willing."

Ben pushed himself to his feet. "Aye, I may be." He held his hand out, and Thomas put three pennies in it. Ben stared at them for some time before putting them on the table. "Add these to our pot, Winnie."

Thomas led the way through the stable and into the workshop, where Eleanor stood waiting. She directed them, and they raised the stone. Thomas felt the weight of it but tried not to let it show because Ben seemed barely to notice. Both men shuffled to the end of the press while Eleanor pointed to where she wanted the stone set. She called the place the coffin, and Thomas could see why because it was a rectangular opening made from thick wooden spars with more wood beneath. The stone fit almost perfectly when they lowered it into place, and Ben nodded in satisfaction.

"He is not a talkative man, is he?" said Eleanor when Ben had gone.

"I have been here three days and heard no more than eight words from him. Perhaps he considers them as coin and is careful with them."

"Unlike you, Tom. Thank you." She lifted up and kissed his cheek, which sparked a familiar unease. "All we can do now is wait and pray Luke has success. What are you going to do, Tom? Do you visit the King again soon? What else do you do? I know little about you and would like to know more."

Her mention of the King reminded Thomas he had not

read his messages yet. He pulled them out, broke the seals, and read the first.

"He wants to know why I have not visited after his last message." Thomas glanced at Eleanor. "A message I never received."

"Your steward does not like you, does he? I went next door to ask after you this morning and was sent away with a scowl."

"I suspect Hardwin likes no one, but you are right. He received an earlier note from Henry and failed to give it to me. Unless it is this other one." Thomas opened the second note and laughed.

"I take it that means it is not from the King. Are you aware you called him Henry? Take care not to do so in front of someone who might take offence at such boldness. I suspect you could be a bold man, but in this city, it can get you into trouble."

Thomas thought of all those he had called by name, kings and queens, princes and princesses. He suspected that having done so did not make him bold. He was fortunate to have been close to them and accepted into their circle. That was not the same with Henry ... but it might be with his son. He knew Harry liked him, and one day, he would be king in his father's place. It would be wise to ensure Harry continued to like him and his family. Which is who the second letter concerned.

Thomas handed it to Eleanor. "See for yourself."

She took the paper and read it.

"Who are Will and Usaden? And whoever wrote this

has an exceptionally fine hand. I could make use of someone like that."

"Its author is no doubt my daughter, Amal. Will is my son, and Usaden my friend."

"Two of them have strange names. How is that?"

"Amal's mother, my wife, was a Moor. And Usaden crossed the narrow sea from Africa to Spain. He was a mercenary soldier but has since become part of my family. A family that has grown more than I expected. You will like them both when they arrive, which should be soon if they left at the same time as this message. Though why they are coming, I do not know. I only hope there is no trouble in Ludlow."

"Yes, I would like to meet your family, Tom. Are they anything like you?"

Thomas laughed. "When Will arrives, you will see he is nothing like me. As for Usaden ... well, there is no one like Usaden." Thomas looked into space for a moment. He wanted to stay and tell Eleanor about those he had left behind in Ludlow, but knew he had matters to attend to.

"You are thinking of something," said Eleanor.

"I am thinking I need to speak to More again. He was going to ask the goodwife about who might have left his copy of the book. I also asked if he could find out who the victims are. I want to know what they have in common."

"I can do nothing here until we have type again. May I come with you? I know Thomas More and would not be turned away."

Thomas could see no reason to refuse her request.

TWENTY-ONE

Thomas and Eleanor passed through Ludgate and made their way towards Lincoln's Inn. When Thomas rapped on the door of More's room, it was opened by the man.

"I take it you have come for a reason?" He looked past Thomas to Eleanor and offered a nod of recognition, if not welcome.

"I know where two locations referred to in your copy of the book are. This information may help us understand the clues in the text."

"Then come in. You too, Eleanor, though how you know this man is a mystery to me."

"He saved my life," she said. It was an exaggeration, but Thomas allowed it to pass.

More glanced at Thomas. "That does not surprise me. Tell me what news you have."

Once seated at the table, Thomas said, "Bear with me, for this needs an introduction. It started on the day I arrived in the city. Eleanor told me men had attacked her and injured Luke. She feared they would return, so we moved her printworks to a new location, next to the house where I am staying. Two days ago, the men returned. They broke her press and stole her type. She cannot work without type. Luke—"

"Who is this Luke?" asked More. "He is not known to me."

"My man," said Eleanor. "He has gone to Flanders to try to buy type so we can work again."

"Before he left, he told me of a tavern where he had seen the attackers drinking," Thomas said. "So I went there."

More stared hard at Thomas, shaking his head. "Are you a fool?"

"I have been called such, but do not believe I am."

"Tom is brave," said Eleanor. "And a good friend."

"Is he. What has this to do with the book?"

"That I do not yet know, but I have theories. I witnessed the men I followed attack a man and leave him senseless. Then they knocked me cold."

More stared at Thomas but said nothing. Perhaps there was nothing to say other than call him a fool.

"It was a soft blow and did not knock me out," Thomas said. "I pretended to be unconscious and overheard them talking of plague pits. Linacre also made mention of one near the site of the murder I witnessed the result of.

"It occurred to me there may be clues to other locations now we know they are linked. I would like to look at the book again. I recall two locations that might be relevant. I intend to follow the men again tonight to discover more sites, but from what I witnessed I am unsure they are who I seek. If we can decipher the entire book, we will be closer to identifying the primary suspect."

"The book is unsuitable for a woman," said More. He glanced at Eleanor, who stared at him with an expression tight with disappointment and anger, but after a moment, she moved away and sat in the corner as if she had been chastised.

Thomas felt bad about it but knew More would not have agreed to let him see the book had she stayed close.

More looked between them, then rose, brought his copy of the book, and set it on the table.

"Show me."

It did not take long because Thomas knew of only two sites, and More was familiar with both. He fetched a sheet of paper, dipped a quill, and started to draw. Slowly, a rough sketch of a partial street plan of London emerged.

More circled two locations. "You mentioned here and here," he said. "Linacre mentioned plague pits to me. They are an interest of his. Both of these locations are on or near the site of a plague pit."

"Plague pits?" said Eleanor from the corner. "Your friend has some strange interests."

More smiled. "Indeed he does, and that is the least of them." He glanced at Thomas. "You and he should talk, for I believe you have much in common."

"Other than the plague pits," Thomas said.

More circled another location to the north and east. "This, I am sure, is also one Linacre mentioned. It is very old and has not been used in centuries, but knowledge of it still exists in some quarters." More could not hide the excitement in his voice. "This is good work, Berrington. Now..." More pulled the book towards him and fanned it open. "... we need to identify which passages relates to these. So, what have we?"

Thomas assumed the question was not meant for him because his knowledge of the streets of London could not match that of More's. When Eleanor rose and brought her chair closer to the table, More glanced at her but said nothing as she sat and leaned forward to study the book. She put her finger on More's rudimentary map. "This location is close to where our first print works stood and not too far from where we are now. Bladder Street and Cheapside are close by, as is The Shambles. The churchyard of St Paul's is but forty paces away. If I am not mistaken, another smaller cemetery stands at this location."

"It is associated with the College of St Martin le Grand." More appeared to have forgotten his reservations about Eleanor seeing the book's pages. "Linacre told me that old plague pits often lie beneath more recent burial grounds, which makes sense."

Eleanor flicked through the pages of the book and suddenly stopped. She leaned forward, her finger on a verse.

"Read this."

Where gilded men gather to fight their foul fight
So demons walk in the dark of the night
Come one, come all to sport, and learn
But beware one false step does not lead you to burn.

"All around this location are the Guilds," Eleanor continued. "Saddler's Hall lies almost on the junction of the roads. Goldsmith's is at the end of Faster Lane."

More nodded in excitement. "Agreed. With the knowledge of the place, the meaning is plain to understand. And the other one? There is less around there because it lies outwith the city wall."

"I do not know London that far north," said Eleanor, glancing at Thomas.

"I know some of the area from a journey last year," he said, "but it was further north than this. I will try to follow the men again tonight and every other night until I know what is going on."

"Do not follow them. They have already knocked you out. Next time they might kill you."

More hunched over the book, a sheet of paper close by. As he read, he made notes.

"I need to see Linacre," he said, straightening up and easing his back. "I understand more than I did, but I need confirmation. Some, if not all of the sites, may be associated with plague pits." He looked at Eleanor, then Thomas. "Do you know some people believe such pits, even when covered over as these are, can create a conduit to hell? But there is more – talk of alchemy, or eternal life, creating gold and gemstones from rock and soil. Linacre gave me a note to give you, Berrington. It is here somewhere, let me look." More rose and fussed about on a side table while Thomas and Eleanor paged through the rest of the book, their shoulders touching.

"I have it," said More, returning to the table. He glanced

at the cosy nature of them both, his face expressionless. He handed a folded sheet of paper to Thomas. "Princess Catherine tells me you have faced evil men before and triumphed."

"I am not sure triumph is the right term, but I have defeated some and stopped their actions. Why?"

"Perhaps you are the right man to stop the killing, for I fear it can only become greater. I implore you not to put yourself in danger. Whoever these people are, they have no humanity. Do not sacrifice yourself."

"They are no demons," Thomas said. "There is a reason they want the streets of London empty. If I can discover what that is, I may learn who is behind the killings. Those men I followed will take their orders from someone."

Thomas slipped Linacre's note into his jacket before rising and offering his hand to Eleanor. As she took it, Thomas saw the expression on More's face.

On the street Thomas took Linacre's note out and read it.

"What does he have to say, Tom?"

"I asked him to see if he could find out the names of each of the victims." He handed the note across to Eleanor. "Do you know any of them?"

She came to a halt as she scanned the sheet and Thomas waited, watching her. There was no surprise on her face, even when she looked up at him.

"There are four names here," she said. "I thought there were only three deaths so far."

"As did I, but Linacre has found one more."

"Three of the names are familiar to me, the first is not."

She glanced at the paper again. "They are all titled men who share an interest in the arcane."

"Are you sure?"

"As sure as I can be. I have seen them at Blackwood's gatherings, and he only invites men of title."

"How can I find out more about each of them? There must be records held somewhere."

Eleanor smiled and shook her head. "You are looking at me as if I might know, Tom. We have just left the man who might be able to find out that information for you. More has access to court records."

Thomas laughed. "You are right. Wait here." He turned and re-entered the house. The door was again opened at once and Thomas thrust the sheet of paper at More.

"Linacre has given me four names. Do you think you can find out more about them? Where they lived? If they were married or had children? Who their families are?"

"I do have my studies and work to do," said More.

"I know, and I apologise. Is there someone you can ask? A junior, perhaps?"

More took the sheet of paper. "That might be possible. Leave it with me. If I find anything out I will send a message."

Outside Eleanor was waiting for him. She slipped her hand into his again and leaned against him. "Did he agree?" And when Thomas nodded, said, "You are so clever, Tom, and so masterful. You can get people to do anything you want."

The way she looked at him made Thomas uneasy about

what she might want him to ask her to do. If it was as he suspected, she would have a long wait.

"Will you come with me to see John Wynkyn again? I intend to press him to provide me with type but know he will not. Perhaps you can look dangerous and change his mind."

TWENTY-TWO

"You are not going to stop your search, are you," said Eleanor as they headed east from the city walls.

"With Linacre's list I am closer to uncovering the guilty party behind all this." Thomas saw Eleanor smile and knew she thought him arrogant. Perhaps he was.

"More is right. The men you followed are dangerous, and you do not know if there are another three, a dozen or a score of them."

"Do not concern yourself about my welfare. I can look after myself. You have enough troubles of your own. Do you think Wynkyn will offer you type?"

"Of course not, but I can at least make him feel guilty for not doing so. And I will never stop telling you what is good for you."

"Then I will continue to ignore your sound advice."

It felt good to be walking alongside this pretty woman, trading challenges. It had been a long time since he had done anything of its like. Thomas knew, other than with

Lubna, he had experienced little true contentment with women. He believed he might have found it again with Bel Brickenden, but she had changed over the last few months. So had he. They had been lovers once when they were little more than children. The memory of it was not enough to maintain a relationship all these years later.

At the Caxton Press, Eleanor's prediction proved correct. Thomas saw John Wynkyn felt some guilt at his refusal, but he would not budge. Eleanor liked the man well enough not to push too hard. After she had gone to speak with some of the workers, for those involved in printing liked to talk of their skill and new devices, Wynkyn ushered Thomas into his small office.

"I cannot offer Eleanor what she wants, but I can tell you how you may be able to obtain what she seeks. Are you and she close?"

Thomas read the implication in Wynkyn's question and shook his head. "Not in the way you might believe, sir. I admire her courage and industry, but she is young enough to be my granddaughter."

"That would not stop most men."

"I am not most men."

"Perhaps you are not, but take care, Thomas Berrington. Eleanor carries enough troubles to drive any man away."

"You have experience of this?" Thomas asked, surprised.

"I do not, unfortunately."

"So you do not know what these troubles, if they exist, are." Wynkyn was starting to annoy Thomas.

"In my profession I hear things. So just beware, sir."

"You hear things? Tittle-tattle and rumour, I expect. Am I to judge a person on such weak evidence?" Thomas tried to push his anger aside. "You mentioned you might be able to help her."

"I know of someone – not a friend nor even an associate, but you get to know many who carve a living in the margins in this trade. Perhaps it is nothing more tittle-tattle, but I sense Eleanor is desperate. There is a man who deals in stolen and counterfeit type. Making type is not difficult if you have the right equipment, but it is expensive and not easy to come by. Printworks are springing up in London, and they all need type. Most last barely more than a few weeks before discovering there is more to it than having a press. The man I am about to tell you of may be able to provide type and the equipment for making it."

"You do not encourage it, do you?"

"Of course not, but as I told you, the girl has spirit. I have read some of her tales and they are not without merit. The subject matter is profane but her wordsmithing is admirable. It is a shame she is a woman or she would be better recognised. In any case..." Wynkyn turned aside and wrote something on a scrap of paper. "You will find the man here. I do not know if Eleanor can afford what he may charge, so I urge you not to let her know what you are doing. A man such as yourself can strike a better bargain than she could. And if you manage to obtain what she seeks, do not tell her my part in it."

Thomas offered a curt nod. "Agreed." He took the scrap of paper, noticing it came from a spoiled sheet because there was print on the other side. No doubt nothing here was wasted.

After walking Eleanor back to her workshop, he made an excuse that he had matters to attend to and entered the stable, but only to emerge at the front of the house. He made his way to London Bridge and crossed the Thames. The traffic on the bridge was heavy as people made their way from one side of the river to the other, and Thomas had to push his way through in places. He was aware the location Wynkyn had provided would take him close to the renegade print works Eleanor had taken him to, but he had no intention of visiting there a second time. He had found Gray distasteful, even as he felt sorry for the boy. There were boys like him all over London, all over England. They scraped enough work together to put food scraps in their bellies, but it was no life for anyone.

The place he wanted lay further south, beyond the last scattered dwellings. Thomas followed a track through marshland towards where a low hill rose. A few wooden houses dotted the slope, and he went to one of these, recalling Wynkyn's instructions. Do not press. Do not antagonise. If you are rebuffed, accept it and turn away. Except Thomas knew he could never turn away.

When he reached the building, there was no door, only an opening on one side. As Thomas approached, a man of middle age, broad, tall, and strong-looking, appeared.

"You are lost, sir?" He looked Thomas up and down but saw no threat.

"Only if you are not Hugh Fletcher."

"Aye, I am he. What is your business?"

"I was told you might be able to provide me with a set of type and punches to make more. English and Latin if possible, but English will do."

The man studied Thomas, lingering on his hands. "You are no printer; I see no ink on your fingers. Do you have a buyer for what you seek, or are you here to cause trouble?"

"No trouble, and you are right, I am no printer, but I have a friend who is. Her type was stolen yesterday, and she seeks to replace it."

"She? I know of few women printers. Does this one have a name?"

"Eleanor Cooper." Thomas saw no harm in revealing her name.

"I know Eleanor and Luke both. It is a shame if that happened, but I have no type here good enough for her. I have some, of course, but it is of poor quality, and some only carved in wood." The man's gaze moved beyond Thomas, who turned to see what had caught his attention. He saw two men in the distance. Whether this was their destination or not, Thomas did not know, but Hugh Fletcher seemed to.

"Go through to the back of the house, sir. You may be in luck after all. Do not show yourself or make any sound until I have dealt with these men. However, if I call out, I ask you to come to my aid. You look like a man who can fight despite your age."

"I have been known to. Who are they?"

"Men you would prefer not to meet after dark. Now go. They have already seen you, and I will have to come up with a story to satisfy them."

Thomas walked past the man. The house was narrow but deep, with only a single expansive room. He went to the far end and crouched behind a table where he could still see. Hugh Fletcher stood in the opening, silhouetted against the brightness beyond. He nodded as the two men reached him. Thomas recognised them both from last night before they donned their satanic costumes.

"Merek, Elias, do you have business with me?"

"We have something you might want," said the older man. "Let him see, Elias."

The other man opened a sack and showed its contents. Thomas could not see what is contained, but Fletcher nodded. "Maybe I could use something like that, but I am not sure I could pay much."

"The quality is excellent. Take some out and see. It is good lead type, and all the extras – I have no idea what they are all called."

"I see a chase, some sticks, letter punches, formers and two sets of type. I do not need to know about quality. Those I deal with do not care about quality. But I might be able to take them off you for a shilling."

The man named Merek laughed. "Five shillings, not a farthing less. We will find someone who wants them if you do not."

"Who will offer you even less or even call the constables. I have heard of type going missing in London these past days, and I expect so have the authorities. I may be able to go as high as two shillings, but no more."

"Four."

"Two shillings and six pence."

"Three and six."

Fletcher shook his head. "My thanks for thinking of me, but two and six is my final offer. Take it or leave it."

"It is robbery," said Merek.

"Aye, it may be, but am I meant to care?"

It seemed Fletcher knew who he was dealing with because Merek nodded. "Two and six then."

Fletcher turned into the house and went to one side out of sight. When he returned, he dropped coins into Merek's hand and Elias handed the sack over. There were no niceties offered before the men turned and walked away.

Thomas waited until they were out of sight before returning to the front of the house.

"Are those Eleanor's?"

"I would say so. Good quality and worth a good deal more than I paid for them, but what choice did they have?"

Thomas could see the two men in the distance and wanted to follow them, but a trade had to be made first.

"You will sell them to me?"

"For the right price."

"Name it."

"Ten shillings."

"You paid two shillings and sixpence."

"I did, but the cost is still ten shillings. I have this house to maintain and food to put on the table."

"Five," Thomas said, and Fletcher laughed. In the end they settled on seven shillings.

Thomas paid the man, took the sack holding the type, and descended the hill seven shillings the poorer. He might have spent longer haggling but the two men were disappearing fast.

He got close to them before London Bridge, then held back, pretending to examine wares sold by the merchants lining both sides, waiting until the men stepped off the bridge. The men turned east towards the Tower but struck north almost immediately. Thomas waited then walked fast to the alley they had entered, but there was no sign of them when he reached it. He followed the alley until he emerged on Eastcheap, but still did not see the men. The road was crowded, making it more difficult. He considered loitering on the corner to see if they returned but decided against it. Instead, he turned west and returned to Milkstrete and Eleanor.

"These are my type and punches," she said when she opened the sack. "Where did you get them?"

"Best you do not know."

"What did you pay for them?"

"Again, it is best you do not know."

"Then I cannot accept them." She made to hand the sack back.

Thomas decided to lie. "I saw the men from last night, those who attacked you and Luke. I followed them to a house near the Tower. I watched them enter, and then when they left, I went inside and found this. I did not know it was yours but recognised it as type."

Eleanor shook her head, whether in disbelief or incredulity, Thomas could not tell.

"You can start work again now?" he asked.

"Yes, I can, thanks to you once more. I do not know whether to be grateful or angry at you."

"Neither is necessary," Thomas said, pleased when she smiled.

"I..." Eleanor started, then stopped.

"You what?"

"I will need help. Could I ask you ... no, I cannot."

"What kind of help?"

"Forget I asked. I will manage. It will be tricky to place the paper, pin it, peel it away, and hang it, but I will manage."

"Would it be difficult to teach someone how to do it?"

"Not that part, no, but I have already imposed too much on you, Tom."

He laughed. "I was not offering myself, but Jack might be willing to help. He has little to do at the moment. He took my horse out for a gallop, and I might get him to do so every other day, but he is at a loose end. I suspect I am a disappointment to him because I make so few demands on his time. Do you want me to ask?"

"I will pay him, of course."

"And he would expect you to. So yes?"

"Yes, Tom. What will you be doing?"

"Searching for the demons of Hell."

TWENTY-THREE

Jack bounced up and down on his toes in excitement at the prospect of working with Eleanor.

"Can I start now?"

"That is up to Eleanor. Go and ask her, not me."

Jack grinned. "I will. And Master Hardwin has a message for you. I told him I would hand it to you but he said it was not my place."

Once Jack had gone, Thomas entered the house and knocked on Hardwin's door. It took an uncommonly long time to open, which he suspected was deliberate. Hardwin did not invite Thomas inside but handed him a sealed letter.

Thomas opened it to find it was from the King, who asked if Thomas was still alive or had he fled London because of the devilish rumours. Which told him that the King, or whoever had written the note on his behalf, knew of the fear that stalked London after dark.

Hardwin had almost certainly broken the King's seal and re-applied it so he would know the message's contents.

The strangeness of the household almost made Thomas long for the Bel Savage.

"Shall I ask Jack to saddle your horse?" asked Hardwin.

"No, I will take a wherry as soon as I have changed."

"I trust you possess attire suitable for an audience with the King, sir?" Hardwin's manner dripped with a disdain he did not attempt to hide.

Before Thomas could respond, Hardwin turned and re-entered his rooms, closing the door behind him. Thomas smiled as he ascended the stairs, amused by the man. He spent several minutes going through the few clothes he had brought. There was one set which he had worn for their first meeting, which he would have to do again. It was dark cloth, a colour the King favoured.

The tide was about to turn, so the wherry rocked and surged as it passed beneath London Bridge. However, the water closer to the Tower was calmer. Thomas climbed to the quay and was admitted at once. He wondered if such speed was deliberate or a comment on his tardiness. Then he wondered if he tended to overthink such things, aware even as it came to him that he was indeed once more overthinking.

The King was in the Queen's Tower, where Thomas had seen him on every visit. It seemed to be the family rooms, for Queen Elizabeth was there with the King's mother, Lady Margaret Beaufort. She sat upright on a hard chair with the King and Queen's daughters beside her. They were reading their bibles, and now and again, Lady Margaret would correct them or explain something.

"What have you been doing? Did you not get my

messages?" asked King Henry. He sat at a table where servants were laying plates and knives. A flagon of rich, dark wine sat near his right hand.

"I received but one, Your Grace."

Henry grunted. "I sent more, but you are here now. I take it you saw Princess Catherine and informed her of my wishes? How did she respond?"

"She is much taken with your son, Your Grace, and not averse to the idea of a marriage arrangement."

Henry's lips thinned in an expression that might have hinted at amusement. "Not averse, eh? Well, I suppose it is a start. You can tell Harry when he arrives from his lessons. And you will eat with us, yes?" It was a statement rather than a question.

"It will be my privilege, Your Grace."

"How is that house I gave you – suitable, is it?"

"Most suitable, Your Grace. Some staff members are stiff around me, but I am a stranger so it is to be expected. However, the location is excellent, and the rooms are elegant and spacious. I have taken a small liberty and offered the workshop adjoining the house to a printer."

Henry shrugged. "Do as you wish. It is your house now. I will have the papers sent across so all is above board."

Thomas stared at the King. "I thought it was a temporary measure, Your Grace, while I am in London."

"Which you will be more often if negotiations regarding the future of Henry and Catherine are to progress. You will need a base, so the house, poor as it might be, is my gift to you."

"And the staff, Your Grace?"

Henry raised a shoulder. "I suspect I am paying them, but eventually, they will become your responsibility. Of course, you only need give them a wage while you reside there."

"What about my responsibilities in Ludlow?" Thomas asked.

"I understand most are conducted by your son, daughter, and the Spanish eunuch. Or have I been misinformed?"

"They are acting as Coroner, Justice of the Peace and clerk at the moment, but I expect to resume my duties on my return."

"I would rather you were closer to me. Ludlow was important only while Arthur lived. Now he is gone it is a backwater, and you deserve better."

Thomas wanted to point out that he had built a house of his own design beside the river Teme, complete with running water and heated floors, but expected Henry would not care what he had done. He cared only about what Thomas could do for him in the future. Thomas also wanted to say he was not sure London was the place he would choose to make his home, but Henry would be uninterested in his opinion. It felt as if his future, whatever there was left of it to him, had been steered along a path not of his making. Thomas knew his entire life had been the same. Taken to France by his father to fight in a battle that took the John Berrington's life and set Thomas adrift in a strange land. He had loved a girl who did not love him in return, and was the cause of him being thrown into a canyon and assumed dead. The Sultan of Granada had chosen him as his physician, another act that had forced him along even stranger paths.

So Thomas nodded and said, "I will do what you request, Your Grace."

"Of course you will." Henry turned his attention to several new arrivals. "And here is Harry. Tell him what Catherine thinks of him as a potential suitor. You can lie if you need to. Then we will eat fine capon, beef and lamb, and drink this rich wine."

When he turned, he saw the young prince appear alongside Thomas More, who seemed surprised to find Thomas with the King. He came forward and offered his hand.

"Well met, Berrington." He lowered his voice. "I was going to send you a note. I have deciphered several more locations, and Linacre informs me all are sites of old plague pits. It is a breakthrough, do you agree?"

"A breakthrough, yes, but to what we do not yet know."

"Linacre also provided me with a list of names of those who died, together with his thoughts on them, which do not make comfortable reading." More reached beneath his coat and slipped a wrapped sheaf of papers into Thomas hand. "Put them away to read later."

Thomas glanced at young Harry, who stared up at him. It was an expression he was used to with the prince. The boy had probably listened to and watched the transfer of the paper.

Thomas More stepped back a little as if to offer them some privacy, but was still close enough to hear.

"What do you speak of?" asked Harry.

"Matters of law, Your Grace. Nothing important."

"Dull then." Harry grinned. "Is that big son of yours with you?"

"Not at the moment, Your Grace, but he will soon join me here."

"When he comes, bring him to see me. I have questions regarding sword-craft, and I wager he is the man to ask."

Thomas suppressed a smile, for Harry spoke of violent matters in his still boyish voice.

"Will is better with an axe than a sword, but he is good enough in a pinch."

Harry laughed. "When I am king – and I pray that will not be for many years – I want him at my side. A man such as him will bring even greater respect for the crown. I intend to ask him next time we meet."

Thomas wondered what Will's answer would be. No doubt he would go along with Harry for now, but he, too, had made his home in Ludlow. Did this family of Tudors expect the entire Berrington clan to decamp to London, where they would live at their whim? Thomas wondered if it was too late to return to Spain permanently, though he doubted life would be much different there. Isabel had poured honours and positions on him he had not welcomed and was glad now for their lack. The magic of al-Andalus had disappeared when Spain conquered its last holdout of Granada. It was why men like al-Timani had made new homes for themselves in London and other northern countries. At least here, they were not subjected to random death.

"You should ask my son himself, Your Grace. He is his own man now."

"I will not tell you again, Thomas. Do not call me your grace. My name is Harry. I am not King yet, so call me by name."

Thomas glanced at More, who appeared surprised at the boy's offer.

"Are you staying?" he asked the man, partly to avoid having to answer Harry.

"I cannot. Linacre has agreed to meet me for an early supper, and then we will explore some of the locations we have identified."

"I would suggest you wait until morning."

"I do not believe demons stalk the streets of London. We will be perfectly safe, and at least there will be no crowds."

"What is this talk of demons?" asked Harry, excitement in his voice.

"It is nothing, Your Grace," said More. "It is merely a conceit for a story I am thinking of writing."

"You are always writing," said Harry. "You need to be more like Tom here and do some fighting."

More smiled. "In future years, when the name Thomas Berrington is not even a memory, the words I set for a printer may still be read."

Harry laughed. "Or not. I have seen none of these scribblings you claim to have done, Master More. I am not even sure they exist."

"Oh, they exist, my prince, but they are not suitable for a young, ah, man." It was clear to Thomas that More had almost said 'child', which would have angered Harry. Fortunately, new arrivals distracted the boy, and he went to Sir

Geoffrey Blackwood, who entered beside an elegant woman Thomas assumed was his wife. She went to speak with Lady Margaret while Blackwood crossed directly to the King and leaned close to whisper in his ear.

When Harry moved away, hovering halfway between the two new arrivals, More said, "Now there is a man who pushes his own interests. Do you know Blackwood?"

"I have had the misfortune," Thomas said. "We have been introduced, but I doubt he remembers who I am. What about you?"

"He is aware I tutor the prince, so he likes to make a pretence of friendship now and again because one day the boy will be the new king, and Blackwood likes nothing better than to be close to the machinery of power, despite his past."

Thomas was intrigued. "What about his past?"

"I cannot speak of it in his presence, but come to my house when you can where we will talk without fear of being overheard. The names Linacre provided for you are all acquaintances of Blackwood. They share the same interests in the arcane." More glanced at the man again. "But enough for now. Call on me after noon, for I am at Lincoln's Inn most mornings."

"When do you visit Catherine next?"

"I go to tutor *Princess* Catherine each Monday, which is when you saw me there."

"I expect she is a good pupil, yes?"

"She is bright and possesses a fine mind. Sometimes, her questions take me by surprise."

"I have known her since she was a babe, so it does not surprise me. She is like her mother in that."

More smiled. "You are a strange man, Berrington. To look at you, most would take you as ordinary. Tall, but ordinary. Yet you are far from that."

"I wish I were ordinary, but the world does not allow me to be so." Thomas saw Blackwood had finished pouring whatever plot he had in mind into the King's ear and now moved away to stand with his wife and Lady Margaret, who greeted him with a rare smile.

"Go speak to the Prince," said More. "And do not forget, tomorrow at noon."

"I will not."

After More had gone, Thomas approached Harry, who was talking with one of his sisters. Thomas had forgotten which of them it was. They all dressed similarly and were close enough in age to make separating them difficult.

"What is this about demons?" asked Harry again. It was clear he had not let the idea go. For one as young as him it no doubt carried an illicit sense of danger and excitement.

"It is nothing, your—" Thomas stopped himself and started again. "It is nothing, Harry. Wild rumours spread by the mob, nothing more."

"See, it was not so hard to say my name, was it?"

"But doing so will cause me to forget myself once you are King."

Harry laughed. "By that time you will no doubt be long dead, Tom, so you have no need to worry on that score."

Thomas saw Blackwood approaching. He assumed the man wanted to speak with the Prince, but he was wrong.

"I have something for you, Berrington." Blackwood reached inside his jacket and drew out a sealed letter. He held it out.

"What is it?"

"An invitation, of course. Do not open it here in case others see." Blackwood smiled without humour. "Some may be jealous if they do not receive one."

Thomas slipped the letter into his pocket beside Linacre's notes, then accompanied Harry to the table.

TWENTY-FOUR

As Thomas walked from the Tower, shadows spread tendrils across the streets and alleys. Full dark lay less than an hour away and people wanted to be safe in their houses before then. His feet found their own way as his mind worked through everything said to him. Prince Harry, King Henry, the Queen and Lady Margaret Beaufort all contributed. But Sir Geoffrey Blackwood's private conversation still occupied his thoughts. He could not decide what to make of the man or why he had spoken with him. As for the invitation offered, it was plain ridiculous. If he were in his house in Ludlow, he would sit and talk with the others. Jorge mostly because he was the wisest of them all regarding such matters, though Amal was fast catching him up. But he did not have them in London, so when he reached his house, he followed the alley to Eleanor's workshop.

Thomas was surprised to discover her still working, even more so to see Jack there.

"Have either of you eaten today?" he asked as he entered, the air thick with the smell of ink and paper.

"Eaten?" Eleanor frowned. "What is that?" She looked exhausted, pale-faced, with a sheen of sweat across her brow. Thomas thought he saw her sway as she tried to stand upright, as if she had difficulty with her balance.

"Jack, go to the house and ask Winnie if she has anything you can bring back. Bread and cheese will do, but I expect there are better leftovers from their supper. Tell her it is for me and a friend."

Jack grinned. "Shall I tell her who the friend is, Master Thomas?"

"I think she may already know." He patted the lad's back. "Now go."

When he had gone, Eleanor said, "I have lost my helper, so now you will have to do. But I doubt you will be as skilled or keen as Jack."

"You look unwell." Thomas went to reach out to touch her throat, then held back. She might misinterpret the move.

She waved a hand in dismissal. "My head aches, I admit, but it is not unusual. It has grown worse of late." She tried to smile but it was wan. "Perhaps I should consult a good physic. Do you know of one, Tom?"

"I will examine you if you wish it." He was unwilling to play her games but was concerned for her. "And try not to tease Jack too much. He is young and, I believe, more than a little besotted with you."

"I will try, but it is so easy to do. He is like a puppy at my feet." Her expression became serious. "What would this examination involve? Would I have to disrobe?"

"It would not come to that."

"That is a shame." She made an effort to pull herself together. "Now, hang this finished sheet over the rail for me. Then bring me another clean sheet, and I will show you how to pin it to the board." She clapped her hands together. "Come on, be quick. You can examine me once we have finished here. Perhaps you can tell me why my head hurts so much."

Thomas peeled the printed sheet away, noticing the metal pins sticking up from around the type. When he brought a new sheet of paper, Eleanor applied fresh ink, using a stuffed leather ball on a rod to roll it across the typeface.

"Go ahead," she said, stepping back.

"Are you sure you trust me?"

"No, but go ahead anyway."

Thomas studied the layout and then carefully laid the paper onto the bed, pushing the iron pins through its edges. He had noted how Eleanor and Luke had used them to mark the exact position so that the pages would line up when they turned the sheet over to print the other side.

"Is that all right?" Thomas asked when he was done.

"Good enough, but I want to see you do better next time."

"Jack will be back by then, and you both need to take a break and eat. And then there is something I need to talk to you about."

"The book?"

"No, not the book, but I will talk of it while you eat."

"How was the King?" she asked.

"Kingly."

"I expect you ate supper at his table."

"I ate little, the food was too rich for me." It was not true, but he did not want her to think that whatever Jack brought would be second best. He expected she would not believe him in any case. "I want to discuss something with you while we eat."

"What?"

"I will tell you when you finally sit and eat something."

Eleanor huffed and wound the press down onto the paper. When she raised it, Thomas peeled the sheet off the bed and hung it alongside the others.

Jack returned with a wooden box and set it on the table. Inside were bread and cheese, the remains of a pie, apples, and pears. He had even remembered to add three knives.

Thomas held Eleanor's narrow shoulders and steered her to the table.

"The ink will dry out, and I will have to clean the type," she said, but her protest was weak.

"Show me or Jack how to do that after you have eaten."

"I can leave if you would rather eat without me, sir," said Jack.

"No, sit with us," said Eleanor. "You have done good work today, Jack. If you ever tire of being a stable lad I will find a job for you."

"What is the pay like?" he asked with a grin, and Eleanor pretended to slap his ear.

"What are you paid now?"

Thomas found plates and put food on all three. He would eat a little to keep them company, but his stomach was already full.

"Nothing," said Jack. "But bed and board are free, and both good."

"Except you sleep in the stables," Thomas said.

"That is true, but the cot is comfortable, and I have blankets and a brazier for the winter months. The horses keep me warm."

"If you worked for me, I would pay you a penny a day, which is not much. But you will get one-twentieth of the profit when we sell our tales."

Jack stared at Eleanor. "How much would that be?"

"It depends. Last time, I printed three hundred pamphlets, which sold for one penny each. So three hundred pennies, less the cost of the paper, the ink, and whatever rent I pay." Eleanor looked at Thomas. "Except I am not paying any rent, am I?"

"I am no businessman," Thomas said. "But I did learn something surprising from the King today. This house and the workshop now belong to me. I had assumed I would live here only until my current task was finished, but that is not the case. Henry is going to send me papers in my name." Thomas looked at Jack and smiled. "You must put up with me a while longer, lad."

Jack tried to look serious. "I suppose you are not the worst master I have had."

"How do you think Hardwin will take the news?"

"It is not my place to say, sir."

"You said you had something you wanted to talk

about," said Eleanor, around a mouthful of pie, spraying pieces of pastry on her plate.

"Do you know a man named Sir Geoffrey Blackwood?"

Eleanor stopped chewing and stared at Thomas. Once she swallowed, she said, "Why do you ask?" Her voice was flat and emotionless. She did not sound like herself, and Thomas saw Jack also note it.

"I have seen him each time I visited the King. It seems he is close to the court, and before I left, we had a conversation that might interest you." He glanced at Jack, wondering if the lad was old enough to hear the subject.

"Why interest me, Tom?"

"He knows of the book."

"The book?"

"Yes, the book."

"What book?" asked Jack.

"One whose name cannot be spoken."

"Ah," said Jack. "That book."

Thomas frowned. "You know of it?"

"All of London knows of it. Why else are the streets empty after dark?"

"Not always," said Eleanor, "otherwise there would be no victims."

"Dudels," said Jack, "getting what they deserve." He glanced at Thomas. "No offence meant, Master Thomas."

"None taken, and if ever I am regarded as a dudel then someone please tell me."

"Knowing how you dress, Tom, it is highly unlikely you will be accused of such," said Eleanor. "And you have still not told me what the dudel Blackwood wants of you."

"I am invited to a gathering of like-minded individuals. Which I suspect will be made up of lords, ladies and gentlemen. Not to mention the occasional duke or earl. Blackwood has been present when I visited the King, so I wager he spends much time there. I have not seen him on my previous visits to London, so his rise may be recent." Thomas was aware of the way Jack stared at him. To mention an audience with King Henry so casually seemed to make an impression. Though this house had been a gift from the King and must have had many men of position stay here before. But none had been made a gift of the house, orchard and workshop.

"You have made a useful connection in Blackwood. He knows everyone important in London. You must go to this gathering, Tom."

"I told him I would consider his invitation. He asked me to bring a female companion, but I do not have one."

"You could hire one," said Jack.

Thomas laughed. "You know all about hiring women, do you?" He was amused when Jack's face blushed a bright red.

"I do not mean a strumpet, master, but a woman of class."

"I suspect it might mean the same thing," Thomas said.

"Ask me," said Eleanor. "When is it?"

"Two nights hence. He was most insistent I attend. Will Luke not object if he returns and finds you planning to attend a gathering with another man?"

"Luke is not the jealous type. Besides, he does what I tell him and allows me much freedom."

"Then you share an unusual relationship."

"That we do. Besides, he will not return for several days. I doubt he has even set foot in Flanders yet."

Thomas expected a smile from her, but there was none.

Jack's eyes darted between them. No doubt he knew he would never rise to a position where he would be invited to such an event. To Thomas, this was a sad state of affairs, but he suspected Jack was content with his lot. And perhaps now that this house was his, he could help improve the lad's prospects. He was bright and willing.

"So you will take me?" asked Eleanor.

"I have not altogether decided if I want to attend."

"What if I say I do?"

"Then I can see why Luke does as you tell him. Let me sleep on it. I will give you and Sir Geoffrey my answer in the morning." Thomas glanced at the abandoned press. "Tell me how to clean it down. Jack, you need to go to your bed once you have eaten. And you the same, Eleanor."

"Are you not going to examine me, Tom?" Her teasing was so blatant Thomas tried not to laugh. Jack looked uneasy.

"You are pale, and exhausted. Sleep is what you need."

Thomas remained in the printworks after Eleanor ascended the steps to the upper floor. He had cleaned following her directions after Jack had left them. Now he sat at the table and spread the papers Linacre had sent him. He heard Eleanor moving around, then a soft thump as she dropped onto the pallet.

He took the top sheet and scanned it. Four killings. Four names. Together with notes added by Linacre. Each was dated, and Thomas assumed it indicated the order in which they were attacked.

May 13. Faster Lane (nPP). Sir Jacob Kell. 55 yo, unmarried, dissolute, known to lie with both men and women. Rich through inheritance. Lives east London near Tower. Rumoured to study alchemy. Killed with multiple blows to the head but skull remained intact. First victim?

May 28. Near Charterhouse (PP). Joseph Nash. 39yo, goldsmith, untitled but wealthy. Beaten about head. I believe his skull was opened while still alive, but died of blood loss. Brain tissue missing. 2 wks after first attack. Chosen to make up for not opening skull then?

July 17. Near Aldgate (PP). Lord Benjamin Kirkbridge, 56yrs, outwardly upright, religious, beneath the surface most corrupt and debauched. Widowed. No children known. Skull removed and never found. Body identified by clothing and a letter in jacket pocket.

September 9. East Smith Field (PPx2). Oliver Warwick, 29yrs, youngest victim. Inherited wealth from father (rumoured to have poisoned him). Gambler, abuses whores, seduces titled ladies and other men's wives. Interest in alchemy.

Thomas read the list three times then sat up, washing his hands across his face. Oliver Warwick was the victim Thomas had heard screaming in the night and whose body he had witnessed. His skull had been opened and his brain taken. Thomas appreciated Linacre's brevity, which covered most of what he needed to know. The lack of any family for those chosen meant it would be difficult to follow up on each of them, but not impossible. They must have had friends, or at the least others who knew them. Thomas rose and found a sheet of discarded paper and a pen. He took it to the table, but before he could make his own notes, he heard a loud rattling from above him. He stopped and listened, unsure what Eleanor could be doing. Then there came a strange wailing sound and he ran up the steps.

Eleanor lay on the pallet, the blanket kicked loose. Beneath it she was naked. Her head was back, her neck taut, and her limbs shook and twitched. There was white froth around her lips.

Thomas rolled her onto her side and pushed his fingers into her mouth to check she was not choking on her own tongue. Then he covered her nakedness with the blanket and held her. There was nothing else he could do, not until the tremors passed. He was familiar with the falling sickness and had treated it in the past with a low dosage of hashish. In at least half his patients it had helped. He had learned the remedy from an ancient treatise penned in Arabia from one of the great Arabic scholars. When Eleanor recovered he would give her a small amount and check on her regularly. It was possible her complaints of headaches were a symptom, but it was uncommon.

When the shaking stopped Eleanor fell into a deep sleep. Thomas brought water and washed her face and mouth. He rolled her on her side again, then sat against the wall. The blanket had worked loose again and he watched the rise and fall of her pale breasts without shame. Eleanor possessed a spirit that attracted men. It attracted Thomas, but he was determined to do nothing about it. His eyes grew heavy and several times he jerked awake with a start. Then sleep came for him too. When he woke grey light showed through the small window and the palette was empty. There was no sign of Eleanor downstairs. Thomas went into the house, stripped and washed himself then climbed into his bed. Only as he closed his eyes did he remember Linacre's notes. He had left them on the table in the printworks. He smiled and let sleep take him again. They would still be there when he woke.

TWENTY-FIVE

The morning was almost finished before Thomas woke, washed and dressed. Then he made up a weak tonic of hashish and herb water sweetened with honey. He descended the stairs without seeing anyone. As he passed the kitchen Winnie had her back to him as she kneaded dough for bread. Jack was in the printworks with Eleanor, who smiled at Thomas as he entered.

He went to her and looked into her eyes.

"If you intend to kiss me, Tom, I shall have to ask Jack to look away." She leaned closer and whispered, "I think it would make him sore jealous."

"I am trying to see if you are recovered."

"Recovered from what?"

"Last night."

Eleanor stared at him. "What happened last night? I slept like someone dead and woke with my head clearer than it has been for days. Did we do something we should not have, Tom?"

"You..." Thomas glanced at Jack. He did not want to speak in front of the lad. Instead he took Eleanor's hand and led her outside, then along the alley until they emerged on Cheapside where the melee of people allowed them a strange privacy. When he released Eleanor's hand she put it back in his.

"Do you want me to come to your room, Tom? Or an inn? You told me you stayed at Bel Savage. We could go there. I want to lie with you something fierce. You might be old but you are strong and handsome."

Thomas pulled his hand free again. "Do you truly not recall what happened to you last night?"

Eleanor shook her head. "But I am sure you are going to tell me. Was I wicked? I can be, you know." She smiled and took a step closer.

"You suffered a frenzy. I came and held you until it passed. You were bad a long time and I was worried, so I made a tincture for you. I have used it before. It will do you no harm and might help to stop their return."

"I had no frenzy, Tom. I told you, I slept without dreams and woke refreshed." She tugged at his hand. "Now stop this foolishness and let me return to work. I have much to do before we visit Blackwood later today. I need to wash myself well. Can I use your room to do that? You can help me if you would like."

"You can use my room, but I have other things to do."

Eleanor shrugged, and he knew she was only teasing. He suspected she found it too easy, and wondered what she did if a man responded. When she started back towards Milkstrete he waited a moment then followed. A boy ran into him, almost sending him to the ground. Thomas caught the lad's shoulder and shook him.

"Watch where you're going, boy."

"Fuck off, old man." The lad twisted loose and ran off even faster than before. What the rush was was a mystery. Eleanor had gone, but he found her in the printworks.

Thomas went to the table where he had left Linacre's notes, but in their place was a wooden chase with a page of type laid out ready to be set.

"I left some papers here," he said.

Eleanor glanced at him from where she was instructing Jack how to lift out the old type and what to do with it. Thomas knew it would be poured into a bucket where it would wait until the small brazier was fired up to melt the lead into ingots which would then be used to punch new letters.

"I saw no papers. Did you, Jack?"

Jack shook his head. "Nothing. You had already tidied everything when I arrived."

"Does Hardwin not object to you spending all your time in here?" Thomas asked.

Jack smiled. "I told him you said I could."

"He had to accept Jack's word," said Eleanor. "You are, after all, the master of the house."

Thomas hoped Jack would not suffer as a result of what he had offered him.

"Did you tidy away my papers?" he asked Eleanor.

"I threw whatever was on there away. It was spoiled print inked on one side and creased. I always clear it away before I start work if it has been used on both sides. Was it important?"

Thomas thought about it. "It was, but I can recall what was written there."

"Was it a love letter from your pretty princess, Tom?" she asked.

"It concerned—" Thomas stopped. He did not want to state what had been on the pages with Jack there. Why, he was unsure, other than talk of murder was too dark a subject for them both. "It does not matter. As I said, I can recall what was there. I will leave you both."

"And I can come and use your washing facilities, Tom?"

"I will have Eliza arrange for a tub to be filled for you."

"And who will wash my back?"

"If it needs washing, I am sure Eliza can do that as well."

Thomas grew tired of Eleanor's constant teasing. He turned to leave, then stopped.

"I will come for you when it is ready, later today. I will also leave your tincture with her. Make sure to drink it all."

Eleanor curtsied and blew him a kiss before turning to Jack. She laid an arm across his shoulder. He would be her next victim.

Thomas returned to his room and wrote down everything he recalled from Linacre's notes. What he would do about them had to wait until at least the morrow. Tonight, he had to attend Blackwood's revels. He might have forgotten his invitation, but he wanted to talk to the man. It was possible he would know some, if not all, of the dead men.

Once he was satisfied, he recorded everything he knew.

Thomas found Eliza and asked her to fill the round wooden barrel with hot water and to tell him when it was done. The bathing room was on the ground floor to save having to carry water upstairs, but at least the room had a sturdy bolt.

When she came to him, Thomas used the tub, then dressed and went to tell Eleanor it was waiting for her. He neglected to tell Eliza she might be needed. It was a moment of spite which pleased him. He was unsure what to make of Eleanor. At times, she was a perfect companion. At others, something took her over she could barely contain. Thomas had seen it before in people who suffered the falling sickness. Often, before a bout, they grew manic and acted out of character.

Thomas returned to his room and took some time to select what to wear. He had asked Hardwin where to find a tailor and purchased new clothes. He suspected others at Blackwood's gathering would like to display their wealth and status. Thomas did not care, but he did want to fit in. People were more likely to talk if they saw him as an equal.

TWENTY-SIX

Thomas's formal invitation from Blackwood had arrived the evening before while Thomas had been with Eleanor. Hardwin had been saved the effort of removing and re-applying the seal because it was nothing more than a hand-written card, which the man handed to him without comment.

The hand that had written it did not belong to a man. It was ornate, bold and precise. He and a companion were invited to Stepney Manor, the home of Sir Geoffrey Black-wood. All food, drink and entertainment would be provided. No finish time had been offered, but the invitation said to arrive before dusk.

When Thomas entered Eleanor's workshop after dressing in his new clothes she was nowhere to be seen. Pages that had hung over rods to let the ink dry had been taken down. In their stead, on the table, sat a pile of pamphlets. Thomas picked one up to find another of her bawdy tales.

"Is that you, Tom?" Eleanor's voice came from upstairs.

"Were you expecting someone else? Is Luke back yet?"

"Luke will not return for at least another week. Longer if he encounters difficulty obtaining the type."

"Which you no longer need."

"Whatever he pays, it will be worth ten times as much here in London."

"Shall I come up?"

The laughter that drifted down the stairs was delightful. "Only if you want to see me half naked. Which you could have done already were you not so prim. Though you said you would examine me, so now might be a good opportunity. But best stay down there until I am ready and decent. Is Blackwood's house still east of the city?"

"It is beyond Smith Field, so yes. Do you know of it?"

"It is some distance so you will need to take your horse."

"Jack is saddling Sombra for me now. I am sure he can find a mount for you."

"I do not ride well. I would rather perch in front of you, and then you can stop me from tumbling to the dirt and messing up my pretty dress. You can even examine me a little." A laugh caught in her voice.

Thomas did not believe a word of what she said but had learned enough about Eleanor to know arguing would prove pointless. He was pleased she appeared to have recovered from her fit without any lasting effects.

"How do you know of Stepney Manor?" Thomas asked.

"Sir Richard Croft took me there when I lived beneath his roof. He enjoyed showing me off. I have been told I am worth showing off."

"What was the entertainment like?"

"I have tried to drive the memory from my mind, so prefer not to say." Her voice was serious now.

When Eleanor descended the staircase, the sight of her almost took Thomas's breath away. Her dress was exquisite, with a tight corset and low décolletage, which revealed the pale upper curve of her rounded breasts. She wore fine leather shoes on her feet, and her hair had been piled atop her head, on which sat a silver tiara.

"Where did you get such things?" Thomas asked and, without thinking, offered his hand, which she accepted, her own small and warm within his.

"I have my secrets, kind sir. If you treat me well, I may reveal one or two. Now, do we mount this horse of yours, or shall I go and change?"

"We ride, if you are ready."

"Yes, I am ready."

Heavy cloud had obscured the sun all morning but had cleared by noon. As they rode east and passed through the postern gate into Smithfield, a pale sun was trying to break through, but it sat low in the sky, and mist rose from the Thames to their right. Thomas had no idea how long the event they were heading to would last but suspected it might be morning before they returned.

Eleanor sat sideways in front of him, one leg on either side of the pommel. Thomas had to wrap one arm around her to keep her safe, and her proximity and sensuality were disconcerting.

As they approached Aldgate, they became aware of other well-dressed men and women heading in the same direction. One or two nodded, but it was not until they passed through the gate and others joined them from the north that anyone spoke.

"Well met, sir," said a portly man astride a tall mount. He had no companion with him. "I do not recognise you. Is this your first time at one of Blackwood's affairs?" He spoke to Thomas, but his eyes lingered on Eleanor.

"Yes, my first," Thomas said.

The man smiled lasciviously. "If you need help call on me." He nodded at Eleanor. "Your companion looks familiar. Is this your wife, or someone else's?" He laughed more than the comment deserved.

"Of course I am Sir Thomas's wife," said Eleanor before he could respond. "He received his invite from Sir Geoffrey while they were with the King."

Thomas saw the man's eyes widen momentarily, but he suspected most of those heading along with them might be familiar with King Henry.

The man laughed. "No matter, many wives will be available tonight, and Blackwood always ensures a surfeit of young women. A man is not expected to sport with his own wife at these affairs." He touched the wide brim of his hat and urged his horse on.

Once he was out of earshot, Thomas said, "Is everyone going to be like that?"

"Did you not take to him, Tom?"

He shook his head. "Did you expect me to?"

"Of course not. And yes, most will be like him, though he was ugly enough to scare any demon, was he not?"

"You did well in answering him."

225

"I know his kind well enough. His hands will be all over whichever woman he is near. Mind, that is what these events are all about."

"You speak as if you know them well, and said this was not your first time at Stepney Manor."

"I told you Sir Richard took me with him now and then when we came to London. He always told his wife it was for my education, but she knew the real reason and was glad his attentions lay elsewhere and not on her."

"It must have been terrifying," Thomas said.

"Not so bad, no, or at least I did not notice. I was young and knew nothing else. All the staff at Croft Manor knew how Sir Richard was. There was an expectation among the women who worked and lived there how it would be. He bedded every woman except for his wife, who none of us ever saw."

"They have several grown children so he must have bedded her a few times."

"That was long before I knew him."

Thomas thought back to when he was a boy before he left Lemster at the age of thirteen. He had probably met Sir Richard Croft because his own father was important in the town, but if he had there was no recollection. Since his return to England, he had had too much knowledge of the man. He understood his nature, but did not dislike him.

"His wife lives in London most of the time. That is what he told me."

"In one of his fine houses, yes."

"I take it you are not one of his bastards. Do you know who your parents were?"

"I do."

Thomas waited, then said, "Do you intend to tell me?"

"No."

"Then tell me when you left Ludlow, and how you met Luke."

"I left Sir Richard's house when I had almost seventeen years, and his attentions turned more demanding. By then, I was working in the kitchen, and it became harder to hide the bruises. In the end, I grew tired of my weakness and left. I stole a little money and one of Sir Richard's books, of which he has many."

"I have seen his library, and he has even more books than I do."

Eleanor laughed. "Indeed he does, but this book was from his private collection, and unless you were a man of similar tastes, you would not be shown it. There are books and drawings there that would make the devil blush. It is where I acquired an interest in the erotic. It is easy to pen, and men and some women are happy to pay a good price for it. As for Luke, we met in London. I worked for John Wynkyn at the Caxton Press, where I learned my skills. He did not work there but would bring rolls of paper. We got to talking. He is good-looking and funny. When I started working for myself, he joined me."

"So he works for you?"

"He does."

"That does not surprise me. You are a strong-willed woman."

"But not physically strong, which is why I need a man to

be with me. You are not young, Tom, but you have great strength."

"Not as much as I used to."

"When you were my age, you must have been magnificent."

"I lived in Malaga then."

"Where is this Malaga?"

"Southern Spain, on the narrow sea. There is nothing south of it until the coast of Africa. It is dry and hot, and I loved it."

"Loved, or love?"

"Loved. To love it now would be pointless, for it is lost to me. Except..."

When Thomas said nothing more, Eleanor twisted on her perch and looked at him. "Except what, Tom?"

"King Henry has asked me to travel to Spain, to speak with Isabel and Fernando."

"Who are they?"

Thomas laughed. "I forget others do not know them as I do. They are King and Queen of a far distant land. Queen Isabel of Castile and King Fernando of Aragon."

"As Princess Catherine is of Aragon?"

"She is their daughter. They have other daughters, and a son, Juan who will be king one day."

"You know Catherine though. What is she like?"

"Once, she was beautiful, carefree and clever. Now she is sad and brave, but still beautiful."

Ahead, a large house appeared, clearly their destination because everyone on the road was headed that way. A clutch of boys stood ready to take horses for stabling. Thomas watched the protocol before slipping two pence to the lad who led theirs away. He had observed some give nothing, others the odd coin.

"You are too generous with your pennies, Tom," said Eleanor. "One day, you will slip a hand into your pocket and find it empty."

Thomas smiled. "That day will be a long time in the future." He offered his arm, and Eleanor slipped hers through it.

Wide stone steps led to a terrace where men and women gathered in groups.

"Is it true what you told that fat man, Tom – you have never attended such a gathering before?" asked Eleanor.

He shook his head. "Never. But you said you have."

Thomas did not want to think about what Eleanor was not revealing. She was sharp enough to know what was on his mind but too polite to lay it in the open. The thought reminded him of what he had witnessed on Burfa Bank west of Ludlow, where men and women disported wildly. Sir Richard Croft had been among them, and Thomas wondered if the man would be here. He looked around, but everyone he saw was a stranger.

"I do not see Sir Geoffrey," he said.

"These people are here at his invitation. He will be inside to ensure the final preparations are being made. He will show himself soon enough."

"You must help me. You know more about this than I do."

Eleanor shrugged a pale shoulder. "A girl learns things." She leaned close and kissed the corner of Thomas's mouth.

She smiled. "Fear not, I will take you in hand." Her eyes met his. "Do you not find me attractive, Tom?"

"You must know how you look and how men react to you."

"In that case, why have you never responded to me?"

"Because you are young and I am old. Besides, I have a woman at home in Ludlow." It was not entirely the truth anymore.

Eleanor laughed. "And I have Luke, but he is not here, and neither is your woman."

Thomas tried to think of an answer but was spared when wide oak doors were flung open, and Sir Geoffrey Blackwood appeared. He was dressed in black satin, the fine material cut to reveal bright scarlet within, flashing as he moved. On his head, he wore an ornate hat fashioned to form two horns.

He spread his arms wide. "Welcome one and all to our wassail. Enter. Eat, drink, do as you want, with whomever you want. Before long, the night will be upon us, and you will have to stay until dawn unless you wish to meet the demons of Hell." He gave a manic grin, his eyes red and bright. "Unless one can be roused from within our midst!"

His exclamation was greeted with a great roar from almost all present. Thomas looked around, aware that some of the attendees were already drunk. He saw a woman with a breast displayed. A man with his hand inside another woman's dress. As Blackwood entered the house and others began to follow, servants appeared carrying trays laden with small food items, but mostly drink. There was little ale but much wine, and small heavy glasses holding stronger spirits.

At least a score of young women, some naked, others barely clothed, moved through the crowd.

"Stay close to me, Tom, and if any men approach with intent, you must make it clear I am yours for the night, not theirs."

"And how do I do that? Punch them on the nose?"

Eleanor giggled. "Most of them would swoon should you do so. Violence will not be necessary. You are to make it clear I belong to you. Embrace me. Kiss me like a lover. You may also touch my intimate parts."

"For all to see?"

"Oh, there will be much to see here, and no one will care, but I will be safe if you do so. And it will not be such a hardship, will it?"

Thomas was less sure. He wondered exactly what path Eleanor expected this night to take. And what path he would allow it to take.

As they entered the hall, a drink was placed in their hands. People approached, curious about who the newcomers were. Most attention fell on Eleanor, but one or two women seemed intrigued by Thomas. Among the effete men present, he stood out as a rugged man, a man of action who had fought and prevailed. Thomas knew he was too innocent, but it was too late to back out now. Blackwood had the ear of both the King and his mother. Why he wanted Thomas in his circle was a mystery. One he might find an answer to before the night was out.

TWENTY-SEVEN

At first, everything was strange. Whenever Thomas was in the company of people such as those flocking into the rooms and chambers of the large house, he felt out of place. He knew he should not, for had he not been the confidant of Queen Isabel of Castile? As he was now to her daughter, Catherine of Aragon? But those friendships were different. They were real. Here, there was little of friendship but a great deal of lust and skirmishing for position.

None of those here were royalty, but many were titled. A glut of Sirs, a smattering of Dukes, and a handful of Earls. Those without titles were wealthy. They were not as wealthy as Thomas, but rich beyond the ken of most ordinary folk, and unlike Thomas, they preferred to flaunt that wealth in how they dressed. They were people like those on Linacre's list of the dead, and he wondered if those had attended Blackwood's gatherings.

With Eleanor on his arm, he spoke with many who questioned him. There was no artifice here. These people went directly to what they wanted. In most cases, they wanted to know if Eleanor was available. A few of the women were intrigued by Thomas, but it was Eleanor that people wanted, both male and female, and Thomas could not blame them.

She shone with a pale beauty, anointed with rich perfume. Her breasts were pale, their upper swell on display, as were those of almost all the women.

"How did you know how to dress?" Thomas asked during a lull in the conversation. An hour had passed, introductions made, and liaisons agreed upon. Several couples – not those who had arrived together – wandered off into rooms at the rear of the house. Thomas saw Blackwood moving through the throng, a word, here, a touch there. He also saw Sir Richard Croft, his arms around two women who brazenly kissed each other.

"I know titled people, Tom, you know I do."

"Are they all like this?"

Eleanor laughed, the sound so delightful several people turned to look at what might have amused her. Their interest soon waned when they saw it was only Thomas.

"Of course they are, or Sir Richard would not have come." Her arm tightened through his, and her slim body pressed close. The sensation was pleasant but disturbing. Thomas could not comprehend that she might want him in the way she hinted at. And even if she did, he did not want her in the same way. He knew he had to speak his mind.

"You have a man in Flanders, sent on a wild goose chase. Your type has been returned and you are printing your tales once more. What will Luke say when he returns from his dangerous task and finds it unnecessary?"

"He loves me, so I will be forgiven." Eleanor looked around the room, several men blatantly meeting her gaze. Heads nodded, smiles were offered.

Thomas had a question but knew he could not ask it. When Sir Richard had brought her to this place, had she participated in the revels that took place out of sight? Even as the thought came to him, he noticed one or two couples locked in heavy embraces and knew how she would answer. He was also aware of how Sir Richard Croft treated women – all except his wife. Thomas glanced in his direction and looked quickly away. How a man could behave in such a debauched way in a room full of others was beyond his ken.

"Fortunately, he has not seen us," said Eleanor, following Thomas's gaze.

"His mind appears to be elsewhere."

"As are his hands."

Thomas laughed. "I wager he may have taken on more than he can handle. He is not a young man."

"He is even older than you, but can still perform. Do not underestimate him. Do you want to stay, or leave before events grow too wild for you?"

"Than this?"

"Oh, this is nothing. The night will grow far more debauched yet."

"We cannot leave. I was invited for a reason and must stay until I discover what it is."

"Invited by Sir Geoffrey?"

Thomas nodded.

"Then he wants something from you – something only you can give him. He will offer you both women and men because he does not yet know your tastes well enough."

"I have nothing he wants. He is already close to the King."

"For him to invite you, he must believe that you do. He may want your body, for he indulges in the pleasures of both male and female flesh. But even he must recognise you are not that kind of man. It will be something else. What is it you know he wants access to?"

"I know many things, but none that would interest a man like him. He plays at power, but Henry sees through him."

"They are different as night and day," said Eleanor. "Sir Geoffrey pretends to be powerful, but all the power belongs to the King. And—" She broke off. "God's scrotum, he has seen us." She began to pull away, but Thomas held her firm.

"Let him come, then I will learn what he wants."

"He brings those libertines with him, so I know what he wants."

Thomas laughed. "Then I will punch him if he dishonours you."

"A fine joke, is it?" said Sir Geoffrey. He stood close, shorter and stouter than Thomas. One of the women with him exceeded his height, the other was tiny. "Do not keep the joke to yourself, Berrington."

"It is not worth repeating," Thomas said, unsure how to address the man. When in the company of King Henry, he always insisted on formality. Here, formality appeared to have been set aside.

"Shame, I heard you were a clever man renowned for your wit."

"Then you have been led astray."

"Oh, I always enjoy being led astray, do I not, my dears?" His gaze settled on Eleanor, rising and falling without shame as he studied her. "I am sure I have seen you before but do not recall when or where," he said to her.

"I doubt you have, sir, for I am a nobody."

"Far from a nobody. A body, yes, but not a nobody." He laughed at his poor attempt at wit before his attention returned to Thomas. "You and I must talk. I have something to show you, but not now. Enjoy yourselves. There are rooms you can use if you wish. If they are not vacant, there will be another free, or you may join someone who is already there. There is food and drink aplenty. I will find you at the stroke of midnight, Berrington. Apt, I think, for what we need to discuss." He did not wait for a reply before turning away.

Thomas watched him work the room. A word for everyone. A touch for most.

"He is a pig," said Eleanor.

"You have no argument from me. I wonder what he wants to discuss?"

"It will be some plot or other. He is always dreaming them up. He might have fought alongside Henry Tudor at Bosworth, but rumour has it his loyalty lay with York until he saw the way the fighting went. Rumour also says he has no love for King Henry and would have someone else in his stead. He finds the man too uncouth, but forgets he rules a quieter country than when first he came to power. Blackwood wants a return to chaos, for in that wealth can be created. But England grows tired of it and begs for peace."

Thomas looked down at Eleanor, surprised at the venom in her voice, equally surprised that she seemed to know enough about the man to make such a judgement. He had again underestimated her. Once more, she revealed how different she was from most people here. She was not content to work day in and day out with no thought of politics or her masters. Life was often a drudge, but most knew there was no escape. It was neither right nor just but the world's way. He also knew that, as a woman, her opinions would hold no sway.

Thomas had hoped they might be ignored by staying close to a corner, but that hope was dashed when two men approached. They ignored Eleanor to stand in front of Thomas.

"You are Berrington, are you not?" said one. He was tall and slim, with a soft, handsome face and blonde hair. His companion was shorter, stockier, dark-haired, and also handsome. Eleanor reached for Thomas's hand and squeezed it as if in support or perhaps merely to indicate her possession of him.

"I am. And you are?"

"Do you not recognise us? We are often present in the Tower with Prince Henry. I tutor him in music – at which he is most skilled – and my companion does the same in dance, which he greatly enjoys. A man of position must know how to make music and dance."

"I am no man of position, so would not know." Thomas felt Eleanor's fingers squeeze his as if she approved.

"And I am afraid I must have missed you when I visited the King."

"But we have seen you, Berrington, and heard tales of your prowess with the sword. They say you are a fighting man."

Thomas laughed softly. "That may have been true at one time but less so now."

"Yet you look strong and hale," said the other, the dance instructor. He reached out, felt Thomas's arm and nodded. "Yes, still strong."

"My mind remains sharp, but I still have no recollection of either of you. Do you have some purpose in approaching me?"

"Oh, a serious question. Do you mean in this life? Or here, in Sir Geoffrey's house?"

"I mean here in front of us," Thomas said.

"Us?" The man doing most of the talking glanced at Eleanor. "Ah yes, both of you. We wondered why you were so prim, standing over here and not joining in the pleasures offered."

"Sir Geoffrey invited me to attend for a reason, but that reason is not to indulge myself even if I wished to do so, which I do not." Thomas turned and led Eleanor away. Once out of earshot, he said, "What was that all about? Did they intend to seduce me? They had little interest in you. Do I look like a man who would lie with another?"

Eleanor giggled, covering her mouth with her free hand. "You do not, Tom, but you are wrong. They were interested in me but would not have objected if we had all sported together. I know them both and they are not what you think, but like to give the appearance they may be. In this company, they can do so without being judged. But if the King knew their natures, he would never allow them to tutor young Henry."

"Do you know everyone here?"

"Not all, but a good number."

"Because you visited with Croft."

"Yes, because of that. Let us pretend we want to be alone. It will prevent a repeat of their approach and any suspicion. Despite dressing as a gentleman, Tom, you look much out of place."

"I cannot help it. I am out of place. I wish Blackwood would tell me what this is all about."

Eleanor shook her head, her blonde curls kissing her face. "Perhaps he wants to know how deviant you are. It may be to his advantage to know it."

"Me?" Thomas laughed so hard that people turned to stare, but they soon lost interest when they saw who it was.

"Yes, you. He does not know you well enough to know you are the least likely to share his interests."

"Tell me of these interests. If I am to wait, I might as well learn something about the man."

"When we are alone. Come, along here. There will be a room we can use. And we must ensure people see us entering so your reputation as a masher is enhanced."

Thomas tried several doors. Some were locked, but others opened, and when they did presented views of various acts of lechery he would prefer not to have witnessed. Twice, they were invited to join the couples but moved on.

"There is a small room around the corner, Tom," said Eleanor. "It is rarely used." She took his hand and dragged him along and around a turn. Once inside, Thomas let go of a breath he was unaware he had been holding. He threw the bolt across the inside of the door. When he turned back, Eleanor was lying on a wide bed, her arms spread.

"Do you intend to ravish me now, Tom?"

"I do not."

She laughed. "Then you disappoint me." She patted the bed. "Come and sit by me. I promise to behave myself."

Thomas remained beside the door. Eleanor sighed deeply and shook her head. "You are beyond redemption."

"You are not the first woman to say that. Tell me about Blackwood."

"Other than plotting against the King, the man is also a dabbler in the dark arts. Alchemy, the ingesting of substances that alter the mind, and the belief in darker powers. Devil worship and demonology."

"I have ingested mind-altering substances myself," Thomas said.

"But I wager you have never worshipped the Devil, have you?"

"Of course not. But neither have I ever worshipped God, so some might call me heathen." Thomas wondered if such a confession might shock Eleanor, but all she did was smile and stretch as Kin used to when he lay in front of the hearth. "I expect he owns a copy of this book of demons, does he not?"

"Oh, more than that. I believe he may be the man behind its creation and distribution."

Thomas stared at Eleanor. "Believe? Or know?"

"Somewhere between. I do not know, but suspect it to be true."

"Why?"

"Do I suspect him?"

"Why would he do such a thing?"

"Because he is evil and wants, as I have told you, to bring down King Henry. And he thinks spreading fear throughout the city will help to that end. As you have already worked out, you and More, those killed so far, were men of position. It is possible they stood in the way of his ambition."

"Is he involved with the killings?" Thomas finally relented and sat on the edge of the bed. When he did so, Eleanor moved closer, her arms circling his waist. Thomas tried to draw away but she would not let him. "I am not here to lie with you," he said.

"I know. And yes, I suspect Blackwood may be involved in the killings. Hence their brutality."

"Then report him to the authorities."

"I have no proof. I hoped you might be useful in that regard."

"I believe you know more than you have told me so far. Tell me everything and I will consider what action to take."

"To do that, I must gather my thoughts, so give me a little time."

"How much time?"

"An hour or two. You can sleep if you want. I will wake you when I am ready." She pushed at him until he lay on his back, then lay beside him. Their arms and legs touched.

Thomas knew sleep would prove impossible.

Someone tried the door, then found it locked and hammered on it.

"Berrington, are you in there? Put your hose on and open this door." It was Blackwood's voice.

"Ignore him," said Eleanor, tracing her fingers along Thomas's chest.

"I cannot. He wants to tell me something, and I need to hear it."

"Then tell him to wait, you need to dress."

"I am dressed."

"But I am not." Eleanor rolled away and in a moment stood naked beside the bed. She laughed, unashamed. "He needs to think we have been tupping each other. Now go, I will bolt the door after you. Knock and call out when you return. I will be waiting like this for you." She slid beneath the covers but ensured her breasts remained on display.

Thomas threw the bolt.

"About time," said Blackwood. He looked past Thomas and grinned. "You are a fortunate man indeed. Now come, I have something I want to show you."

"If it is more debauchery I have no interest."

"It is more important than that. Come."

TWENTY-EIGHT

Blackwood had dispensed with the cloak and ornate horned hood. Now he was dressed simply in hose and a white linen shirt. He strode along an empty corridor revealed after he used a key to unlock a door.

"How long are we going to be?" Thomas asked.

Blackwood laughed. "Want to get back to your strumpet, do you? I cannot blame you. She has a look about her that speaks of sin, and Croft told me she will do anything. We are almost there."

Another turn, another locked door. This one led down steps into a cellar. Thomas stopped at the entrance while Blackwood went to a long bench.

"This is what you want to show me?"

"I hear you are a physic and a man of learning. I thought you would appreciate what I have here." Blackwood used his arm to indicate the array of glassware, bottles, braziers, tongs, knives and pots.

"You are an alchemist?" Thomas said.

"Trying to be, with little success. Which is why I wanted to bring you here. I thought you might be able to tell me what I am doing wrong."

Doing wrong? Thomas thought. *The whole idea of what I see here is wrong!*

"I do not believe I am the man you think I am," he said.

"But you cure people. You have seen inside their bodies. Have you ever found anything while looking there? A soul? God? The Devil?"

"What are you trying to achieve here?" Thomas asked. "Are you one more fool looking to turn lead into gold? It does not work. Will never work."

"I agree. My ambition is far more than that."

Thomas laughed. "The big one, is it? Eternal life? That, too, is impossible."

"Have you not read your bible?" said Blackwood. "Methuselah lived 969 years!"

"A fairy tale."

"Are you ungodly?" There was no judgement in Blackwood's voice as Thomas expected.

"As you said, I believe in science and logic."

"But not God?"

Thomas shook his head. "Judge me all you want, I do not care."

"And if I told King Henry you were a godless heathen, would he be so enamoured of you? And enamoured he is. Why, I do not know. I was his closest advisor not long since, but now you take up half his attention. You and that whore Catherine."

Thomas crossed the space between them and slapped

Blackwood hard across the face. The look of surprise turned quickly to anger.

"You would raise your hand to me? Are you mad?"

"No, but I suspect you are. Take the name of Princess Catherine in vain again and I will more than slap you."

"Would you kill me?" The idea did not appear to worry Blackwood, but perhaps it should.

"I have killed many men, but they all deserved to die. Do you?"

Blackwood stared at Thomas. He raised a hand and stroked it across his cheek, which was bright red.

"I believed you and I might have had something in common. Men of science. Men seeking wisdom. I see now you are wrong. Go back to Eleanor. She is a fine filly to ride. I have personal experience, and hope to do so again. You are nothing. A mere will-o-wisp, gone tomorrow with the coming of dawn."

"And if I tell Henry of what you have here?" Thomas said.

"Tell him. He will not believe you. Apart from which half the titled men in London are acolytes of the alchemical sciences."

"Beasts of the city," Thomas said.

Blackwood did not react. Or rather, he did, but not as expected.

"If you imply we are masters of this city you are not wrong. And that foul book has nothing to do with it. We control London. Soon we will control the King, or another who sits in his stead. Henry is not a healthy man. When Harry comes of an age it will be alongside men such as me who have raised him the right way." Blackwood smiled. "No doubt you have already heard the rumours of the boy. He likes women a great deal and is advanced for his age. Some say too advanced, but I would disagree. A man must follow his nature. Harry follows his." Blackwood laughed. "As your sweet Catherine will discover when they are man and wife. I expect Arthur was too unworldly to teach her much."

Thomas wanted to hit Blackwood again but held back, knowing it would do nothing unless he hit him hard enough to damage him. He disliked the man, but not enough to kill him.

As he turned away Blackwood called out. "Mount her hard and fast, Tom. She likes it that way. Though she may be too much woman for someone like you."

Thomas continued. As he followed the empty corridor back to the room he was aware of an arousal growing in him. Blackwood's words, the violence he wanted to inflict, the memory of Eleanor naked beneath the bedcovers. Would it be so wrong? He had done much worse in his past. Had had no qualms about taking women, but at least all had been willing. There were times he regretted it. Other times he justified it because he had been young and the sap rose hard through him as it often did to men and boys that age. As it seemed it did in Prince Harry. Another reason Thomas had to remain alive to look out for Catherine. Except, once she was married she would be distanced from him. So, he would keep Harry close when he could. The boy already liked him, and that might be enough. A trusted adviser. Which meant, if he went to Spain on the King's order he would have to return. And that might prove hard.

When he reached the room the door was unlocked and the bed empty. Eleanor's fine dress still lay on the floor, but she was gone. Naked? Had someone come and taken her by force? Or had she gone willingly?

Thomas turned and stalked the corridors, opening doors, until he heard a scream from outside and began to run.

TWENTY-NINE

It had taken Will Berrington and Usaden several days longer than expected before they passed through Ludgate into the city. They had encountered some small trouble outside Oxford. It had not been targeted at them, but they had responded in any case, as they always did.

A thatched house a quarter mile from the road was burning, and people were trying to quell the flames with wooden buckets filled from a well. As always, Usaden was first to see it, and both galloped across flat farmland to offer help. The fire was smaller than it had looked and been put out within the hour. But a section of the roof had fallen in, and an inner wall was damaged, so they stayed to help with repairs.

Then, as they worked, they discovered that the fire had been started by a group of renegades terrorising the locality, demanding money for allowing folk to farm in peace. Some paid. Others did not. Will and Usaden waited for the men to return, as they knew they would.

It had ended as they expected, with some deaths, some injuries, and others running for their lives. Neither Will nor Usaden suffered a scratch, which they also expected. The farmer's eldest daughter offered herself to Will in thanks, though he suspected thanks had little to do with it. Will was familiar with how women reacted to him. His size. The way he offered protection. Also, he was handsome, a trait he had inherited from his mother, who had been a harem concubine and, briefly, his father's wife.

Will had been tempted, for the girl was pretty and her figure lush. But in the end, he had seen sense. A moment's pleasure would not keep him there but might unsettle her. So they had mounted their horses and headed east once more, two days later than they intended. Will only hoped his father had not managed to find trouble. Usaden did not comment nor show any expression, but there was a connection between them that could only be broken by death, and neither expected that for many years to come.

Once through Ludgate, they called at the Bel Savage, where Peggy Spicer welcomed Will warmly, ignoring Usaden, who stood to one side so as not to draw attention to himself.

"Your father stayed but one night, and then King Henry offered him other accommodation." Peggy spoke as if such was to be expected, but it was a surprise all the same.

"Do you know where?" asked Will.

Peggy started to shake her head, then stopped. "I do not know where, but Tom left a note in case anyone came asking for him. Let me go and see if I can find it."

Peggy was gone long enough for Will to order a jug of

ale for himself and Usaden, who had learned to enjoy the taste. This was mainly because, as in the rest of England, Ludlow offered little else.

Eventually, Peggy returned and passed Will a grubby sheet of paper that looked as if it had been opened and closed several times.

"We are not the first to ask?" Will asked.

Another shake of the head. "No, you are the first."

Will looked at the creased paper and then unfolded it to show a roughly drawn map and the names of three streets. Will knew where one of them, Cheapside, was.

He thanked Peggy, refused her offer of more ale, food and a whore – hopefully, had he taken her up not all at the same time – and went outside. The light was fading and a man with a long pole walked the streets to set a light to oiled torches perched on high sconces, but they saw no one else. They retrieved their horses from the stable and headed deeper into the city. The spired St Paul's Cathedral passed on their left before they turned north to reach Cheapside. It took them several attempts to find the house, partly because as full dark fell, the streets emptied completely, and there was no one to ask directions from. In the end, it was Usaden who found it. He did not say how, and Will did not ask, knowing that Usaden could find anything anywhere.

When they rapped on the ornate front door, no answer came, even after five attempts, each louder than the last. Usaden stepped away, and after a moment, Will followed. Along a narrow side alley they came to a stable, a wavering light coming from within a wooden structure leaning against the house.

This time when Will knocked on the side of the wall, a young lad appeared.

"If you're looking for Tom or Eleanor, they have gone to a party."

Which told Will they had come to the right place.

"Thomas Berrington?"

The lad nodded. "Who is asking?"

"I am his son, Will, and this is his friend, Usaden."

The lad's gaze took them both in.

"And I am Jack." He wiped his hand on his shirt and held it out. Will shook it. So did Usaden. He had learned to be polite in England, but it had taken a while.

"What party, and where?"

"East of the city, beyond the wall. They went some time ago, before night fell. Do you want to stay until they return? I am sure Master Tom would welcome you under his roof."

"Who is Master Tom?" asked Will, which brought a frown to Jack's face.

"Did you not say he was your father?"

"But this is not his roof."

Another frown. "It is a gift from King Henry, who has been most generous. If you are Tom's son, I expect it is your house too, so I will tell Wilkin you are here, and he will arrange rooms."

"I prefer to stay outside if I can," said Usaden, his accent thick with the tones of the deserts of North Africa.

"If you do not mind being with the horses, there is another cot in the stable."

"I do not mind," said Usaden. "And we will not be staying yet. Do you know where Thomas has gone to?"

"He showed me an invitation he received. The name on it was Stepney Manor."

"Which is where?" asked Will.

"Go north of here to Aldgate, then take the first road going east. The manor house lies less than a mile in that direction. But take care in the dark, it is not safe."

Will laughed. "Oh, I think we will be safe enough."

As they passed through Ludgate, Usaden said, "It does not sound much like your father to attend a party." He spoke in Arabic because it came more easily, though his English was much improved. This was mostly because his woman, Emma, had tried to learn a little of Usaden's language before he learned enough of hers not to make it necessary.

"No, it does not. And who is this Eleanor he has gone with? Pa already has a woman."

"Are you sure of that?" said Usaden. "He and Bel are more like you and Silva these days. How long since you have seen her?"

Will shrugged. "Three months."

"At one time, Emma was sure you and she would last forever. Thomas and Bel were also like that, but no more."

Will smiled. Usaden spoke rarely, but when he did, it was always a surprise how capable he was of analysing what lay in people's hearts. He did it almost as well as Jorge.

"I think Pa is too old to take a new lover at his age."

"He is not so old, and Bel is not a new lover, is she?"

Ahead lay flat ground, a deep ditch to the right, farmland on their left, inhabited by only a few hogs rooting in the clay soil for stray turnips. Moonlight filtered through a light cloud to offer enough illumination to make the animals out.

"Pa has three-score-years and three. He is old enough to be dead long since."

"It will take a lot to kill your father," said Usaden.

"You may be right. All the more reason for him to seek love somewhere."

"But not with Bel."

Will shook his head. "You amaze me."

"Good."

Will laughed. "Silva was not right for me, just as it seems Bel is not right for Pa. What Silva and I had was great sex, but we are too different for that to be enough. Besides, I intend to have great sex with as many women as I can now I have decided never to marry."

"I once thought the same as you," said Usaden. "But all that time, I knew it was not enough. Now I have found enough with Emma and my baby girl."

If Will did not know Usaden so well, he could almost imagine a hint of emotion in his voice – and then it was dashed away in an instant.

"Someone is coming." Usaden eased his horse to one side, leaving enough space between them to use their swords if necessary.

"How can you tell? I can barely see my hand in front of my face."

Usaden seemed to consider no reply necessary as he drew a short knife. He preferred the shorter blade to a sword because it was easier to wield. Will slid the axe from behind his back and twisted the leather thong around his wrist.

Both men held their weapons down so they would not be seen by those approaching.

Slowly, two horses appeared through the gloom. As they came closer, Will swung his axe back over his shoulder. He assumed Usaden would sheath his knife, but perhaps not. He knew the man felt unclothed without a weapon in his hand.

Will began to make out the riders. Two men, one tall and skeletal, the other shorter and stout.

"You are late for the revels, gentlemen," said the stout one. All the wenches will already be taken, though I expect they can be taken again." He gave a coarse laugh. "There will still be plenty to drink, I wager." He raised a hand, which made Usaden tense, but it was only a wave of greeting, then departure, as they passed.

The tall man said nothing, his face grim as they rode on.

"Revels?" asked Usaden. "What has Thomas got himself involved in?"

"No doubt something he shouldn't, as always," said Will.

Before long, light showed ahead, flickering and golden. As they came closer, both made out a substantial building lit by myriad torches. Closer still, they made out two figures on the terrace.

"People may believe you have been invited if you change your clothes," said Usaden, "but never me. I will slip into the shadows and keep watch." Usaden dismounted and opened one of the two saddlebags on his horse, which held some of Will's clothes, some of which he had brought in the unlikely event he would need to meet with Catherine or the King.

Once Will had removed his travel-stained clothing and dressed like a gentleman, he handed the reins of his horse to Usaden and walked towards the terrace, not expecting to be admitted. But either everyone was too distracted, or Will managed to look better than he imagined. It was his height and bearing that allowed him to walk inside unmolested. Nobody could believe him to be other than titled.

THIRTY

As a second scream split the night, Thomas broke into a run. He almost lost his footing as he rounded a corner to find a score of revellers asleep on couches or indulging themselves. He lost his footing again as he slid on a pool of spilt wine. He would have fallen had a strong hand not gripped his arm.

"I thank—" Thomas stopped dead because the hand belonged to his son, Will. He was taller than anyone else in the room, broader across the shoulders, and looked like a warrior even in his smart clothes. Another scream came, less strident, more desperate.

"We should see what is going on," said Will, releasing his grip on his father's arm.

Thomas had questions but knew now was not the time. "It came from the terrace. Are you on your own?"

Will grinned. "Usaden is outside somewhere."

They fell into step as they crossed the hall, then passed through the wide doors. On the deep terrace, they saw a group gathered around something on the stone slabs. Eleanor stood to one side, looking away. Thomas pushed his way through and saw what the screaming was about. A woman lay on her front, her face hidden. The back of her skull was a mess of blood, bone and brain matter. Not enough of the latter to have filled the skull, but it was not empty. To Thomas, it looked as if whoever had bludgeoned her had done so in haste, unable to finish their task fully.

He knelt and gently turned her over. From the front, if her eyes had not been wide and staring in terror, she might have been sleeping. She was elderly, dressed in fine linen clothes. A hat lay nearby, damaged and marked with blood.

"Who is she?" Thomas asked one of the men.

"Lady Harrington," the man said. "Wife of Lord Harrington." He glanced around as if only now able to tear his gaze from what lay before him. "Someone should tell him what has happened. He will be here somewhere."

"Go then," Thomas said. "I would not recognise him."

The man looked at him briefly, his face slack with shock, then nodded and moved away. Several others followed. Then, Sir Geoffrey Blackwood approached from the rear of the house. He stopped and stared at the dead woman before shaking his head.

"Who did this?" he asked Thomas. "I hear you have a reputation for punishing the wicked. Find out who did this and I will pay handsomely."

"Who would want to kill her? Did she have enemies? A jilted lover?"

Blackwood shook his head. "Matilda is the sweetest creature ever to walk this earth."

"Is she not rather old to be involved in your revels?" Thomas asked.

"Matilda rarely indulged anymore, but she liked to watch her husband with other women." Blackwood glanced quickly at the body, then away. "I cannot think who might have hated her enough to do this. Unless it is meant as a punishment against Joshua. Or a judgement on their actions."

"Who is Joshua ?"

"Lord Harrington. He must be told of what has happened here."

"Someone has gone to do that. I need to question people. Find out if anyone witnessed this act, or if they saw anyone come this way with her. Can you inform your guests and have them gather in the main room? Bring everyone."

"They will not welcome being disturbed so early in the night. Can this not wait until the morrow?"

"I do not care what they welcome. Do it, or I will have the King send his men here. They will use all their means to get answers." Thomas waited, and eventually, with one last glance, Blackwood walked away. Only Thomas, Will, and Eleanor remained. Will glanced at her and raised an eyebrow in a question, which Thomas chose to ignore.

"You said Usaden is with you. Where is he?"

"No doubt watching." Will put two fingers in his mouth and whistled, the sound piercing. Within a moment, a shadow formed from the darkness, and the shadow became Usaden. Dressed as always in black, his dark skin offered even more cover. He leapt onto the terrace and looked down at the body.

"Did you see anything?" Thomas asked.

"Everything," said Usaden, "but whether I understood it is another matter. What I saw was a creature. Ten feet tall, with talons and horns. It was naked, its cock engorged, its eyes red as if a fire burned within."

"Why did you not try to stop it?"

"I was too far away. I ran, but stopped when I saw the woman was dead."

"A demon," said Eleanor. "Another demonic death. Every copy of the book must be burned."

Will frowned. "What book?"

"The Beasts of the City," Thomas said.

"Do not name it!" said Eleanor.

"Its name has no power. Only the words inside it do."

"I have no idea what you are talking about," said Will, "but God's teeth, Pa, it takes you no time at all to find trouble, does it?"

"I never seek it."

"But it always seeks you." Will looked down with interest at Eleanor. "And who is this?"

"A friend, nothing more."

"You do not believe it was a demon, do you?" Thomas asked Usaden.

"Of course not. It was a costume. It could have been anyone beneath it, man or woman. I came as fast as I could, but was too late. Whoever it was wore a mask so their eyes glowed. They walked on stilts to make them tall and carried a hammer to break this woman's head open."

"Where is this demon now?"

"Gone. When I saw she was beyond any help I went to

the back of the house where the demon fled, but there was no sign. I took a torch and tried to track it but it was gone. I did find the costume abandoned on the grass."

"I would like to examine it." Thomas turned to Eleanor. "Can you arrange for torches? Then stay here while the three of us go to see this costume."

"I should come with you," said Eleanor. "I mean no insult, but you are men. It will take a woman to recognise who might have created such a costume. I can think of few in London capable of such craft. Though when I see it it might be crude." She looked at Usaden. She seemed to have accepted him because he was a friend of Thomas's. "Would you say it was fine workmanship?"

Usaden shrugged. "I am not the kind of man to be able to answer that. Best to see it for yourself."

While Eleanor was away arranging for torches, Thomas removed his outer coat and laid it over the head and torso of Lady Harrington. He was still kneeling when a man approached at a run.

"Take your hands off my wife!"

Thomas rose fast as the man swung at him, a knife in his hand. Will stepped between them and plucked the knife away.

"I take it you are Lord Harrington," Thomas said.

"What have you done to her?"

"I have done nothing. I merely want to protect her in death."

The man went to one knee. He drew the coat back and moaned.

"Oh, Mattie, who did this to you?"

"That is what I intend to find out, sir. Do you or she have any enemies who might have done this?"

"Who are you to question me? Do you think I had something to do with this butchery?"

"I would say no from your reaction, but you might know who did. My name is Thomas Berrington. I am a friend to—"

"King Henry, Prince Harry, and the Spanish Princess. Yes, I have heard of you, and your reputation. It claims you are more than capable of killing." He stared hard at Thomas. "But I also hear you punish wicked people, and my wife was not wicked." He waved a hand. "Leave me to take care of her. Geoffrey will have a cart and men to carry her home. Go, Thomas Berrington, and find out who killed my Mattie. Bring him to me so I can cut his heart out."

When Eleanor returned with torches, Usaden led them into the darkness. He told them they would not need horses because the discarded outfit was not far away. Thomas smiled when he saw Eleanor walking beside Will in the wavering torchlight, questioning him.

They crossed flat ground, marshland to the north, then jumped across a narrow water-filled ditch. Thomas stopped to examine the ground, but no footprints showed in the soft mud other than theirs. They went on, following Usaden as he led them to a low rise. When they reached it, there was nothing to see except flattened grass.

"It was here," Usaden said. "I almost brought it with me, but I knew you would want to examine it where it had been left."

"You are sure this is the spot?"

Usaden gave the question all the attention it deserved. Thomas knew he had been stupid even to ask. He took a torch from Eleanor, held it over his head and circled the low rise, moving out with each pass. But it was Usaden who found what he was looking for.

"There was a horse here." He pointed at some disturbance Thomas could not make out, but he knew better than to doubt Usaden. The man walked to one side and pointed again. "It came from this direction and left the same way."

"They came and took the costume?"

"Or came here with the costume," said Eleanor, "dressed in it, killed Lady Matilda, then fled on the horse."

"If that was the case, how was the costume left here for Usaden to find? Thomas looked in both directions. "You are sure they came this way?"

Usaden nodded.

"The manor house lies in the other direction."

Usaden nodded again. He had grown more talkative than he had once been, and his English was now good, but he was never one to speak when an answer was obvious.

"We need to return and question Blackwood, but I want you to track that horse and whoever rode it. Then go to my house where we will meet you. Do not let them see you."

Usaden smiled as if the idea someone might be able to see him was ridiculous.

"Do you think Sir Geoffrey is involved?" asked Eleanor once Usaden had disappeared into the darkness.

"The woman died on the terrace of his house. If he did do it, he is even more stupid than I already take him for. You have known him longer than me. Is he capable of murder?"

"I told you, he is a student of the arcane, but he dabbles rather than practices. I can see him taking an interest, but having a hand in a killing?" She shook her head. "I do not see it, even less with the damage done to Lady Matilda. You saw another killing, Tom. Was it the same as this?"

"Close enough to assume the same killer. Someone who is obsessed with the human skull."

"Or what lies within it?" Eleanor said with a shiver.

Thomas almost reached out to comfort her, but Will's presence stopped him.

"I am trying to see what this method of killing has to do with the book. Is it a mere distraction to draw suspicion in another direction? You told me you suspect Blackwood might have a hand in the book. He took me to his cellar and showed me his equipment. He is a dabbler in alchemy, which hints he might well be involved in producing the book. I need to speak with Thomas More and examine his copy of the book again. I want to see if this area is mentioned as a location."

"The time has come to stop what is happening in the city," said Eleanor. "I will tell those men who threatened me I will print their foul words. Then I can gift you a copy. We can work on it together."

"How will you find them?"

Eleanor smiled. "They will approach me again soon enough. They are not the kind to take no for an answer."

"When I followed them, they came to your new printworks and watched you work. They know where you have moved to, but I do not know how. I was ready to protect you if they came at you again, but they did not and moved off."

"And you forgot to tell me this?" Eleanor's anger showed in her voice.

"You came to no harm."

She punched Thomas's chest. "But I could have." She turned and strode away, taking the torch with her.

Will laughed. "I see you have not lost your touch with women, Pa."

Thomas said nothing as he started after Eleanor.

As they approached the manor house, Thomas saw people streaming away in the other direction.

"I asked Blackwood to keep everyone in the house. The fool."

"I doubt he even passed your message on," said Eleanor, who seemed to have forgiven Thomas. "Even if he did, these are not the kind of people who accept orders from someone they consider lesser than themselves."

"Do you want me to herd them together and drive them back, Pa?"

"It would be an impossible task even for you, but Blackwood will answer to me."

Except, when they reached the house, the lamps and candles had all been extinguished, and the halls were empty. Sir Geoffrey Blackwood, along with his guests, had fled the scene.

THIRTY-ONE

Thomas saw Jack emerge from the stable when he heard their horses. His gaze took in the three of them.

"I see your son found you, Master Thomas. Leave the horses, I will take care of them."

"I assume the household is asleep?" Thomas dismounted and reached up to help Eleanor from where she sat in front of Will. Thomas was amused at her sudden change of affection.

"I expect they are at this hour, sir."

"Has my friend returned?"

"The dangerous-looking one?" Jack shook his head. "I have not seen him."

Thomas glanced at Will, who was staring at Eleanor. "I assume there is little point trying to find him, is there?" There was no need to ask if Usaden might need their help.

"He could pass within ten feet of us in the dark and we would never know he was there, so no."

"I need to find a room for you, but that can wait until

morning. We can share my bed for one night. It will not be the first time."

"There is a spare cot above the workshop if Will prefers," said Eleanor, and Thomas turned away to hide his smile.

Will showed some sense when he said, "My thanks, but we need to talk before we sleep." He glanced at Jack. "What hour is it?"

"The church bells struck four a little while ago, sir."

"I am no sir, lad. Call me Will. And the dangerous one is Usaden. If he returns, send him up to us, though I suspect he would prefer to sleep in the stables."

Thomas led the way to his room on the second floor. He removed his boots and coat and lay down fully dressed, a great weariness flooding him that he attempted to ignore. Will took the chair beside the fireplace, where still-warm embers glowed.

"You appear to have found yourself in another mess, Pa. And not for the first time. Where did you find the woman?"

"If you mean Eleanor, then I helped her after she and her man were attacked by a group of rogues." He slightly emphasised the word man so Will might show some sense, but if he did, it would be for the first time where women were concerned.

"Same as ever, then. Did you kill any of them?"

"By the time I got there they were nowhere to be seen."

"Where is this man of hers now?" asked Will. "She was showing interest in you when we first met, but now…" Will shrugged.

"I noted she is showing interest in you." Thomas

laughed softly, which was all his body could manage. "She as good as offered you a seduction."

Will smiled. "That is true, but then I am young enough to fully satisfy a woman such as her, whereas you are—"

Thomas reached for his discarded boot and flung it at Will, who plucked it from mid-air so fast the movement could barely be seen. He set the boot down. "You might need that come morning. I should have taken her up on her offer. She is no great beauty but there is something about her that attracts a man. There is also something strange hidden under her looks, and I have given up on strange women. What does she do? She is no whore, I wager."

"She is not. And you already have a woman."

"I follow Jorge's philosophy these days when it comes to women. Besides, just like you and Bel, Silva grows tired of me. I am too unadventurous for her."

"Is she mad?"

Will laughed. "Yes, I believe most of the time she is. She eats the mushrooms that bring visions almost every day. She is a beauty like no other, and adventurous in matters of love, but she is hard to live with. We agreed to take a break from each other, which I suspect will be a break forever. I do not think she is disappointed."

"And you?"

"I am also not disappointed. Are you and Bel truly having problems? She has been staying in Lemster a great deal these last months."

"I do not know if we are or not. When we found each other again, it felt like we could carry on where we left off all those years ago, but too much time has passed. We have lived different lives and loved other people. Bel has hardly set foot outside Lemster. I think she even found it hard to live in our house at Ludlow. She told me I have seen too much of the world to be able to settle."

"She may be right," said Will.

"Yes, she may. I have not told you what Henry has asked of me."

Will said nothing, waiting. The noise of an object being dropped came from within the house, followed by someone shouting to tell whoever dropped it to go back to bed.

"He wants me to return to Spain," Thomas said.

"Has he also grown tired of your company?"

"He needs someone he trusts to negotiate with Isabel and Fernando so his son can marry Cat. He has a surfeit of mediators but does not believe they serve his best interests."

"He is King, so that goes without saying. Have you seen Cat? What does she think of this plan?"

"She has little choice in the matter, but she did tell me she likes Harry and is willing to be an obedient wife."

"Then one day she will also be Queen, as she was meant to be." Will showed no expression.

"Harry likes you," Thomas said. "He even asked after you when I saw him two days ago. Now I have this fine London house there is an expectation for me to spend more time here – perhaps for all of us to spend more time here. You could become part of his court when he is king."

"London stinks," said Will, which made Thomas laugh.

"Yes, it does, but so do most places people live. Ludlow also stinks, but I admit not so badly."

"All of which is beside the point, Pa. Tell me what trouble you have found, and how we can end it."

So Thomas laid everything out. Will listened in silence until he had finished. Then he sat some more, mulling over what had been said.

"This book – it is the one Eleanor mentioned? The one the men who attacked her wanted her to print? "

"The book is, yes. I have made a new acquaintance, a man by the name of Thomas More, who also shows interest in the book. Not because he believes in what it claims but as an exercise in deciphering its clues. We have, between us, managed to identify some of the locations mentioned in its pages. Four of them have seen deaths, all close to site of old plague pits. Five deaths now, if Blackwood's manor house is included. I do not yet know if it should be. If Eleanor finds me a copy, we can study it."

"You can study it, Pa, not me. It is a shame Amal did not come with us."

Thomas smiled because Will always claimed he lacked the cleverness of his sister, but he was far from stupid.

"You mentioned plague pits," said Will. "Are they significant?"

"That I do not know, but have been told some regard them as conduits to Hell. A place where Satan's demons can rise to this world. Eleanor seems to think that whoever is doing the killing believes in these demons."

"And you, Pa? It would surprise me if you said you believed in demons."

"Of course I do not, but it seems others do. In particular, the kind of people who are friends of Blackwood.

Damn, but I would have welcomed questioning him about what happened. No mind, he has always been at court whenever I visit. I will take him aside and question him tomorrow. Henry is expecting me again."

"You said Harry likes me. Is it worth me coming with you?"

"It may be if they let you in. He asked after you when I saw him. I noticed you wore the clothes of a gentleman tonight. Brush the dirt off them and they should be good enough."

"Amal told me I might need them. And Jorge is upset he was not allowed to come."

"I need someone to hold things together in Ludlow."

"Amal does that. I provide the threat and Jorge the amusement."

"He sees into people and speaks soft words that make them do what he wants. Few men possess his talent. Do not underestimate his skills because they are not yours."

"I have known him my entire life, Pa. I love him like another father, but you are right. We are chalk and cheese. You said four men are dead—"

"Tonight's death was a woman, but all have been killed in the same terrible way. It is meant to look like a demon had slaughtered them and eaten their brain. Their wicked work was interrupted tonight so she was saved that humiliation. Each death is associated with a location in the book, which becomes clear only after the event. I want to see if I can work out other locations in advance and keep watch on them."

"Usaden said the man who killed the woman tonight dressed as a demon. Why?"

"Fear," Thomas said. "People are superstitious and easily made afraid. The streets of London are all but abandoned after dark. I followed three men who may be those who attacked Eleanor, and they dressed as demons. They whooped and barked like dogs and chased people away."

"Do you think they are doing the killing?"

"They bludgeoned one man's head and left him unconscious. They tried to do the same to me. But if they were the killers they would have done more. They are there to spread fear. They will be following someone else's orders."

"Why does he want to spread fear? And who would want to do such a thing? What benefit does it bring them?"

It was a good question that Thomas had not considered, but knew he should have. He had been drawn once more into protecting someone and giving no heed to why they needed protection, or from whom. The men who attacked Eleanor and Luke were not those who created the book; they were merely underlings carrying out orders. With luck, Usaden would have followed them to their lair, and Thomas, Will, and Usaden could confront them to find out who their masters were.

"I believe that person may be Sir Geoffrey Blackwood, but if I am to confront him I need proof. And why? Clearly he wants the streets empty, but I can think of no reason other than without people on the streets, the killer's work is easier and there are no witnesses." Thomas stretched out. Now, let us try to get a little sleep before Usaden returns."

Except when Thomas woke, daylight streamed through

the small, mottled glass in the window. Usaden had not disturbed them, and a note had been pushed beneath the door telling him the King wanted to see them at once. Thomas woke Will and both went down to the stables, half expecting him to be there, but Jack told them he had not seen him.

"He should have returned hours ago," Thomas said. "Do you think he ran into some kind of trouble?"

"What kind of trouble could he possibly find he could not handle?"

"We do not even know where he might be."

"He will return," said Will. "Do not concern yourself with Usaden. There will be a reason. Now, did I smell fresh bread when we passed the kitchen? I need food. And then you have to visit the King, and I, your brave and trusted son, will accompany you."

THIRTY-TWO

The King's message stated Thomas must call at once, but he had no idea when it had been received. Thomas and Will walked across the city to the Tower once they had broken their fast, only to be told the King was expecting them at Westminster. They descended steps to the river and paid a wherryman to take them upstream. Fortunately, the tide had only recently turned, so the current was with them, but not so strong as to make negotiating between the buttresses of London Bridge dangerous. Even so, as they approached the wherryman made several manoeuvres while deciding which gap to take. Will looked up at the buildings that seemed to perch impossibly, as if hanging from the edge of the bridge.

He pointed. "Is that not the opening you fell from a few years ago, Pa?"

Thomas looked up and nodded. "It could be, but there are several others like it. I only saw it from up there, not down here."

"How you did not die, I do not know," said Will.

"Neither do I. It seems I am hard to kill."

"Which is fortunate for you and the rest of us."

The water was rough, tossing the wherry about as they raced beneath the arches. Beyond the bridge, the river calmed, and the wherryman used his oar to keep them in the centre of the stream. Thomas paid the man at Westminster, and they climbed steep stone steps to the palace. It lay beyond the city walls and was more extensive than the Tower but less impressive. It served as a seat of government but also provided lavish accommodation for the court.

Thomas was informed that the King was indeed present, and they were asked to wait on a stone bench.

"So much for rushing across the town," said Will. "Is dealing with kings and queens always this much trouble?"

"They are not like the rest of us," Thomas said.

"Cat was like us once."

"That was long in the past. Gods, we could have slept longer if we had known we would be kept waiting."

"Tell that to Henry and see what he says."

Thomas laughed and stretched his legs out, trying to find comfort and failing. An hour passed, then another. The bell in the King's Chapel rang noon before an equerry appeared to take them inside. The King sat at the head of a long table with two men standing on either side of him. There was no sign of the Queen or Prince Harry.

"Ah, there you are, and about time, too," said Henry, as if Thomas had kept everyone waiting. He did not even glance at Will, though he was difficult to miss. "Do you know these men?"

Thomas inclined his head towards the man on the left of the King. "I am familiar with Rodrigo de la Puebla, Your Grace, but the second is unknown."

"Both are ambassadors for King Fernando, and the man you are unfamiliar with is Gonzalo de Heredia, who recently arrived from Spain. Both are here to negotiate the remainder of the dowry for Princess Catherine. We are having difficulty reaching an agreement."

Thomas said nothing. He knew he was not expected to and was unsure why he had been admitted when such negotiations were ongoing.

It seemed both men agreed with him, for Rodrigo de la Puebla said, "I know Duque Berrington, Your Grace, and am surprised to find him here. I hope you do not think he can use his position with Queen Isabel to influence negotiations."

"Thomas is here on another matter entirely," said Henry. "And I believe we are done for now. You may both take your leave. I have more pressing business to attend to with Thomas." Henry waved a hand.

Both men stood rooted to the spot, as if being dismissed in such a fashion was alien to them. Henry ignored them as he came around the table and embraced Thomas before shaking Will's hand.

"You are Thomas's son. I recall you were here when Princess Catherine married Arthur. You are welcome. Come through to the family rooms. My Queen, Prince Harry and my daughters will be there." Henry looked back at the two ambassadors. "I take it you know your way out?" Then he put his arm through Thomas's as if they were close friends, and led him from the room.

"They will come around to your way of thinking," Thomas said.

"I know, but seeing the annoyance on their faces gives me much pleasure. Both are too stuck-up for my taste. They think Spain is in the ascendancy because they have brought much gold from across the ocean. Some of that gold is mine by right, and it will come my way, or Harry will find another bride. One more acceptable to me."

"Catherine would be sorely disappointed if that were to happen," Thomas said.

"I know you are close to her, but this is about politics and power." They entered a corridor which led to a smaller room where voices sounded. As they crossed the threshold, the King visibly relaxed. As always, he smiled with pleasure at his wife and kissed her cheek. Thomas again noted the swell of her belly, reminded she was due to deliver another child in the new year. A child everyone prayed would be a boy. Young Harry was a strong and healthy lad, but the King had already lost one heir to the throne and would welcome having another available in reserve.

Harry caught sight of Will and ran across to him. "I remember you. You are the giant. Do you want to see me fight?"

"Not at this moment, Your Grace, but perhaps later."

"Yes, later. Do you know my sisters?"

Will glanced across to where they had each modestly lowered their gaze.

"I do not believe we have met, but they are all most pleasing to the eye."

"Yes, I suppose they are."

Thomas let the chatter fade into the background as Henry led the way to a table where platters of fine food, ale, and wine were laid out. He had something he needed to say but was unsure how it would be received, so best get it done at once.

"Did you hear there was another horrific death last night, Your Grace?"

"Blackwood told me. Lady Harrington was beaten around the skull until dead. Do you know who did it?"

"I have someone following a person seen nearby. I asked Sir Geoffrey to tell everyone to wait in the house so I could question them. Someone must have heard or seen something, but when I returned all were gone. Including Sir Geoffrey himself."

"I doubt he would have fled," said Henry. "That manor house is his main residence. I suspect these events happened late at night, yes?"

"They did, your Grace. The death happened soon after the strike of midnight."

"So people would be tired and ready for their beds. You are seeing too much in what happened. No one was trying to avoid you. It was an unfortunate death. Blackwood was here this morning and told me Lady Matilda might have fallen from one of the upper floors of the house and received her injuries that way. I know the house, and there are several balconies at a height sufficient to be the cause."

"Blackwood was here today, Your Grace?"

"He was, at an unseemly hour. He told me what happened, but not that you were there. I will have to speak with Lord Harrington and offer my sympathies. Lady Matilda was a friend of Elizabeth's and a frequent visitor."

Thomas wondered about the connections. He was sure Eleanor had said the deaths might be carried out to humiliate the King, to reduce his power and perhaps even replace him. The populace of London would expect him to offer them some protection. If it was not forthcoming, they might demand someone replace him who could.

"Perhaps you can arrange for more watchmen to walk the streets after dark, Your Grace. I am sure it would set people's minds at ease."

Henry looked Thomas in the eye. "You think that, do you?" His voice was cold. "And where will the money come from to pay them? From your pocket or mine? The streets are safe enough, I have been told, because they are empty. Those foolish enough to wander them after dark deserve their fate. Whoever, or whatever, is doing this will soon tire, and life will return to normal."

"I do not believe Lady Matilda deserved her fate," Thomas said, unwilling to back down, knowing he was treading on dangerous ground. People did not challenge the King.

"She was at Blackwood's house, yes?"

Thomas nodded.

"At one of his ... gatherings?"

Another nod from Thomas.

"In that case, she was no doubt punished for her sins, as was her husband for losing her. I know full well what Blackwood's nature is, but he is useful to me. Should he overstep the mark, he will be dismissed from my presence or worse. Men have lost their heads for less, and he knows that full well. So, Thomas Berrington, concentrate on what I have asked of you and forget this other matter."

The message was clear: Do what I ask and nothing else. Except Thomas knew he could not turn away. He would need to be more careful in his approach to the King and give more thought to Spain.

Thomas wondered if Henry had ever been invited to one of Blackwood's parties. Though he had trouble reconciling the King with such actions. It would be too dangerous because those present would only have to spread the rumour to make Henry even more unpopular than he already was.

"I assume you do not wish to hear if I find anything out, Your Grace?" The question was impudent, and Thomas saw the King make note of it.

"It has nothing to do with me, and as I have already said, you have other more pressing matters to attend to. I need to know how soon you can leave for Spain. I must have someone I trust to speak with the King and Queen and knock some sense into them."

"I may not be the right man to do that, sire." Thomas knew he should stop but could not.

"I have decided you are. It would be best if you left before the end of September. After that, the weather worsens and I hear that crossing Biscay can be rough."

"Your son is several years shy of reaching an age to marry, Your Grace. Why such haste?"

"Because this has been going on long enough!" Henry banged his fist on the table, making knives clatter and drawing the attention of the others. "I want matters settled. An agreement reached. And if one cannot be found, I will look to other suitors. There is a glut of princesses scattered across Europe, all of whom will be happy to marry the boy who will be King of England. Go see Catherine on the morrow. Press her to reveal her heart and mind to you. I can think of no one else she might confess her true feelings to. None that will report them to me. When she has done that, return here and tell me whether she will marry Harry or not."

Thomas knew there was no point asking whether Catherine had any say in her future, whatever lay in her heart. Frustration boiled through him, but as always when in the presence of the King, he could do nothing to express it. He knew he had to stop now before things went too far. He would put off the journey to Spain as long as possible – though the prospect of standing in the presence of Queen Isabel filled him with great pleasure. King Fernando less so, but he could not meet one without the other, not on this occasion. And he would not take any cutter through Biscay. He would ride through France and Spain to Andalusia, if that is where they were. It would be safer and take less time if the western storms came early. So he sat with Will and made small talk with the Queen, her daughters and Harry. Later, Harry got his way, and Will showed him several moves unsuitable for a lad of the prince's age.

The day was edging into dusk before they were allowed to leave. Another wherry took them partway downriver but left them before London Bridge. They walked in growing darkness through streets absent of people. Shops were shuttered, windows barred, and doors locked. Even the inns and taverns appeared closed up, but they heard the sound of voices and laughter as they passed them. Thomas wondered how those enjoying their ale and wine would return to their houses. In large groups, he imagined, believing numbers might protect them. Which, if they truly believed the deaths were the work of demons, would offer no protection at all.

"What were you arguing with the King about that angered him so much, Pa?"

"The deaths. He wants to know nothing about them. Wants to take no action."

"Is it not to his advantage to be seen as strong? To take matters in hand and be seen as the saviour of London streets?"

"It appears he does not care." Thomas's tone was enough to elicit more questions from Will.

And by the time they reached the house on Milkestrete, Usaden had returned.

"I followed the tracks into the city," said Usaden. It became harder once they were within the walls and I lost them a few times. Fortunately, the horse had a damaged shoe, so I picked it up again. Then I lost it altogether at the river. There are stone slabs set above the water, and I believe either horse and rider took a boat to the other side or rode along the stones for some time."

"It is not like you to give up," Thomas said. "Tell me what you did then. You have been out a long time."

"Not long enough because I failed."

"No, you have not. What else did you discover?"

"Nothing, only some guesses. I went along the riverside in both directions until the stone slabs stopped but found no indication of the same horse. Which makes me think they crossed over. So I did the same, hoping to pick their trail up on the far bank. I failed to find it again." Usaden sat back, exhaustion on his face.

"So whoever he is has gone south?"

"Perhaps," said Usaden.

Thomas wanted to press him, but now was not the time.

"It was only one man? Did they meet anyone else?"

"No. I checked for that and would have said if they did."

"Of course."

Thomas looked between Usaden and Will.

"Where does that leave us, Pa?"

"Nowhere we want to be," Thomas said. He dragged a hand across his face, aware of his exhaustion. "We should try to sleep and see if the morning brings a revelation. I am too tired to come up with anything now, and even you must be beyond tired, Usaden."

"I was thinking of returning to that man's manor house to see if he has gone back there."

"And then?"

Usaden shrugged.

"Not tonight." Thomas rose. "To our beds. I am going

to arrange another room for Will. I can find one for you if you wish."

"Ask them to find me a cot. I can sleep in Will's room."

Thomas arranged a room for Will and Usaden, which was done with far less fuss than expected. Perhaps Will's size impressed Hardwin. Whatever the reason, the assigned room was better appointed than Thomas's. He wondered how little regard they had initially held for their new tenant and whether that opinion had changed. But he had been absent too often to know the answer.

THIRTY-THREE

Thomas woke late as a fleeting shaft of sunlight lanced through the small window and danced across his face. He put a hand up to stop the glare, only then opening his eyes. He found himself fully dressed on top of the covers. He wondered how long he had slept, then had his answer as the bells of the churches at each end of the street chimed the hour of ten. He swung his legs to the floor and rose slowly, aware of aches in his body he would not have felt a few years earlier. Time passed and brought such intimations of mortality.

Thomas checked on Will's room but their he nor Usaden were there. He went outside and through the table towards Eleanor's workshop, but Jack came out and said, "You might want to wait, master Tom."

Thomas stopped. "Whatever for? Have you seen Will or Usaden?"

Jack stood there without saying anything. When it was clear he did not intend to, Thomas went on.

Inside the workshop the printing press lay quiet. Yesterday's prints hung from wooden rods, swaying in a light breeze that came through the wide opening to the yard. He was about to turn away when he heard a noise from upstairs, a rhythmic thumping sound. His stomach chilled when he heard Eleanor cry out. Thomas feared more thugs had been sent and were beating her. He ascended the steps three at a time, but as his head emerged into the room, he stopped dead. The sight that greeted him shocked him almost as much as that he had witnessed at Blackwood's manor house.

Eleanor had her back to him. She was naked, straddling a man. From how she continued moving, it was apparent she did not know they were being observed. He also assumed Luke had returned and they were reacquainting themselves with each other. It was none of his business, so he turned to leave, which is when one of them saw him.

"God's teeth, Pa, can you not wait? I'm almost done here."

"No you are not." Eleanor half twisted to look at Thomas. She openly displayed her breasts as she did so. "Leave us to finish here, Tom. Your son is a skilled lover, and it has been some time for me."

Thomas backed down the steps and went to stand outside. He did not know what to do.

Jack approached. "I am sorry sir, I did not know what to say. He went in there an hour since. I knew what they were doing, but..."

Thomas shook his head at Jack's expression – disappointment, anger, almost rage. The lad was young and besotted. He would never understand why Eleanor did not choose him. Time would change that. Jack was not a bad-looking lad, and as he grew taller and broader, women would regard him differently – but never Eleanor.

Thomas patted Jack on the shoulder. "I expect there is something else you can do."

Jack stared up at Thomas. "Master Hardwin has a message he wants delivered. I will do that." Jack's expression was blank as he fought to control himself. He turned and strode to the house, his back straight.

Thomas sat on the wall, waiting for Will and Eleanor to finish.

It took some time, but eventually Will emerged, tucking his shirt into his hose. Thomas rose, unsure how to react to what he had seen, but Will seemed oblivious. He slapped his father on the shoulder and said, "I am starving, Pa. Have you eaten yet? Do you think Winnie can find us something?"

Thomas knew Will had quickly grown comfortable in the house, and the staff seemed to like him.

"I need to speak with you first."

"I trust it is not regarding what you just witnessed, because that is none of your business."

When Will walked away, Thomas followed. An unease filled him. He could remember when Will followed him, not the other way around. But he also knew it was the way of the world. Parents taught their children and hopefully got the lessons right. If children grew and applied those lessons then the day arrived when they exceeded their teacher. Despite her lesser years, Thomas knew that day was also close for Will. Thomas had found a form of maturity even earlier, but only because it had been forced on him by the death of his father, finding himself an orphan in France. He could not blame Will for what he had done, for he had done worse himself.

He found Will seated at the kitchen table, with ale in a mug and meat, cheese, and bread on a plate. Winnie fussed around him like a mother hen. Eliza stood in a corner, a bucket of wood for the fires in her hand and her mouth open as she stared at Will.

Winnie pushed her towards the door. "Come on, girl, let these men eat in peace. Help yourself to whatever you can find, Master Thomas."

A moment after they left, Eleanor entered the room. She sat beside Will and started to eat.

"Is Usaden still in your room?" Thomas asked Will.

"He rose before dawn and told me he was going to Blackwood's house to watch it."

"For what?"

Will shrugged and swallowed a mouthful of ale. "He thought that is what you would want him to do. Was he wrong?"

"No. But..." Except Thomas could think of nothing.

"Do you visit the King again today, Tom?" asked Eleanor.

"Not today, for which I am grateful. He demands too much of my time with everything else that is going on."

He is the King," said Eleanor. "He does not care about your needs, only his own. And most people are glad to be summoned into his presence and do whatever he asks."

Just as my son has answered your summons, Thomas thought. Though he doubted there would have been any reluctance by Will. Thomas wondered, foolishly, if he was jealous. Eleanor had made it clear that he could have her if he wanted, and he had ignored her.

"I intend to use my time finding out more about each of the victims, now Linacre has provided me with their names. I need to know if any had a connection to Blackwood. He showed me his workshop and he will not be the only man in London searching for eternal life." He looked at Eleanor. "Did you know of it?"

"Know of what, Tom?"

"What he has in the cellar at his house."

"There are rumours of chains and dungeons where he takes his pleasure, but that is not what you are talking of, is it. And who would want to live forever? Life is sweeter to know it is short, and we have to make the most of each moment." She reached out and touched Will's hand, but he ignored her. There was something wrong, but Thomas could not work out what.

He rose and ascended the stairs to fetch the copy of Linacre's list of names he had made from memory. Except when he went to the table beneath the window where he had left them, the papers were not there. He checked below and behind it but found nothing. So he searched the bed, the small wardrobe, under the washing bowl. He turned, intending to find Eliza to ask if she had put them somewhere when there came shouting from below, Will's voice the loudest.

"One more step and I run you through!"

Thomas went down the stairs three at a time. He emerged to find Will standing at the back door leading to the stable, a sword in his hand. Eleanor stood behind him, her hand on his shoulder. Of the rest of the household there was no sign.

Beyond the door stood five men dressed in the livery of the King's guard. Two had unsheathed their swords. The man at the front held a sheet of paper.

"What is going on here?" Thomas demanded.

"They claim they are here to arrest you, Pa, but they will have to come through me first. Get a sword. Stand beside me."

Thomas pushed past Will and stepped down to stand in front of the lead man.

"What is this all about?"

"You are Sir Thomas Berrington?" said the man.

"I am."

"I have an arrest warrant from King Henry for you. You can come with us peaceably, or we take you by force." He glanced beyond Thomas to Will, who filled the entire doorway. "We can take two as easily as one."

Thomas turned back to Will. "This will be a misunderstanding. Stay here, wait for Usaden to return. If I am not back by dark find Thomas More. He knows the law, and will know someone who can help." He stared into his son's eyes. "Do not attempt to free me. Understand?"

Will made no response and Thomas knew, understand or not, what he asked was not in Will's nature. This was different. Will and Usaden were ferocious, but the Tower of London was impregnable.

He turned back to the guards and held his hands out. "Do I need to be shackled?"

"You are a gentleman, I have been told, so unless you intend to run or fight you can remain free for now."

As the King's guard walked through London with a lone figure between them they drew attention. People stopped to stare. They put their heads together and whispered. Who? What? Is that the killer who stalks the streets?

They entered the Tower through an entrance Thomas had never seen and he was led through dank corridors whose walls were sheened with water to emerge close to the Queen's House. Three of the guards left. The lead man took Thomas's elbow and led him inside to where King Henry stood alone, his face as dark as thunder.

"I received two notes this morn' regarding you, Berrington." He waved a paper in his hand. "This from Hardwin Steward, complaining about your actions and attitude. He says you have exceeded your responsibilities and must be ejected from that house at once." Henry tore the paper in two and tossed it aside. "The man is an arse, and I pay him no heed. He detests you, so I advise terminating his service immediately. The other concerns me more." Henry raised a hand, and the guards left the room. "It is from Geoffrey Blackwood and makes an accusation of murder against you."

Henry's cold eyes met Thomas's. "What say you to that, Berrington? Have I placed my trust in a murderer? And a worshiper of the Devil at that!"

THIRTY-FOUR

"Does Sir Geoffrey say who I have murdered?" Thomas asked. "I admit I have killed men in the past, but only to protect myself and those around me. I do not recall having killed anyone recently."

"We have all fought, Berrington, have all killed. It is how battles are won. But outside of battle, brave men will sometimes have to fight and kill. A King even more so than common men. It is a responsibility I do not bear lightly. Blackwood claims you are responsible for the deaths in the city these last months. Responsible for the fear that stalks its streets and makes men and women refuse to leave their houses." Henry banged his fist on the table. "It is not good for trade, and not good for the reputation of my constables. Why would he make such an accusation if he has no proof?"

Thomas knew he was about to walk on thin ice. One wrong move and the King would have his head jammed on a spike on London Bridge before nightfall.

"Has he shown you his proof, Your Grace?" Thomas saw from Henry's expression Blackwood had not, which emboldened him. "I have been accused of being clever, but could I be clever enough to hatch such a plot from Ludlow? In my experience, a man who accuses another of a crime without proof wants to deflect attention from himself."

"Blackwood says you have been living in London the whole time, and I admit that any correspondence I have had with that town has been answered by your daughter in all instances. What credence am I meant to give your opinion?"

"Amal deals with all correspondence, Your Grace. Did she not, no one would be able to read it." It pleased Thomas to see the King smile. "You appointed me Justice of the Peace in Ludlow, and it seems the work I do has met with your approval because you then appointed me Coroner. If I now displease you, I will return to my family and trouble you no more. Unless you prefer to throw me in a dungeon now."

Henry sighed deeply. "It is always a problem when an honest Justice is appointed. I should have known better. Life is far easier when I work with men who want something. Strength of character is more difficult to dispute."

"Does Sir Geoffrey have strength of character?" Thomas asked, and the King laughed.

"Sir Geoffrey lacks many qualities expected in a man of position. Strength of character is but one of them, and not his worst. However, what he does have are powerful friends. Men I must keep on my side if I am to remain King and ensure the succession."

"So why does he maintain his position if he cannot do it justice? And these friends of his. If they are so powerful you should exile them. Or kill them."

Henry laughed. "Now, *that* would spark an uprising. Let me ask you something, Berrington. People say you held several positions of rank in Spain after the heathen were expelled, duke being one of them. Knowing you, I expect you carried out your duties confidently and earnestly. But tell me, of the other men of position around you, how many did the same?"

"I respected their positions, Your Grace." Thomas saw where the King was going, and the sharpness of his questioning told him something else – that Henry was clever and deserved his position.

"That is not what I asked. How many of them could be replaced by dragging a man off the street and putting him in their place?"

"A few."

Henry laughed. "You are being too coy, Thomas. I suspect you mean most." He leaned forward. "And that is why Geoffrey Blackwood has a position. He comes from a long lineage of fools with positions and was in the right place when needed. In his case, on the battlefield at Bosworth. I am sure he intended to fight for York, not Lancaster, when he arrived. But I found him at my side when it mattered, and he killed men who might have killed me. So I let him continue the family tradition and become someone respected. It is how things work, as well you should know. Position is not meant to be a stamp of approval you deserve but one that carries the crown's power behind it. And Geoffrey Blackwood does what is required of him when needed. He is pompous, disliked, and lacks true friends. But he has power. He believes himself clever, which is always dangerous in a powerful man, but he can be controlled with barely a crack of the whip. "Henry smiled again. "And yes, I know he welcomes more than a small crack of the whip, but that knowledge only adds to my power over him. Now, what do you say to this accusation, Thomas? Shall I call my guards back to take you to a cell?"

"My son would be most vexed if you did that, sire."

"I expect he would, but for all his prowess he can never reach me in the Tower. I have a mind to fetch Blackwood so you can face each other with your accusations. Though I suspect I do not need to. I am unused to having an honest man working for me. Do you want this confrontation, Thomas?"

"Not yet, Your Grace. I am still looking into matters concerning Blackwood and others."

"Can you put an end to this fear?"

It was the first time the King had openly referred to the killings, and Thomas thought for a moment before nodding. "I believe I can."

He wondered if he spoke the truth, but the words were out there now, and he knew Henry would not forget them.

The King clapped his hands together. "Excellent. Now, do what you must, but do not forget you are my man, and do not forget what is even more important than Blackwood. You must deliver Catherine of Aragon on a silver platter, with her father's gold in my coffers. Do that and there will be a position for you in my court." Henry laughed. "You already own a suitable house in London, so it will be convenient."

"And Ludlow?" Thomas felt the conversation slipping away from him.

"Ludlow is a backwater since Arthur died. London is where important matters happen. London is where you should be, with your family alongside you. Is the house big enough for them?"

Thomas considered the question. "The house I built in Ludlow is larger, but I suppose this one might suffice."

"Damn it, but you are an argumentative individual. If the house does not suit, there are others. But only if your journey is a success."

"And the Spanish ambassadors?"

"You will allow them to believe any success is entirely theirs. Argumentative as you are, I do not take you for a precious man. I will know who takes the credit when I get what I want. Let the ambassadors believe what they will. I want you to visit Catherine again when you leave here. Talk with her. Persuade her."

"She needs no persuasion, Your Grace. And if I am to do that I assume Blackwood's accusation has been set aside?"

"Of course it has. The man is a gilded fool."

"If I may ask, Your Grace, if that is the case why did you send men to arrest me?"

"I wanted to look you in the eye when you refuted his allegations, Thomas."

"I trust I satisfied you?"

Henry waved a hand. "You are a free man, so do not push me. Now go, talk to Catherine."

"And Blackwood?" Thomas could not set thought of the man aside.

"He is beneath contempt but, as I say, useful at times. Ignore him."

THIRTY-FIVE

As he made his way out from the Tower on his way to Durham House, Thomas wondered what he had just done. He had argued with the King, stood up to him, and, in the end, buckled to his will – or at least gave the appearance of doing so. Except, he wanted to do as the King asked – return to Spain, even if only briefly. But the return would also involve politics, and Thomas hated politics.

As he passed the stables he looked over the horses, pacing and whinnying in the yard, but knew he would not make out if one of them belonged to Sir Geoffrey even if it came and stood on his foot. He considered the promised confrontation between himself and Blackwood, but it did not concern him. The man was all bluster and cowardice. He did ask one of the stable lads if he had seen the man, sure each would know the steeds men of position rode, and was told he had not been present for a few days.

He expected resistance to him entering Durham House but was fortunate that, as he approached, so did More and

Linacre. All three were admitted together. They were ushered into a sunlit room looking across a paved courtyard to the river. Slabs had been lifted where trees and shrubs grew, others rose from pots. More trees rose beyond a line of houses on the far side of the river. Thomas recalled that the rogue printer Eleanor had taken him to in her fruitless search for type worked not far from the opposite river bank.

"Did you find the names I sent useful, Berrington," asked Linacre as they waited for Catherine to be ready for them.

"Most useful, but I appear to have mislaid them, or someone has considered them waste and thrown them out. Most likely the latter. But I recall them. Is it strange all of them were unmarried?"

Linacre shrugged. "Not particularly. Many men remain unmarried. More for one, though I know he likes a pretty face."

"They were all students of alchemy," Thomas said, and Linacre laughed.

"I am not sure you could call them students when the study lacks any scientific rigour."

"No, perhaps you are right. You heard there had been another death?"

"At one of Sir Geoffrey Blackwood's gatherings, yes. A woman this time. Do you consider that significant?"

"Not at the time, but then I did not have your list then. It may be it is not connected, but a man who was with me saw someone dressed as a demon attack her. And if you do not already know, Blackwood has an alchemical laboratory in his cellar. He says he is searching for eternal life."

Linacre scowled. "It is against the will of God for man to live beyond his allotted years. Search all he likes he will not find it."

"I spent some time last night studying the book," said More. All three stood side by side, looking through the windows, waiting for Catherine and her chaperones to arrive.

"Did you discover anything new?"

"One or two things, perhaps. It helps to have an equal mind to discuss such matters with. Perhaps we can sit together later and discuss them. You said there had been another attack. I had not heard that?"

Thomas realised news of Lady Matilda's death had not yet spread. Or had been deliberately withheld.

"If I may ask," said More, "what were you doing there, Thomas? Blackwood's gatherings are no place for a man of God."

"I was in search of the truth, nothing more. Otherwise I would never have gone. There was much debauchery."

"Which I have heard. Did you question those there? Someone must have seen something."

"A man on stilts dressed as the devil. He broke Lady Matilda's head into pieces. I believe he would have taken her brain but fled when he heard others coming."

More crossed himself. "A demon."

"Dressed as, but not an actual demon," Thomas said. He saw Linacre nod in approval. They were both men of science.

"What if this is truly the work of the Devil?" asked More.

"You cannot believe that," Thomas said. "It is men who do these deeds. Men who spread fear through the city. What their reason is, I do not know. I believe Blackwood is involved, but he cannot work alone." Thomas studied More as he spoke, still uncertain of him. He wondered if the man himself could be involved. He was close to power and deeply religious. Was that reason enough? Was a belief in the Devil so different to a belief in God?

"We should speak again when—" Thomas started, but was interrupted when Catherine of Aragon entered the room, accompanied by Doña Elvira and two ladies in waiting, both of whom Thomas recognised from the Spanish court and Catherine's brief time at Ludlow Castle.

"What are you doing here, Berrington?" asked Doña Elvira, her voice sharp. Her dislike of him, even hatred, had not softened over the years.

"The King has sent me to speak with Princess Catherine," Thomas said. "He was most insistent. It is a matter of state."

Doña Elvira glared at Thomas. "The Princess is due her lessons with these men. You will have to wait." She turned to the ladies in waiting. "Make sure he does nothing more, or I will punish you both."

Both curtseyed. Doña Elvira glared again at Thomas, but it appeared she had nothing else to say before she strode from the room.

"Behave yourself," More whispered to Thomas when she was gone.

"I am familiar with both Maria de Rojas and Catalina de Molina. These ladies know I hold Catherine's well-being close." Thomas smiled and spoke the words loudly enough for both women to hear, and they smiled back.

Catherine approached Thomas but as she did so Doña Elvira called her away. "Your lessons, Princess, are more important than that man."

Catherine pulled a face before turning away to speak with More and Linacre. "Now, gentlemen, what torture do you have in store for me today? Latin or Greek? I would much rather sit with Thomas and talk of old times."

"Perhaps later, my lady," said Linacre. "And today, it is indeed Greek, for much of the knowledge in the world can be found in Greek texts. Please, come through." He glanced at her ladies in waiting. "And you may also sit and wait." It was clear from Linacre's tone he did not expect them to understand a word of the English he used. Thomas knew different.

Even so as he sat between Catalina and Maria, he spoke to them in Spanish. They replied softly as he asked them how Catherine was, discovering her health no better. He wished he was allowed to examine and treat her but knew such was impossible. The drone of the voices of Linacre and More from the other room faded into the background as Catalina and Maria brought to mind the heat of Granada and the pleasure of his time there. Maria was in her forties and married to a man who remained in Spain. Thomas wondered if she missed him. Catalina was younger, in her twenties, handsome and dark-haired. She was unmarried, which was unusual among Catherine's ladies.

An hour passed, then most of another.

"I understand you like books," said Catalina. "Would you like to see our collection?"

"Please. Anything to break this boredom."

Catalina smiled and rose. Thomas walked beside her, the voices of More, Linacre and Catherine fading. They entered a large room with more windows facing the river, but here, almost every free space was lined with shelves, and on the shelves sat what must have been over a thousand books, leaflets and pamphlets. Thomas wandered the shelves, picking out the occasional volume. Most were in Latin or Greek, which would delight Linacre, but a few had been translated into Spanish. Even fewer were penned by a native of that land. Catalina went to sit by the window, perfectly calm. She must be used to waiting. Used to the closeted life she and her mistress led.

"I am returning to Spain soon," Thomas said, feeling the need to make conversation.

"Then you are fortunate."

"Do you miss it?"

Catalina offered a sad smile. "Do you not?"

"I have made my life here in England now, but yes, I miss it."

"And Queen Isabel?"

Thomas looked at her, but if there was anything deeper in her comment, he could not see it. He was sure no one knew the truth about what he and Isabel had done one afternoon before the fall of Granada. He was not even sure he believed it himself. In memory it seemed a dream and, if so, he was content with that.

"Yes, I miss the Queen," he said.

"I believe some of her words are here somewhere. Perhaps on one of the high shelves." Catalina rose and walked to him. She stood close as she pointed to a corner. "There is a step over there."

Thomas retrieved it. He climbed until he could reach the upper shelves.

"Which one is it?"

"I do not know, but I am sure Princess Catherine told me it was here somewhere."

Thomas ran his finger along the edges, then stopped. He had felt something different, unsure exactly what it had been. He moved his hand back until he touched a leather-bound volume. It was slim, the leather old and worn. It felt as if it gave off a warmth, as though the leather still was wrapped about the beast it had once been part of. He pulled the title out and almost fell off the steps.

"Take care, Thomas! Is that the one?"

He looked at the cover. "No, it is something else. Something I have been searching for. Do you think I can keep it for a while?"

Catalina laughed. "Nobody comes in here other than Masters More and Linacre, so of course you can. She held a hand out as he descended even though there was no need, but all the same, Thomas accepted it. He passed the book to her as he finished his descent. Catalina took it and then dropped it almost at once. She swayed.

Thomas gripped her shoulders. "Do you feel faint?"

"No, it is nothing. The book surprised me. Perhaps I am a little tired, for I was sure it moved when I held it." She made no move to pick it up, so Thomas did.

Catalina stepped away and stood at one of the tall windows. "I like to look at the river and think of it running out to sea. To think of following it back home."

Thomas sat and opened the book. He wondered how it had come to be in this room, in this house. As he read, the words and images drew him in as if they contained an unknown power he had never felt before, certainly not in the copy More owned. Some of the passages differed to those he had seen in that. They were darker. more profane, and disturbed him.

Only when Catalina screamed for the second time did he hear her. Coming back from the book felt like an effort, but finally he stood and went to her and gripped her satin-clad shoulders.

THIRTY-SIX

Catalina startled before turning to discover it was Thomas. She melted against him, her head on his chest and he had no option but to comfort her.

"What is it?" he asked.

"A dead man," she replied. "Out there in the water. I saw a dead man."

Thomas released her, though she clung to his arm. He leaned close to the window and looked to where Catalina pointed. At first, he saw nothing, then a shape rolled to the surface, and he saw it. The body rolled again before sinking beneath the stained water.

Thomas took Catalina's hand and led her away. "She is unwell," he called out to the others. "I will take her outside for some air. Continue your lessons."

Beyond the door, she resisted, her hand slipping from his. "I do not want to go out there, Thomas."

"You do not have to. Is there somewhere you can go where you will feel safe?"

"My lady's chamber."

"Then go there, but on your way tell Linacre what you saw. He is the tall one."

She hurried away.

Thomas found the courtyard exit, then stone steps set into the wall that led him down to the muddy foreshore. He stood for a moment, waiting. The shape appeared again, and he waded into the river, where the current tugged at him and mud slid beneath his feet. He reached out, but the figure was too far to grasp. He went further, letting the river to take him. The current was stronger here, but he struck out and grabbed the figure's coat, then kicked hard. He knew he could not fight the river and let it carry him downstream. The shoreline came closer until his feet found purchase, and he hauled the body out. He turned it over so it faced the sky, and as he did so, he recognised who it was. Despite the bloating of the face, which indicated the body had been in the water for several days, he saw it was Luke Thatcher. Thomas wondered if he had made it aboard whatever ship was to take him to Flanders. Or had he boarded and then fallen over the side? Or been thrown? Considering the attack on both Luke and Eleanor, it was a possibility. Thomas knelt and pulled Luke's hair back, looking for any sign of a blow to the head, but found nothing.

He would have to tell Eleanor of her lover's fate. As the thought came to him, he wondered why she had seduced Will. Was it a sign the relationship between her and Luke was not as strong as Thomas had believed? Or nothing more than lust for Will? She would not be the first woman to throw herself at him and undoubtedly not the last.

When Thomas heard the suck of feet approaching through the mud, he turned to discover Linacre making his way towards him. He stood close and looked down at the body.

"Three or four days, I would estimate," he said.

"The man was alive four days ago, so you are right."

"Do you know him?"

"His name is Luke Thatcher. He was a printer, meant to go to Flanders to buy type." Thomas glanced at the body, a deep sadness filling him. Eleanor had to be told, and a burial arranged.

"Did he fall in?" asked Linacre.

"I would not expect to find him here if he fell from a boat. Ships to Flanders anchor downstream, beyond the Tower."

"The Thames is a fickle river," said Linacre. "A body might fall in there, and if the tide rises hard, it can be carried beyond this point. I have known some that washed backwards and forwards for weeks. But I agree it would be unusual. Not knowing exactly when he went into the water, we might never find out. Can I remove his coat? I would like to examine him."

"Why?"

"Curiosity, nothing more. It is in my nature, but also part of my profession. Examining the bodies of the dead helps me to become a better physician. Do you disagree?"

"No, but I am surprised to find an English physician who professes such an opinion."

Linacre offered a wry smile. "Not all of us are as ignorant as you make out."

"As I am discovering. Let us examine him, then."

They both went to their knees, which again impressed Thomas. Linacre was not afraid of getting down in the mud, which stained his hose to the knees. Between them, they stripped Luke of his clothes, and once they had done so, both stared at two gaping wounds in his chest.

Linacre touched one of the wounds, inserting his finger to the knuckle. The stink of decomposition rose from the body, but it did not appear to bother the man.

"He was never meant to rise to the surface," he said. "Two knife thrusts, one to each lung to deflate them. And then there is this." Linacre put a finger on the rough stitching of Luke's earlier wound. "It was made before the others."

"He was attacked by a band of men. I stitched his wound, but it is not my best work."

Linacre smiled. "No, it is not, but even I get my nurses to do the stitching. They have a more delicate touch than us men."

"Luke's belly is bloated. It is what brought him up," Thomas said. "Another day, and he would have sunk again."

Linacre nodded. "I agree."

Thomas pulled at Luke's coat. He reached into each of the inside pockets, unsure what he was looking for until he pulled a stone from one. He held it up to show Linacre.

"I wager others filled his pockets. The tides dragged him to and fro along the river bed and must have dislodged most of them, leaving only this, which was not enough to keep him down. We were never meant to find him."

"Murder then," said Linacre, and Thomas nodded.

"Yes, murder. Another one. Though this is not the work of the so-called demons."

"Princess Catherine often mentioned you when she spoke of her past life in Spain. I think it soothed her to recall it. She told us you are a righter of wrongs. A punisher of evil men."

"Not through choice," Thomas said, "but yes, I have done so most of my life."

Linacre laughed and offered his hand so they could support each other to stand. "Then I would say it has chosen you, and chosen well. Come, we will find someone to bring the body up. Is there someone he should be returned to if you know him?"

"There is."

"Good, but we should clean him before you do that. They must not see his body in this state."

"I can do that, but it might be a problem because the woman he lived with resides close to me. And you are right, she must not see him until he has been prepared."

"I know of somewhere we can work," said Linacre. "I will help you prepare him.

THIRTY-SEVEN

Daylight faded as Thomas led a small cart through streets where people scurried to their homes before full dark fell. No one as much as glanced at him or his cargo. In the bed of the cart, Luke lay dressed in fresh clothes Linacre had provided. When Thomas asked where they had come from he told him off another corpse, one which had died a natural death.

They had taken Luke to the infirmary of Elsyng Spittal at Cripplegate, where his body had been washed. As Linacre examined the knife wounds he had called Thomas closer.

"Do you recognise these?" He pointed to small lesions on one of the lungs.

"I have seen them before. Tapeworm, yes?"

Linacre nodded. "Yes." He glanced at Thomas. "Small, though. Are you squeamish?"

Thomas laughed. "You want to check his bowel for something larger?"

"Tell me if you would rather I not. It is not necessary.

We know what killed him even if we do not know who. But I find it hard not to follow something through."

"As I too will not stop until I find his killer," Thomas said. "Go ahead. I am also curious." He stood while Linacre opened Luke's abdomen and palpated his intestine.

He stopped. "There is one here." He sliced along the coiled grey flesh and reached in. The stink was pungent, but both men ignored it. Linacre pulled out a long, pale parasite. He dropped it into a bottle of alcohol. The creature was already dead.

"Are there more?"

"Possibly, but my curiosity is satisfied. You knew the man. Were there any indications he carried a worm inside him?"

Thomas shook his head. "I heard him once complain of a belly ache, but other than that, no. I have not known him long."

"He has a woman, yes? You should check her. Often they pass from one to another in a family. It is difficult to stop the eggs getting into food when it is being prepared."

Once Luke's openings had been stitched shut, Linacre brought a nurse who applied rouge to the cheeks and neck, which created a more lifelike appearance, but there could not be a moment's doubt he was dead. Which is why a rough blanket covered him as Thomas took him to Eleanor's workshop.

He left the cart in the stable yard and walked to the workshop. Eleanor was hanging up a sheet of paper, both sides now printed. Will was holding the bar for raising and lowering the platen, and Jack was inking the typeface. He was keen but not as adept as Eleanor, so his hands and lower arms were almost black with ink. Thomas doubted soap and water would get it off. He would have to wait for a week or two and the natural sloughing of skin before they looked normal again. Unless he continued to work with Eleanor, in which case the stain would most likely be permanent.

"Tom, where have you been?"

"Can we talk outside?"

Eleanor frowned. "There are no secrets between the four of us."

"I need to tell you bad news, and best done in private." Thomas turned and walked out, hoping Eleanor would follow, which eventually she did.

"What is all this about, Tom? I hope you do not mean to berate me for seducing your son. Or have you news about the book or who is behind it?" As she asked the question Thomas realised the copy of the book he had found in the library of Durham House still sat on the table where he had been reading it. It was, he considered, a minor matter compared to what he had to tell Eleanor.

"Luke did not go to Flanders, and will not return."

"Of course he will." Eleanor pushed her fists into her waist and scowled. "He will be back any day now."

"Come with me." Thomas walked away from her and she fell in beside him.

"What is this about? You are scaring me now."

When they reached the cart, Thomas pulled the blanket back and waited.

Eleanor looked in as she was meant to. A hand flew to

her mouth to stifle a cry. She turned to stare wide-eyed at Thomas.

"What is this? What happened?"

"It is Luke, is it not?"

She glanced at the body. "Of course it is Luke. Who else could it be?"

"I pulled him from the river earlier today. He was murdered. Weighed down with rocks, his lungs punctured. He was never meant to surface, but he did."

"That is Luke for you. He never does the expected." It was a glib comment, but Thomas understood it was a result of her shock. "Where in the river?"

"His body washed up near Durham House."

"Of course. I suppose you were visiting your princess again." There was an edge of spite to her comment. More reflection of her anguish.

"If you mean Catherine, then yes. Be grateful I was otherwise he would never have been found. As it was, I almost drowned myself getting him out."

"Yes, he is heavy. I suppose I had better arrange to have him buried. Can you help? I have never done it before."

"I know how it goes," Thomas said. "And Will is used to death. You can stay here if you wish. There is a large burial ground north of the wall. We will shroud the body and take him there. Six pennies for a gravedigger."

"I can pay."

"Then pay." Thomas was sympathetic to her loss, but her attitude was starting to annoy him.

"And I will come with you," she said. "After living with him all this time, I should see him in the ground."

Thomas bit his tongue when he almost said, "Yet you allowed my son into your bed after only three nights alone," before thinking better of it.

Perhaps she saw something on his face because she said, "Do you judge me? Now?" She glanced at Luke's corpse. "I suppose I had better dress appropriately." She turned and walked away. Thomas watched her go with a frown. It would take some time for her to come to terms with Luke's death, but he was sure she would. She had displayed a coldness today, which came as a surprise to him. He also noted she seemed incurious about the manner of his death. There would be time to question her later, to try to discover who might want him dead.

After a while, he returned to the workshop, where Jack was laying paper beneath the platen, and Will held the handle to lower it.

"Ellie's gone upstairs," he said.

Ellie? "She has had a shock. Come with me."

"Both of us?" asked Jack.

Thomas thought a moment, then nodded. "Yes, both of you."

Back in the yard, he revealed Luke's face once more.

"Who is it, Pa?" asked Will.

"Luke Thatcher. Eleanor's lover. He might even have been her husband, but I do not think so."

"He was meant to go to Flanders."

"And never made it." Thomas recited his story once again. The river. The unintended swim. The discovery of the wounds. He made no mention of the worm because it was a common enough parasite and many lived with them.

"Eleanor is changing. As soon as she is ready, we will take him to the graveyard and have him buried."

"You had best be quick," said Jack, glancing at the sky. "Twill be dark soon, and the gravediggers do not work at night, not in these times. I hear some of them even refuse to work in daylight. The sooner this scare is ended the better."

"It does not bother you, does it?" Thomas asked.

"Fool's superstition is all it is," said Jack.

Thomas almost corrected him, then knew there was no point.

They waited, and eventually, Eleanor turned up dressed head to toe in black. A hat covered most of her blonde hair, which she had tied up, and a veil draped beneath it.

"Let us get this done," she said, "so I can return to work. I will need the pennies to pay the gravedigger."

"Has he any family?" Thomas asked as Will pulled the cart out from the yard. "Parents, brothers or sisters?"

"None. He was an orphan, so at least I need write no letters."

When they reached the extensive graveyard north of Charterhouse Priory, it was almost dark, and they discovered Jack had been right. A lone man passed them as they approached, and when they asked him about someone to dig a grave, he laughed and said, "God's luck with that, sirs," then walked on.

"Do we wait here until morning?" asked Jack.

"We take him back to the house, then return on the

morrow," Thomas said. "We will have to cover him with canvas tied down hard to stop rats or vermin getting at him, but he is not going anywhere on his own, is he." He wondered if Eleanor's uncaring manner might be rubbing off on him.

Back at the house, Eleanor entered the workshop, and Will and Thomas went into the house, where they found some food and drinkable wine. They sat at the kitchen table, the room empty other than for them. The remnant of the fire was little more than ashes but still offered some warmth.

"Do you think his death is connected to the others?" Will asked as he bit into a chicken leg.

"It is different, but I believe it likely is connected to the book. He and Eleanor were threatened before. Luke was stabbed the first time, both were assaulted, so yes. Whether he was killed because he was trying to obtain type, or because it was a job left unfinished, I do not know."

"We need to stop this, Pa," said Will. "Stop it now before more die. Do you know who is responsible?"

"I suspect Sir Geoffrey Blackwood has a hand in it some-where, but finding proof might be hard. Presenting it before the King even harder. Blackwood told Henry I was the killer stalking the night-time streets. Fortunately, the King believed me, not him."

"You would have found it hard to kill people in London while you slept in Ludlow, Pa. We should pay this Black-wood a visit."

Thomas looked around. "Usaden is still watching him?"

"Of course. That is what you asked him to do. He will be hidden somewhere near the manor house, watching and waiting. No one will see him, no one will hear him, not until it is time to act."

"Then we go there tonight. This time, I will not be weak. Tonight, he will talk and reveal all, whatever it takes."

Thomas cut a hunk of cheese and chewed on the corner as Eleanor entered the kitchen.

"Will, I meant to say to you, but with everything going on, I forgot. You will be made welcome if you want to come to me again tonight."

She offered a smile, turned and left.

Thomas looked at his son, waiting a moment to make sure she was out of earshot before saying, "Her man lies dead in the back of a cart, and she asks you to fuck her? That is what she said, is it not?"

"It is. And you know as well as I that closeness to death can bring arousal to those left behind. We have seen it often enough in battle, and I am sure you have experienced it, too, Pa."

Thomas considered his son's claim. He was not wrong, but Thomas had no intention of confirming it. Yes, he had sought solace in a woman's arms after killing or witnessing death, but he did not consider it healthy. That Eleanor had offered the invitation sat uneasily with him. He wondered if it was jealousy, but he had no reason to be jealous. He was old. Will was young and strong. It was nothing other than that. Within his arms, Eleanor might find a safe haven and comfort for a few hours.

"Do not worry, Pa, I have no intention of accepting her invitation. We have other matters to concern us this night."

Thomas stood. "Yes, we do, but not what you think. I

will ask Jack to find us a spade. You and I will return to the burial ground and dig Luke's grave."

"Can it not wait until morning?" Will made no move.

"For all her bluster, Eleanor feels his death. You are right. It is why she came to you. The sooner Luke lies underground, the sooner she can begin to heal."

"Silva and I are no longer together," Will said, "but were she to die, I would be a great deal more upset than Eleanor appears to be."

"We are all different," Thomas said. "Some feel things more than others. We all deal with grief in our own way. This is hers. There is no right or wrong to it. If you want to stay here I will bury him on my own."

"And kill yourself doing it?" Will rose, but not to his full height or his head would have cracked against the ceiling. "But in the morning we talk long and hard about what we must do next."

THIRTY-EIGHT

Full dark still cloaked the city of London as Thomas and Will returned with the empty cart. The air had turned chill but Luke now lay in the ground. Eleanor had returned to her work with a vengeance, as if trying to avoid thinking about Luke's death. When Thomas entered the printworks, she looked unwell, pale-faced and sweating, her eyes narrow as if she fought against some inner pain. She refused to meet his gaze, and after a while he returned to his room. He knew he would not sleep. As he stood, numb, he heard the nearby church bell strike the hour of six. Soon, the sun would fully rise and a new day begin.

Early September was too soon for frost, but as Thomas walked out of the city through Ludgate it felt as if a hoar should lie on the grass. The last year or two the weather had been strange, with long, cold winters and wet summers. Thomas wrapped his coat closer about himself as he made his way through almost deserted streets to More's lodgings.

When the door opened to his knock More ushered him inside.

"I was about to send a message," he said. "I have been studying the book and have new thoughts regarding it. We have an hour before I must leave for the Inns of Court. We are to have a moot today." He inclined his head towards a piece of dark furniture against the wall. "One of Princess Catherine's ladies told me you were studying something before you were drawn away. She asked me to hand it to you. It is over there, inside that leather wrap. More smiled. "She also told me how handsome you looked while you read it."

Thomas glanced across. "Did you look inside?"

"Why would I do that? Whatever lies within is not mine."

Thomas brought the wrap across. "You might be interested, however. I found a copy of the book for myself and spent a little time studying it. Here, let me show you." He put his hand on the back of a chair. "May I sit?"

"Please." More took another chair and leaned close as Thomas opened the wrap. When the book was revealed, he reached out and then stopped. "May I?"

Thomas offered a nod. More drew the book closer, a strange grimace on his face as he started to page through it.

"Where did you obtain this? They are scarcer than hen's teeth. And this copy differs from mine."

"It was in the library at Durham House."

"The Princess Catherine would not have acquired such a profane title," said More.

"I suspect it has been sitting there, ignored on a top shelf for many years. Decades, even. It feels old, does it not?"

"I see you have made many notes." More glanced up to meet Thomas's gaze. "Or was that not you?"

"It was me." Thomas reached for the sheets of paper which Catalina had thought to slip inside the covers. He considered it fortunate she would have been unable to read them. He laid the pages beside the book. "Each page is numbered to keep them in order, and you will see another number corresponding to the book's page. I numbered those as well because they had not been done."

"I did the same to my copy. I believe it is to add a layer of mystery." More spent some time comparing Thomas's notes with the cross-references in the book before sitting back. "You have done good work here, better than I have."

"My mind is used to solving puzzles," Thomas said. "Particularly puzzles of a criminal nature."

More laughed. "Mine is meant to if I am to prove a skilled lawyer, and I pray that will come in time. Fetch us two mugs of ale while I go through these again and make my own notes."

Thomas went to The Bishop on the corner of Holborn and asked for a jug of ale. He expected More would possess cups. When he returned, More was still bent over the pages, making his own notes, so Thomas found flagons on a shelf and poured the ale.

He sat and waited. Eventually, More sat up.

"Your copy of the book is different. It has several pages mine does not possess, but I cannot tell if they are significant or not. And, of course, it is hand-written, not printed.

It appears to me to be a product of a monastery. Though what manner of monastery would pen such deviance is beyond me."

Thomas knew of at least one such place, buried among the high hills on the borderland between England and Wales, that would be capable of doing such a thing. No longer, but possibly in the past.

"Show me which they are." Thomas waited while More marked each with a small tear of paper before pushing the book across the table.

Thomas studied each of the marked pages in turn, cross-referencing with his notes. When he was done, he said, "Seven additional descriptions of locations and seven additional demons. You have bested me to name them. You know your bible and apocrypha well."

"I was raised in the expectation I would join the Church, so the study of both was ordained by my family. Were you not?"

"I was, but left England when I had but thirteen years, and only returned two years ago. Before then I lived in Moorish Spain, and the bible was not much studied until ten years ago in the parts where I lived. But I can name several Islamic demons and identify them in this book. They have names in the Christian faith as well and are the same creatures, though Islam does not consider them fallen angels, but Jinn."

"The term is not known to me, nor the concept. If they are not demons and slaves of Satan, what are they?"

"Jinn are considered demons, but they are not fallen angels. In Islamic belief, Allah created angels from light, the jinn from fire, and humans from dirt. It is a different set of beliefs, but it surprises me how much the two share in common."

"Not me," More said with a sour expression. There is only one true God, and one true faith – the Catholic faith."

"I have identified thirteen named demons so far," Thomas said, not responding to More's comment, hoping the man would assume he shared that same faith. "The book has thirty-three pages. One is an introduction to the others, and the final page is a summary. Which means, I believe, it names twenty-nine demons. I identified less than half."

"I know you have tasked yourself with ending this darkness that plagues London," said More. "Does the information you now have help you do that?"

"I believe the demons are less important than the locations," Thomas said, "and I have identified more of those. Fifteen so far, and like the ones you found, they are all near plague pits.

"I would offer to help, but I am not the same as you, Thomas Berrington. Princess Catherine has told me of your exploits, and Prince Henry is in awe of your son and also a little of you."

"My son Will is indeed awesome. I would want no one else beside me in a fight. And my friend, Usaden even more so."

"Usaden?" said More. "That is a heathen name, is it not?"

"He is from Africa," Thomas said, "so yes, he would be considered a heathen in many eyes. But he is the best of men."

More looked thoughtful. "There are some who would claim those two statements are contradictory. A man cannot be good unless he is Christian. I am not one of those men." More smiled and leaned forward. "Also, I am not a stupid man. I have noticed how you failed to answer when I left a clear path for you to do so. Do I take it you converted to this heathen religion?"

"I did not, though my now dead wife worshipped Allah, and at one time so did my daughter. But I believe she has now converted. She seeks faith in her life and takes comfort in attending service at the church in Ludlow."

"That is good, Berrington, but you still refuse to state your beliefs."

"Would we still converse if I told you my true feelings?"

"Until I know them, I cannot say. Do you believe in God?"

Thomas was surprised at the turn the conversation had taken. He wondered if he should lie or tell the truth. But the truth would end what small friendship he had forged with More. He liked the man. Respected him, even, and believed he might grow to become someone of note. But was that enough? Thomas knew that he had few friends outside of his family. Catherine, yes, but any others lived far to the south in Spain. Then he thought of one who lived close to where he had built his new house. He had known Abbot Bernard all his life and respected and liked the man. And yes, he was sure they were friends. And if so, what would Bernard counsel him now? For he knew Thomas's heart. Knew he did not believe in the Christian God, or any god. Bernard had forgiven him this sin. He claimed it was a small sin, balanced by the good Thomas did. But others would disagree.

So Thomas said, "I worship the same God as you," to More, relieved when the man accepted the lie as a truth. In some men, that lie would burn through them, lodge in their hearts and cause an ache. In Thomas, it did none of those things because, in his mind, it was truly a small lie. He now lived in England, which the Catholic Church ruled. Abbots and Bishops, priests and laymen, kings, queens and princes, none were above the Christian God they all worshipped. Thomas smiled. No doubt More, if he knew what lay in his mind, would condemn him and say he was damned.

Just as those who had been murdered were damned? The thought came to Thomas in a moment, and he wondered where from, and if it was worth pursuing.

"It has occurred to me I have been considering these atrocities from the wrong viewpoint," he said.

"Explain."

Thomas liked that More did not waste words he considered unnecessary.

"I am searching for a culprit. One man – and I believe it is a man for the nature of the injuries could never be committed by a woman, the strength needed to crush a skull would be too much . But I need to know more about the victims. What they have in common. Are they good people or bad. Linacre's list helped, but I need to dig deeper."

"Linacre attends Princess Catherine with me tomorrow afternoon. Come to Durham House and perhaps he can provide you with the information you seek. I glanced at his list of names and two are known to me, but not well and not their private lives. And I take it their private lives will have something to do with their deaths, yes?"

"If what I suspect is true, then yes. They will be deviants. Believers in alchemy and the occult. I may not be able to visit Durham house on the morrow. The King demands an answer from me regarding Cat." Thomas saw More's eyes widen at his use of the special name he and his family used for her. It had been a mistake to use it here.

He glanced at the book and scattering of papers on the table. They represented random thoughts he had not yet worked into a rational shape. He gathered them up and folded the linen wrap around them. Best not to let anyone see what it contained.

"You are a strange man, Berrington," said More. "A violent man, I wager, and I do not usually take to such men. But you are different to others, and I admit I have taken to you. I like how complicated you are."

Thomas laughed. "My life does not feel complicated but seems too often guided by others."

"I do not believe that either. You have fashioned your own destiny, your own place in the world. You have a position many would envy, me amongst them. So go, do whatever you must. If you can, come to Durham House an hour before noon on the morrow and you can ask Linacre your questions. If he is willing to answer them, for he, too, is a complicated man."

THIRTY-NINE

When Thomas emerged onto the street, rain had come again, and he was growing tired of it. For some reason, when it rained in Ludlow, he never minded. Here, in London, it felt like a punishment. And perhaps it was, for in the city, life was lived more in the raw, closer to the edge. Greed, riches and poverty rubbed together everywhere he looked. Even so, he had to deal with the rain, so he pulled his tagel-must, usually hidden beneath his jacket, over his head and tied it in Moorish fashion so only his eyes showed. Back at his new house he went upstairs to leave the book and his papers in his room. As he came back down he found Will outside as Usaden held the reins of his horse, which sheeted water onto the cobbles.

"Where have you been, Pa?" asked Will.

"Talking with a clever man."

Will laughed. "Where did you manage to find one of those in London? Usaden has some news that will interest you."

"What?"

"I went to watch Blackwood's house," said Usaden. "I did not see the man himself, but three rough-looking men rode up and went inside. They were there more than an hour. When they emerged, I decided to follow. They did not look like the kind of men Blackwood would mix with, and I wondered what the connection was."

"And did you find one?"

"Not yet, but I did find out where they drink, which is where they are now."

"We intend to go there and follow them, Pa. How many men did you say attacked Eleanor when first you met?"

"Three, she told me."

"Then Usaden will take us to where these three men are drinking. Will you recognise them?"

"I did not see the attack on Eleanor, but have seen the men who stole her type and also who accosted me. So yes, I will recognise them."

They started walking, and Thomas followed, assuming Will and Usaden knew where they were going.

"They called into a drinking house, but I believe they are likely to leave soon. Even men such as them can only consume so much ale."

"Would this inn they are slaking their thirst in be called the Saracen's Arms, by any chance?"

Usaden cast a curious glance at Thomas. "It would. Why?"

"Before you arrived in London I followed three men who drank there. They left when it grew dark and donned outfits to make them appear as demons. They used cudgels to knock people out. Including, they thought, me."

"Your head was too hard, I take it," said Will with a laugh.

They left the city and as they approached the Saracen's Arms Usaden raised a hand to halt them. Three men had staggered out from the open door of the inn. It was not yet noon, but all three were in their cups.

"Are they the men?" he asked.

Thomas narrowed his eyes before nodding. "I think so, but they are all of a type. There are a hundred of their like in London, but I am sure it is them."

They sank back into an alley from where Thomas had a good view of the men's faces as they passed, sure now. He also recognised two as the same men who had ascended the hill to sell Eleanor's type.

"Both of you stay here," said Usaden. "Or go into the inn if you want. I will follow them. Better I go alone than all of us. I will not be seen."

"They spent an hour with Blackwood," Thomas said after they found a nearby stone bench to sit on. Neither wanted to enter the inn. "They are the same men who I saw disguise themselves as demons. There has to be a direct connection back to that man. Everything fits. His study of alchemy. His deviant nature. What I do not yet know is how he chooses his victims. They are all gentlemen, apart from the last, and she could have been killed to punish her husband. Might they be chosen from those who have visited Blackwood's gatherings?"

"Is it not too ornate a way to kill?" Will asked. "The

detail of the demons. It requires disguises and a story strong enough to empty the streets at night. I barely met this Blackwood, but is he a clever enough man to come up with such a plan? Why not just use a knife? Why crush their heads to a pulp?"

Thomas smiled. "It is all to do with the book. With the story created. Though you are right that Blackwood does not appear to be clever enough to come up with such a plan."

But the more Thomas thought about it, the more Blackwood came into focus as the man behind the terror stalking the streets of London. Thomas had seen three men dressed as demons running wild. What he did not know was why Blackwood wanted the streets empty. Thomas did not know the man well but well enough to consider him arrogant without cause. He was the kind of man who would not dirty his own hands with killing. Three men would be enough. After they attacked Thomas he had heard them say it was not them who killed but their master. Was that how it worked? The men stunned their victim and Blackwood administered the final blow? And the damage done to the skulls, the taking in most cases of the brain. Was it part of his experiment? Did Blackwood believe that using others' brains was a means to some demonic power? Or did he distill them into a liquor to consume. A liquor he believed might offer him eternal life.

He wondered if Blackwood was the author of The Beasts of the City? If the three men worked for him and they had tried to beat Eleanor and Luke into printing more copies it might make sense. Except ... the copy

Thomas had found in the Durham House library had been far older. Much older. It had the feel of something a century old, if not more. Had Blackwood seen the same copy? Had he copied it, making alterations to suit himself? It explained the differences between the two versions. But why?

Thomas knew he needed to speak with Eleanor again, to press her for information on Blackwood and possibly Croft. They had both been with Henry when Thomas first called on him. They had both been at Blackwood's gathering. But those questions would have to wait because Usaden came running towards them.

"They have entered a house not far from here," he said. "I waited long enough to gather they intend to stay. If they do their work at night it makes sense they will sleep through the day." He smiled. "And they were drunk enough not to have bolted the door to the street." He stared at Thomas, waiting.

"Show us," he said.

The house was one of a row, each with a door and window on the lower floor, a single window above.

"Are we going in?" asked Usaden. "The door is an open invitation."

"We wait for now," Thomas said. "I want to question them and get to the truth, but let them sleep deeply before we go in."

"I think we should cut their throats," said Usaden, and Thomas knew the man he had first met all those years ago on the dockside in Malaga was barely concealed beneath the surface.

"We wait and watch," he repeated. "I need them alive if I want to find out Blackwood's connection."

"We wait in the pissing rain?" said Will.

"It does not need all three of us," Thomas said.

"Yes, it does," said Usaden. "Two of us could return to your fine house and sleep, but it is too far to fetch us if anything happens here. So we wait. Besides, it is only rain. I am even getting used to it since coming to England."

Which, as if the rain had a mind of its own, increased in ferocity. Water bounced up from the dirt of the alley to filthy their boots and hose. Time passed and eventually, as the light thickened, the rain lessened. As dusk crept across the city, the rain stopped altogether, but each of them remained where they were, soaked. Thomas wondered if it had been wrong for all three of them to stay. He shivered inside his wet clothes and felt too stiff to fight. He hoped Will and Usaden felt better than he did.

A short man with a paell covering his head came scurrying along the now almost deserted street. He stared at the unlatched door, then pushed inside.

Usaden smiled. So did Will.

"Perhaps someone has come to save us the trouble," said Will, disappointment in his voice.

Once the streets were fully dark and empty, four men emerged from the house, all dressed as demons.

Thomas, Will and Usaden followed. Usaden roamed ahead, invisible among the shadows between torches. Will stayed behind Thomas, who pretended he was just another nervous man out too late and trying to get home.

The men entered the city through Ludgate and then

continued east. So far, they had encountered no one, and each removed their ornate hoods so it was easier to breathe. When they reached St Paul's Cathedral, they struck north and followed an alley towards the rear. It was empty when Thomas reached it, but Usaden appeared as if by magic.

"They took steps and went underground. I could hear them talking and their feet on stone before I came for you." Usaden looked beyond Thomas as Will appeared. "Do we follow?"

"Give them a little time, then yes, we follow. We finish this tonight if we can."

Usaden smiled again.

"I do not want them killed unless there is no other choice," Thomas said, but Usaden's expression remained the same.

They stood beneath a canvas awning over the shuttered entrance to a butcher's shop. Rainwater from the roof ran pink from in front of the door where animals had been slaughtered.

"Time to go?" asked Will after a while.

"Yes, time." But as Thomas stepped out, Will grabbed his arm.

"Wait. Someone else is coming."

Thomas turned but saw no one.

"Where?"

Will pointed. With his other hand he put a finger to his lips.

Thomas waited and then saw them – two people. One he recognised, the other, a woman, he did not. So wrapped was she in heavy cloaks with a wide-brimmed hat pulled low over her face that he could not make her out or even judge if she was slim or overweight; or even a woman. The man though was clear. Sir Geoffrey Blackwood. He was grinning, walking fast as if eager to reach his destination.

As soon as they were out of sight, Will tugged at his father's sleeve.

"Not yet," Thomas said. We have seen four men and Blackwood, but who is the woman?"

"Their next victim?" said Will.

"She went willingly enough, so I would say not. I suspect she is another acolyte. Though for all I know those killed were also acolytes."

"If not her, who is the victim?" asked Will.

"That is what we wait to see. These are preparations. If I am right at least two of the men we saw will emerge to find their victim." Thomas did not believe the night's events had started yet. He tried to think of any pages in the book that mentioned St Paul's Cathedral, particularly the extensive catacombs beneath. He could think of two or three More had deciphered, with their call to those who sought magic and power.

"What if no one comes?" asked Will.

"Then no one comes. There must have been other nights when this group gather and find no victim."

Usaden stepped away and almost immediately disappeared into the dark.

"Where is he going now?" Thomas said.

"Where we should be going." Will's voice showed impatience. He was not someone made for waiting. He lived to throw himself into action. Thomas had seen it in him repeatedly, even when Will was too young to do so. Even then, he had triumphed. Much of that was Usaden's doing. The hours, days, weeks and months of training resulted in a savage skill, but also a gentle one. Thomas knew they trained the same way now, but Usaden could no longer best Will.

"Do you think I want to wait if something is happening down there? I know enough that these people wait for the curious to arrive and then kill them."

"Do you also know why?"

It was a good question, and Thomas considered it before shaking his head. "Sometimes a reason is not needed. You know that as well as me. Sometimes evil seeks to destroy without reason. It is possible whoever is behind this believes in the creatures of Hell, in demons, and is trying to entice them to the surface to do their bidding."

"Or they are mad," said Will. "We have seen that before."

"Yes, and I admit it is more likely explanation. But, mad or not, they attract others who help them. Those three men are wicked but not evil in the same way as whoever gives them their orders. From what I have seen, that person is Blackwood."

"He does not strike me as mad. I only met him briefly, but he had his wits about him."

"He does appear that way, but I hear things when I visit King Henry. Blackwood fought for him at Bosworth, but his conversion to the King's side came late. Before that, he was a Yorkist through and through. He is welcome at court because his family is close to the Queen's. Henry seems to trust the man and has bestowed several tracts of land on him, together with positions in government and parliament. Blackwood has spoken to me on several occasions, and each time I can tell he is sounding me out. What exactly for is unclear, and will never be made clear until I show enough interest. I think the gathering you found me at was his most explicit attempt yet. He wanted to judge my nature."

"Perhaps you could make a pretence, Pa. You are good at lying."

Thomas suppressed a laugh. "Not as good as Jorge, but then Blackwood would never want to be close to him." Thomas shook his head. "I do not know, Will. I truly do not know. But it may not matter. If we can link him to the killings, even his closeness to the Queen will not save him."

FORTY

Usaden appeared from an alley that ran alongside the cathedral. "They have two victims down there already. A man and woman, both naked and tied to iron hooks set in the walls. The new arrival, the plump man, is reciting some words, but not in any language I know. You need to come, Thomas, you might understand. You need to come now before they start their work."

Thomas followed Usaden, with Will in the rear. Stone steps led down to a surprisingly high tunnel. Torches were unnecessary because a faint illumination came from the distance, together with the sound of voices. As they progressed, other tunnels led off to their left, taking them through the catacombs beneath the cathedral. The tunnel reached a fork, and Usaden took the left path. The light grew brighter, and Thomas made out a voice.

"You have come in search of knowledge, yes?" The voice was low, coarse, and guttural.

Thomas was sure the speaker was not Blackwood.

They reached a point where iron bars gave a view into a circular chamber below.

"Is this where you watched from?" Thomas asked Usaden in a whisper.

"They came this way. A little further along, there is a gate that leads to steps, but I thought you would want to see what was happening before we attack them."

"Keep them alive, if possible. And whoever their victim is, we cannot wait until they kill them. Go and make sure the gate is open then return."

Usaden padded away.

Below, it appeared as if an entertainment was being played out on stage. Blackwood stood to one side, an observer. There was no sign of the woman who had entered with him. A naked man and woman had their hands bound behind them, attached to hooks in the wall. The three costumed men stood in the shadows. A fourth figure, the person who had accompanied Blackwood, stood before the two victims.

Two, Thomas thought. *Is that new?* Or was Lord Harrington meant to die alongside his wife at Blackwood's house? He glanced along the ledge, wondering where Usaden was. They needed to be down there, stopping what was about to happen

"Tell me your wish." The cloaked figure with the coarse voice spoke again.

"I seek the knowledge of our dark master," said the naked man.

"We welcome our dark master," said both the woman and Blackwood.

"Knowledge comes only through pain." The speaker had his back to Thomas. He was dressed entirely in black, an ornate hood topped with curved horns covering his head.

"We welcome both knowledge and pain."

One of the men from the house approached with a curled whip in his hand. He shook it loose and lashed out. The tip touched the man's chest and he jerked as it opened his skin. Blood ran across his fat belly and down his legs, but his manhood stood erect. The whip cracked again, and the woman cried out, but it was in pleasure, not pain. Blackwood was ignored.

"Do you love our dark master?"

"Our master is everything. We are nothing."

"Will you do his bidding, whatever the cost?"

"We will." Both spoke. Blackwood kept his silence. Thomas realised he was here to watch his wicked plan, whatever it was, come to fruition.

"Are you ready to meet your master?" The voice remained coarse but became increasingly false. Beneath the black robe, hands moved, making the cloth billow and shimmer, the torchlight adding its own glimmer.

"We welcome our master."

"We need to be down there," Thomas said. "Where is Usaden?"

"There." Will nodded along the ledge.

Usaden ran to them on silent feet. "The gate is locked, but I have found another way. Be quick." He turned and dashed off. Thomas followed, no longer caring if they were heard or seen. As he ran he glanced down into the pit to see the cloaked figure raise its staff. It approached the chained man, raised the staff and brought it down in a heavy blow. The man's knees went limp and he hung from his bindings.

"Now," the figure said, the voice different, lighter.

One of the men approached and passed them a heavy, curved blade. It was a tool a woodsman might use to cut branches. That was not its intended use now.

Thomas almost ran into Usaden, who stood waiting for them at the head of a set of steps that led down.

"Quickly," he said and descended.

When Thomas came out into the pit he saw he was too late. The cloaked figure swung the blade down, but it was not the first blow. Blood flooded the stone floor, and the naked man now hung completely limp. The figure scooped its hand into the open skull and withdrew the damaged brain. Then it turned to the woman, who screamed.

Thomas ran to stop another death, but was confronted by the three men, each with a sword in one hand and a wicked knife in the other. Three against three. It was not a fair fight.

Usaden struck first, taking two of them. Will went for the third, and Thomas shouted, "I want him alive!"

Will glanced at his father, a scowl on his face. He tried to do as asked, but the man kept advancing. Will parried his thrusts but had to step backwards. Thomas came in from the side. He used the hilt of his sword to crack against the man's skull, then did it again harder when he remained on his feet. The second blow was enough.

Thomas turned away but saw he was too late. The woman hung slack like her husband, but her skull remained intact. Nothing could be seen of the cloaked figure or Blackwood. Thomas stood and listened. Were those feet he could hear running away, their passage echoing through the underground chambers? He could not be sure.

The woman groaned.

Thomas used his knife to cut the rope binding her arms. She fell like a sack of grain. The jolt brought her awake. As she turned her head, she took in the man with his skull broken and empty, the lake of blood surrounding him, and she fainted away with a cry.

A fire burned in Thomas. He wanted to track Blackwood and his supposed demon and punish both. But a woman lay comatose at his feet, and his instinct was to care for her. Thomas knelt. He felt her neck, relieved to find a pulse there.

"Me and Usaden should follow," said Will.

Thomas looked up at him. "Not yet. We know where to find Blackwood. I have two jobs for you first. Carry the dead up to the streets and lay them out as if they have been fighting. Put them in front of the cathedral where they will be seen as soon as dawn breaks. Leave those dressed as demons as they are, the dead man too. Try to make it look like the demons have been defeated by some force. If they are outside the cathedral it will be worth starting a rumour God defeated them. With good fortune, when they are found, people will see they are nothing but men dressed as devils, and the fear that stalks the night will start to abate."

"And the one that is not dead?"

"Come back here when you have taken care of the others. I would question the last of them. Are you sure he is out cold?"

Will went across to the man and kicked him between the legs. There was no reaction.

"He's out, Pa. What are you going to do?"

"Take this poor woman to our house and ensure she is safe. Once she has recovered her wits, I will ask her what she and the man were doing here. It sounded as if they were willing participants, but I need to know for certain."

"What if we meet resistance?" asked Will.

"That resistance lies on this cold, hard stone. I have only heard of three men, so do not expect you to be troubled. Blackwood cannot hurt you, but I would like to know who the other was. Acolyte or master?"

"Blackwood is weak and a coward," said Will. He turned away and went to the first dead man. Between him and Usaden, they lifted him and carried him to the steps.

Thomas knelt and lifted the woman, then put her down again. He went to the comatose man and stripped the bright red demon's cloak from him, then wrapped it around her small, slim figure. He carried her out into the night. He detoured to the front of the cathedral and watched as Will arranged the dead men on the steps leading to it. It would have been better if the victim had bled there, but Thomas doubted most people would notice. If Linacre was called, he might, and Thomas determined to check with him and offer an explanation. The man might also know who the victim was. Thomas was aware he should feel some measure of guilt at the coldness of his actions but did not. This terror had to end, and this act was a start. It angered him that nobody had done anything about those terrorising the streets, and wondered why. Was there a deeper plot at work?

Blackwood had influence throughout the city. Was it possible he had used that to ensure no action was taken?

"Usaden, go to Blackwood's house and see if he is there."

"Do I kill him?"

Thomas shook his head. "If he is not there, return and tell me. Otherwise, once dawn breaks, Will and I will join you and all three of us pay him a visit." He turned to Will. "Go down and bring the other man back to the house. When he wakes we will question him."

Thomas turned north and carried the woman through the streets, grateful they were empty. He did not enter his house but took her to the printworks, which was the safer choice.

"Eleanor!" he called out, but there was no reply.

He set the woman in a corner and climbed the stairs. He discovered Eleanor on the bed. She, too, was naked, her pale skin glistening with sweat, her hands clutched to her head. She half sat up when he appeared, a rictus scowl on her sultry mouth.

"Thomas, help me. They are eating me alive. Stop the voices. Please, stop the voices!"

FORTY-ONE

Thomas knelt beside Eleanor. When her hands came out to clutch at him, he grasped her wrists, uneasy to be so close to her nakedness.

"Hold me, Tom. Drive the demons away."

Her skin was cold, her pupils blown wide.

"What have you taken?"

"Nothing. Only what Timothy gives me for my headaches."

"How much?"

"Enough, but it has not worked. Help me. Save me."

Thomas tried to wrap the blanket around her but she threw it off.

"Lie atop me, Tom, make it stop." She tried to pull him down but he leaned back, then rose to his feet.

"I have to do something. I will be back soon. Go nowhere."

He was conflicted with which of the two to deal with first, but the woman downstairs might possess information he needed to know. So he descended. Instead of lifting her he went to the stables and woke Jack.

"Master Thomas, sir, are you aright?"

"I am, but others are not. Is there anyone awake in the house?"

"At this time of night? Of course not. Why?"

"I have witnessed a killing, but one survives. I need to take her somewhere safe. And I need you to watch over her and fetch me if she wakes."

Jack struggled to his feet and pulled on a shirt. "Where will you be?"

"Dealing with Eleanor. She is unwell."

"More of her headaches?"

"You know of them, then."

"She never lets me forget. She complains about them all the time, but I do not believe she can suffer as badly as she claims."

"If you saw her now you might change your mind. In fact, I want you to go to her while I take the woman to my room."

"Your room? Is that proper?"

"Perhaps not, but it is right. I warn you, Eleanor has lost her wits and her clothes both. She is naked. Can you manage her?"

Jack stood tall. "I can, Tom. I will be a perfect gentleman."

"She will beg you not to be."

"I am no beast."

Thomas left Jack to ascend to the upper floor. He lifted the woman, barely any weight at all, and carried her into the house. All around was quiet as he ascended the stairs. He took her into his room, laid her on the bed and covered her with a blanket. Her breathing was steady. Her heart beat quickly, but that might be expected after what she had witnessed. He left her, descended the stairs silently, and crept out to the printworks. When he reached the bedroom, Jack was holding Eleanor down. She writhed beneath him, uttering vile curses and invitations to mount her.

"I have never seen her this bad. What is wrong with her?"

"I do not know. She has complained of headaches ever since I met her. I have also witnessed her suffer a bout of the falling sickness, but this is different. I believe she has imbibed too much of the medicines al-Timani gives her. I left her something for them as well and she may have taken both. I need you to go to my room. You will find the woman there. If she wakes, you must come for me at once."

Jack nodded and almost fell down the ladder in his haste to leave. Thomas believed Eleanor in this state scared the lad.

"Help me, Tom. Drive them from my head." She writhed on the bed, her legs trapped in the tangled covers. Her hand was raised to ward off something only she could see.

Thomas reached out and took the hand, which resisted with surprising strength.

"There is nothing there. It is all in your mind."

"In my *head*, Tom! They are in my head!" She growled, a long, guttural cry for help.

Thomas had witnessed madness before, but those he

had treated in the past showed little rationality. Eleanor's condition was different. Most of the time, she was bright, calm and in control. But no longer. He wondered if this was a delayed reaction to Luke's murder. A reaction to the danger she was in. She had accepted it well until now, but had it arrived like a thunderstorm to overwhelm her senses? Normally, he would administer a little hashish and poppy mixed in wine, but he suspected she had already taken too much of both. What she needed was time. And comfort. So he lay beside her and held her in his arms. He stroked her face and neck. He covered her breasts with the blanket and held her tight. Slowly, she stopped writhing and stopped trying to throw the blanket off.

"Save me, Tom." Her voice was a whisper now. Her breath had slowed.

Thomas continued to stroke her face. It took time, but eventually, she slept. Now and again she would twitch and mutter words that made no sense. Thomas stayed with her in his arms until Jack came for him, then slid away.

"She is awake?"

"Waking," said Jack. "Who is she?"

"That is what I am about to find out. Stay here with Eleanor. She is sleeping now. Do as I did and just hold her. She needs to be comforted. Can you do that?"

Jack nodded.

"When she wakes, she may ask you to violate her."

Jack stared at Thomas. "What do you take me for?"

Thomas returned to the house, hoping Jack could cope with Eleanor. The lad had matured a great deal recently, and Thomas trusted him. The woman was sitting up in bed when Thomas entered the room. She cowered away from him, clutching the blankets to her chest.

"Who are you, sir, and why am I here? Do you intend to violate me?"

Thomas suppressed a smile. The woman was not ancient, neither was she young, but as far as looks went, she had been handed a poor hand at birth.

"My name is Thomas Berrington, and you are in no danger from me. You are?"

She stared at him and he could imagine the struggle going through her mind.

When she said nothing, he said, "Do you recall what happened beneath St Paul's?"

She shook her head. Slowly, her face seemed to crumple from within.

"John," she said, her voice barely a whisper. "What that devil did to John...." She looked up at Thomas. "Were you there? Is that what you plan for me?"

"I was there, yes, but watching from above."

She scowled. "Are you a peeper?"

Thomas had not heard the word before but could work out the meaning. "Not in the way you mean, lady. I would have intervened had I been able to descend to the pit sooner. He was your husband?"

She nodded.

"You called him John."

"Sir John Tanner, friend to King Henry and his Queen. He is well respected in Parliament."

"And you are?"

"Lady Tanner, of course."

"Your given name."

"Clemence." It took an effort for her to force the word out. She was undoubtedly unused to being on first-name terms with strangers. "What are you going to do to me?" She coughed, her pale face turning paler. She clutched the bedclothes even tighter against her chest. "I have a great pain, sir. I cannot—" Before she could say more, her eyes rolled back in her head and she slumped to one side.

Thomas rushed to her. He searched for the pulse in her throat. When he failed to find it, he cursed. He formed a fist and punched between her slack breasts. He had been taught it many years before when he was little more than a lad and had used it more than once since. This time, it did nothing. Thomas cursed again. Any chance of finding what she knew had gone.

He arranged her on the bed and drew the covers up so she was completely covered. In the printworks, Eleanor lay whimpering. Jack knelt beside the palette, his hands gripping one of hers.

"She is quieter?" Thomas asked.

"She is exhausted. I did not know what to do so held her hand. It seemed to help."

"You did well."

"How is the lady upstairs?"

"Dead. I would return her to her family but her husband also died. I do not know anything about either of them. Do you think Hardwin might recognise their names?"

"It is possible, Tom. What are they?"

"Sir Jacob Tanner and his wife, Lady Clemence."

"There is no need to ask Master Hardwin, I can tell you a little about them."

"Because stable lads talk amongst themselves," Thomas said.

Jack smiled. "We do, sir. You would be surprised at the secrets I could reveal."

"I don't believe I would, but a conversation between us at some time might prove fruitful. I am a stranger in London and need to know more about those who inhabit it."

"You mean ladies and gentlemen?"

"And people like you, Jack."

Jack shook his head. "I am nothing. You know I am. No one sees the likes of me or the other staff. You are the first master we have ever had in this house that even meets our eyes. I should warn you it is not always wise. You need to keep a distance from those such as us."

"I was like you once, Jack, and could never do what you say. Now tell me what you know about the Tanners."

"They have a fine enough house in Laurence Lane, where they live with their children. Two girls and a boy. The eldest, I think, has no more than nine years. If both the Tanners are dead, you need to speak with their relatives. The brother of Sir Jacob lives on Lothbury. The others are close together, north of there on Colman Street." Jack hesitated, then said, "I doubt Sir Jacob's brother will take in the children or bury the body of Lady Clemence and Sir Jacob."

Thomas stared at Jack, who had once again surprised him.

"The lady is in your bed," said Jack. "Where is her husband?"

"At St Paul's Cathedral."

"He is praying for her?"

"He is beyond praying. I hope he might make a statement to help end this terror stalking the streets. The man is dead, Jack, as are two of those who attacked him."

There was a noise below and Thomas reached to his waist for a knife.

Then a voice called out. "Are you here, Pa? What do we do now?"

Thomas went to the top of the ladder. "I have one more task for you. Lady Clemence died. I need you to find someone to take her body for interment. She also has children who need to be taken into care. Jack can show you where."

Thomas stayed with Eleanor after Will left with Jack, who knew where to go. He wetted a cloth with cold water and wiped her face. She did not stir. He suspected she would sleep now until morning, if not longer. He checked her pulse frequently, satisfied it did not race nor beat too slowly. He stared at her strange beauty and wondered how so much pain could reside in her. Was it madness or real? He knew of several infections that could cause an apparent loss of a person's wits. Knew of parasites that lived within bodies that could do the same. Linacre had found a worm inside Luke. Did Eleanor carry the same? They had been lovers, so it was possible. When he heard Will and Jack return he went downstairs.

"Do you want me to sit with Eleanor again?" asked Jack.

"There is no need, she is sleeping peacefully now. Go to your own bed, Jack. You have done well tonight. I will not forget it.

"You have taken to him," said Will once they sat at the kitchen table and picked at cold chicken and bread about to turn stale.

"He is clever, resourceful and brave. Like someone else I know."

"Do you mean Amal?"

Thomas threw a chicken bone at his son, but he swatted it aside with a grin.

"Do you need to check on Eleanor before we leave, Pa?"

"She will sleep like the dead now, so no. Best to leave her rest."

"You know what we have to do, then. Do we wait until dawn or go now?"

"Which would you do?"

"I would go now, of course. But if you are too tired we can wait a few hours."

"No. This cannot be put off."

"Will you be hard on him, Pa?"

"As hard as necessary to get to the truth, yes."

"Let Usaden loose on him. No man can withstand that."

Thomas knew it was the truth, but a savage one.

"I will offer him the chance to talk before that last resort." Thomas put his fists on the table and rose. They went into the stables where Jack slept on his cot like someone dead, not stirring as they saddled their horses and led them out. A third horse, which Thomas assumed belonged to Hardwin, was not in its stall, and he wondered if the man was spreading his evil words again.

FORTY-TWO

They took the same road Thomas had on his first visit. They left their horses in a small copse a quarter mile from Blackwood's house. This time as they approached, there was no line of torches to guide them, and only a few windows showed lamplight. As they came closer, Usaden appeared from the gloom and fell into step beside them.

"What has been happening?" Thomas asked.

"A few people came and went, but nothing like the other night."

"What kind of people?"

"Rough-looking, for the most part. Three went inside and stayed for several hours. Two came out looking the worse for wear."

"Drink, or something else?"

"They were not staggering and spoke softly, so not drink. Another horse arrived at speed not long before you. The rider dismounted and went inside. I did not see them leave again so assume they remain there."

They reached the broad steps leading to the entrance door, but it stood firm when Will tried to open it.

"I can get us in around the back," said Usaden. "I slipped inside and stole a little food and drink."

"I take it you were not seen and left no trace?"

Usaden raised an eyebrow. It was answer enough.

"Show us," Thomas said.

Usaden led the way around the side of the house, ducking each time a wash of light came through a window. There was no sound from within, and Thomas saw no one inside.

"How many staff?" he asked, his voice low.

"Less than you might think. There are two women in the kitchen, a footman, a steward, and two girls who do the fires and make the beds."

"And Blackwood's wife?"

"No sign."

"Is Blackwood in there?"

"I saw him twice when I was inside, several more times from without. The first time was after the rough men left. He was padding along a corridor naked. He had been to bathe or was returning from one of the servant's rooms. Men of position come with an expectation their advances will not be rejected. The second time, he wore a long black robe fashioned from silk. Jorge would have approved."

"Did you see where he went?"

"There is a door near his quarters which leads to a cellar. I was unable to follow. I waited as long as I could, but he did not reappear."

"Could there be a way out without being seen?" asked Will, who had listened silently to that point.

"It is possible, but if so I have seen no sign of one. There is no lower door from the cellar and no means of coming out other than the door at the front and another on the side to the kitchen."

"Blackwood took me to his workshop in the cellar," Thomas said. " It is possible that is where he has gone. I take it the rest of the household have gone to their beds?"

"They went there hours since," said Usaden. "All except Blackwood and his new mystery guest. The windows are large, and the quality of glass good, so I had a clear view inside which is how I could watch Blackwood. I tried to see who the new person was but could not. I take it you want to go in and confront them both?"

"I do."

"Then I will take you. We should watch for a short time. If no one appears, we go in. I will check the back to make sure there are no surprises."

Thomas nodded. He wanted to get inside at once, but Usaden made sense. He knew the ways of the house. A fox came to investigate, unafraid and docile. It sniffed the air, cocked its leg on a bush, then wandered away. An owl hooted and was answered. A moment later, the soft sound of its wings reached them but they did not see the bird.

Thomas's head grew heavy, and he fought to stay awake. He rose and walked out from their cover, sure he would not be seen. The house sat in the distance, almost unreal in the flat, featureless landscape. A quarter moon sailed through ragged clouds to offer a little illumination. This, he thought, could truly be the Devil's playground, with no one to witness what happened here. Except, he was still not convinced Blackwood was the main instigator of events. Yes, he was an observer at what had happened below St Paul's Cathedral, but it was another who did the killing. Blackwood abused others and used his position to take what he wanted. But he was also weak, twisting whichever way the wind blew. He lacked an inner core of courage.

When Thomas glanced around, he discovered Usaden had returned.

"Someone left the house a little while ago," he said.

"I saw nothing."

"I know, but I did."

"Blackwood, or his mysterious guest?"

"I saw only from a distance, so I cannot say for sure. Whoever it was they were on horseback, heading west. There must be a tunnel of some kind from the cellar because nobody emerged from the house. Should I follow them?"

Thomas considered the question. It would mean sending Will or Usaden, and Usaden knew the layout of the house. But Will was less adept at tracking than Usaden. It made sense all three of them should stay together.

"It might have been a servant," said Usaden. "But most likely it was Blackwood's guest leaving."

"You saw the figure who killed Sir Jacob Tanner beneath St Paul's," Thomas said. "Could it have been the same person?"

"We only saw them from above, so I cannot be sure, but it is possible."

"If so, they were not here long. I do not want us to lose Blackwood again. He may have been giving orders for another killing. He takes no action himself, but likes to tell others what to do. The man is a coward. I am not sure I recall where the entrance to the cellar is, so I need you to show me. After that, you must follow whoever left." Thomas knew that Usaden could track a someone even through total darkness. "Watch them, but do nothing."

"And if they intend to kill again? Do I allow it?"

Thomas knew he could not countenance another death if it could be stopped. "If you think you can do so without danger to yourself, then stop him. But I suspect he will have joined up with his companions, so there will be be four of them."

"If that is all I can take them. Let us go inside so I can return before they travel too far." Usaden walked away. After a moment, Will came from the bushes, and all three approached the house. Usaden led them around the back, where an unlocked door admitted them to a storage room. Another door took them to a second room lined with coats and, beyond it, a long corridor.

"The cellar door is at the end," said Usaden, padding forwards silently.

Thomas followed, trying to recall if this was the way Blackwood had taken him when he showed him his work-shop, but could not. They had entered from the large main room that time.

Will took up the rear, occasionally turning to walk backwards so he could check behind them. They entered another hallway where a low door stood in an alcove. It looked familiar to Thomas. When Usaden tried it, the door opened.

"This is the same way Blackwood took me through to his workshop, but it was locked then," Thomas said.

"That was at your gathering?" asked Will.

"It was."

"There were a hundred or more people here then. Blackwood would not want anyone wandering down there alone. With only him and the few staff here he likely does not bother with the lock."

"We are a mile from the nearest house, and I expect the staff know not to venture anywhere their master does not allow them." Thomas smiled, the excitement of the chase on him now. "Unlike us."

Usaden went first into the darkness. Thomas waited until, as expected, a flare of light appeared. When he descended the stairs, he found Usaden holding a lantern. He saw a small collection of them on a shelf built into the wall, waiting for whoever came down here.

The stone floor of the first chamber was swept clean. Thomas did not believe Blackwood would have done that, so he must admit some staff.

"Do you want me to go now?" asked Usaden.

"No, stay with us in case we need you," Thomas said. "Blackwood is more important than whoever rode off. He can tell us who it was if we need to find them. I expect the man himself is in his workshop in the next room."

Except he was not, but another door led them into a wide corridor which ran in a straight line. Thomas tried to picture where they were beneath the house but could not. Still within the confines of the walls above, but other than that he had lost his bearings. He expected Usaden had not.

They reached a parting of the ways and stopped.

"I have not been this way before," Thomas said. "There must be another entrance from above."

Thomas looked both ways and then asked Usaden to lower the lamp. Once he did, he saw a faint illumination from the corridor on their left.

He started along it.

As they walked, the distant light grew brighter. Then they heard a soft but definite groan, and halted.

"He is torturing another victim," said Will. "We must stop it now."

Another groan came as they reached the entrance to a chamber and discovered its source. Not one of Blackwood's victims, but Blackwood himself. Half the space was taken up with more of Blackwood's jars, urns, phials and mortars. Jars with mysterious contents lined two shelves and a work-table stood beneath them. Blackwood was held between two stone pillars, chains from each wrist snagged onto iron hooks screwed into the pillars. They were all that held him up because his legs could not. Someone had cut into his skull and removed the top, yet still he lived. His brain had not been torn out as with other victims. It sat within his open skull, pulsing. Blood pooled at his feet.

As Thomas approached, Usaden moved to one side,

Will to the other. Blackwood's head rose, and he stared at Thomas.

"You again." His voice was barely a whisper, and Thomas was surprised the man could talk at all.

"Who did this to you?"

"You know who did it. The Devil. He lured me down here and opened my head with his forked tail."

"I do not believe in the Devil," Thomas said. "It was a man who did this."

"No, not a man. Show me mercy and kill me, Berrington, for the pain is all-consuming. My body burns."

"Not until you tell me who is behind the killings. I thought it was you, but now I see it cannot be. Have the others turned against you?"

"It is all the fault of Croft," whispered Blackwood.

"Sir Richard Croft?"

Blackwood could not nod for fear of what the movement might do to him. Could Croft be responsible? It was hard to believe. Croft debauched himself and openly admitted doing so, but Thomas liked the man for all his faults. Yet it made sense. He wanted to talk with Eleanor, who knew Croft better than he did. She had studied the books in his library and hinted at their bawdy nature. But did they contain more profane texts? If so, was it even possible to punish the man? Croft was close to King Henry. He was a Marcher Lord, a ruler in the borderlands between England and Wales. As good as a king in his own domain and above the law.

"Why did he do this to you?" Thomas asked.

"Others..." Blackwood gasped, fighting for breath. "...

others do the work. But … it is not…" Blackwood shuddered and took another breath. Death was coming for him.

"Not what?" Thomas showed his knife to Blackwood, who only smiled at the release it would offer.

And then he died, his eyes wide open, his body unable to take any more.

FORTY-THREE

They left Blackwood in the cellar but released his bindings so he lay on the floor. Thomas searched for the rest of his skull but could not find it. Instead, he placed a cloth from the worktable over his head. Eventually, someone would come looking for him.

"Do you know where Croft's London house is?" asked Will as they rode west, the approaching dawn casting their shadows ahead.

"I do not. He has mentioned it enough times but never offered its location. Someone working for the King will know. I will go to Westminster first thing and find out.

"Do you truly believe he is behind all of this?"

Thomas considered the question before replying. "Yes and no."

Will laughed. "Ah, well then, everything will be fine."

"He is a Marcher Lord," Thomas said. "He has immense power where he lives but less so here, close to the seat of the real power in the country. I have always found him an amenable companion, but there is no denying he is a man driven by an unnatural lust." He glanced at his son. "There is a sense to it. Not devil worship, not demons, but I believe he could use the threat of them and the fear generated to..." Thomas's voice faded.

"To what, Pa?"

Thomas shook his head. "That is the point. I do not know. I cannot see what advantage it brings him. His position is already exalted. He is entitled, vain, selfish and deviant, but I have never considered him a cold-blooded killer or torturer. It does not sit well with me."

"So Blackwood was lying?" said Will.

"You saw him. Do you think he was capable of lying? What would be the point? He knew he was beyond all help."

"Then he was telling his own truth, but it was not real, only something he had convinced himself of. Perhaps helped by Croft, or someone else who wants to taint Croft, to implicate him in the deaths."

Thomas's mind spun possibilities as the day grew brighter. People started to appear from shacks and hovels beside the road. Here beyond the city wall, men, women and children scratched a living from the ditches and unclaimed land.

"Will, ask if anyone saw a man riding past during the night. If Croft came this way, it will be easy to confirm from their description."

Will rode off to one side, Usaden the other, which left Thomas alone to pursue his thoughts. He recalled Croft and Blackwood deep in conversation when he met the King.

And the man had been at the debauched gathering. Were the two men friends? Conspirators? He thought back to his conversations with Croft to see if anything implicated him. The man was not ordinary, but was he this wicked? Once again, Thomas returned to the question: What benefit would it bring? And for that, he had no answer.

Will and Usaden returned with the news that nobody had seen anyone passing during the night, but few had ventured out until dawn broke. Even out here, people kept their doors locked and their gazes averted. Whoever was guilty of the plot and deaths had seeded the ground well. There would be no witnesses.

"If Eleanor has recovered, I intend to ask her about Croft. She lived under his roof for many years, but it would be cruel to do so while she is unwell and grieving for Luke."

"And what do me and Usaden do?"

"I do not know. Until we find Croft, there is nothing for you to do. Take the opportunity to rest, for we do not know when the next chance might come.

Will laughed. "You are telling me to rest, Pa? Look at you. When was the last time you had a full night's sleep?"

"I will sleep when we have captured our killer, and with good fortune that will be today."

When they reached the house, Thomas went straight to Eleanor's workshop, but the place was deserted. A sheet of paper was pinned to the platen but had not been printed. He went up the stairs to find the bed unmade. When he returned to the stable yard, he asked Jack if he knew where she was, but he shook his head and said he did not.

"She must have taken a horse for one is missing," said

Jack. "She was gone when I woke, but I did not hear her leave during the night. I am sorry, Master Thomas."

"You carry no blame. You did not hear us go either. You were exhausted. She will return soon enough, but I worry about her after last night." Thomas patted Jack's shoulder. "I need to visit Westminster. Would you like to come with me?" He did not know why he made the offer, only that Jack had impressed him. He would turn into an honest and hard-working man with a little encouragement.

Jack's mouth dropped open. "Westminster Palace? They would not allow a lad such as me to enter there."

"I do not intend to visit the King. I need to speak with someone who keeps a list of London houses used by knights, dukes and earls."

"Like this one?" said Jack. "We have had such folk stay here. Do you have a title, Master Thomas?"

"I was once a duke, but that was in far-off Spain, not England."

Jack frowned. "You cannot stop being a duke, can you?"

"Perhaps not. So you will come?"

"Yes, sir." Jack looked down at himself. "Can you wait while I find better clothes?" He looked Thomas up and down. "And perhaps you should do the same." He blushed at his temerity in suggesting such, but Thomas laughed.

"Yes, if I am a duke I should dress appropriately. We shall both change. Meet me here in a quarter of an hour, yes?"

"Yes."

When Thomas returned to the yard, Jack was waiting, dancing from foot to foot as though his thin frame could barely contain his excitement. He wore dark hose, clean felt shoes, and a white shirt over which lay a dark jacket that was too large for him. He had wetted and combed his hair and scrubbed his face so hard crimson patches showed on his cheeks.

"I saddled Sombra and another horse if you want to ride, Master Thomas."

"Yes, if we are to be gentlemen, we should ride."

Thomas felt a little like a gentleman as they left through Ludgate, the throng parting to allow them to pass. They followed Strande until the river turned south in one of the large, looping meanders the Thames was fond of, before entering the Palace of Westminster. Two guards nodded Thomas and Jack through because he was familiar to them now. For a moment, Thomas wondered who else they would nod through and whether some men might be a threat to King Henry. He was not a popular ruler, and no doubt others believed they, or someone they knew, would be a better monarch.

They left their horses tied to a rail because Thomas did not expect them to be long, and then he asked where the office of the Seneschal could be found. He did not want the King's man himself but those who worked under him. They would keep a record of titled men and their places of residence. It did not take long before they were directed to the correct office, and fortunate that when they arrived, one of the junior administrators recognised Thomas.

"Are you on the King's business, Sir Thomas?"

Thomas saw Jack's eyes widen at the use of his title, which was rightly earned even though he rarely used it.

"I need to speak with Sir Richard Croft, but I do not know where his house is. I have visited him at Lemster many times, and he is a fine host, but he sent me a note to come to see him here in London, neglecting to tell me where his house lies."

"Wait here. It may take me some time to find it. Give me an hour. Perhaps you can walk the path along the riverside and take the air."

Take the stench, more like, Thomas thought, but it was a chance to impress Jack some more with the size and majesty of the palace. As it was, Jack barely had chance to study the building. As they emerged onto the walkway, they discovered a party of ladies approaching, also taking the air and making the most of a rare day of sunshine. A westerly breeze carried most of the stink of the river across to the Southwark side.

"Is that you, Sir Thomas?" asked the Queen. "Are you here to see my husband?"

Thomas bowed deeply, then nudged Jack to do the same. "Not today, Your Grace. I have a boring administrative matter to take care of, nothing more. I trust the King is well?"

She smiled. "He complains of a surfeit of maladies, but I believe he makes the majority of them up."

Thomas glanced at Jack, who was staring open-mouthed at one of the younger ladies in waiting, who returned his stare with interest. Thomas wondered if it had been a mistake to bring the boy. Meeting such people might bring discontent with his lot in life.

"I understand Thomas Linacre attends his majesty. He is a fine physician."

"I have heard him say the same of you. Have you seen Lady Catherine recently?"

"It has been a day or two, Your Grace. She too complains of aches but is healthy enough."

"Harry talks of her constantly." The Queen looked around. "He was here somewhere a moment ago. Where has the boy gone to now? Alice, run and find him before he falls in the river." When the girl Jack had been staring at ran off, the Queen said, "Harry believes himself invulnerable." She lightly touched the swell of her belly. "I pray I carry another son for Henry." She did not need to state that one heir was regarded as insufficient.

"Tom!" A streak of red slammed into Thomas, almost knocking him from his feet. "What are you doing here? Father is with his advisers, but I am sure he will admit you."

"I am here on other business, my prince."

Harry slapped Thomas on the chest. "What have I told you? Use my name."

Thomas glanced at the Queen, but she smiled indulgently at her son. "You are much honoured, Sir Thomas," she said. "Harry insists on being called by name only with those he respects."

"Which is why it puzzles me he does so with me," Thomas said, which made the Queen laugh.

"If you do so, I will not tell my husband. Now come, ladies. We must complete two circuits of the palace before I can rest. I am sure Harry will be able to catch up with us."

The prince remained behind once the Queen had gone.

"Have you seen Catherine?" he asked the same question his mother had. "Does she ask after me?"

"Constantly."

"Mother says we will visit soon. She says Catherine needs amusement, and I believe I am just the boy who can offer that."

"I believe you are, Harry, I believe you are."

"Indeed. Who is your companion? He is very thin."

"As are you, but yes, he is thin. This is Jack, a friend of mine."

Harry offered his hand. "Any friend of Tom's is a friend of mine. Welcome to Westminster, Jack."

Jack bowed so low he almost fell over, but he managed to grasp the Prince's hand. Thomas saw Harry's grip tighten, a test of strength he had no doubt witnessed in grown men, but Jack's hard work had given him strength, too, despite his thinness, and the match was equal. Harry offered a nod of respect.

"Come with Tom next time he visits, Jack. We can fight each other. Now, I had best catch up with Mother before she sends someone to find me again." Harry slapped Thomas on the arm and ran off.

"Was that Prince Henry?" asked Jack when they were alone.

"It was indeed. I like how you did not let him squeeze your hand but squeezed back. Most people would not do that."

"I did not know I was not meant to, Master Thomas. I am sorry."

"Do not be, lad. I saw Harry admire you for it."

"He will be king one day, yes?"

"A long time away, but yes, he will be king. And Princess Catherine of Aragon will be his Queen."

"Why did you bring me to this place, sir?" Jack's expression was sombre.

Thomas looked at him, surprised at the question. He wondered if he had done so deliberately to impress him. Except he had not expected to meet the Queen or Prince Harry. He had wanted to enter and leave unnoticed, but that had not happened, and he had possibly set a discontent in Jack.

"I wanted you to see how those who rule us live."

"I would say they live well."

"Indeed they do, but they are men and women like everyone else, with aches, pains, and worries. Being King is not all ceremony, with people prostrating before you. A King must make decisions and act on them. It is not always easy, and even harder to satisfy everyone."

"People complain about taxes," said Jack. "Master Hardwin grumbles all the time."

"Running a country as important as England requires funds," Thomas said. "Soldiers must be paid, swords made, arrows fletched, and fighting ships built. The men and women in the street do not see that, but they will welcome it if we are attacked."

"Who would attack England?"

Thomas laughed. "Oh, more countries than you can imagine." He patted Jack on the shoulder. "It has not been an hour yet, but let us see if that man has found what I need. Then we can get away from here. Have you seen enough?"

"More than enough, sir, and thank you for bringing me. It has opened my eyes to many things."

When they returned to find out about Sir Richard Croft's residence, the man who had offered to help was waiting for them outside.

"I am sorry, Sir Thomas, but I could not find what you asked for."

Thomas was disappointed, but said, "No mind. My thanks for trying."

"It was not through lack of effort, sir, but I was told you could not be given the information you seek."

"Told by whom?"

"That I cannot reveal. I am truly sorry, but you have stirred a hornets' nest with your innocent request." The man started to turn away, then stopped. "Take care, Sir Thomas. You have upset important people."

FORTY-FOUR

"Who is this man you seek?" asked Jack as they rode towards the city gate. His question distracted Thomas from his thoughts. He had been trying to determine who did not want him visiting Croft. He might have suspected Blackwood, but the man was dead, and the administrator made it clear he had received the instruction only that morning – no doubt caused by Thomas's request. Croft himself might have stopped the information being divulged, which made discovering his address even more of a priority before other deaths occurred.

"Why do you ask?" Thomas said.

"Lads talk among themselves. Tell me more about the man, and I will try to get the address you seek."

"My thanks, Jack. Sir Richard lives part of the year in Croft Manor in Herefordshire, between the towns of Lemster and Ludlow. He is married and has grown children. The man himself is tall and has seventy-five years." As

Thomas spoke, it occurred to him that a man of Croft's age could not inflict the damage done on Blackwood without assistance. He did not expect the man would do the killing himself, but no doubt he would want to be close to observe, just as Blackwood had been beneath St Paul's. The men Usaden had seen enter and leave had no doubt committed the killing, but Croft would want to hear the screams of pain. Which raised the question of whether he had been in the catacombs of St Paul's when Sir Jacob Tanner died. Was he standing close, watching the death? Watching Thomas, Will and Usaden as they reacted? The man would know who they were. Had it amused him to see their confusion and lack of progress?

None of which helped unless he could find out where he lived.

"Is that enough to go on?" Thomas asked Jack.

"Enough for now, sir. I will go to ask my questions now. Will you be at the house if I find out what you seek?"

"I need to speak with Eleanor again, and Will and Usaden may have other ideas about how we can progress. If I am not there, leave a message."

"I cannot write, sir, but I will tell Eliza. She can be trusted to pass the message on to you and no one else."

Thomas watched Jack ride away, a short, slim figure atop the large horse. Because of how he was dressed, the crowds parted for him, just as they did for Thomas. Jack had surprised him today with how he coped with the unfamiliar, and his sharpness of mind. The lad had been awed by Westminster but had risen above his initial fear and handled himself well. Thomas knew he wanted to help him all he could. Find a better position for him. Then he smiled and shook his head because he was mapping out the lad's future. Jack would have his own ambitions. Even so, Thomas would try to discover what they might be and offer any help he could.

At the house, he found Usaden sitting cross-legged on the stable wall as if he had been carved from stone.

"Where is Will?"

"Sleeping. Do you want me to wake him?"

"Not yet. I did not find what I wanted at Westminster, but Jack thinks he may be able to get the information we need."

"Do we kill Croft if he does?"

"Not unless we have to. He will no doubt have men around him, and we may have to injure them, but I want Croft alive to stand before the King and admit to what he has done, and why. For it is the why that puzzles me most."

"I do not understand the why of it either," said Usaden.

"I have some thoughts on it. Only men of position or their wives have been killed. He may want them removed to increase his status, or he views them as rivals and wants them gone. I do not yet fully comprehend what benefit it brings him. I assume the demonology is nothing more than a deception. He uses it to draw in others such as Blackwood. Uses it to entice his victims."

"You are a man of position, Thomas. Perhaps he will come to kill you."

Thomas laughed. "Then you will have to save me again."

"Yes, I will save you. But Croft is older than you by a

dozen years, and softer in the body. You could defeat him without trying. I will keep watch, just in case."

"My thanks. I have changed my mind. Go and wake Will. I want us to work on a plan between us, which might be a waste of time if Jack fails to return with what we need to know, but at least we have the time to waste until he does."

Thomas poked at the ideas circling inside his head as he waited, all connected to the big question. What advantage would Croft gain? Slowly, something came to him, and it was because of what Usaden had said. Thomas had a small position now, a place at court. If Croft had him removed, what benefit would he gain? Most likely land. Thomas's land, which was now more extensive than it had been. He wondered if it was possible to find out what lands those who had died owned and what would happen to them. If they had children, he expected it would pass to them. The conjuring of demons to tear people apart seemed too ornate a plot unless Croft believed in it, and Thomas found it hard to accept he did.

When Will appeared, they sat around the kitchen table with mugs of ale and Thomas told them of what he had thought of so far.

"I have the same questions as Usaden about Croft," said Will. "The man is strange – we have all witnessed that – but his age would prevent him from wanting to exert control over much more than he already has, which is already significant."

"He has children," Thomas said.

"Five, and four of them girls."

Thomas laughed. "Can girls not have ambition?"

"Of course they can, but we all know it is often discouraged. I do not know if any of Croft's children are grown, married and have their own children. Grandchildren even, for he is old enough. He may want power and land for them."

"I wondered the same," Thomas said, "but he is already powerful, rich, and owns vast tracts of land. He is also strange enough to believe in demons. You witnessed him at Burfa Bank. He lost control. He let the visions take him. Too much mushroom can do that to someone. What if his mind has slipped, and he believes in what he is doing?"

"Then he is more crazed than I took him for. But I agree the visions the mushrooms bring can change someone. It has changed Silva, which is one of the reasons we are no longer together. She was strange to begin with but even stranger now. She is also close to Croft. Is it possible they have hatched some madness between them?"

Thomas was unaware of any change in Silva, but he had not seen her since she helped him recover his family's bones. A memory came to him of her emerging naked from a pile of skulls, her eyes bright with an inner fire – or madness. Yes, it was possible she could believe in demons. Also possible she and Croft worked together.

"If that is the case, we might expect her to be near," Thomas said.

"How do we know she is not? I have not spoken with her in a month and a half, or have you not noticed?"

"I have been busy with work, but you do seem to have been around the house more than usual. Besides, it does not matter if she is here or not. Blackwood named Croft, so it is Croft we must go after. But I would still like to know what his purpose is."

"With good fortune, you can ask him yourself before the day is done," said Will. "We should tell Eleanor what we are going to do. She used to live under Croft's roof, and she told me she hates the man."

"Was that when you lay beside her?"

Will stared at his father but said nothing, and eventually, Thomas looked away.

"I am sorry, it is none of my business."

Will laughed. "It *is* your business, Pa, because I am your son. We are family – you, me and Amal. Oh, there is also Jorge and Belia and their children, then there is Usaden and Emma and their child, but we three are the only Berringtons left in the world. I would be concerned if you did not worry about my welfare. There is no need. I am almost full-grown and can look after myself."

"I still apologise. You are indeed full-grown and must lead your own life. Perhaps you should go and tell Eleanor what we intend to do. She will be pleased if she hates Croft as much as she claims."

Will rose without further comment and left the kitchen.

"It is nothing, him and the woman," said Usaden when Will had gone. "Women like him. He would be a fool not to respond to them."

"I agree," Thomas said. "It is difficult to let go, but I must try harder." He almost spoke of how he had behaved when he was Will's age, but it would add nothing. "Do we wait until dark before going to find Croft?"

"If the lad returns in time," said Usaden. "And I agree with Will about Croft. I also saw him at Burfa Bank, and he was beyond madness, as were many others that night. Mad enough for him to recruit acolytes to do his bidding."

"It still does not explain what he is trying to achieve."

"As Will said, you can ask him when you have a knife pressed to his throat." Usaden smiled, but Thomas suspected few others would recognise it as such.

Jack was with Will when he returned, and the lad was grinning.

"I have the information you seek, Master Thomas. This Croft is a tall man and has much age?"

"He does."

"He has two houses within the city walls, but my contacts tell me he is staying at a house outwith them. He has a place he uses that is close to Charterhouse Priory. It is no great house but he spends much time there because it is private." Jack bounced from foot to foot, excitement running through him. "I would like to come with you, sir, if you will have me."

"No." Thomas watched Jack's excitement fade. "It will be dangerous work and I will not put you in harm's way."

"You will not be, sir, I can take care of myself."

Thomas took a breath, ready to disappoint Jack, but Will spoke first.

"Let him come, Pa." He looked at Jack. "But you must stay back. Watch the horses. Keep a lookout for anyone approaching. And obey any of us when we ask you to do something. The three of us are enough for what needs to be done. This is the kind of work we are good at, but it needs someone else to help us succeed. Can you be that man?

Jack straightened from his disappointment. "I can, sir."

"One condition," said Will.

"Anything, sir."

"You are never to call me sir again. Nor my father. You know our names, and we consider you an equal. Agreed?"

"Agreed," said Jack, but it was clear he could not bring himself to use their names. Not yet. Perhaps by morning, he would.

"Was Eleanor back?" Thomas asked. "Did you let her know what we have planned?"

"Yes, she is back, and yes, I told her what we planned. She was printing and offered no response. I expect she is trying to take her mind off what has happened. I told her we would likely be out all night."

"We need to prepare," Thomas said. We should have weapons and dark clothes. We go tonight once it is full dark. Which means we should all try to get some sleep." He looked at Will. "In our own beds. Jack, you say you know where this house is that Croft stays in?"

"I do, sir."

Thomas waited, staring at him.

"I do, Tom." The name came out as little more than a whisper.

"Then prepare our horses and one for yourself. Ask Winnie if she can put some food together that we can carry, then rest until the sun sets. We will do the same."

Jack nodded and ran off.

"He may be a distraction to us," said Usaden.

"It means one of us does not have to keep watch, so we take him. I will have another word before we go to impress on him the dangers and what he must do."

"He is your responsibility then," said Usaden, and Thomas knew he was right. One more responsibility, of which he had too many these days.

FORTY-FIVE

The bell of the squat St Anne and St Agnes Church struck ten times as the four of them passed through Aldersgate and followed a rutted track north. Jack rode ahead with Usaden. Will had been unusually quiet beside Thomas.

"What is wrong?"

Will glanced at him, only his pale hair and face visible in the darkness. "Nothing is wrong."

"You visited Eleanor before we left. Did you argue?"

Will shook his head. "Far from it. She asked me to join her in bed when our work is done. Whatever time that is, she said."

"What was your reply?" Thomas glanced to his left as a man appeared from a house carrying a lantern. He saw the four of them and darted back inside. Even out here, fear of the night prevailed.

"I told her I would see."

"You would see."

"Yes. Are you sure you can hear all right, Pa?"

"Perhaps not," Thomas said, "because, for a moment there, I thought you made sense."

Will did not reply because Usaden had turned back and was approaching.

"Men are coming," he said. "They have not seen us, and best they do not." He turned his horse aside and rode out onto a flat field where Jack told them fairs were held. Beyond lay a baker's shop, which threw light across the road. As they circled to avoid it, the scent of bread drifted across to them. They dismounted and calmed their horses, confident they could not be seen from the road, but concerned any stray noise from their steeds might give them away.

Their first indication of the men was the sound of hoofs on hard-packed soil, then men talking. Whoever they were, they did not mind being heard. As they passed the splash of light from the shop, Thomas saw five men, three of them dressed as demons in red, black and yellow robes. Their heads were uncovered, but ornate masks hung from the pommel of each saddle. Which meant the killing of the others had not stopped the terror.

"They are on their way to attack someone," Thomas said, his voice low.

"Do we follow or keep going?" asked Will.

Thomas had to think about the best approach and, in the end, made a compromise.

"Two of us follow them. Once they know what is happening, come to Croft's house to report. I go on and confront Croft himself. I am sure that is where the men have come from, and dressed as they are, we know what their business is."

"Which two?" asked Will.

It was a more difficult decision than the first, but in the end, Thomas knew there could be only one answer.

"Usaden and Jack, follow the men. Usaden, I do not need to say this but make sure you are not seen. If anything happens and you need us, send Jack to fetch us. Me and Will go after Croft."

Thomas could not see Jack's expression in the dark but imagined his face pale, trying to show courage. Usaden said nothing. A decision had been reached. Thomas had made it. That was more than enough for him.

He handed the reins of his horse to Will, then motioned for Jack to do the same. They would be less visible without the horses. When Usaden ran off into the night, Jack remained where he was, uncertain.

"Follow him, lad," Thomas said. "He will not allow any harm to befall you. If you need us, come to the location you told me about and we will be there. Do not enter, but wait outside."

Jack swallowed his fear and ran after Usaden. Thomas hoped he had not made a false promise.

He and Will mounted their horses and led the other two back to the road. They passed the bulk of Charterhouse Priory, only one or two narrow windows showing candlelight. Beyond lay fields, shacks and, further on, hamlets and villages. They crossed a stretch of fallow land which Thomas had identified, from his study of the book, as the location of yet another old plague pit. Now it was nothing more than marshgrass and brambles, cut through with drainage channels leading west to the Fleet. More buildings appeared from the gloom, one with lights showing. The Knights Hospitaller's Priory of St John of Jerusalem sat squat and solid, but most of the illumination came from a surprisingly modest house.

Thomas and Will tied all four horses to a rail in front of the Priory, there for visitors' use, then walked on to the other house. Thomas pointed Will to go to one side while he took the rear. He came to a high wall and followed it until he found a gate. It was locked but easy enough to climb over. He dropped into an orchard and vegetable garden mostly filled with cabbages and turnips. A set of windows and a door gave a view into a dimly lit, empty kitchen. Thomas tried the door, then hesitated when it unexpectedly opened. He waited, listening, but heard nothing. He did not expect Croft to be on this side of the house because it was where the servants worked, but did he dare enter in search of the man? He would no doubt have men protecting him, but how many and how good? Thomas would only know if he ventured further into the house.

He took a breath and stepped into the kitchen, closing the door behind him and dropping a wooden bar across it. At least he could not be attacked from behind. Beyond the kitchen lay a short corridor ending in another door, presumably this one at the front of the house. Thomas realised he had calculated wrong. The place was not large enough to offer separation of master and servant. To one side, a staircase rose to an upper floor. On the other stood two closed doors. Thomas went to the first and pressed his ear to the wood. He heard nothing. He tried the next with the same result. He went to the front door, which, in this case, was barred. When he opened the door, Will stood on the other side. Neither of them said a word. None was needed.

Thomas pointed to the stairs and went first. He weighed less than Will and was quieter. He would beckon Will up if he found who they sought on the upper floor. It would not matter if he made a noise then because the game would be on. How many men, Thomas wondered for the second time? Five had gone into the city. How many more would Croft have with him? Most likely the same number, in which case they could handle them between himself and Will.

He motioned for Will to wait, then crept along a narrow hallway. One side had a single door leading into a small washroom that jutted out from the rest of the building, a round hole in the floor and a makeshift seat fashioned above it to squat on. Three doors gave off on the other side, and Thomas again pressed an ear against each to listen. When he reached the last, a sense of futility grew in him as he wondered if Jack had led them wrong. Then he heard a male voice he recognised, together with that of a female laughing. He waited to hear someone else, but several minutes passed, and all he heard was Croft. No men. One woman.

Thomas opened the door.

A naked Croft spun around at the interruption, a cry of anger coming from him. Beyond him, an equally naked young woman knelt. Neither of them made any effort to cover themselves.

Croft frowned.

"Berrington, what in the Devil's name are you doing here?"

It was an apt turn of phrase, Thomas thought.

"I could ask the same of you, though exactly what you were about to do is obvious." He waved a hand at the women. "You, dress and leave. If Croft has not yet paid you, I am sure he will send coin."

"She is not a whore, she is an acolyte," said Croft.

"A devilish acolyte?"

Croft frowned. "An acolytes of the church of pleasure. You know I am a worshiper of that religion." He smiled. "She will be willing to take us both if you want to join me. You are welcome once you have told me why you are here." Croft walked unashamed across the room and took down a robe. He wrapped it around himself.

"A dying man revealed your name to me." Thomas heard a noise from behind and assumed Will had ascended the stairs to join him, but when he saw the expression of fear on Croft's face he realised his mistake.

He turned fast, but too late. Four men surrounded him, and a blade touched his throat. Croft's men, Thomas was sure, but what the man said next came as a surprise.

"What is this?" Croft's voice showed both anger and fear. "Who are you? Unhand this man and leave this instant!"

"Shut the fuck up, old man," said one. He might be their leader, but each had been poured from the same mould, four inches shorter than Thomas, gaunt-faced, with muscled bodies and dead eyes. Men of experience. Dealers in death.

Thomas held his hands out, knowing he could let them take him because Will was downstairs and would be the last thing they saw. He let them tie a rope around his neck, then his wrists which they strained behind him. Each time he tried to move the rope at his throat tightened. One man on each side led him from the room.

From behind, he heard a man say, "You saw nothing, old man, understand?"

"Thomas is my friend."

"Was your friend. Nothing, remember, or we come for you next. We will gut the woman after we defile her, then unman you."

At the head of the stairs, Thomas saw there would be no rescue from Will, and a sharp chill ran through him. His son lay on his side, blood pooling beneath his head. He could not believe someone had got the better of Will, but there was no other explanation. He also knew he had made a mistake in sending Usaden away.

"What do you want of me?"

The leader laughed. "We want nothing from you. It is someone else who wants to watch you burn in the fires of hell. We are only the flint that lights the spark. Keep your mouth shut and lift your feet, or we drag you on your back."

Outside, the night was as dark as ever. Thomas half expected to see Usaden come flying out of the gloom, but no rescue came. He and Jack would be within London's walls, deliberately led away. Someone had known they were coming. But who? He was aware too many people had been told. Winnie had overheard them while they sat in the kitchen, as had her husband, Ben. Either could have told

Hardwin Steward. The man at Westminster might have lied, and known where Croft lived and passed word to others. Thomas had sent notes to both More and Linacre telling them he believed he had discovered who was behind the killings, and that if he failed to return they must inform the King. He had never expected he might be grateful for having done so, but he suspected by the time help arrived it would be too late for him.

The men threw Thomas over the back of a horse and retied his ropes so he could not work himself free. They mounted their steeds and rode east across the fields, not a glimmer of light from the sky.

They took him to Blackwood's manor house and led him inside, where someone waited for him. It was not who he expected. Not who he expected at all.

FORTY-SIX

Will came conscious in an instant. There was nothing, and then he was awake. His hand reached for a weapon only to have his wrist grasped. He tried to twist away, but another hand gripped him and pressed against the wound in his scalp. For a moment the world swam away again. Only when he opened his eyes did he find Usaden looking down at him, an expression of amusement on his face.

"It is not like you to be taken by surprise, Will. What happened?"

"I do not know." Will tried to sit up and his senses swirled. "They must have come at me from behind while I was listening to Pa upstairs."

Usaden glanced at the staircase. "It is still not like you. Is he still up there? He has been some time if he is."

"I do not know that either." Will saw Jack standing behind Usaden, his face a sickly grey, and knew he must look a fearsome sight with blood covering his face.

"I will go and see as soon as you can stand and hold your axe."

"You can wait until morning, can you?"

Usaden grinned and turned to Jack. "Help Will stand if you can. Do not let him go outside without me."

"How do I stop him if he tries?"

"If he does and you cannot hold him, then he is well enough to go on his own. I will not be long."

Usaden ran up the stairs but was gone barely any time. When he returned, he said, "There is a naked man and woman going at it up there. The man is Croft, and he said four men took Thomas away. When I asked why he had not reported it to the authorities, he said he would in the morning, but there was no point now, and it would be an equal crime not to take advantage of the woman until then."

"The man is a fool led by his cock," Will said, who was on his feet but leaned against Jack, who looked as if he might buckle under the weight.

Usaden stared at Will as if to say he was not the only one.

"I am all right now," Will said. "Come on, we have to find Pa."

"I need some light," said Usaden. "Jack, go find something we can use, but not candles."

Jack ran off as if grateful to get away from them, and Will wondered if the lad would ever return. No doubt he had seen more tonight than he ever wanted to.

"What came of the men you followed?" Will asked. "Did you kill them?"

"No need. They are not part of this, only fools. They

ran through the streets screaming like hags, then went to a whorehouse on this side of the wall and started shouting and whooping some more. We came back. It is fortunate we did." Usaden reached out and touched Will's head, who jerked away. "The blood has not yet thickened, so you cannot have been out long, which means whoever took Thomas is not far away either. Ah, good," he said as Jack returned with a good lantern already lit.

"I checked the oil and topped it up," he said, which brought a nod from Usaden. High praise, even if Jack was unaware of it.

Outside, Usaden had Jack take the reins of their horses, then helped Will into the saddle. He walked ahead, holding the lantern high as he stared at the ground. After a while, he said, "Five horses, riding this way. Croft said four men took Tom, so he must be on the fifth horse."

"Did Croft say if he was knocked out like me?" Will asked.

"Said he was tied tight but awake."

"Then there is hope."

"There is always hope until there is none," said Usaden. "And so far in this life all three of us have been fortunate."

They went north of the large Priory of Charterhouse and then out across fields. After a while, Will said, "You know where we are heading?"

"Blackwood's house," said Usaden. He stopped and mounted his horse, then nodded for Jack to do the same. They urged them into a canter.

"Why there? Do they know the man is dead or not?"

"Perhaps it is they who killed him and know the house is

now a safe refuge," said Usaden. "We will discover the answer when we get there."

It took a quarter-hour before the house emerged from the gloom. Several lights showed through the ground-floor windows. They dismounted and handed the horses to Jack, telling him to stay with them. Then Will and Usaden walked into battle, and God help those they found.

They expected five horses to be tied outside but found a dozen. Will went to each until he came to one without a saddle. When he ran his hand along its flank, he felt residual warmth but no blood.

"Pa was on this one, and they are not far ahead of us." He nodded at the horses. "And best if we assume there are more here than the four who took Pa."

"Can you fight?" Usaden asked.

"Of course I can fight. My head throbs and I may throw up, but I can fight well enough. This is Pa we are going to free, and once we do he joins us in the fight."

Usaden turned and climbed onto the terrace. One of the wide doors stood ajar, and he slipped inside. Will leaned close to Jack and whispered, "Take their horses and ours and lead them well away from here, then stay with them. Do not approach the house or try to follow us." He waited until Jack started to do as asked, then followed Usaden inside.

He found him at the foot of an ornate staircase, but he was looking away from it. He raised a hand to his ear and tapped it to show he wanted silence. When Will joined him Usaden pointed to the left, where several doors stood closed. As Will checked each of them, Usaden took the other side, but all they found were empty rooms. If there were any staff in the house they did not show themselves.

Usaden pointed to the upper floor, and Will nodded. They ascended the staircase in silence and, once upstairs, were rewarded with the sound of voices from the far end of a long corridor. Will went ahead, hoping he had not lied about whether he could fight or not. The voices grew louder, and as they did he made out several men, but also a female.

"We should kill him now," said a man, and Will held a hand up to halt Usaden. They were close to the door, and the conversation came to them clearly.

"We need to take him to the city and make a spectacle of him, you know that." It was a female voice and Will frowned at its familiarity.

"Where tonight?" the man asked. Were these the people behind the terror? It did not seem possible. Was the woman truly leading the planning?

"Put him somewhere many will discover him when dawn breaks. Somewhere close to the seat of power."

This brought a laugh. "Are we not the seat of power now?"

"The power that holds us down, along with all the other good people in this land. I think you should take him to Smithfield and gut him like a pig. Hang his carcass for all to see when they arrive at dawn. Open his skull and place a bucket beneath his head to catch the blood."

Will stepped back and motioned for Usaden to follow him. Neither spoke until they were outside on the terrace.

"They will have to come out this way to get their horses," Will said. "We take them here. You one side of the door-way, me on the other. I sent Jack away with their horses, so they cannot flee. How many do you think?"

"The men hardly spoke, so I cannot tell, but going by the number of horses we should assume eight or ten men."

"Even ten will be easy between the two of us. The woman will be no trouble."

"Agreed," said Usaden. "No mercy?"

"No mercy," Will said.

"You do your berserker thing as a distraction, and I will free Tom. Then he can help us if he has not been injured."

It was a plan, so they separated and waited. Time passed. Too much time, Will thought, but he dared not move from their position for fear it would be the moment people emerged through the door. More time passed, and still nothing happened.

"I will check the back in case they went out that way," Will said, "but I think we would have heard them if they did."

"I give you to the count of three hundred, then come and find you."

"I will be back before then."

Will ran off, swaying slightly but not aware of it. At the back of the house, he found another rail and more horses, and in the distance, he saw a mounted figure racing away. It was too far away for him to make out who it was, but the slimness of the body suggested it was the woman he had heard. He stood for a moment, trying to decide whether to follow, but freeing his father was more important. He returned to the front of the house. He was climbing onto the terrace just as both doors were thrown wide and six men came out, dragging Thomas between them. Will smiled. Only six.

The distance gave him the advantage. His axe slid from his back and into his hand as if with a mind of its own. He bellowed as he ran, the axe swinging from its leather thong around his wrist. He took one man across the throat before removing the arm of another at the shoulder.

When he turned, Usaden was among those around Thomas, his knife darting as he got in close. Then he was close enough, and he passed the knife to Thomas before twisting away. A sword cut through his shirt but did not touch flesh, and the holder of the sword fell dead to the ground. The other men moved away, giving themselves space to recover, but Will did not allow it. Once more his axe flew, and the sight of the wild Northman was too much. They stumbled over each other in their haste to escape.

Which is when Jack stepped onto the terrace. He had a sword in his hand but it looked as if he had no idea how to use it. Two of the fleeing men saw him and turned aside to take advantage of an easy target. Will called out for Jack to run, but Usaden had already seen the danger. His feet flew across the stone slabs and he took one of the men in the back. But the other had Jack around the waist and held a knife at his throat.

"Want your boyfriend back, do you? Then come and get him."

Usaden heard others coming up behind him but gave them no heed. Will was back there and would take care of them. His eyes were locked on the knife at Jack's throat. It had not drawn blood, but the blade was wickedly honed and would require barely any effort to end the lad's life.

Usaden took a step forward, then another.

He saw the man's arm tense and launched himself. Jack raised his sword and tried to jerk away, but the blade caught in something, and he could not lift it. Then Will came past them both, and the attacker's head came off his shoulders and rolled away after cracking on the stones.

At once, it was only the three of them, then four as Thomas came to join them. The last of the attackers fled to the back of the house. Five horses raced away as fast as they could be ridden.

"Are you all right, lad?" Thomas asked as he approached. He worked his arms, still stiff from being bound.

"Still alive," said Jack. He tried to smile, but the expression refused to come. His face and shoulders were dripping with the blood of the man Will had killed. He turned aside and threw up.

"Tom?" said Usaden, his voice coming oddly.

Thomas looked at his friend, who had once been an enemy but not for long. He was holding his side, and blood ran through his fingers to pool on the floor beneath him.

Thomas grasped his shirt and tore it open, then went to one knee and drew Usaden's hand away to reveal a deep wound in his side.

He cursed.

"Jack, go inside. Fetch curtains, anything I can bind his wound with. I need it fast. Will, bring our horses onto the terrace."

Thomas tore the two halves of Usaden's shirt into strips. When Jack arrived with a thick drape, he cut sections from it, put them over the gash in Usaden's flank, and then wound the strips from the shirt as tightly as possible. When he stood, he turned Usaden's head and looked into his eyes.

"I am still here, Tom."

"Which is what I am checking on. Yes, you are alive now, but unless I deal with your injury you will not be within an hour, likely less."

"You know I cannot die," said Usaden.

"You are dying now. Will, get him on a horse and sit behind him, he cannot ride. Jack, mount up. We ride west to Charterhouse Priory. There is a man there who has everything I need to save Usaden's life."

Except, as they raced through the darkness, Thomas did not know if he could save his friend. The wound was deep, and there was a great deal of blood. Something had been punctured inside, and until he looked, he did not know if he could fix it. All he could do was hope.

FORTY-SEVEN

Al-Timani opened the door at the second knock and
Thomas carried Usaden past him, only speaking once he
had lain him on a bench.

"I need whatever you have," he said. "My friend is
injured. I want a great deal of light, a glass so I can see better,
poppy and hashish, blades, gut and needles. And salves to
stop the infection if he does not die."

Al-Timani turned and started putting together what
Thomas had asked for. He said nothing because there was
nothing to say, and Thomas was grateful that the man knew
exactly what to do.

He removed Usaden's clothes and washed him with
warm water. When he untied the bandage, the wound
began to bleed even more, but there was nothing he could
do but open it further. Without needing to be instructed al-
Timani stood on the other side of the bench to offer
assistance.

Will stood against the wall, watching, while Jack went outside to throw up again.

Thomas needed to tell Will what he knew, but not yet. If he did, his son would pursue the person, and Thomas needed them all together until he had saved Usaden or he died. If the latter, then he would send that person to Hell himself.

Time passed.

Thomas widened the wound so he could work more easily. The flesh would knit together, but he needed to see the damage if he was to repair it. Al-Timani held the lamp close and Thomas used the proffered glass. He called Will over to hold the light and asked al-Timani to wash and clean the blood from within the wound. When he did, it revealed a blood vessel that had been sliced clean through. Thomas clipped and traced it before deciding it could be closed off altogether. He doubled one end over and stitched it, then did the same on the other side. The flow of blood lessened. He cleaned within again and used more water. The large dose of poppy and hashish he had been given meant Usaden barely winced as the work went on. Thomas doubted he would have even without the aid of the poppy. He found three more blood vessels, none of them completely severed, and closed them up. Eventually, he looked up, unaware of how much time had passed, but when he glanced at the window, night still held sway beyond it.

"Do you have honey, cobweb and dried moss?" Thomas asked.

"All of them, of course. I will make them up while you finish cleaning his body. You will have to leave him with me until he can move, and you will have to bring a cart when you come to take him away. He will not be able to ride for several weeks."

"I can do that. And my thanks."

Al-Timani smiled. "It is what we physicians do, is it not? Help each other heal the sick."

"It is what physicians such as you and I do, my friend, but I know others who are not so generous."

"Those we ignore." Al-Timani stared into Thomas's eyes. "I thought I was a good surgeon, Thomas, but what I witnessed here is beyond anything I thought possible. I do not believe anyone else could have saved your friend."

Thomas continued his work while al-Timani prepared what was needed to prevent the wound from festering. By the time they finished, darkness continued to hold sway outside, and Thomas wondered how he could still stand. His head swam with exhaustion, and when he looked across to Will, his son looked no better.

"Will, come here. I want to examine your head."

"I am fine, Pa. It is nothing."

"Let me be the judge of that. Here. Now."

Will came slowly. Thomas sat him down and washed the matted blood from his hair before drawing it apart. The wound was deep, but when he pressed on it he felt nothing to concern him. Will yelped and jerked away.

"I will apply honey to it and then a bandage, which I will change three times a day for two days. You will do this once as your father says." He turned to Jack, who sat against the wall. "What about you, lad? Are you injured?"

Jack swallowed and shook his head. "I am sorry, sir. It is my fault your friend was hurt."

"No, it is not. Never think that way. Usaden would not want you to. It was the fault of the man with a knife at your throat, not yours. Do you want to ride back to the house now?"

"I would rather wait for you, sir."

"I may be some time yet."

"I will still wait."

Thomas was about to turn back to Usaden but saw Jack had something on his mind.

"What is it?"

"I do not know if I should say."

"Say what?"

Jack took a deep breath and paled even more. "I saw the woman who rode away. I was holding our horses and she came right past me. I am not entirely sure, so may be making a false accusation."

"Tell me who you think it was," Thomas said.

"She looked like Eleanor," said Jack. "Dressed as a demon."

Thomas smiled. "Yes, I know it was her. Good work, Jack. Now all we have to do is find her." He glanced at Will. "You do not have to come, you are injured."

Will returned Thomas's gaze. "Yes, I do. I knew I recognised the voice. She has betrayed not only you but me and all of London."

Thomas put a hand on his son's shoulder as he felt a welling of love for the boy who had become a man.

"I want you to return to the house with Jack. There is something I have to do first."

"Croft?" said Will.

Thomas nodded. "Yes, Croft."

"Do you intend to kill him?"

Thomas laughed. "That depends. You and Jack stay here. Croft's house is not far. When I am finished with him I will return here and we can ride into London together."

Croft was waiting for him when Thomas reached the house. The main door remained unbarred from when they had left. It made Thomas think Croft was not concerned the men might return.

As he entered, Croft called from upstairs. "Is that you, Thomas? Come up, it is perfectly safe. The girl is gone. We are alone."

Thomas glanced around, but knew in the darkness anyone might have watched his arrival. Life always carried risks, but Thomas had learned to ignored them. He trusted in his own ability to survive.

Croft was dressed, but barely. He wore a long silk robe as he sat in a wide chair in a room next to the bedroom. A log fire burned and an open bottle of wine and two glasses sat on a table between him and another chair, which Croft indicated with a finger for Thomas to sit.

Croft poured wine for them both and took a long draught of his. Thomas left his glass where it was.

"Were you expecting me, or someone else?" Thomas asked, nodding at the two glasses.

"Knowing you, I thought you might return. Tell me what you want to know and I will answer if I can. I assume this is about Eleanor?"

"Did you know what she was doing?"

Croft stared at Thomas for a moment, then shook his head. "I had suspicions, but no proof. I hoped I was wrong. She was such a sweet girl once."

"Do you bear any guilt for her actions?"

"Why would I?"

Croft was too civil, too reasonable, leaving Thomas unsure. Not for the first time in the man's presence.

"She told me you took her in. Did you also defile her?"

Croft smiled. "It was the other way around, but I could have said no. She seduced me when she had but fourteen years, but told me I was not her first. She was so beautiful. She still is. Are you going to kill her, Thomas?"

"I am going to arrest her."

"You have no power in London, for all Henry appears to find you amusing. Do you have proof? Witnesses?"

"You would see her walk away without punishment?"

"I am fond of the girl, even now."

"Do you know what she has done?"

"I do now. None of it is her fault. She had no chance in life, not with who her parents were."

It was Thomas's turn to stare. He knew what Croft was leading up to. He recalled the staff leaning in a corner of Eleanor's printworks. He had remarked on how it looked

404

like an abbot's staff and she had laughed and made light of it. "A girl needs some protection," she had said.

"Both of them?" he asked, and Croft nodded.

"You know how it was before you put an end to it. Shame that you did, mind, but water under the bridge now. Those midsummer nights on Burfa Bank were a wonderful amusement. The Marches is not ready for an honest man such as you, Thomas, but at least I am old enough not to have to worry about it much longer. Though you grow older, too."

"But not my son or daughter."

"No, not them. Ah, but your daughter is also a great beauty. Even more so than Eleanor or her mother. You should find her a husband right quick."

"Amal makes her own mind up."

"There you go again, being reasonable. It is not seemly in a father. Eleanor was not my daughter but there were times I felt fatherly towards her."

"Not enough to refuse her advances."

"No, not enough for that. Her mother was a great beauty, as you know. She was also mad, as was her father, as you also know. I took her in when she had but eight years. I saw how her life would be had I not. Already Felicia was talking of introducing her to the men who called at the Nunnery. I paid them for her. They thought I wanted her for myself, which in truth I did not.

"As the years passed, I began to see she was growing to be more like her parents. She possessed both Felicia Hughden's obsessions and Abbot Haylewith's violence. I forgave her much because she was a demon in bed – in fact, a demon anywhere I wanted to take her. But when she tried to kill me I disowned her. She used her father's staff on me." Croft touched the side of his head. "She stunned me, but I was stronger than her. All she did was laugh and try to get me to mount her again.

"I did not know whether she lived or died, and did not much care. I discovered she came to London when I ran across her one day selling pamphlets. She told me their content was my fault because of the books I read. I accused her of stealing a special one from me."

"The Beasts of the City," Thomas said.

"Yes, The Beasts of the City. Though in truth it might have been hers all along. She brought it with her when she came to my house. I believe she stole it from the Abbot. That at least is what she claimed. It was old. Very old. And contained great power."

"You should have destroyed it," Thomas said.

"Yes, I should have. I tried twice to do so. Once with fire, but it would not burn. Once in water. The Lugge carried it away, but a week later I found it back on a shelf in my library. Eleanor said nothing and I did not ask. By then I was afraid of both her and the book. I was relieved when she left and discovered she had taken it with her."

"There must have been another and I now possess that copy. I believe it is the original that Abbot Haylewith found, for it has a feel of great age to it."

"I did not know you had a copy, Thomas. Or should I use your title now? Sir, or Duke? It seems Henry has plans for you. He has gifted you a fine house, much against my advice, but he follows his own mind in such matters.

Beware, because he wants to own you heart and soul. I am not sure you are a man who can live under such an expectation."

"Did you introduce Eleanor to Blackwood? She told me you did. That you took her there several times and offered her to others."

Croft smiled. "You may not believe me, but I did none of that. Oh, I attended his gatherings for many years, of course, but never took Eleanor with me. It surprised me when I saw her with you. I made enquiries. It seems she approached Blackwood some time ago. She was aware of his interests in the arcane and demonology. The man, like others, was searching for eternal life. I cannot think of anything worse. The boredom."

"And the killings?" Thomas asked. "Did you know they were her doing?"

"You must remember I do not spend most of my time here. I have holdings that need managing, and a man cannot let others do that for him. You will know that. So no, I was unaware of them until I arrived a month ago. And truthfully, they did not concern me. But..."

Thomas waited, but when Croft remained silent, he said, "But what?"

"Blackwood was excited by the killings. Of course he was. He—"

"He watched her," Thomas said. "I witnessed it myself only a few nights since. He said nothing to you?"

"He made attempts to recruit me to his cabal. He showed me his workshop, but I was not impressed. Toys, they were, nothing more. He warned me to keep away from

Eleanor. He knew our background together. It was she who seduced him, as she did me. She is a very busy girl indeed."

"And the men?"

"What men? Those ruffians who took you from this house? I have never seen them before. I am pleased you escaped, Thomas. The world would be a less interesting place without you in it. I take it your son and that man of yours freed you?"

"They did. But now Usaden hovers between life and death. He was struck down while trying to save someone else."

"I am sorry to hear that. Do you intend to kill her?"

"That is not my way."

"Is it not? I have seen you kill many men. Scores of men."

"All of whom deserved their fate."

"Does Eleanor not deserve that same fate? You know ... there was always a suspicion while she lived under my roof. Animals. And later, other children. At one time she was close to the witch who lives in the woods above my land. Another beauty. I believe she and your son are together now."

"No longer."

"Perhaps that is for the best. It does not surprise me Eleanor kills. It would surprise me more if she did not, considering who her parents are. So kill her, Thomas, before she does more evil."

"She is sick."

"I know, which is why I said it."

"Not in the way you mean. She will die soon without

my raising a hand. I have seen her worsen in the few brief days I have known her, and her end is near. Did she ever complain when she lived with you?"

"Not at first, but later, in the year before she left she did. Headaches. Sickness. Sweating. What causes it? You are a man who might know."

"There could be a surfeit of causes, but I believe it is a parasite. Pork would be most likely. The meat, if not fully cooked, carries a number of parasites that can take root in a human body. In this case it is in her brain."

"Would that be the cause of her madness?" Croft appeared genuinely interested.

"It will have made it worse, but I suspect it has always been there. Everything you have told me – and I thank you for your honesty – only confirms it. Eleanor is bad to the bone. Wicked inside. I will not kill her, but I will hand her over to the authorities. She will end up on the gallows or worse. It is what she deserves."

"And the terror in London will end?"

"Yes. The terror in London will end."

FORTY-EIGHT

Jack rode ahead of Thomas and Will, as if he wanted to separate himself from the danger they represented. He was a vague shape in the darkness. Each time they passed a shack or hovel that showed light, he had gained a little more distance.

"He was brave to come," said Will, "but he did not expect the violence. I do not think he will volunteer again."

"I would not ask him. Not everyone is like us, Will."

"How Usaden managed to get injured is a mystery to me."

"He was protecting Jack. He has done the same for both of us in the past, but perhaps, like me, he is growing older and slower."

Will laughed. "It was a misfortune, nothing more. The only surprise is why it has not happened before. Both of us injured on the same night. Who could imagine such a thing? Does it mean the men we are up against are different? More skilled? More ruthless? *Better* than us?"

"Ruthless, certainly, but I doubt they are better than you or Usaden. As you say, it was misfortune." Thomas rode on for a moment then said, "You realise what we have to do about Eleanor."

"She fooled me."

"She fooled everyone."

"Why did she do it?" asked Will. "Kill all those people, and in that way? Create such a crazy scheme to cover her tracks? Did your conversation with Croft throw any light on it?"

"She already told me Croft took her in, but never said where from. I assumed she was one of his bastards, but no. Her mother was Felicia Hughden and her father Abbot Haylewith."

Will chuckled. "That explains a lot."

"It raises a question we do not have an answer for. Are children made in the image of their parents, or do they acquire who they are from others? Eleanor lived at Elmbrook Priory until she had eight years. Then Felicia planned to sell her to the men who called. Croft took her in."

"To abuse her, no doubt." Will's face showed his disgust in the slowly growing light.

"According to him she was the seducer."

"And you believed him?"

Thomas shrugged. "I can believe it of her, yes, but I don't suppose Croft put up much of a fight."

"She is an unusual beauty, Pa."

"She is. Croft doesn't know everything, but enough to convince me Eleanor is as much a slave to her own self as to anyone else. Blackwood might have believed he corrupted her, but again I think she corrupted him."

"And these damned men who keep cropping up?" Will rubbed his head, which was still sore.

"I think Blackwood recruited them, not Eleanor. Though it might have been at her bidding. They are troublemakers, only too willing to use a knife or sword. It would have been easy money for them to dress up and terrorise the streets."

"They did the killings as well?"

Thomas teased the answer out from the skeins of thoughts in his head. "I believe Eleanor killed them. She used Haylewith's staff to knock them out, then either cut them or continued to beat them with the staff. It sits in plain sight in her workshop."

"I have seen it. If what you say is true, there will be blood on it."

"She will have washed it well after each use. It is probably what she knocked Luke out with when she claimed men came to threaten them. I saw no men. I do not believe there were any men, not that time."

"We saw them later."

"Looking into her workshop, yes. Looking, but not acting. Not threatening her. The same men who were beneath St Paul's Cathedral. Eleanor was the cloaked demon who killed Sir Jacob Tanner. It was she who killed Lady Merryl on Blackwood's terrace."

"The voice was not hers," said Will.

"People can change how they sound." Thomas glanced at Will. He felt a pain in his chest. A sadness that his son was growing into adulthood. "Did she ever display any of that when you…"

Will laughed. "When we fucked?"

"Yes," Thomas said. "When you fucked."

"A little. She was wild and demanding. She … no, you do not need to know what we did."

Thomas shook his head. "I prefer not to. She as good as offered herself to me, too. I believe it is what she does. Something inside her is broken."

Will drew his shirt down to show his shoulder to his father. "She did this to me."

Will sported a bruise on his neck, and when Thomas leaned closer he saw the skin was broken. A bite, made with small, sharp teeth. "At the time in the throes of passion I barely felt it. I have been marked by women before, but never as badly as this. Later, when I stood to leave, she grabbed me and told me not to go. When I told her I had to she drew a knife that had been under the mattress the entire time. The thought occurred to me she could have used that instead of her teeth. It would not have surprised me if she had."

"Do you believe the bite was deliberate, to harm you?"

Will shrugged.

Thomas looked ahead but could no longer see Jack even in the growing light. "If Jack saw her tonight she may have also seen him. He might be in danger if he arrives at the house alone."

"She would be a fool to be there," said Will. "Despite everything you say, she is no fool. If she saw Jack she would know he was with us. I even told her where we were going."

"I am going to ride ahead and try to catch him. If not I will go to the house. Follow me at your own pace."

"I can keep up, Pa."

"No, you cannot. You need a day before I trust you to fight. Do as I say, for once."

Before Will could offer any further objection, Thomas kicked his heels and Sombra broke into a canter. It was only possible because the road was deserted. It was less than a half mile from the gate to his house but he did not see Jack. When he arrived, he dismounted and left Sombra in the orchard to graze on fallen apples. Jack's horse was nowhere to be seen, but when Thomas entered the stable he found Jack grooming it. The lad turned sharply at the sound of Thomas's entry.

"It is you, sir. I am sorry I rode off but I was sore afraid. Have you been to see if she is in her workshop?"

"I wanted to make sure you were safe first. Leave that and go into the house. Lock all the doors. I will knock when I want entry, but you must ask who it is."

"I am not allowed into the house at this time of day."

"If anyone tries to stop you tell them I allow it." A thought occurred to Thomas. "You said you have a group of lads you meet now and then. Was that where you got Croft's location from?"

"Yes, sir."

"I want you to go and ask them if they know of a good, honest Steward. This house is going to need one."

"Master Hardwin will not allow himself to be replaced."

"That is my decision, not his. Now go inside. If you want to sleep, use my room."

Thomas stared at Jack until he stopped grooming the horse. He led it into a stall and hung a bag of hay over the side then, with a glance back, entered the house.

Thomas waited until he heard the bar drop over the door then turned and strode along the alley to Eleanor's workshop. It was still shaded inside, so he found a candle and lit it, then used that to light a lamp. The printworks looked almost the same as the last time he had been there, but now there was no paper hanging from the wooden bars. Stacks of unprinted sheets lay on a shelf, but of the finished pamphlets there was no sign.

Thomas took the lamp and climbed the stairs. He did not expect to find Eleanor, but if she was here he knew what he had to do. Ignore her lies, which would come, and take her into custody. But the single room lay empty. The bedclothes were tossed aside. When he knelt and felt the coarse mattress it was cold. He reached beneath but there was no knife there. He stood and looked around, not fully seeing anything as his mind played through what Eleanor had said and done. The bite on Will's neck had been deliberate, not done in passion. The teeth marks were almost directly over the main vein running along his neck. He suspected only Will's unnatural muscle had saved her from opening it. Her intention had been to kill him. She would have to flee after, but would be prepared.

Yes, prepared, Thomas thought.

It was she who had killed Luke. Had she always meant to, or was it nothing but convenience? Eleanor enticed men to her will. She had done so with Blackwood, Luke, and then Will. Thomas knew she had tried to use it against him, and admitted he had been tempted. Any man would be.

He considered all of her lies.

And then he wondered why she had chosen him. If she had chosen him. The chance he should be walking across the entrance to the alley at the exact moment she came running out and knocking him down seemed too thin. He recalled the man who rushed past him as he left the Tower and wondered if he had been going to Eleanor to tell her Thomas was on his way.

Which would mean she *had* chosen him. But why?

The how was easier to understand once he accepted she wanted him involved. Blackwood was with the King most days. He would overhear Thomas was on his way to London. It would be simple to have someone watch the Bel Savage and tell her he had arrived. The rest was simply waiting.

The why slowly formed in Thomas's mind, but he was aware he might be wrong.

Was he meant to be punished, or was he chosen because Eleanor knew she needed help. Or both? Earlier in the year Thomas had been responsible for the deaths of Eleanor's mother and father. She would not have forgotten them when she went to live with Croft. If she had inherited their madness, would she still feel close to both? She would have heard of their deaths. It was no secret. And no doubt among those around King Henry it would have been a three day wonder, the death of both an Abbot and Abbess.

Eleanor's trade was in words. Had she written anything down that might answer all Thomas's questions? He looked around the sparse room. A pallet. A wash basin. A chair. There was nothing else.

He started to turn away then stopped.

There was something else. He had stubbed his toe on the chest. Had even asked Eleanor if it contained her wealth and she had laughed. "No, not my wealth, my future," she had said. He had assumed she meant papers, writings, books. And yes, coin. She sold her pamphlets for a penny a piece, and she printed hundreds of them a day. She would be wealthy enough not to work.

He descended the stairs to break open the chest, but it was not there. He found pamphlets stacked in numbered order in a cupboard and realised they were a copy of everything she had ever produced. He left them where they were, but wondered if he read all – a task he would not relish – they might offer some clue to her state of mind.

He leafed through the stack of virgin white paper, but nothing was concealed among it. If she did not return, he would offer it to another printer. Perhaps he could offer the premises as well. Then he wondered if Jack might like to try his hand at the trade. He already knew how the press worked, and if he was willing, he could learn the rest.

Thomas ran his hand over the printing press. A small thrum of tension ran through it, or so he thought, but suspected the vibration came from him. Then he cast one last look around and saw what he had missed.

There was no type anywhere. The thing that had started everything: the theft of the type, the search for its recovery, Luke's supposed journey to Flanders to obtain more. Except he had never taken ship. It had all been about the type and the ability to create more – to pour molten lead into ingots to be used in a punched matrix to fashion letters, to create words from those letters, then pages and ... ideas to twist a reader's mind. To make them fear the demons that stalked the city night.

Now Eleanor had taken her type and fled. To where?

Thomas smiled.

Of course.

FORTY-NINE

The streets and alleys grew busy as Thomas walked south to the river. Those who had cowered in their houses during the night emerged as though fear did not exist. Life was starting anew once more. He wondered, if this was the end of the demons, how long it would take before men, women and children gained enough courage to venture into the dark again. He hoped it would not be long, because already the days grew shorter, and soon night would hold sway over daylight.

At the river, he descended to a narrow quay where several wherries were tied up.

"Do any of you know where a ship would set sail from if it was on its way to Flanders?" he asked.

Several of the men laughed.

"Who are you running away from, sir? A scold of a wife or the husband of another?"

"Three pennies for a man who gives me a sensible answer to my question."

Four men pushed against each other in their rush for the spoils. Thomas chose the strongest because he would be the best to take him where he wanted to go.

"The Hanse control most of the trade with Flanders and elsewhere, sir. They are based at the Steelyard on this side of the bridge. It will be another three pennies to take you there."

Thomas knew it was daylight robbery but nodded and climbed into the rocking wherry. The man pushed out into the current, then steered so the outgoing tide carried them downstream.

"Do you intend to take passage to Flanders, sir?"

"Not me, but I seek a woman who is."

"We are all seeking a woman, sir, even if we already have one to scold us day and night." The words sounded heartfelt but were none of Thomas's business.

"I believe this one is heading for Flanders. If you take me to this Steelyard, I will ask there."

"If she is going today, she will have already gone. The galleys and carracks set off at the turn of the tide, which was an hour since. The tide will carry them along without setting sail until they reach Woolwich."

"Can you take me there?"

"The water will be rough under the bridge, but I can for three pennies more."

Thomas reached inside his jacket and pulled out a handful of coins. He threw them across the floor of the boat in a fit of pique. He did not care about the cost, but he did care about the man's attitude. He wished now he had chosen another boatman. The man stared at the coins.

"You can pick them up when you have taken me down-river," Thomas said. "If you can negotiate the bridge, that is, and not tip us into the tumult."

The man pulled on his oars and looked over his shoulder to judge the best arch of London Bridge to run through. Whether he chose right or not Thomas did not know, only that they barely made it. Water washed over the sides, and the man kicked a bucket at him, which Thomas used to bale with.

They continued, faster than the falling tide, and after some time three large ships appeared ahead. None had yet raised their sails, but Thomas could see men working in preparation to do so. He narrowed his eyes, scanning the figures on board each.

"Can you get us closer? And if you say it will be another three pennies I will throw you overboard and do it myself."

The man glowered but said, "Perhaps a little closer, but on your head be it. There is danger getting too close to ships that size."

"Once their sails go up, we will never catch them. Do it, man."

The wherryman heaved on his oars, and Thomas changed his mind again. He had chosen right after all. And then, as he looked up, he saw Eleanor. She stood at the stern of the boat, staring upriver, no doubt checking that she was not being followed. She seemed to be satisfied because she turned and walked to the prow of the ship and disappeared from view.

"Closer," Thomas said. "I need to board that ship."

"No matter how many coins you throw at me I cannot do it. We will both perish."

"Then get me close enough." Thomas stood and pulled off his boots. His coat followed, leaving him in only shirt and hose. "Tell me when we can get no closer."

He stood in the swaying wherry as it approached, and then the man said, "This is as far as I go, sir. If you mean to drown yourself, now is the time to do it."

Thomas dived into the muddy water and struck out hard. He had always loved to swim, but that had been in clean water, and clean the Thames was not. But he could not let Eleanor escape justice.

He reached the ship and grabbed for rope webbing hanging over the side, presumably for the purpose should someone fall overboard. He pulled himself up until he could almost see over the gunnels, then rose more slowly. Sailors were hauling on ropes to raise the sails. A westerly wind caught in the canvas, and the boat heeled over hard, almost throwing Thomas back into the water. He pulled himself onto the deck and stood, swaying and sheeting water onto the boards.

Two sailors approached.

"Did you fall out of something?"

"My daughter is aboard. I was meant to join her but was late for the dock at Steelyard." He believed a lie might carry more weight than the truth, and it seemed to work.

"She said nothing about anyone joining her. She has taken the captain's cabin below. Paid well for it, too. I will show you the way."

Thomas was surprised and relieved the lie had worked.

He followed the man along the rocking deck, staggering from side to side, unlike the sailor ahead. It made him consider King Henry's request, and the long sea trip from England to northern Spain. He had not made it before, but he did recall taking passage to France when he was little more than a boy. It was a journey that did not end well, but at least left him alive and changed his life. Whether for the better or not he did not know; but he believed it had.

The sailor stopped at a narrow doorway set beside the thick mast. A maze of ropes ran down and across from the sails, making progress hazardous.

"She will be below, sir. Foot of the ladder and go forward as far as you can. The master's cabin is tucked beneath the prow. There might be enough room for two, but you look like a big man. Watch your head."

Thomas found himself unexpectedly alone. He looked into the dark belly of the ship, then carefully descended the ladder. At the foot, a narrow passageway led both forward and back. Openings on each side held supplies. Barrels of water, spare rope, and boxes of hard biscuits. The ship was well provisioned for the relatively short crossing to Flanders, but he supposed it might pick up more cargo there and carry it elsewhere. The crew could be at sea for weeks or months.

There was a door, as promised. It stood ajar, and Thomas pushed it open and ducked as he entered the cabin. Eleanor had her back to him, naked to the waist, and her hands went to her breasts as she spun around.

"What do you think you are—" She stopped when she saw who it was and lowered her hands, unashamed in his presence. "Did you miss me so much you had to follow, Tom? Well, here I am. Give me a moment, and you can join me in this bed. There may be just enough room if I lie atop you."

"Why?" he asked, knowing there was no need to explain.

"Sit down. I do not like how you loom over me that way."

"When you put some clothes on."

Eleanor smiled. "Do you not like what you see? Your son did. I could pleasure you as I did him."

Thomas resisted the sudden urge to slap her. "And try to tear my throat open?"

"It was a token of love, nothing more. Sit. I will do as you ask, this once." She turned away, picked up her shirt and slipped it on but left the buttons undone.

Thomas looked around for a stool but discovered something better. Eleanor's chest took up most of the space to one side of the bed and he sat there. Her knobbed staff leaned in one corner, the top almost reaching to the low beams of the roof. Eleanor sat on the bunk and drew her legs up. The ship rocked in the current as the wind caught in the sails, the river turning and winding to the sea.

"You know why," she said.

"Croft. Your parents."

Eleanor nodded. "Yes, Croft and my parents, but mostly Croft. For what he did to me." She gave a tight smile. "Even now, men are going to his house, the one you visited to cut his belly open and hang his lights around his neck. The same with whatever woman, or women, are with him. That house is where he takes them. Where he took me when I had but twelve years."

Thomas knew she was lying. If she meant to kill Croft her men would have gone there the night before.

"People have died in terrible ways."

"All of them guilty of sin and avarice. Blackwood was among the worst, so I kept him to the last. He knew someone was coming for him, and the fear was exquisite to watch as it grew."

"He named Croft in his final breath to me. Why did he do that?"

"Because he did not know it was me 'neath the costume. It was Croft who introduced him to the illicit pleasures of the flesh, though not to the other deviant hobbies Blackwood followed. He lay with both women and men, and he liked to hurt people. They call us the weaker sex, and that is what men like Croft, Blackwood, and all the others want. A weak woman they can impose their desires on. But not all of us are weak." She put a hand to her head and tilted it to one side.

"Does it hurt?" Thomas asked.

"You know it does. I thought you were the clever physic who could cure me but you are useless. Worse than useless."

"I stopped you. Why the reign of terror?"

Eleanor laughed. "Why not? It was easier to carry out my plans if the streets were deserted, so I penned tales of demons and gave them away free. I had boys who pushed them under doors of the homes of dissolute men. The book–" She laughed "–no, *The Beasts of the City,* was my masterpiece, deliberately made scarce so the right kind of people would seek it out the more. Or perhaps I mean the wrong kind of people. I knew who they were and ensured they obtained a copy."

"What was your plan?" Thomas asked. "I see no plan in what you did, only butchery."

"I was seeking the one," said Eleanor, her face tight with pain.

"Which one?"

"*The* one, of course! Among all the pretenders and liars, there must be a true acolyte, a true believer who can cure me. It takes someone like Blackwood to do it, but he was not strong enough, so I killed him. I thought he was the one, but I was wrong. My search goes on. You could be who I seek, Tom, if only you loosen the ties that bind you so tight. I could help you do that, and you could help me in return. It is why the book found you."

"Did you take it from my room?"

"I did, once I realised you could not be turned. It now lies in the trunk you sit on."

"How did you manage to get the copy into the library at Durham House?"

Eleanor stared at him. She gave another shake of her head, as if a fly bothered her. "I did not. I was surprised when you told me you had found it."

"I do not believe you. Everything was your doing."

"My parents carry more guilt than do I. The copy I stole from Croft was gifted him by my father, Abbot Haylewith. But that was a copy of the original. After you told me you had it I thought long and hard how it came to be there. The only thing that came to me was that Durham House belongs to the Church. Bishop Cuthbert Tunstall gifted use of it to your Princess. Or rather to King Henry, who allows her to live there. My father visited London several times that I know of. He would likely have stayed at Durham House."

"Why would he lodge his original copy of the book there?"

"What better hiding place than to put it in plain sight in a library no one ever uses."

Thomas shook his head. He did not believe her explanation, but neither could he think of any other reason for the book to be there. Unless more in the Church were involved with Abbot Haylewith and his deviant plans.

"Those men you used, are they a part of it all or nothing more than fools?"

"They are hard men, all of them, but also weak men. You saw some. They are bullies. They like to drink and whore and attack anyone they consider weaker than themselves, which is most of London. There are always men such as them. My folly of having them dress as demons amused them."

"What was done to your victims, did that not disgust them?"

"Some, of course, but not all. They are not men who think deeply about the pain of others, and I chose them well. My plan has been hatching for many years."

"Why?"

"Because I am searching for the answer."

"To what?"

"To what ails me. To what lies in my head and tortures

me night and day. The killing eases the pain, but only for a short while."

"Where do you flee to? Flanders, to start over again? Do you have your type and the makings of more in this chest?" He stood and flung the lid open. It did reveal type, but also a costume laid beneath it. Thomas reached in and pulled it out. A cloak, a mask and a knife.

"Put those down. They are mine. *Do not touch them!*" Eleanor's voice ended in a high pitched scream. She launched herself at Thomas but he pushed her back to the bed.

"Abuse me then, Tom. Do it now." She pulled at her clothes to once more reveal herself. Then her voice changed and became guttural and dark. "Do it now. Take me!"

Thomas stepped away as far as he could.

"You are dying," he said.

"No, I am on the cusp of finding eternal life. The book tells me how. The demons will show me how. It is all in the book." Her eyes went to the chest, and Thomas glanced down and saw it.

The book that had sat in his room now lay beneath her costumes. He reached for it, then stopped. He had intended to throw it into the Thames until he recalled what Croft had told him. How he had tossed it into the Lugge only to discover it back in his library within days. Except the book held no power. It could not. Still, Thomas was unable to bring himself to touch it.

"Pick it up, Tom." There was the fire of madness in her eyes. "Shall I summon a demon of the river to join us? To tear your body limb from limb and feast on your guts? I can do it. You know I can."

"Do it, then," Thomas said.

Eleanor rose and removed the last of her clothes until she stood naked. The roof was low, but she was short so that she could stand upright. She gripped the beams and began to ululate and curse, raw words spilling from her lips.

She called out louder, but all that happened was the ship tacked again and she staggered as it heeled hard over. Thomas rose, caught her and spun her around, his arms gripping her tight.

"Do it, Tom. Impale me as so many men have. It will give me power over you. Then the demon will come to open my skull and heal me of this pain."

"You mistake me for some other kind of man."

"No, all men are the same. Filled with lusts and anger." She shook her head once more and sat hard on the bed. Her hands gripped her skull. "Make it stop, Tom. Heal me."

When Eleanor cried out in pain Thomas almost felt sorry for her.

"It is too late for me to visit al-Timani," he said. "Or I would have him provide poppy for you, despite all you have done."

"The chest," said Eleanor. "There is poppy in the chest. I asked him for enough to last me until I could find another Moorish doctor. Make me a tincture, Tom. I cannot stand the pain or the voices in my head. It makes them go away."

Thomas lifted out some dresses, then found outfits of a different kind. Silks and linens. Bright colours. And another horned mask. When he looked Back at Eleanor, she was smiling.

"Yes, they are all mine, Tom. You know they are mine, but I wanted you to see them. I also want the pain to go away."

Thomas moved the clothing aside until he found a cedar box. Within it lay dark poppy resin. Enough to last someone a month or more.

"Do you have wine?"

"Over there." Eleanor pointed to a small cabinet. When Thomas opened it he saw six bottles of ruby-red wine. He uncorked one and poured some into a cup, then he heated the poppy over the swinging lamp and crumbled it into the wine. He kept his back to Eleanor so she could not see how much he added. More than enough, he believed. And then a little more.

He stirred, turned and handed the cup to her.

"Hold it for me, Tom. I am fear I am too weak to do so."

He sat on the edge of the bed and tipped the cup as she drank deeply of it, hungry for the relief it would bring.

She emptied the cup and lay back, her hand beneath her head under the small pillow.

"Come close so I can whisper to you, Tom."

"It is too late for confession."

"That is not what I offer. Come. We could have been together. I wanted us to be. Let me whisper what you need to know."

He leaned over and placed his ear close to her lips even though nobody could hear them with the splash of the waves against the bow beyond the small window.

"I will see you in Hell!" she said, her voice filled with spite.

Thomas jerked away, and the knife she meant to slash across his throat missed by barely any distance. He grasped her wrist and took the knife from her.

He remained where he was, stroking her face as the poppy started to do its work.

"Soon," she murmured. "Soon I will kill you. Do not sleep, Tom, for I will come for you in the deepest dark."

Thomas waited as her breathing grew shallow, and then stopped altogether.

He felt no guilt, but neither did he feel triumph. He had thought of letting her escape, despite all she had done. She had been a victim too. But the knife had been too much. Besides, whatever ailed her, worm, parasite, simple madness, was killing her anyway. He had only hastened her end, and done it with a mercy she did not deserve.

Eventually he rose and went back to the deck, where a short, bow-legged man wearing a three-cornered hat approached.

"Is your daughter happy with the accommodation, sir?"

"She is most pleased with it but has asked not to be disturbed until you dock. She has food, water and wine and prefers her own company."

The man offered a nod. "I will do as she asks."

"Are you the master of this vessel?" Thomas asked.

"I have that honour, sir." He held his hand out, and they shook.

"How long to Antwerp?"

"Two days with a fair wind. Three if we have to use the

431

oars. Are you accompanying us as well? I have no other cabin, but you can bunk in with the men."

"I would have you set me ashore if such is possible."

"You are in luck, sir. We have cargo for Benfleet, and it is arranged for a cutter to meet us off Canvey Island. I am sure for a few pennies they will be happy to take you as well. And your daughter?"

"She stays."

At the dock, Thomas bought boots to replace those he had lost to the river, then he turned west and started to walk. It was a long way back to London, and then a long way back to Ludlow. Henry expected him to respond to his demand, and soon, but he had other matters to attend to first.

FIFTY

It was a week before Thomas judged Usaden well enough to travel. Al-Timani provided enough salve, poppy and hashish to last the journey, and Thomas knew there would be more once they reached Ludlow.

Home. And what he had to face when he reached there. The beasts of London had been despatched back to Hell where they belonged. Thomas and Will had spent the week hunting down the men Eleanor had recruited. Some had fought and died, but most had submitted and were taken into custody. Thomas suspected they would come to regret their choice. A swift death with a knife would have been preferable to what the authorities would do to them. Thomas had told Will and Usaden what he had done with Eleanor below decks in the vessel she planned to escape in. He did not want them concerned she might return and seek them out. There had been no hue and cry when she was found, and he suspected the sailors assumed she had died a natural death.

They travelled slowly so as not to jar Usaden's wounds and, each night, found a Tavern or Inn with comfortable beds. Often it meant an early stop for the day, but none of them minded. For Usaden it was a time to heal. As for Will ... Thomas did not know, only that Will was content to let the days pass without the need to rush back home. The slow passage of days allowed Thomas time to think about what Henry had demanded of him. His world was changing, and he lacked the understanding of how to prevent it, or even if he wanted to. Henry's request offered him a return to Spain. For how long he did not know, nor did he even want to consider it. The idea of Spain sat sweet on his tongue, like honey.

There would have to be a conversation with Jorge. Belia too. She might want to return to Granada. Then there was Will and Amal? Except if they all went south, who would provide judgement in Ludlow? There was no time to find an honest replacement even if such a rare beast existed. Thomas had a plan, of sorts.

Will and Amal would remain in Ludlow and manage affairs. He would ask Jorge to travel south with him – just the two of them. He thought he might agree, as long as they were not away too long. Belia and the children would have to stay. Thomas would offer Usaden the choice but believed he already knew his answer. South might be where he came from, but these days Ludlow and Emma held his heart.

The journey north and west lasted ten days. It took three more before Jorge came to Thomas with his answer.

"I will come to Spain with you on two conditions." Jorge sat across from him in the kitchen, only the two of them present, other than Kintu, whose slim, sleek length lay across the wide hearth where embers of a log fire settled and sparked. It was gone midnight, and around them the house lay silent.

"Which are?" Thomas had drunk more wine than was good for him, but he poured more into his cup and did the same for Jorge.

"Say no to either and you go alone."

"I am still waiting to hear what I am meant to say yes to."

Jorge smiled. The firelight caught his face and hair. He was still handsome, still turned the heads of most women and fascinated most men.

"The first is that you do what you are being sent to do and, once finished, we return here." Jorge held a hand up as Thomas started to reply. "I know Spain is where I was born, but my home lies here now. And one more thing."

"You said two."

"Two and a half, then. I do not want you finding trouble when we are there, like you always do."

"I never—"

"No! You always say you never seek it. This time, turn away when it comes knocking at your door."

"What is your second, or third, demand?" Thomas asked, amused.

"Belia tells me she is growing older and would like one more child while she still can."

"I see. And exactly how is this miracle going to happen?"

"Do not be awkward, Thomas. It will happen the same

way it has three times before. She would have asked you herself but did not think she could while Bel slept under our roof."

"And if she returns?"

"She will not. I went to speak with her when you told me you must revisit Spain. She wishes you well, but has learned that both you and she have changed too much. You are not children anymore. Too much time has passed. She told me she will remain a friend if you wish it, but she would prefer not to. I believe it is difficult for old lovers to become friends."

Thomas absorbed the news, trying to measure his reaction. He felt nothing. Which meant it was time to move on.

"Henry wants me to sail before the end of the month. The weather grows worse after that and makes the crossing more perilous."

"You make it sound less and less appealing."

"I intend to ride, not take sail. But we will still need to leave at the end of the month."

Which means you have two weeks with Belia. That should be enough. It always has been in the past."

Thomas smiled. "You forget I grow old. Though, apparently, you do not."

"But I cannot give her what she wants. You can. I can give her everything else she needs, but not that. Please, Thomas, for me and for her. I know you love us both. Also, do it for yourself. She says she will never ask again, and is not even sure the time has passed when she can set a child inside herself. But she wants to try. One more child to love." Jorge stared into Thomas's eyes. "It will not be so bad, will it?"

Thomas thought of the boy he had unmanned and turned into the eunuch that now sat before him. How they had formed a fragile, awkward friendship that turned into love. He thought of how he had lain with Belia three times before, and yes, Jorge was right. It had not been a hardship – none at all. With anyone else, it would have been awkward, but not with Jorge and Belia, because sometimes it felt as if the three of them were married to each other.

"Two weeks," Thomas said. "We will not be here to know if my seed has set, but Amal will help if and when Belia's time comes. I hope we will return before then. Nine months would be a long time to stay away."

"Even if you do not return, Thomas, I will. I suspect you may remain longer. I suspect you may never return once the Spanish sun shines on your face again and you smell the dust in the air."

"I will return," Thomas said, wondering if he spoke the truth. England had been his home, but so had Spain. There was a choice, and he did not know if he wanted to even contemplate making it. Time would tell. Time always did.

"Tell her yes," he said.

Jorge smiled and drained his cup. "Tell her yourself. She is still awake and waiting for your answer."

HISTORICAL NOTE

As is often the case with my books, the title *The Beasts of the City* came to be before the plot. However, one of the central elements was always going to be the nascent trade of printing in the city, brought to London by Wilhelm Caxton.

The inclusion of Thomas Linacre into the story was made after much petitioning by a good friend of mine. She knows who she is.

Thomas More is well known as Henry VIII's chancellor, but at the time of this book he was much younger and training to be a lawyer, as well as tutoring Prince Harry and Catherine of Aragon.

For reference to street names and locations in this book I used the excellent map *Tudor London, The City and Southwark in 1520,* provided by the Town & City Historical Maps Society. While it shows the city eighteen years after the events in *The Beasts of the City* my hope is enough remained the same to provide the information I needed.

I have used the name John Wynkyn rather than Wynkyn de Worde for the man who took over Caxton's printing press after his death. Some sources indicate the 'de Worde' was used as a descriptor as many last names were at that time. Others sources indicate a number of different names.

The concept of using plague pits as an association with the crimes committed came about after discovering, while doing the random disjointed kind of research writing a book such as this often entails, a website listing many of these sites within the then city of London and around it. This can be found at https://www.historic-uk.com/HistoryMagazine/DestinationsUK/LondonPlaguePits/

RESEARCH SOURCES

Thomas More, Peter Ackroyd

Catherine of Aragon, Giles Tremlett

Studying Early Printed Books: A Practical Guide by Sarah Werner

The Dictionary of Demons, M. Belanger.

As promised, Thomas and Jorge will appear again soon, next time in Spain.

ABOUT THE AUTHOR

David Penny published 4 novels in the 1970's before being seduced by a steady salary. He has now returned to his true love of writing with a series of historical mysteries set in Moorish Spain at the end of the 15th Century, and 16th Century Tudor England. He is currently working on the next book in the series.

David also writes The Izzy Wilde Crime Thrillers series under the name DG Penny.

Find out more about David Penny
www.davidpenny.com

Printed in Great Britain
by Amazon

52368903R00256